Busting Billy's Butt
ISBN 978-1-909934-07-8
Copyright©2013 Barry Lowe
Cover art and design by Dawné Dominique

First published by loveyoudivine Alterotica

Published by
Lydian Press 2013
Find us on the World Wide Web at
www.lydianpress.com

Busting Billy's Butt

Barry Lowe

Lydian Press

CONTENTS

All previously published in eBook format by loveyoudivine *Alterotica*

Is voyeurism such a crime – especially if watching your own boyfriend in action with strangers turns you on big time?

Steve and Billy's monogamous relationship has gone stale until Billy, ever the exhibitionist, shows them a way to spice up their sex life.

Billy has the most coveted ass in the city and Steve loves to watch him secretly spread it open for strangers. But can their relationship survive when Billy goes too far and offers himself to Steve's worst enemies?

For Wally,
who lets me release my inner slut
when I feel the urge

FOUR ON THE FLOOR

When you find your relationship going stale and your boyfriend spends more time watching the hunk across the street through binoculars than he does with you, how can you get his attention back? How about a sexy strip in front of him and his sleazy boss and two of his horny buddies?

Steve is bored with the same old/same old in his relationship with Billy and gets his kicks by spying on the slut in the apartment across the street, whose anal gymnastics get him hard. Billy is pissed at the lack of attention and when Steve's sleazy, ugly boss arrives with two hot buddies in tow, he decides to put on an anal show of his own. But things get out of hand and Steve is forced to watch as money changes hands and Billy spreads his cheeks for anyone who wants him.

"*H*oly shit, man, get a load of that ass." Jerry focused the binoculars on the fourth floor apartment across the street. With the magnification of those suckers, he could see straight into the living room through the wide-open balcony doors. As wide open as the guy's butthole, if I had my guess.

"Here, let me see." Mike snatched the glasses from him.

"I told you he was something out of the box," I said from the corner bar where I was topping up our drinks. I threw the empty Bourbon bottle in the trash to join the earlier one we'd already polished off.

Jerry, my sleazy boss at Klassic Kars where I worked as a detailer, came back to get his glass. He's chunky, in his early forties, shaven head and a splash of body hair across his chest; definitely a daddy type, but not exactly "attractive" to go with it. "You weren't kidding, Steve. That guy has it all. I could fuck that."

I knew for a fact that Jerry wasn't fucking anything at the moment. He was always at me to set him up with one of my single friends. It wasn't gonna happen.

Billy sneered. "I don't think there's anything special about him." He hated it when he wasn't the centre of attention.

"You're kidding, right?" Mike relinquished the glasses to Jerry, who definitely wanted another look. We'd met Mike at the showroom a few weeks earlier, when he'd come in to give a newly arrived 1956 Buick Century Riviera Four-Door Hardtop the once over. He'd bought it on the spot, counting out the price from a huge wad of high value banknotes he said he always carried in case of emergencies. This guy was seriously wealthy—or a braggart. Maybe both. And dumb as shit to carry around that much cash. Both Jerry and I had pegged him as gay, and Jerry had pegged him as available, something I wasn't, and flirted accordingly. Mike wore baggy blue jeans, navy sneakers and a black cotton T-shirt that hugged his chest so tight his hard nipples could have poked your eye out if you got too close. He looked to be around thirty with shaggy, black hair that he flicked with his fingers to keep it out of his hazel bedroom eyes. I would have been flirting as well, if I hadn't already been in a relationship, although said relationship was as rocky as a row boat in the North Atlantic at the moment. However, we liked to give the outward impression we were the perfect couple.

We had been when we first started out five years before. Billy was the five-feet-eight, tanned skinned, blond haired, blue-eyed beauty with the snug little body that had only gotten better and more defined when he'd 'discovered' the gym. I would have said 'obsessed' with the gym since his retrenchment as a sous-chef in a restaurant that didn't survive the economic downturn. That was just one of the problems. I was the other. I'm slightly taller, thinner and two years older at twenty-eight, with dirty blond hair matched with dirty blond eyes. That's what Billy called them when we first met at a bar that was so humid inside we didn't know whether the air conditioning had failed or whether we were so hot for each other we were producing our own power surge.

By the time we'd both emerged from our sex-addled euphoria, we found ourselves saddled with a substantial mortgage on a fifth-floor apartment in a high-rise development full of gay couples and solos, with minimalist but classy furniture, expensive cultural and social tastes, and maxed out credit cards. There is no way we could afford a separation, even if we'd wanted one.

We didn't. We were still comparatively happy together. We fitted, in the parlance of our friends and neighbors. We were popular. A little too popular. The apartment complex was a breeding ground of temptation and infidelity: attractive, buff boys of every color, class, creed and combination. I was like a kid in a rainbow hued candy store, and I wanted a taste of everything. Billy, however, was all eyes front, prim as a Sunday-go-to-meeting front pew fundamentalist.

Trouble is I was finding it hard to, well, get hard for the same old/same old boyfriend after all these years. No one wants to eat meat and potatoes year in year out, so why would they want to fuck the same ass regardless of how cute? The solution, we'd decided, was Paris, and not because of any overt familiarity with the city, but just a general romantic longing to spice up our lovemaking, which had become as stodgy as porridge. But financially, Paris was as far away as Mars.

That's why we'd been sniping at each other all afternoon, the atmosphere taut as tensile wire across a paddock, when an uninvited and unwelcome Jerry, with two new buddies in tow, arrived for an up-close-and-personal look at our exhibitionist neighbor.

"What's he doing here?" Billy hissed when I told him who had just buzzed our apartment. "You know I can't stand the ugly toad."

"I didn't invite him," I snarled back.

Just then he barreled through the open front door, and we both beamed our best imitation smiles at him. He was too crass to notice, but his buddies did.

"Knew you wouldn't mind," he said. "You know Mike already, and this is his young mate, Raoul. Where're the binoculars?" Jerry was all couth.

Raoul, about the same vintage as Mike, tattooed and twice as good looking, had an attitude to match. "If he's as hot as Jerry here says, why don't we go jump him and tattoo his ass with our spunk!" One look through the binoculars was enough to convince him.

"You sure you don't know his number, man? Or even his apartment, so I can go buzz him." Unluckily for Raoul, our neighbor lived in a security building, but that didn't prevent him from shouting obscene invitations across the street to zero success, and to my utter embarrassment.

"You should have bought extra binoculars and installed cinema chairs for the show." Billy was at his sarcastic stage.

"Hey, chill out," Raoul said. "This is some show."

"Tell me about it," Billy said. "I got up the other night for a drink and came out here to find Steve fully naked and jerking off while he watched pretty boy over there in action. He didn't even realize I was watching him until he blew his load in the Zamioculcas zamiifolia. And it's not the first time."

Raoul was getting irritable and horny. "In the fuckin' what?"

"Those plants over there," Billy said, pointing at our Zanzibar ferns.

"Sick, dude," said Mike.

"It's not like I do it every night," I said, trying to placate Billy and keep the evening peaceful. I didn't want an argument in front of the guests. "Anyway his show that night was something else. There was a group thing going on, and I was hard as steel."

"Glad something can still make you hard because it sure isn't me," he said.

"Oh, shiiiiit," Jerry said. "He's got company."

Even Billy moved to the balcony to have a look. Our neighbor never did it in the bedroom, always in the living room, either for our benefit, because he appreciated an audience, or maybe because he never washed his bed sheets. His brazen behavior encouraged mine and I no longer tried to hide the fact I jerked off to him.

Not any more than our little group was attempting to hide the fact we were watching him as closely as teen sci-fi geeks at a Star Trek convention.

Raoul moaned. "That's a great ass, dude."

"Not what I'd call a great ass," Billy said.

"Fuck, I'd slip him a bit any time," came Jerry.

I tried lightening the mood. "You'd slip anyone a bit any time."

"Just exactly what would you class as a great ass then?" Mike asked with an arch of an eyebrow.

Billy shrugged. "Mine, for example." He patted his butt.

If I'd been honest I would have agreed with him, but in a stale relationship the ass across the street was more appetizing than that readily available in my bed.

Mike laughed. "Yeah, right."

"We'll have to take your word for it," Jerry said.

Billy smiled. "Don't believe me?"

Mike looked from Billy to the exhibitionist across the way. He turned the binoculars on Billy. "I guess Steve will have to be the judge because he's the only one who's seen both."

I was angry our private life was being aired in front of my boss and virtual strangers. "Leave me out of it."

"You'd be biased anyway," Mike chipped in.

"There's only one way to settle this," Raoul said eagerly. "He'll have to show us."

I didn't like where this was heading.

"His visitor is porking his ass. Fuck, that is so hot." Jerry had turned back to the free show across the street.

There was a scramble. We grabbed the binoculars from one another for a close up of our neighbor bent over the back of his divan, a hung top pounding him from behind. Even without the aid of glasses, we could see it was quite a performance

"I could give you a much better show," Billy said.

Mike chuckled. "Man, there's no way. That guy is hot. Just look at him."

Lightning fast, Billy had his tank top off to reveal his marbled six pack with the small fluff of blond hair that snaked down under his army fatigues, which just as quickly dropped round his ankles. All that separated him from total nakedness was his navy striped briefs that clung to his bulging package and hugged his ass like toffee to an apple.

"Fuck, I thought I was ripped," Raoul said and flexed his arm. His bicep was good enough to lick.

I gulped my bourbon. I was losing control of the situation.

Billy dimmed the lights and programmed the CD player. Suddenly, "Sin" by Nine Inch Nails thundered through the apartment. I watched horrified as he slowly gyrated his body and wagged his ass like some cheap pole dancer, miming the lyrics about being 'defaced' and 'disgraced' as he swayed around the room like an Indian cobra under the influence of a Hindu snake charmer. Mike and Raoul were in party mood, whooping and hollering. As my lover swept his hips tantalizingly within reach, Mike opened his wallet and tucked a note into the band of Billy's briefs. Raoul was keen to join the testosterone melee that was engulfing the room and grabbed a handful of cash to shove down the front of Billy's increasingly revealing underwear while taking the opportunity to cop a feel. Jerry, as usual, was content to sit on his wallet.

I was acutely embarrassed. On the other hand, Billy's eyes shone. Before I could scramble to retrieve his clothing and drag him into the bedroom, even before telling everyone the party was over, he panted and patted his butt cheeks.

He smirked. "Well?"

Jerry adjusted his cock in his pants. I turned away, disgusted.

"Not bad. Not bad at all," Mike said. "But we still haven't seen the real thing."

Jerry sneered. "I can get ass and a blow job anywhere else for what you guys just paid."

Billy extricated the cash from his briefs and flourished it in the air. "You think I'm some two-bit whore?"

But even from where I was seated I could see it was a substantial wad.

Mike dared him by counting out two one hundred dollar bills. "How about this?"

"That's a lot of money just to look at someone's ass," Jerry said. He'd always been a mean bastard.

"What about me, man?" Raoul pleaded. Mike counted out another two hundred.

"You want to see it?" Billy asked Jerry.

The idea of my plug ugly boss ogling my boyfriend's ass turned my stomach. When Jerry hesitated, Mike snapped, "It's only fuckin' money. For that, you get a moment in ass heaven. Or else, you get your money back. Right?"

Billy nodded.

"What about him?" Jerry said, nodding toward me.

"Forget about him," Billy said. "He doesn't matter."

My presence was dismissed so completely, I was momentarily castrated of my balls and my ability to speak.

Jerry thought about it for a split second before reluctantly counting out his cash. "I'm in."

I finally found my voice. "Come on, guys." I tried to push the cash back into their hands, but there were no takers.

Mike smiled. "Hell no, the night just got real interesting."

"Now we can judge for ourselves whether this ass you're always bragging about is as hot as you think," Jerry crowed.

Billy took control. "Get them another drink, Steve. None of that cheap shit either. That good Scotch you save for special occasions."

I poured way too much liquor, hoping they'd pass out. Me, I poured an even stiffer one. I gulped it down at once, and it burned my gut like humiliation.

Billy lowered the lights further, small consolation, cleared a spot and had the visitors seat themselves on the floor around the edge of the rug that he was about to use as his stage. To catcalls and whistles, he ramped up the music and Nine Inch Nails, his favorite band, spewed out "Closer" as he circled the area, ferociously bumping and grinding to the anthem about wanting to violate, to desecrate, to penetrate, before hooking his fingers in the band of his briefs. Sidelined, I held my breath. Teasing like a professional stripper, Billy slid his hands down until he was stark naked, waving his hard cock close to the visitors' faces. But that's not what they'd paid to see. He swirled around and bent over, parting his perfect muscled asscheeks, daring them to touch him while, with perfect timing, he mouthed the lyrics "I want to fuck you like an animal." Raoul had already succumbed to a pheromone rush and was openly stroking his cock in appreciation, while Jerry kept looking in my direction, frightened of any repercussions.

Billy lay back on the coffee table. He raised his legs over his head, spread his butt cheeks with his hands, singing "my whole resistance is gone". All attention focused on his smooth, hairless thighs leading to that inviting pink, puffy hole. He licked his fingers and started to prod them into his sphincter. He looked so fuckin' hot burying three up to the second knuckle. "I guess I win," he said as he finger fucked the ass I had neglected of late.

I suddenly got my balls back and went to the CD player to end the charade, but in my confusion, all I did was bump the disc up louder. Billy raised his voice over the music, "Are you sure all you want to do is look?"

I could not believe what I was hearing.

"Add another five, and I'll let you fuck me right here."

Mike didn't hesitate. He peeled off five hundred and placed it on the coffee table, then smugly peeled off another five hundred for Raoul. Turning to Jerry he asked, "You in?"

Jerry's lust to pork my lover overcame his natural stinginess. His voice cracked as he told Billy, "Come by my office tomorrow and I'll pay you what you're worth."

The hypnotic song had been edited so that "I want to fuck you like an animal" was on a loop, a constant sexual command, cock hardening and orgiastic. Billy writhed to the pulse of the music as Mike leaned forward, pushing his strong, thin cock against his well-lubed sphincter. He slid right in.

Mike gasped. "Oh fuck."

Raoul moved quickly to hold Billy's legs to give Mike better access. He sank right down to his balls.

"Oh, man, you gotta try this fuckin' hole. Hot as hell, dude. Fuckin' ace."

Billy groaned as Mike slid in, a sound I remembered from the first time I pressed my come-drooling prick inside his eager guts. I shook my head in agony. Mike pulled out, hesitating a split second before lunging back into that slick ass chute. Raoul, not to be denied, slipped his cock into Billy's hungry mouth.

"That wasn't part of the deal," I mumbled.

Jerry was contemptuous. "Who gives a fuck? Always going on about how perfect your fucking relationship is and all the time your boyfriend's a come dump. Panting for cock from every sick bastard in the neighborhood. Well take a good look when I shove the cock that was never good enough for you up your sweet little boy's fuckhole." Jerry waved his ugly, drooling, stubby cock in my direction.

"This–mouth–was–born–to–suck–cock," Raoul panted. "His–throat–is–slick–as–pure–fuckin'–velvet."

"So is his asshole, man." Mike was battering my lover's ass like a tornado in Kansas. "Sweet asscunt."

"I bet the fuckin' slut could take two in his sweet boy pussy at the same time," Raoul said. "That way we can all do him together."

"I want the fucker's asshole," Jerry said. "No way will I settle for a blow job. This was about his ass."

Mike assumed control. "Okay, but you'll have to take sloppy seconds."

Jerry nodded. "No complaints from me. I'll just get his mouth to slick me up while I'm waiting."

Mike pulled out and lay on the carpet, holding his hard, slimy prick upright so Billy could skewer himself on it. Once successfully kebabed, he leaned forward to make his ass vulnerable to Raoul's liberally greased, uncircumcised weapon that he squeezed against Mike's, already buried up the battered asshole. Raoul, straining against his elastic ass muscles, made Billy cry out in pain before he relaxed, murmuring with pleasure. Jerry moved round to the only hole still available. I watched, repulsed, as he forced his thick cock between Billy's lips.

Incredibly, I was harder than I had ever been in my life. Harder than when I jerked off watching our neighbor take cock with considerably less skill than Billy. Harder than when the two of us first met and went at it like proverbial rabbits. Fuck, the realisation was like a cartoon light bulb in my brain: I got hard on watching. Sure, I was pissed big time about my lover slutting his body to two strangers, as well as my disgusting boss, but I was more excited than I ever had been when I fucked him. I liked, no, I fuckin' loved watching him take cock in his ass and his mouth. Cocks of strangers. Cock of an ugly brute of a man.

Billy was taking on three, severely stretching his limits. Stretching mine. My cock was feeding directly to my brain, admitting this new experience was the ultimate pleasure. There was no thought about the repercussions of what we were doing to our relationship—was it over? But all anger and frustration left me.

Raoul took over the rhythm of the assfuck, penetrating deeper and deeper, opening Billy wider.

"Fuckin' sensational," he praised as he slid his tan cock along the length of Mike's shaft, Billy's ass muscle stretching to take the two greasy pricks.

Jerry sounded like a bad porn movie as he viciously fucked Billy's mouth. "Fuck the little slut. Bury your cock in his guts. Ram his asshole."

Mike massaged Billy's slobbering cock as he and Raoul raised the momentum. I moved in closer to watch the two amazing slimy, hard pricks shafting their way into the needy hole. It was hot enough to be a porn movie; but knowing it was my boyfriend's ass that was copping a battering sent the sexual mercury through the roof. I was painfully hard. I stripped off my jeans and briefs and began to spit slick the knob. Mike smiled knowingly.

Jerry saw me as well, and encouraged by Billy slurping on his ugly prick like it was prize caviar, kept up his verbal humiliation. "Your sweet slut likes real man cock in his cunt mouth. Watch me slide it down his throat."

Billy didn't seem to care the real ugly fucker he was sucking was my boss, a man with biggest mouth for gossip in the county. It would be all over the showroom tomorrow that he'd fucked my boyfriend. Slamming into Billy's mouth, he held the back of his head, pinning him like a trophy butterfly. "Nasty. Just the way you like, eh boy?" Billy was turning purple from the fat fucker holding his face firm against his belly suffocating him with cock.

Billy gasped for air as gag puke drooled off his lips when Jerry finally let him free. He just wiped his mouth and plunged right back around Jerry's prick. He was oblivious to everything but cock.

The onslaught of Jerry's verbal abuse, plus the friction against his sphincter and his prostate knob buried inside his fuck canal finally pushed Billy to explode all over Mike's belly. That in turn contracted his ass muscles, squeezing his two synchronised fuckers until they screamed out their pending orgasm and shot almost simultaneously into his guts. They slumped, exhausted, until their shrinking cocks slipped out of Billy's well-fucked hole. Knowing how impatient Jerry was for his turn, they helped Billy back on to the coffee table and went to clean up, all the while keeping a watchful eye on the action.

Billy held his legs apart, his slimy ass canal dripping sex juice and begging to be filled again. Jerry grabbed me by the hair and pushed my face toward his prize. "You always thought this asshole was too good for me. Now look at it." Jerry shoved in his fingers, scooping out come and forcing it into my mouth. I sucked his fingers clean.

"Too good for anyone but you. Now it's dripping with other fuckers' spooge. Not too good now, is it?" He pushed my face into Billy's crack, smearing my face in the ass spunk. I tasted Mike and Raoul. He yanked my hair again; my face was level with his prick.

"Now get me slicked up Mr. High-and-Mighty. Too fuckin' smug to suck the boss's prick, but now look at you." He shoved it between my lips.

I tried to make him blow so he wouldn't plough Billy.

He must have guessed my intentions because he pushed me away. "That's enough! Beg for it, baby."

Billy whimpered. "Fuck me, fuck me now. I need you inside me,"

"You want my cock, baby? You want my hard man cock?"

"Rape my fuckin' ass! I need cock bad!"

Jerry gave what sounded like a strangled rebel yell and plugged Billy like he was plugging a dam, knocking the wind out of him.

I watched, fascinated, as this ugly fucker rammed into my lover. No finesse, just raw animal fucking.

Jerry cursed the slut, keeping up a string of filthy talk until it became so rancid I knew he was shooting his comesnot in Billy's asshole. He shuddered the last of his juice into Billy, then pulling out, he wiped his slime over my face.

Now that it was over Jerry could not look me in the eye. He dressed quickly, mumbled his farewell and headed for the door.

Billy lay exhausted, his asshole gaping and dripping spunk. Raoul and Mike, now cleaned up and fully dressed, stood surveying the scene as if it were a disaster zone. I was so shell-shocked by the whole experience I feebly offered them coffee like a good host. They politely turned it down and headed for the door.

"Worth every penny." Raoul adjusted his crotch, and was gone.

Mike hesitated at the door. "He's right you know. One of the best asses I've ever had. You're a very lucky man, Steve. I envy you. And Billy's a lucky man to have you."

When Mike closed the door, the silence was deafening.

Billy lay naked and still, his arm across his eyes, waiting for the storm he knew was coming. I picked up the cash and counted it.

"With that bastard Jerry's money tomorrow that gives us just about enough to take that trip to Paris we were planning for our anniversary." I said, scarcely daring to breathe.

Billy took his arm away from his eyes and looked at me, stunned. I smiled.

He returned my smile. Relieved. He looked at my aching cock. "Why don't you fuck me now."

Damn. We were back to the same old routine. I regretted we'd lost the moment for a new beginning as I slid into his sloppy asscunt.

Then Billy said, "I hear those French boys are really something."

I fucked him with a vigor I hadn't felt for a long time.

JOLLY ROGERING

What's a guy to do when his lover joins a band of pirates, but the only booty they're interested in is the boyfriend's?

After selling his ass to three sleazebags in revenge for Steve's neglect, Billy puts further pressure on their relationship when he joins an amateur production of Gilbert & Sullivan's *Pirates of Penzance.* The pirate chorus has definite designs on Billy's booty that will culminate in his getting it in the aft from all of them at the closing night party…if they can just get rid of Steve for an hour or two.

"General dogsbody is not what I signed on for," Matt shouted at the pirates. "I've had it up to here with too many sweaty leather pants and pissy jockstraps. They can wash their own fuckin' undies from now on." Matt threw the offending items in Colin's general direction and stood with his arms dramatically on hips. It was a Bette Davis moment.

I heard Vern whisper, "With a performance like that she could be an overnight sensation."

"She bellows and screams like an A-grade diva," Richard guffawed.

I hate it when gay guys call each other 'she.' Granted, it was old-fashioned gay Polari, but I hate it.

Matt was steaming. "As for you, Miss Digit Dick," he said, turning on Richard, using the disparaging name everyone, including his best friends, used behind his back, "You might try wiping on the odd occasion so I don't have to scrape the skidmarks off your tights before I send them to the laundry." He stormed toward the exit.

There was an audible gasp. You just don't speak to pirates in this manner. No siree. Not if you wanted to survive for very long. Even if the pirates in question were part of a production of Gilbert and Sullivan's The Pirates of Penzance. Even if they were an unruly chorus of street trash, ferals and narcissistic bodybuilders.

I stood in shadows at the back of the rehearsal hall watching the drama unfold, already having decided to keep my presence unobserved because no one likes their dirty laundry aired, least of all when it seems to be as stained as this group's.

Colin, the young Goth director, looked up from the script he'd been studying with a concentration I'd never seen him employ before, his shoulders heaving in an attempt to stifle giggles. Colin giggled, he never laughed.

"Rightio, love, I think we get your point." His attempt to restore calm was met with the slam of the auditorium doors as Matt made his dramatic exit. Colin sighed loudly.

From the gossip that Billy delighted in relaying when he came back from rehearsals four nights a week, this tension had been festering for some time. He'd auditioned for the disparate group of small-town theatricals who came together, sometimes, it was rumored, in more ways than one, three times a year to present an orgy of culture, usually some out of copyright musical extravaganza.

Billy, whose total on-stage theatre experience up to that point had been a brief stint as third pumpkin from the left in a grade school production of Cinderella, which he confessed he gave up because "the orange make-up gave me hives", had taken on the challenge because he had been unemployed so long his self-esteem was suffering. We both thought the audition would be a good way to ease back into selling his abilities and his personality when it came to job applications. We were both equally amazed by his success. Billy had, it transpired, a lovely, untrained tenor voice, was an adequate enough actor, particularly in a pair of tights and with his shirt off, and looked amazing next to the huge brick shithouse of a guy who was playing The Pirate King to Billy's Frederic.

With an enthusiasm that pleased me, Billy embraced the role and was a conscientious study. He would return from rehearsals buzzing with gossip and gripes, although there were few enough of the latter and mainly concerning members of the cast, especially Vern and Richard, who couldn't keep their members to themselves. They were looking for bed, not wed. A one-night honeymoon. No matter how shaky our relationship had become, Billy was very definitely wed.

It was about six months after Billy peddled his ass to my butt ugly boss and two of his buddies in revenge for my obsession: jerking off to an exhibitionist neighbor. We'd sidetracked talking about the momentous event, mainly because Billy felt like a slut. I had convinced myself that because I'd enjoyed the experience as a voyeur I was a pervert, until our relationship began hemorrhaging and we were forced to sit down and confront our action. There was lots of sobbing, begging for forgiveness and heartfelt promises that we would never allow ourselves to get back to that situation again.

Now, here we were, back to the same old/same old. At first, we intended using the bundle of cash he'd made for a trip to Paris to rekindle the spark of our romance, but the dollar to euro exchange rate, the exorbitant surcharge for aircraft fuel, and the fact a bit of infidelity performed in front of me furnished my fantasies for a number of months, meant our invigorated love life was better spent at home. Spent in all senses of the word. I spent my seed vigorously in Billy's hot, insatiable ass, visualizing his nasty defilement by the three guests, until we were both spent of energy and flopped exhausted in bed. And our limited resources were spent, albeit more sparingly, on the day-to-day necessities of life, but the savings did, eventually, begin to dwindle.

I'd been paid out by the aforementioned boss, who had been too embarrassed, as shame was not in his vocabulary, to keep me on after he'd fucked my boyfriend in front of me in an act of defiant humiliation, even though I was the best detailer at the showroom. Unemployment and a large mortgage on our luxury apartment had eaten into Billy's ass-earned money. It didn't help matters that he was also unemployed, sous chefs not being in particular demand in an economic downturn. Billy still spent his days at the gym finessing his already magnificent body to chiseled perfection and his evenings at rehearsals, particularly now that opening night was rapidly approaching. I would drop in occasionally to see him after the rounds of employment agencies and car dealerships.

Billy threw himself into research, becoming more and more confident, as stacks of books on acting, which he never got around to opening, battled for attention with a collection of swashbuckling movies starring such stalwarts of the genre as Steve Reeves, Gordon Scott and other actors more noted for their muscular bodies than the subtleties of their acting skills. We would watch those curled up on the lounge in our spare moments, and Billy would get hard watching pirates stripped to the waist, young men kidnapped by pirate hordes and made to suffer at their hands—in fact, just about anything semi-naked and piratical. I reaped the benefits in a more willing and pliable Billy, who would do just about anything for his pirate king—me.

I just wondered what Billy would do for the show's Pirate King, the brick shithouse bodybuilder named Pernel. They looked so cute together, so hot, and in fact, the company had decided to go with Billy and Pernel on the posters: big, black Pernel with bulging muscles and a chest dripping with perspiration glancing down at an adoring blond, blue-eyed Billy. It pushed the buttons on a few racist fantasies, but it showed two hot men at the peak of their perfection lusting after each other.

"Sailors and pirates always used to fuck the cabin boy in real life," Billy told me one night while I had my fingers embedded in his hot asshole.

"Aren't you the cabin boy in this production?"

"Yes, but it's a comedy. Colin just wants us to bone up on the background and try to incorporate that as subtext." Billy's eyes glazed over as he thought of the subtext.

Pushing my fingers in harder until I triggered his orgasm by playing with his prostate, I asked, "Is that your fantasy? Having Pernel and the pirates gangbang this cute little ass?"

I had to admit, if only to myself, even I had fantasies about Pernel, and the pause before Billy answered, spoke more eloquently of his feelings than his feeble denial. Later, as I tormented his ass with my cock, he admitted he had often jerked off to fantasies of pirates dominating him. But not make-believe theatre pirates, I hoped.

Colin's retro take on the hoary old G&S classic was to explore the homoeroticism of pirate culture, as well as going for the gritty realism of pirate life by casting as many actors who looked like street rabble as possible. Admittedly, he'd had problems because not only did they have to look like rough trade, they had to be built, ruggedly good looking, and be able to at least hold a tune. The approach had created a buzz in theatergoing circles, in the gay community, and sneers among the G&S aficionados and the old guard of the theatre company who began dropping out as Colin's vision unfolded. So many had departed the sinking ship that only a six pirate crew remained.

I was becoming concerned myself, not at the interpretation, but at Billy arriving home later and later after socializing to wind down after rehearsals. He was forever at me to come and meet 'the guys'. On the one occasion I had taken him up on the offer, I was made anything but welcome. It was obvious to all, but the blithely unaware Billy, that the clique was strictly members only—theatricals. I didn't mind. I was picking up a bit of part-time employment here and there, often coming home buggered, in the fatigued sense rather than the sexual meaning. Sometimes, if I'd been working late, I would call in to rehearsals to see if Billy wanted a lift home. It was those occasions he would try to drag me along to the pub or someone's home to debrief on the night's activities.

This was one such night. Colin, the young drama tyro from the local university, dressed goth-like in basic black, his left earlobe sporting a plug that stretched it like some tribal warrior's, his eyebrows pierced with silver bars, as well as, so rumor had it, piercings in more intimate areas, called everyone's attention back to the rehearsal. The pianist rumbled the keys on the old upright, and what was left of the pirate chorus assumed position.

The Pirate King himself stood centre stage, as magnificent a specimen as you were ever likely to see. If Broadway ever started casting purely on the size of pecs, abs and biceps, Pernel was Tony Award winning material. But that body was matched with a voice just as impressive, so deep you could have thrown a bucket down it and never hit bottom. Not only that, he was married to the fiercely protective actress playing Mabel, who thwarted his every attempt to get Billy alone. I was grateful for her interventions. As was Billy. Or so he said.

This was the first costume rehearsal, and I had to say the pirate chorus was outstanding. One by one, they stepped forward to show their costumes. The rugged look had certainly paid off. If there was a shortage of tops in any city all you had to do was send for this motley pirate crew. Then Billy stepped forward. He took your breath away. His torso had been oiled, and his muscles glistened under the work lights, the shadows emphasizing the curves of his chest and arms. His tights were low slung and the apron, rather than the blacks and tans of the somewhat anonymous rabble, was a startling deep blue that matched his eyes and highlighted his blondness. When he turned, there were squeals of admiration. The designer, bless him, had highlighted Billy's curvy ass, the tights squeezing between his butt cheeks so that if he leaned forward I'm sure we would have seen his puckered hole outlined in the fabric—that's how snug was the fit. It was inspired, too, that the back of the tights were cut in a V to reveal the cleavage of his tantalizing butt crack.

But even Billy paled into insignificance when Pernel strode forward. If Billy glistened, Pernel gleamed, his muscles reflecting light like the sun on a winter's morning. All movement in the hall stopped. In a coup so inspired it was the main reason advance bookings for this production had outstripped any of the company's previous, Colin, a believer in non-traditional casting, had recruited the black bodybuilder over his wife's objections, for she knew the predatory nature of show queens well. It didn't hurt that his voice was swoon-worthy, that he looked the part in his tights and cummerbund, and, not least, what a sword! Everyone noticed Pernel's weapon, including the director.

"I appreciate good advertising as much as the next man, but you could have someone's eye out with that," Colin said as he poked said appendage with his finger, giving a surreptitious thumbs up, meaning 'it's all real' to those cock cognoscenti present. "The only weapons I want to see on stage are of the plastic variety being swung about your heads, not stuffed down your tights."

He whirled around and called, "Matt, do something about the bulge, love. Matt?" Then realising his costume designer had walked, he cursed and strode toward where Matt had been last seen, dismissing the company with, "Take ten. I'll go and placate Matt. Meanwhile, Billy, go and relieve Pernel." The cast guffawed. "Of his costume, love. Get him a tunic or something off the rack to cover his modesty. Or lack thereof."

The chorus wandered away, some to the dressing room to go through their lines, others to the back alley behind the theatre to indulge their tobacco addiction, while Billy and Pernel slipped among the racks of costumes offstage left.

Keeping to the shadows along the side walls of the auditorium, I slipped closer to the stage. The cover of the curtains hid me as I clambered up the rehearsal steps opposite Billy and Pernel, who were now whispering conspiratorially among the racks of costumes that had been scrounged from op shops and other theatre companies waiting to be tried on by various cast members and then taken in, let out, or whatever was needed by the ever-eager Matt once Colin could lure his return.

I climbed silently up the metal ladder to the walkways from which the lights were hung above the stage, giving me an unobstructed view of everything below. Pernel was beetroot with embarrassment. "My fucking cock is always getting me in trouble. It's these fucking tights. They rub against my dick and, hey, what guy wouldn't get hard?" As if to prove his point, he rolled them down, his cock springing free. Billy demurely looked at the floor. "It'll never go down in time for rehearsal."

But I bet Billy will, I thought.

"Come on, Billy." Pernel waved his cock in the air. "I'm due back on in ten."

Billy stared at the bulging black shaft while Pernel caressed it invitingly, the vein running over his huge biceps throbbing. Billy stood mesmerised as Pernel, moving slowly closer to his target, worked himself toward orgasm until he was close enough to put his hand around the back of Billy's head, easing him to his knees and his mouth on to his cock.

There was no resistance as he slid his monster between Billy's lips. It took only a few strong thrusts before Billy had swallowed it all the way, his mouth stretched in that startled O reminiscent of plastic blow-up dolls. Part of me marvelled at his skill in swallowing the enormous cock; another part of me was pleased to have such a great vantage point for the live porno show, but a smaller part of me was furious at Billy for reneging on our agreement. I wrestled my outraged sense of morality into perspective, especially as I now had leverage over Billy in future disagreements. I adjusted my cock, which had hardened as a result of the cocksucking exhibition.

I lay down on the metal walkway to be less obvious and peered through the spaces in the metal slats. Billy endured a few more throat fucks before pushing Pernel away, his cock plopping from my boyfriend's mouth glistening with his saliva.

"You're married," Billy spat. "You shouldn't be doing this."

"You've got a boyfriend," Pernel said with no sense of contrition. "What they don't know—"

"Oh, they'll find out all right. This place lives and breathes gossip."

My stomach lurched. Billy was more concerned about being found out than about any moral dilemma.

Pernel crushed Billy against his massive chest, cupping his butt in his strong hands, squeezing and massaging in an attempt to get him to change his mind. He looked into Billy's eyes. "Your boyfriend knows you're a slut, right?"

I saw Billy tense then glare at him. "What gives you the right to say that?"

"Come on, Billy, everybody's heard about you putting out for your boyfriend's boss and his buddies. Must have been quite a party."

"I was drunk," Billy snapped, pushing the man away.

Pernel shrugged. "Not what I heard, but if it makes you feel better."

Billy flew at him, pummeling his chest and his arms in anger and frustration. Pernel allowed the first few blows then held him at arm's length. "Whoa, mate. Sorry. Sorry. I didn't mean to upset you. You say you're not a slut, I believe you."

Billy calmed down and Pernel released his grip, pulling my boyfriend to him and cuddling him protectively. "But, hell, babe, it's not easy having you so near knowing I can't touch. You get me hard. All the time. I don't know how I can get through a performance without getting wood, especially when I see your spectacular ass in front of me."

"You think my ass is spectacular?" Billy sounded surprised.

Pernel purred, running his hands over it. "One of the natural wonders of the world. Listen, I'm really sorry for what I said earlier, but I gotta get rid of this hard on before Colin gets back with Matt."

Billy tried to interrupt.

"No, hear me out. I don't want you to do anything you're uncomfortable with, but how about you just let me look at your ass while I jerk off."

"I don't know," Billy said, his conflicting desires written all over his face.

"No touching. I promise."

Billy looked skeptical, but I knew it wouldn't be long before Pernel persuaded him. All it took was a hangdog look from Pernel with a half-hearted pull of his prick.

"Okay, where do you want me?"

"Just on this chest with your legs apart." Pernel led him to an old wooden chest that served as a set dressing and repository for various props. He helped Billy remove his tights before pushing him over on to his back and posing his legs so his juicy butthole was visible and agonizingly vulnerable. Leaning against the theatre's side wall, Pernel concentrated all his energies on Billy's hole, his gaze searing enough that I thought for sure Billy was in danger of his butt combusting spontaneously.

Pernel moved closer, all the while stroking his cock. I was interested to see if he would keep his word. No sooner had the thought entered my mind than Pernel was rubbing his big hands over Billy's gorgeous butt and flicking his finger at the inviting hole. Billy told him to cut it out, but made no effort to push the hand away. In fact, his eyes glazed over, his head went back, and he moaned quietly, playing with his own stiffening prick.

Pernel, transfixed by Billy's ass, began a deep chant that was barely audible where I was crouched. "That's a beautiful asshole, Billy. One of the best I've ever seen. It was made to be fucked. To be shared around. One man will never satisfy you. You're a cock whore. You need regular fucking. You should be a real pirates' slut. You should let the pirates gangfuck you whenever they get horny. You'd love to feel pirate cock in your mancunt, Billy."

I could tell from the way Billy writhed he wouldn't last much longer. It was an amazing sight. My boyfriend lay out below me, his legs in the air, displaying his cunthole, while a mammoth black pirate massaged his cheeks and fingered that hole while jerking his own throbbing meat.

Hearing other sounds, I scanned the backstage area. I saw Matt, his professionalism obviously getting the better of him, watching from between the costume racks, consumed with excitement, longing for an opportunity to join in.

"You need come, slutboy? You want to lap up my manjuice? All over your face? You worship cock. You're a good little come lapdog, aren't you, slutboy?"

"Yes, sir," Billy grunted as he blew his load, shooting high in the air, landing on his chest and on the floor. Pernel moved closer and aimed his come at Billy's hole, squirting a huge load all over his ass and balls. He scooped it up with his fingers, pushing it into Billy's asshole then, moving to his face, he forced Billy to lick his slimy cock clean.

Pernel pulled up his tights, tucking his now soft cock discretely to one side, selected a leather Tunic from the rack and tugged it over his head. "Thanks, Billy boy. You were a big help. See you on stage." He slapped Billy's butt hard as he exited.

Billy still lay dazed until a shout from Colin in the auditorium reminding the cast they were now due back on stage galvanised him to action. Not finding a cloth of any description, he wiped the sticky come on his fingers and sucked them into his mouth, missing a few spots so that his skin glistened where the spunk still dripped. He yanked up his tights and ran back to rehearsal. I remained in position, lest I be discovered, and watched as Matt came out of hiding. He walked over to the scene of the action and kneeled to examine something that had taken his interest. Seconds later, his face was on the stage floor lapping away at the puddle he had discovered. I would have to watch Matt more closely in future.

Eventually, when all was clear, I left my perch, clambered down, exiting via the stage door, re-emerging through the front of the theatre as if I had just arrived. I sat quietly at the back of the dark auditorium watching the production take shape, admiring Billy's blossoming talent, and carefully watching the pirate chorus. A distracted Billy decided to accept the lift I offered rather than go drinking with his stage buddies, giving me the opportunity to quiz him about the night's proceedings.

He was morose in the car on the way home, clutching my thigh tightly. "Steve," he said barely audibly. "Do you think I'm a slut?"

If I hadn't witnessed the exchange between Billy and Pernel in the theatre I would have been tempted to laugh, but I treated his question seriously.

"No, I don't," I said without having to weigh up my answer. If I paused, he might be suspicious. "Why do you ask?"

It all poured out. The insinuations from the other cast members, their constant unwanted harassment, then, reluctantly at first, his infidelity with Pernel. I pretended a concern I did not feel. I told him the act had been forced upon him.

"But I enjoyed being forced," he admitted. "It made me feel wonderfully cheap and nasty. I know that's unfair on you." There was much moralising and apologising until we reached home.

Once inside the apartment, I swept sweet Billy into my arms, kissed him gently before carrying him to our bedroom, and laying him on the bed, stripping his rehearsal sweats from him, I knelt between his thighs as I hoisted his legs over my shoulders. "I love you, Billy," I said as I plunged into his luscious asshole. "Just remember that. Whatever you do, as long as you remain true to yourself, I will always love you. If you think you need forgiveness then you've got it. I give it to you in advance. If you think you have to live by some set of rules that other people want to impose on you, you'll just tie yourself up in guilty knots. Life's too short. My only hope is that you'll keep on loving me." He got misty.

While I pumped my cock in and out of his asshole, I thought of how he looked as Pernel towered over him, feeding him massive black prick. I'd swear Billy was fantasising about the same thing.

The opening night was soon on us, and I was going with two of Billy's best mates, Vince and Andy. Vince was an ugly fucker. The remnants of a rugged handsomeness still faintly apparent under the patina of acne, booze and drugs, he ran a leather fetish retail outlet that specialised in slings, handcuffs, harness and hoods, was a leather top, and was a good thirty years older than either Billy or me. You can tell I don't like the guy. Oh, he's always pleasant enough to my face, but I knew he was a backstabbing bastard. He tormented his partners like young kids torment ants. Andy was just as obnoxious, although better built, and was the key designer in Vince's workshop. They prowled gay bars together, both often working over the same bottom. I knew they had designs on Billy, and I also knew they thought I wasn't good enough for him. They, of course, thought they were. Up to date, they hadn't convinced Billy himself, but they kept working on it. We observed an uneasy truce.

They were already in their seats when I arrived. I'd been back stage telling Billy how proud I was, how Johnny Depp would be on the phone hiring him for the next Pirates of the Caribbean once word got around, all in an attempt to calm his jitters. I wished all the pirates in the dressing room the best, without using the dreaded word 'luck', and I could sense they were glad to see me go. They began circling Billy like sharks before I'd even closed the door.

I barely had time to greet Vince and Andy before the overture began, the curtain went up on the pirate ship, and it was immediately apparent where this show was headed. Ten pirates, as near naked as legally possible were strutting their pirate stuff. Colin had augmented the crew by the simple expedient of sending out press releases to the print and electronic media that this particular cruise was looking for a few good men to join the search for pirate booty. And to highlight that booty, they'd used a revealing photo of Billy's ass being lovingly fondled by Pernel.

Ticket sales had shot up accordingly, and there was an avalanche of applications to join the crew. Colin had sole discretion in wading through the competition entries, only he knew the rules—if there were any—and he'd found four of the nastiest looking animals you'd find on a stage, the sorts of guys who'd play rapists and perverts in the movies. Their saving grace was their bodies, and unless they had been artificially enhanced, their packages, which promised mouth-stuffing delights. Colin had gone for authenticity because these guys had enough studs and jewelry to set off a metal detector at a hundred paces. But, god, did they look the genuine article. The fact they couldn't sing a fuck didn't matter. They mimed while the six theatrical pirates did all the vocal chorus work. It was a brilliant touch and the audience applauded spontaneously. And they kept applauding, and gasping, through Billy's entrance as the indentured pirate who has just reached his 21st birthday. And finally, the entrance of The Pirate King, whose present to the young cabin boy is a symbolic sword. Colin made sure the audience was acutely aware that the sword Pernel, as the Pirate King, really wanted to give Billy's Frederic was the one between his thighs.

The night was a triumph. At interval, the audience began texting and ringing people on their cell phones, partly in a display of one-upmanship, but also because of genuine delight at a theatrical surprise. After the show the hubbub increased, people thronging to be invited to the opening night party, which was transferred to the theatre when it was realised Vern's apartment could no longer accommodate the crowds. He looked anything but pleased when he was told of the change. My suspicion that he'd planned something nefarious that involved Billy was thus confirmed. I had a quiet chuckle to myself.

Backstage was a madhouse as well-wishers milled about until the lead actors deigned to appear before their adoring public. Colin had decreed that as the party was at the theatre, and the crowds were threatening to overwhelm the little security available—the doorman—they should emerge from the safety of their dressing rooms and mingle as soon as possible.

Vince and Andy found the whole evening a bit too 'girlie' for their leather tastes, but they did enjoy the pirates and thought Billy was superb. They declined an invitation to come backstage and said they'd have Billy over for a debrief and 'whatever', that was their word, when the season was over. I was glad of their reluctance to stay. I soon became part of the crowd backstage, pushing my way toward the pirates, when I heard a cheer go up. I pulled Billy into my arms, planting a sloppy kiss on his sweaty mouth.

"Mmmm." He broke for breath. "Does that kiss mean I didn't embarrass myself?"

"You were brilliant," I said. As if to confirm my opinion, a number of people slapped him on the back offering their congratulations. More than a few people, I noticed, slapped him lower down. If Billy noticed, he didn't let on because he was glowing in the accolades that were flowing his way. He told me Colin had been the first to burst into the dressing room, so hyped up the cast thought he would explode.

Billy, too, was high on the audience adulation, as if he'd taken speed. He held my hand, always introducing me as his boyfriend or lover, to the chagrin of a few men, and women, who had been intending to make a play for him. I congratulated Vern and Richard on a job well done, as well as George and Peter, the only two straight pirates remaining. Then I was taken to be introduced to the four newbies who stood somewhat apart, surly and unappreciated.

Their attitude didn't help. They ranged in age from their twenties to their forties, and were incredibly belligerent, probably a defence mechanism, just as intimidating in the flesh as they were on stage, but they softened when Billy approached.

"Hey, Billy. Great fuckin' job, mate," the older of the group said. I was introduced to Deuce. It was obvious he and the others had a soft spot for Billy.

The others were Hal, Spike, and the youngest was Lorrie. Their conversation dried up pretty quickly, then Billy dragged me along to meet more of his new friends. The atmosphere was electric. I shook so many hands, got so many "you lucky fucker" from people who envied my relationship with the star of the moment, it was becoming tedious. Pernel's wife was coping a lot less graciously as adoring queens pawed her man.

The backstage crush began to thin out as people realised they had no chance with Billy or Pernel, although I noticed the other pirates had collected a swag of phone numbers; even the four ring ins. Vern suddenly appeared and suggested now was a good time to toast their success in the dressing room. "I don't drink. I get silly if I have too much," Billy said. Vern looked pleased, but replied, "Just one little champagne. It never hurt anyone. And you can't toast your success with a soda." When I looked as if I might join in, Vern said, "I hope you don't mind sharing Billy just this once, but it's only for cast. " I didn't like his tone.

I smiled. "I understand. It's a group thing. Been there, done that. Outsiders don't understand it."

Vern looked surprised that I would relinquish Billy so readily. Crushing my mouth against Billy's and squeezing his delectable ass proprietarily, I let him go and turned my attention to Colin, who was attempting to set up party food for the masses on a trestle table on the stage. He was grateful for the assistance because everyone, including Matt, was busy swanning about or else had tasks to perform. Matt was busy getting the costumes ready to clean for the following performance. I made sure I told him how much his designs added to the production, giving him a hug and a more than social kiss. He was surprised but pleased I'd singled him out. As I turned to walk back to Colin, Matt stopped me. "It's none of my business," he stuttered, "but I wouldn't leave Billy alone in the dressing room too long."

I laughed. "You don't want to fuck him, too?"

He was embarrassed. "I'm a bottom."

"Not a state secret, Matt." I grabbed him and stuck my tongue in his mouth, startling him, while I squeezed his butt cheeks tightly. When we broke our lip lock, I said, "I bet you're good at it, too." I slapped his ass.

He went back to his costumes…smiling.

Colin and I chatted away as we set up. He was an ambitious young man and, to my surprise, straight. He'd seen the hoary old Gilbert and Sullivan warhorse as an opportunity to show off, and he'd gone for it. Against all odds, it had worked.

We finished fairly quickly and went round each of the dressing rooms, telling people all was ready for the main celebration. I left the pirates until last. Knocking briefly, I entered. Animals caught in the headlights would be an apt description. The laughter dried up and people sprang apart. Billy was snuggled on Spike's lap, crowded on the battered old lounge suite in a corner of the room. The whole room was dim with most of the lights having been turned off and the only real illumination coming from a lamp at the far end of the room and a few globes above the actors' mirrors. I could see that Billy was out of his tights, but his pirate apron still covered his groin. A small table in front of them was covered with cans of soda and a number of bottles of spirits, mainly vodka and rum. Vern was pouring cola into a glass, which I noticed had a large portion of clear liquid on the bottom. When the glass was filled, he handed it to Billy.

Billy was unfazed and did nothing to disguise the fact his naked ass was wedged against Spike's lap, perhaps because Spike was fully clothed. "Hello, love," he said. "Having a good time?"

I acted as if nothing were amiss, smiled genially at the company. They all visibly relaxed. "Colin says you can come out of hiding now. The crowds have thinned and the party can begin."

"We're having a party here." Billy was already two sheets to the wind, but I pretended not to notice. What I did notice, however, was there were friends of the cast in the room, after I had been specifically excluded. "Move over," Billy said as he shoved Vern to make room. "Come and sit here, Steve." Vern looked most unhappy.

"No, love, it looks a bit cramped. I'll stay over here." Billy got up reluctantly, revealing the bulge in Spike's costume, but I said, "Stay there, Billy, if you're comfortable." He attempted to sit down again, but wobbled until Vern put his hands out to steady him, managing to guide him on to his own lap. Billy put out his hand for balance. It landed on Spike's crotch. In the shadow, Spike put his big hand on top of Billy's, trapping it there, manipulating it along his cock. Billy looked too out of it to notice.

"Where's my drink?" Billy asked. When he'd stood up to join me, he'd placed it on the far side of the small table. He rose unsteadily, leaning over the table to retrieve it, Vern holding his waist. I winked at him. His eyes opened wide in surprise then he made an almost inaudible purring sound. I recognised it immediately for what it was. Billy had something pleasurable wedged in his butt. It was difficult to make out at first until I noticed Vern had only one hand on Billy's waist, which meant he was pushing the fingers of his other hand into Billy's vulnerable asshole. He was being secretive about it, so he obviously thought I wouldn't notice. Before Billy could start moaning, Vern removed his fingers to help him retrieve his glass before guiding him carefully back down on to his lap. This time Billy did gasp. Spike attempted to cover it by faking a coughing fit, as if his drink had gone down the wrong way. Billy attempted to escape, but Vern held him tightly. I guessed he'd guided his cock up Billy's ass as he sat down. In his struggle to get up, Billy was milking Vern's prick.

Everyone in the room watched my reaction to gauge if I knew what was going on. I gave no indication, chatting amiably about the production and how good they all had been. Billy's eyes rolled, which meant he'd given up struggling. Smiling weakly in my direction—that was his guilty look—he bobbed as unobtrusively as he could, putting his hand back in Spike's lap, jerking him in the shadows. I was amused that they thought they'd get away with it, and that they'd all get a turn. I would have broken it up there and then except Billy was enjoying himself. They'd obviously laced his soda with vodka or rum, so he was blithely unconcerned about anything but pleasure at the moment, except for keeping it secret from me.

I stood up. Everyone froze. "Well, I'm going out to join in the fun at the party. You guys coming?" It was an obvious pun, but I couldn't help myself.

Those not involved in the action got up, crowding me to the door. "Don't be long, Billy. And put some clothes on before you come outside."

"Give me five, and I'll be right with you, love," Billy mumbled.

I'd be willing to take a bet there were five who would readily volunteer even though he obviously meant minutes.

It took him a minute or two longer, but he was dressed and had sobered up a little. Maybe he realised what he was doing and felt guilty. I pulled his face over to mine, pushing my tongue between his sweet lips as I ran my hands down his back and under his belt. He tried unsuccessfully to fight me off, but I could taste the residue of spunk in his mouth. My finger found his funky hole and slid right in without resistance to the sperm porridge in his guts.

Billy whimpered. "What's got into you tonight?"

"Just making sure my boyfriend is having a good time and that I'm part of it."

He pouted. "I think the guys must have put something in my soda. I feel a bit light-headed."

"It's all the excitement."

The remainder of the night passed without major incident except that as Billy sobered up, he became much more aggressive at rejecting unwanted passes from cast members, including an attempted toilet cubicle grope by Robert, who ended up with a swollen lip when he wouldn't accept Billy's forceful rejection. They also kept trying to fool him with sodas laced with alcohol, but he wised up and began pouring his own drinks. Eventually, their lack of success frustrated them, and they turned on one another, and more particularly, on Vern and Spike, who had managed to have their way with drunken Billy. We left them arguing loudly in the dressing room.

The next morning Billy's triumph was offset by his piercing headache. He wasn't so stupid not to realise he was hung over, although I had seen him, once or twice, fake a hangover to excuse outrageous behavior. This one, I knew, was the real thing. I cocooned him as best I could by lavishing as much healing aspirin as praise, but the telephone was insistent until he answered it. He turned down an invitation from Vince and Andy for a two-on-one debrief, pleading alcohol poisoning, stalled the local gay paper who requested what would probably be an ass-to-face interview, was pleased Mike and Raoul had liked the show 'even though we're not into musicals', and was generally gracious to fans who found his number on Facebook or in the telephone directory. At this rate, we'd have to move. In the end, I took the phone off the hook to give him some relief.

"Those bastards," he said when the throbbing in his temples began to subside. "They obviously laced the soda."

"Uh huh," I said. "The dressing rooms were littered with empty vodka and rum bottles."

"They know I can't drink without..." I saw the sudden realization cloud his gorgeous face. He lowered his face into his hands in shame. "What did I do? I'm so sorry, Steve. Please forgive me." He knelt beside me with those puppy dog eyes of his, admittedly a little bloodshot, pleading. "I promise I won't do it again. Promise."

I ruffled his silky blond hair. "Firstly, you didn't do anything to be ashamed of." I had chosen my words carefully. "Secondly, even if you had, it was not your fault. The lesson here is not to trust those bastards."

The remainder of the three-week season went off without a hitch. They had to extend the show by a week to cater to the demand for tickets, Billy was careful what he drank, and I went to every performance. I'm not a control freak because I know Billy can look after himself—and how! No, I enjoyed watching him perform, developing the role so that by the end of the first week he was acting and singing up a storm. I usually sat with Colin, who presided over every aspect of the show like a proud father. And so he should have been. On the strength of this production, he won a scholarship to a prestigious campus with an even more prestigious theatre department.

As closing night approached, Billy became a little despondent, as if all vestige of self worth would disappear along with the applause. But first, he had to negotiate the usual promise of revelry and larrikin behavior at the after-show party. I was less worried because it was being held at the outer suburban palatial home of one of the city's major cultural philanthropists, an elderly heterosexual couple, about whom there was not so much as a whisper of scandal let alone a breath. But first, the cast had to clear up their dressing rooms, the backstage crew had to strike the set ready to send to storage, the musicians to clear up their instruments and music stands, and Matt to collect the costumes for cleaning and returning from whence they came.

The final performance, the proceeds of which were earmarked for local gay charities, surpassed even the opening night for glitz, glamour and standing ovations. The audience didn't want to let the cast go, and they were obliged to return for so many encores they might just as well have repeated the entire show. People seemed reluctant to leave the theatre, milling around in the auditorium talking to friends, lingering in the foyer and at the bar.

Backstage was a hive of activity as people hurried to make a quick exit to the party to catch up with friends and get stuck into the grog and the promised canapés. All except the pirates' dressing room. Billy was excited. "They want us pirates to entertain at the party, so we're keeping our costumes."

"What do you have to do?"

"Just some little pirate thing we're supposed to ad lib, and then sing a few songs."

"So, you're ready to go?"

"Soon, but…"

I didn't like the sound of this particular 'but'.

"I thought, if you didn't mind, I'd head out to the party with Pernel and his wife, so we can run through a few ideas on the way. Don't want to be totally unprepared. It's for charity, after all."

Knowing how much this meant to Billy and knowing that there would be a woman in the car, I agreed. "Maybe I could give someone a lift." The offer wasn't totally selfless as it was a good forty-five minute drive to the party and company would be a pleasant diversion.

Robert stepped forward, "Well, I…" I didn't like the man, but I couldn't very well refuse him. "I was supposed to take out the keyboard for Stan, the musician. He's a friend of mine, but my car's ratshit, so we have to go with

Vern, but there's no room for it. I was wondering if you'd mind, now that your car is free."

It would fit on the back seat. "Sure," I said, although I wasn't.

I hugged Billy, whispering, "I love you, pirate Billy," before Robert helped me carry the instrument, already wrapped and tied in a thick blanket for protection, to the car park. He seemed nervous, agitated, but I put it down as fear that I would say something about his groping Billy early in the run. I tried to relax him by praising his performance and the whole show in general, asking what he was doing next. That seemed to make him more jittery, so I finally gave up, walking the rest of the way in silence. After we'd placed it carefully on the back seat, he fled back to the theatre in case the others didn't wait for him. The car park was already half empty of cast vehicles, so it's true what they say about actors—they sure are party animals.

Wondering whether Billy would have had a surfeit of theatre now or whether this could become an ongoing passion, I drove off slowly, careful the keyboard not be jolted. I knew musical instruments were sensitive, and I didn't want to be responsible for ruining this one. The radio was cold comfort for human company, but the time passed quickly enough. I'd been driving about fifteen minutes when I discovered I'd need gas to make it there and back. I didn't know the area well enough to take a chance there would be a gas station farther out.

I pulled in to top up the gas tank, thinking it was a ridiculously long way to go for a party, when the blat of a horn woke me from my daydreaming. I looked up. A member of the show was waving from the other side of the highway.

"Don't tell me the party's over already?" he called.

I'd finished filling the tank and walked over to the car. My heart sank, the blood in my veins ice. "Where are you off to?" I asked, trying to keep my voice steady.

"The party. I had to take my keyboard home first, as I don't like leaving it in my car in case it gets broken into. I live down there a few blocks." He pointed in the direction I was heading.

I tried to keep my voice calm. "Which party you going to?"

He was genuinely surprised. "Is there more than one? Isn't it still at Pernel's? His wife's on the committee, as well as being lead actress, so they're always at her place."

I faked my good humor, "Yep, that's where I'm headed. I'd just found myself low on gas and pulled in to fill up."

"I thought you would have stayed for the charity show back at the theatre, seeing as Billy is the lead. Sounds like fun," he said and winked. "See ya."

My first reaction was stunned silence, then anger, then a deep, deep ache. I ran back to the car and ripped open the blanket to discover a few bundled sheets of timber and metal rods. With a roar of frustration, I yanked it from my car, discarding it beside the road. Speeding back, I took deep breaths to calm myself; after all, it could have been a genuine mistake. Strike that idea. They wanted me out of the way, which meant only one thing—gangbang Billy. My only problem was to find out who 'they' were. Could I trust Billy not to have been involved in the ruse?

I'd seen a side of him I'd never known before when he slutted himself to my sleazy boss Jerry and his two buddies, Mike and Raoul. Maybe he was a Jekyll and Hyde character, a monster who craved cock so badly he would do anything to get it, including conspiring against his boyfriend.

No…I shook my head to clear it. I would have to play this carefully. My relationship, if I still had one, depended on it. I would adapt to circumstances. First, see what was going on. Slamming into the car park, a few dozen slumbering vehicles confirmed that a number of cast and audience members were still in the theatre.

Creeping through a side door into the semi-darkness of the foyer, I pressed open the auditorium door, hoping it would not squeak. Seated in the front few rows, I was surprised to see between thirty and forty men, only men, whom I recognised as respectable married businessmen and gay glitterati. There was an aura of decadence to it.

At first, I could not see Billy, but I heard one of the pirates cursing profanely and the audience applauding. Then there was a shout of 'Five' from those in the front rows, and the sound of a whip hitting flesh. I saw now that it was Lorrie, the youngest of the new recruits who was stripped to the waist, wearing his pirate tights and brandishing a lethal cat-o'-nine-tails.

"Six," the audience counted as Lorrie brought the leather fingers down on a naked back, striping it red. The back was Billy's. I saw him now, hoisted by his wrists locked in leather cuffs, his legs spread apart, locked just as securely in ankle bracelets.

I was about to scream for them to stop when I heard Lorrie shout, "Will you tell me where the captain's treasure is? Or do I have to punish you some more?"

He raised the whip and brought it down again to the cries of the audience. "Seven."

"I know nothing about the missing treasure. I love the captain more than I love my own life. I would never harm him." I recognised Billy acting and relaxed. I stood in the darkness to observe. The other pirates were lounging on the deck of the ship, watching the action with scant interest. Vern and Robert were there; so were Deuce, Hal and Spike. Plus an actor I knew as Kern. There was no sign of Pernel.

The interrogation continued apace, as did the whipping, with Billy whimpering each time the leather caressed his back. Watching had got me hard, but my secret vantage point did not give me a good view of the action. I knew Billy would be loving it, for he'd confided a fantasy of being the captive of a pirate crew who all had their way with him. I hoped he had not confided it to any of his fellow actors.

Deuce stepped in. "That's enough for now." He went to examine Billy, whose head was drooped as if unconscious. Deuce yanked it up by the hair, half turning him toward the audience. "The poor lad is near death from his wounds. This rum will revive him." He put a bottle to Billy's mouth and poured. The liquid overflowed his mouth as fast as he swallowed, only to cough it up, the remainder running down his chin and over his chest. The way Billy reacted it had to be real spirits of some sort. He sounded as if he were choking.

"Drink it, lad, if ye know what's good for you."

The next words really caught my attention. It was Vern. "Aye, lad. It will help you endure the pain that is to come." He rubbed his hand across Bill's butt cheek to a rousing cheer from the audience who, I noticed, had their own supply of ready liquor they were imbibing in rather copious amounts.

Sneaking back out through the doors at the back of the theatre, I went to the manager's office where I found what I was looking for. I took a few moments before I was fully prepared. Out the side door of the foyer I went, and then ran around to the back of the building. The stage door was unlocked, so I let myself in quietly. I heard the action on stage more clearly now, and it was obvious Billy was slurring his speech. So obvious it could still be acting. I did not want to make a fool of myself by interrupting something for charity, especially if it were legit.

My earlier hiding spot above the stage was out, as the actors would see my ascent. Instead, I descended the cold concrete steps to the basement, a graveyard of old costumes and dusty props, and the stage above me creaking as the pirates moved about. I switched on the work light and a feeble blue glow cast ominous shadows across the forgotten characters stored here. I ducked down to avoid low beams and dusty cobwebs, picking my way across the room toward my goal.

The theatre had been built in the early part of the twentieth century, so it still had a functioning prompt box, although it was seldom, if ever, used these days. It was a little ornamental hut jutting up at the front of the stage, traditionally used to prompt actors or conduct opera singers out of sight of the audience. For Pirates of Penzance, it had been incorporated into the set as part of the design.

I clambered inside the booth, which was fortunately curtained at stage level. Parting them slightly with my hands, I had a perfect view. Billy was definitely starting to look the worse for whipping, and if they were pouring real liquor down his throat, he would soon be a quivering mess. Just enough, Billy lost all inhibitions. Too much, he shut down totally and fell asleep.

"Now, slag, where did you hide the treasure?"

"I don't know what you're talking about," Billy shouted in character.

Lorrie began to loosen his cuffs. "In that case, we'll have to fuck the information out of you."

A cheer went up from the crowd, and Billy began to struggle. I heard him hiss at Lorrie, "Remember, no penetration. You promised."

"We won't really fuck you," Lorrie said, keeping up the acting by running his hand over Billy's rump.

Billy relaxed. "Okay, then."

"Help me, boys," Lorrie called to the other pirates. In no time at all, they had unstrung him, manhandling his body above their heads.

Vern took control. "Over here, lads." They roughly tossed Billy face down over a barrel that was part of the set, securing his ankle and wrist cuffs to hooks, which had been recently hammered into the floor. Billy's tantalizing butt had suddenly become available.

Serious preparation had gone into this production because mirrors had been previously angled so that Billy's face and his ass were reflected to the eager audience even while he was side on to them. Slightly upstage of my hiding place, I, too, had a perfect three-sided view of my captive lover

Vern yanked his hair bringing his face up. "Right, lad, are you willing to tell us?"

"I don't know anything about your stupid treasure," Billy spat.

"Then we'll fuck the information out of you!"

Vern strode around to Billy's ass to run his finger along the crevasse.

"Fuck him!" someone shouted from the audience.

Vern produced a lethal looking pirate dagger, sliding it under the waist of Billy's tights and, with a deft stroke, sliced the fabric open, revealing Billy's smooth, blond butt. Vern ran the blade gently across that ass before poking the inviting puckered entrance.

"This is your last chance to come clean."

Billy struggled valiantly. "I'll never tell you. Do your worst, but my lips are sealed."

Vern crowed, "Your lips won't be sealed for long!" He cut his own tights off in one smooth motion to show he was already hard as a pirate's sword, and twice as shiny from the slick precome that caked his cock. He stroked it slowly for the audience. It was a great prick, and under different circumstances, Billy would have welcomed it up his ass, but Vern was a bastard, a bully, and a cheat. Besides, Billy was spread-eagled over a barrel being watched by a coterie of some of the most important gay businesspeople in the town, people who might one day employ him or be paying customers for his culinary skills. Guys who obviously didn't mind a bit of fantasy non-consensual role play. But what the hell; it was for charity.

After displaying his cock to the very vocal approval of the crowd, Vern spat in his hand and massaged the shaft. As he ran one hand up and down his beautiful weapon, he prised Billy's moulded cheeks apart with the other, displaying Billy's most intimate crevice to the audience. Vern would obviously slide his hard cock between the butt cheeks to give the appearance of fucking, and Billy would scream as the cock supposedly tore his asshole. In the hush that followed, I thought I could hear the throbbing heartbeats of the men in the audience, until I realised it was my own heart pounding in anticipation, and the throbbing, my own cock, rampant at the scene unfolding before me.

Vern aimed his slick cockhead at Billy's sphincter. I realised too late that the shine on his cock was not precome, but lube. The bastard had already greased his cock for the performance. Billy's scream of pain confirmed my fear; the look of surprise on his face, reflected in the mirror, was not part of the agreed scenario.

A long, deep collective breath from the audience, ignorant of the twisted sexual dynamics of the performers, believed it to be hardcore playacting, which meant they were buying the fantasy.

"Fuck, you're hurting me," Billy screamed. "Take it out. You fuckin' promised."

"A pirate's word ain't worth shit, slut boy." Vern grunted as he thrust brutally into Billy's ass, as if trying to punish him for his previous rejection of the pirate chorus. Then he whispered loud enough for me to hear, "Just enjoy the fuckin' ride, Billy. That way it won't hurt so much tomorrow."

The other pirates moved in, their cocks out, jostling to be the first to be taken care of. "Just open your mouth slut; there's a good pig," Vern demanded for the benefit of the audience. "Fuck his face, Deuce. Slam your cock down the fuckin' fag's throat. Choke him on your pirate dick."

Deuce was a big, black fucker, but a few bricks short of Pernel.

"Put your tongue out, Billy. That's a good slut. Give Deuce a launching pad." Billy did as instructed, giving Deuce the opportunity to slide his prick into his gullet, gagging him momentarily. "Mmm, taste good, Billy? Don't even think about biting or anything nasty because if you do, we might just have to invite the audience up on stage to teach you a lesson."

The men in the theatre cheered.

Billy could take anything dished out to him. He enjoyed cock, but he was not consenting to this, and he wasn't drunk enough not to care.

Yeah, I could have stopped the show. But I didn't. Deep down, I was good and pissed off with him. Pissed off that he fucked my sleazy boss in front of me all those months ago, that he encouraged him and two mates to use him like a whore, just because he'd caught me jerking off. Pissed off that his actions had shown me an aspect of my personality I was not at all sure I liked. Why else was I huddled in a theatre prompt box perving on my boyfriend being taken? I'm no psychiatrist, but even I could see that sort of behaviour is fucked! I was pissed off, too, that in the dressing room he had allowed himself to be used in front of me, used to humiliate me, allowed himself to be fingered and fucked while I sat there and watched other gross men give my lover pleasure…as if I accounted for nothing.

Sure, I still loved the fucker, but love fluctuates, and right now, I was getting major wood from watching Billy reap the results of his slutty behaviour. Anyway, he said he had fantasies about being fucked by pirates, so what if the reality was a little less to his liking and a great deal more painful? I smiled at the thought.

Billy wasn't smiling though, not with Deuce's thick, black fucker hammering his mouth, stretching his lips wide to take the black shaft skewering his throat. Deuce was cutting off his air so that every time he pulled his cock out, Billy gasped for breath, his eyes watering, his nose running, gag juice drooling down his chin.

"What do you think of pirates now, fag boy?"

Vern obviously wasn't expecting an answer because Billy's face was in Deuce's vise-like grip, his mouth stuffed full, and he could scarcely move. Vern packed his cock even harder into Billy's asshole

There was a bull roar and all attention turned to Deuce, who had Billy headlocked against his prick as he pumped his spunk down his throat. Applause broke out from the audience while Deuce, his cock still embedded in Billy's craw, struck a pose flexing his biceps. His cock popped free. Billy puked up spunk and gag while other pirates headed for the vacant mouth.

Robert grabbed his hair, pouring liquor into his open mouth. "Here, slut. This will get rid of the taste."

In between swallows, he tried to turn to the audience for help.

Vern, his face contorting, pulled Billy's ass back against his groin and held him there. It was obvious he was blowing his load. The audience cheered and the chant of "Fuck him! Fuck him!" reverberated through the hall.

Vern pulled out, and Robert immediately took his place, once again leaving his mouth free. Kern stepped up, his body a mass of thick, black hair, his cock barely visible in the mat of pubes around his groin. But it was deceptive, and soon the long, thick pole sprouted like a primed weapon from its camouflage.

Again Billy struggled, shouting, "Leave me alone. You're fuckin' killing me!" but to no avail. The audience whistled and stomped in appreciation of his 'performance.' His face was about to take another battering, from Kern this time.

It was apparent that Richard's nick name of Digit Dick was a misnomer as he had an above-average length, if not thickness, way above average, and was having difficulty getting it all into Billy's dripping asshole, which flexed against him. Robert savagely slapped his butt cheeks. "Open up, slut, or I'll make you very sorry." Robert held Billy's body and crammed his cock in to the hilt. Billy's cries of pain were muffled by Kern's prick lodged in his throat.

The pirates circled like sexual vultures waiting to use and abuse his body until one-by-one they all took their turn. Or turns. His face was sticky, and his hair was matted with spunk. Juice from the guys who had blown their loads inside his butt dribbled down his legs. The pirates had synchronised so that as the final two dumped in his throat and ass, the others moved in close to shoot a second string of sperm on his face. Vern, keen to make Billy's submission total, unclasped his cuffs, insisting the pirates carry his limp body to the front of the stage. Then he pulled Billy's head roughly by the hair so everyone could see the slime oozing in his eyes and mouth. He turned Billy over, pulled his legs back, and exposed his gaping asshole with come puddling as it was expelled from the swollen anal chute.

There was dead silence in the theatre.

I heard someone say in horror, "They really fuckin' tagged him. It wasn't acting."

There came the sound of seats creaking and mumbled discussions. "I can't afford to get involved in something like this."

The auditorium door banged shut as some of the audience escaped.

The pirates did not look at all chastened when Vern stepped forward. "Gentleman, isn't this what you all came here tonight to witness?"

There were calls of "Fuck, yeah!" and "Do him again!"

"Now, gentlemen, we come to the highlight of the event. Pirates, your places please."

Billy groaned. "Where's Steve?"

Vern laughed. "Who's Steve?"

Billy looked puzzled. "You know Steve. My boyfriend."

"You're a pirate slut. You don't have boyfriends. You have fuck buddies."

Billy became more demanding. "Where's Steve?"

"Don't you remember?" Robert said. "You sent him on a fake errand to the other side of town. By the time he realises his mistake your ass will be mincemeat."

"You guys tricked me. I said no penetration."

"Hey, Billy. It's for a good cause," Vern whispered, grinning. "You get all the cock you could possibly want, we get our rocks off, plus enough cash for a hell of a lot of party time. And there's a bonus. We get to stick it to your interfering boyfriend. He gets to come back to find you tied up and covered with other men's slime. Won't be much left of your relationship after that, eh, Billy? If you're lucky, one of us may take pity on you and fuck your slack asshole once in a while, for old time's sake."

The audience lapped it up.

Vern kept at it, like an old-time carnival spruiker. "Don't sweat it, pretty boy. It's been a rough trip, but it's not over yet. It must be weeks since you had good, hard cock. You miss cock, don't you, Billy? I bet your boyfriend isn't half the man we are. You're our good little slut cock boy. Your ass was made to fuck. You're the best we ever had."

That penetrated Billy's befuddled brain. "The best?"

I sensed something spark in Billy. His body tensed, as if he liked what he heard, liked what he felt. Maybe the Hyde coming out in Jekyll. Whatever it was his confidence returned. The audience murmured their approval, and the performance had just gone up a notch.

The fantasy was overriding the reality in Billy's mind. "Really?"

"Fuck, yeah. Your booty is known all over the world. We have people lining up to fuck you." Vern winked at the audience.

Billy's eyes glazed over again. "Cool. I love new cocks."

"Your boyfriend is a selfish bastard. He won't share you. Won't let strangers' cocks in this sweet asshole of yours. Say you need it, slut boy. Come on, say it."

Vern pushed two fingers into Billy's sloppy hole, fingering it like a precious sculpture. All eyes concentrated on that entrance to paradise, overflowing with cock cream. "Men want that mancunt of yours the instant they see it."

There was a sudden murmur of excitement from the audience. From backstage, strode Pernel, a wall of muscle in his Pirate King's outfit. Wolf whistles and foot stamping greeted his arrival.

"You want him, don't you, Billy?" Vern whispered in his ear. "You wanted him since the first day you saw him."

For an instant, the old Billy kicked in. "What about Steve?"

"What about him, slut Billy." Vern offered him the half-empty bottle of liquor they'd used earlier. "He's not here to see you is he? We saw to that. Remember?"

Billy smiled. He took the bottle and quaffed a good mouthful, coughing as it went down his throat. He took two more in quick succession.

Throwing his head back, he arched his body and grabbed his legs, bringing them back up and over until his knees were almost beside his head. Billy screamed, "Bring it on!"

The audience erupted. I almost did as well. I undid my jeans for comfort, releasing my cock, sticky with the jizz that had oozed from the shaft while I'd been watching Billy.

"Where's the treasure, slut?" Pernel boomed, getting into character immediately.

Billy looked up at the hulk of a man, and in response, opened his asscheeks wider.

"I see my men couldn't fuck the answer out of you. Well, maybe I can." He dragged his long, black cock out of his costume. Here in front of him was the ass he'd wanted a crack at three or four weeks ago. Now Billy was primed and eager. Pernel leaned over and spun Billy around on his back, so the audience had a perfect view. He then kneeled between his legs, sinking his mammoth prick into the warm, inviting depths, pistoning to his balls in Billy's slut hole. He rammed hard and fast. "I managed to get away from the party, but she'll wonder where I am if I'm away for too long, so I gotta make this quick," he whispered to Vern.

"Not too quick," Vern warned. "They want to get their money's worth."

Pernel slowed his pace and started on the dirty talk. "You take cock like you were born to it, slut boy. Your cunt is slick with so much juice I can slide right in. I can feel the pirate loads sliming my balls."

Billy's reply was a grunt every time Pernel's body bore down on his own. "My pirate crew fucked you good, pretty boy. But still you want more. You want my big, black meat sliding into your guts."

I took my hand off my prick so I wouldn't blow prematurely. Suddenly, I felt a breath a second or two before a warm, wet mouth engulfed me to the balls. Startled, I looked down to see a young head bobbing on my cock. It was Matt. I lifted him off.

"I saw you come in," he whispered. "I thought you would stop the show. When you didn't, I knew you'd need some other sort of help."

In response, I pulled his face back onto one of the hardest erections I'd ever sprouted. Watching Billy eagerly fuck while I was being blown by a cute guy—did it get any better?

Pernel huffed and puffed, and blew. It had taken less than five minutes, an eternity on stage if you don't deliver the goods, but he had, and I marvelled he'd held out so long. He grunted his orgasm, then said to Billy, "Fuck, boy, that's some ass. I could fuck that for hours if you can get away from your boyfriend some time." Pulling out, he wiped his cock on Billy's ass cheeks. Then with a theatrical flourish, he squished his fingers back in Billy's well greased hole. "What have we here?" He produced two small numbered balls as if from the ass he'd just fucked, but I'd seen him palm them from his boots. "So that's where you hid the treasure? Clever, slut boy."

A raucous cry went up from the audience as if this was the moment they'd been anticipating all night.

Pernel stood, legs akimbo, over Billy. "You betrayed me, slut. Broke my heart. I banish you. You will be sold off to the highest bidder to spend your life in servitude." So saying, he instructed the pirate band to drag Billy away, which they did with great alacrity. He placed the numbered balls in Vern's grasp, and strode majestically from the stage to wild applause to return, I assumed, to the cast party where just about all those in the theatre would venture shortly.

Matt took his mouth off my cock long enough to utter a single word, "Ham," before returning to his oral ministrations.

Vern took centre stage. "Okay, gents, this is the moment you've all been hanging out for." There was a shout of agreement. "The drawing of the two prizes, the reason you paid such a premium for tonight's, ahem, extra special charity event. Two of you will have a prize you'll talk about for the rest of your lives, and you others will be purple with envy. Without further ado, please check the number on your ticket. The winning number for second prize, the runner-up goes to…" He dragged it out like a game show host. "36."

A whoop of joy, hearty but envious congratulations, then the crowd fell silent. "The major prize, and what I wouldn't give to have the winning ticket for this one…the major prize goes to number…drum roll, please." One of the pirates beat out a rhythm on the barrel, "Number 9."

From the audience came, "Fuckin' yeah!"

I knew that voice, and I didn't like it. I hadn't seen him in the theatre, otherwise I would have decked the bastard.

"While the winners are being prepared, let's bring out the prize." He clapped his hands, which was the signal for the pirates to reenter. They arrived, holding the naked Billy aloft. He'd been cleaned up and was now less the ragged sex slut and more the sexy bottom the audience had paid to see demeaned and degraded.

The audience was restive: "Fuck, he's gorgeous."

"Look at that ass."

"I want a piece of that."

"I'd sell my mother to get inside him for just one night."

Vern called for the runner up to be brought out.

A thin guy in his thirties made an entrance in a brocade dressing gown to the cheers of his mates. He smiled confidently, sauntering across to Billy, who had assumed the position, on all fours. The runner up dropped his robe, standing naked and erect in front of Billy's mouth.

Vern called for the winner. I nearly puked when Jerry, my butt ugly former boss, bounded out on the stage, totally naked, and eager to get to work. I was about to pull Matt off my cock and disrupt the proceedings when Billy looked up, the shock of recognition registered all over his pretty face. Jerry smirked. I had Matt's mouth off my dick, ready to bolt upstairs and on to the stage until I saw Billy's sly grin.

"It's good to see you again, Jerry."

Jerry was flummoxed, thinking there was an ulterior motive. "There's no backing out."

I wanted to poke my ears out rather than listen to what Billy was saying. "I have no intention of backing out. I have fond memories of our last meeting. Extremely fond memories."

That was music to Jerry's ears, and unless Billy was a better actor than I gave him credit for, he was telling the truth. He picked up the bottle and took a giant swig of the alcohol to fortify himself for what was to come.

Jerry liked what he was seeing. "I just wish that smug boyfriend of yours was here to watch me plug you again, making you beg for it, Billy."

"Me, too," he said.

"Sweet Jesus, I really hit the jackpot tonight."

"You and me both."

"If you really mean that—"

"Oh, I do," Billy assured him.

"You hungry for cock tonight, Billy?"

"Always, Jerry."

"Hot damn."

The runner-up took the pause as an opportunity to claim his prize, ramming his cock into Billy's mouth and holding the back of his head to support his fucking action. Not content, like experienced tops, to let the bottom control the action, he was fucking his way to a quick orgasm, rather than going for a lengthy tongue and lip rub.

Jerry grabbed him around the waist and sank his thick, stumpy cock into Billy's steamy pudding of an ass and, although still slick with pirates' come, I knew he felt every inch of its penetration. As I watched Billy's defilement, I shook with…I didn't know what it was. Was our relationship all lies? Was Billy so off his face he would say anything to get cock?

Matt stopped sucking, and I wanted to flee. I didn't want to see or hear his defilement at the hands of my butt ugly boss again. I didn't want to be angry with Billy any more, but I was prevented from leaving when I felt Matt back his ass against my cock, sinking against me without obstruction. Had the whole world gone cock mad? Ass mad?

The guy being sucked didn't last long, and he pulled his cock out to jerk over Billy's face.

Jerry panted as he worked over Billy's ass. "That's fuckin' so hot. You love it, don't you, slut?"

"Uh huh," Billy said, licking as much of the come off his face as he could manage with his tongue.

"On your back, fag,' Jerry demanded. Billy flopped over, and Jerry immediately wedged his cock back in. "Such a sloppy ass, Billy. Full of slime. Running into your guts. I wish I could breed you so the whole world could fuck a Billy. I feel sorry for you; you'll never know what it's like to fuck a sex pig as good as you are."

"But I know what's it's like to be fucked close to death by an expert slut tamer like you, Jerry."

"You think I am, fuckhole?"

"You know I do."

"Tell me, asscunt."

"You make my ass tingle. I love the feel of your hard cock scraping against my asscunt. You hit spots I can only dream about. I want your cock inside me, fucker."

"Tell me, slut."

"You're the best, Jerry."

"Tell me, Billy. Tell me what I want to hear."

"I've never had anyone like you. My boyfriend is shit compared to you. I've felt your cock inside me every night since you first fucked me. I dream about your cock, Jerry. I need your cock. Please, please fuck me forever."

"You fuckin' mongrel, fag slut, cunt ass," Jerry screamed as he grinded his hips into Billy like he wanted his whole body inside.

Billy screamed, shooting his bolt without even touching himself. I emptied my balls deep inside Matt's tight asshole.

Jerry collapsed on top of Billy until his cock slowly softened and popped out, then he opened Billy's butt cheeks and turned to the audience. "Come on, guys. I don't think he's satisfied yet. Who wants a turn?"

I stood rooted to the spot while I watched close to a dozen guys from the audience fight over Billy's mouth and asshole as if he was just a come dump for their enjoyment, while Jerry encouraged them with some of the filthiest talk

I'd ever heard. Vern joined in again, but the other pirates had long since drifted off to the party.

"I wish your boyfriend could see you like this, Billy. It's your natural state. Taking cock. No matter how old, ugly, smelly, or thick, you beg for it. I want to see the look on his face when he sees you covered in spunk, sees it dripping from your fucked asshole. Sees you being humiliated like a pig."

I knew I should have gone up on stage and put a stop to it, but I also knew these people who were taking advantage of my lover, degrading him like an animal. I detailed their vehicles, I mixed with them socially. So why was my cock still rock hard?

Time slowed, and I had no idea how long I watched as the horny group dumped in, on and over Billy until he resembled the sluts in bukkake porn movies. One by one they gathered up their clothes and left for the party or went home to their wives, leaving an exhausted Billy propped up against the barrel, tenderly fingering his asshole, which must have been rubbed raw.

I climbed down from my perch. I couldn't put it off any longer and walked back up the stairs. It was too much to hope that Jerry would have pissed off by now. I slammed the stage door as if I were just making an entry. Matt told me later that he'd been watching from the wings where he'd escaped after I loaded his ass with my come. Billy had winced visibly at the sound of my entry, but had made no effort to clean himself.

I stood calmly, surveying the scene. Jerry moved away in case of violence.

"Hi, Billy."

"Hi, Steve."

"Seems I got sent on a wild goose chase, just to get me out of the way so you could party."

"I didn't think you'd approve of the special performance. I know you don't like Vern and Robert, and some of the others."

"Looks like I had good reason."

"I don't suppose you'd believe me if I said it wasn't supposed to be like this."

"As a matter of fact, I would."

Billy looked up at me with tears forming in his eyes. "I couldn't help it. Maybe what they call me is true. Steve, I'm sorry. So very, very sorry."

"Nothing to be sorry about."

"Steve, once it started, I didn't want it to stop."

"Alcohol."

"I'm as sober as anything, Steve. I tried to get drunk to justify it in my mind. It didn't work."

"Come on. Let's get you home." I went to pick him up.

"No, Steve. Leave me alone. I can't bear it. The shame I've brought on you. The humiliation. I've done it to you before. I can't guarantee I won't do it again.

"That doesn't matter."

"It does to me. I can't live knowing that I hurt you. That my behaviour humiliates you in front of your friends."

Thinking he just needed a little recuperative time, I asked, "Are you going to the party?"

"Not after what happened here tonight. You don't know what went on. How bad it was. Pity there isn't a movie. Then you'd see why I can't come home again. Ever."

I felt my heart tear in my chest. I stood with my arms dejectedly by my side. Gutted.

"Take me back to your place, Jerry. It's where I belong."

The look of triumph on Jerry's face made me want to smash it in, but I just stood my ground, watching helplessly as he walked Billy, still naked and covered in sperm, to the entrance. The last glimpse of my lover was of Jerry shoving a finger into his sloppy ass.

THE DEVIL HIS DUE

What's a guy to do when his boyfriend runs out on him, ashamed of being a slut and a plaything to every stray cock in town?

Billy has moved in with Steve's sleazy former boss, ashamed of his behaviour at a party in which he was forcibly gangbanged by a band of pirates, but Steve is determined to win him back. His task is made all the more difficult when Billy changes masters and is introduced to the pleasures of submission. If he is to convince Billy he is the right master for him, Steve must make a superhuman effort, diving down deep into the dark recesses of his ex-lover's fantasies.

"*You* can't let it go on like this, Steve. He's running the poor kid ragged. There'll be nothing of him left soon."

I appreciated Mike's concern, and that he'd called in to warn me. I was grateful, but I had to ask. "Did you fuck him?"

"Hell, yeah. He's the most fuckable bottom I've ever met, bar none. But he won't be much longer. Jerry's turning him into a bucket ass. It's starting to be like poking your cock in pig slops."

I didn't know whether to thank him or smash his face in. Sure he was concerned for my former boyfriend, my now non-existent partnership, but not enough to refrain from blowing his load up Billy's butthole which Jerry, my repulsive former boss and currently Billy's what, protector, hardly, pimp more like it, was making available to anyone with the right bank balance or social influence. If Jerry was ugly as a hat full of assholes, his personality was downright hideous.

He'd been part of the group that brought about the destruction of my relationship. Billy was feeling shame because after the closing night of Gilbert & Sullivan's The Pirates of Penzance in which he'd played cabin boy Frederic, he'd been gang fucked by most of the pirate chorus in front of a select paying audience. Later he had spread his legs for the musical's leading man and his body had been auctioned off and won by the repulsive Jerry. Not only had Billy taken him on willingly and dared to say he was a better fuck than me but he had gone home with him. He was still there, albeit not on the happiest of terms if Mike's pleading was anything to go by.

I was hardly blameless, having watched the whole fucked enterprise from a secret hiding place, still unbeknownst to Billy. No wonder I was grinding my teeth. No wonder I threw my cell phone across the room on the umpteenth time I was informed Billy's was 'switched off or out of range.'

We'd been separated for almost two months now. I was jittery. Billy and I had a mortgage together on a luxury apartment which I could not afford to pay on my own, hell, we had a life together and I didn't want to give that up. Matt, Pirates' costume designer, was the only thing keeping me sane, and keeping me from stomping around to my former boss's house and beating the shit out of him. I'm not a violent person normally – but these weren't normal times.

I had received so many phone calls and visits of commiseration, all of them about as sincere as a politician in the lead up to an election. While professing concern for my well-being they all eventually got around to asking where they could contact Billy for one reason or another when the reality was they wanted to fuck him. Even the bottoms.

"It's like the spark has gone out of him," Mike continued. "You know that look he gets when he's being fucked?" Like I needed to be reminded. All Billy's looks and foibles were etched on my heart. That sly smile when he was guilty about something he was engaged in. The look of shame when he was caught out. The way his eyes rolled back in his head when he had something special wedded to his insatiable butt. No, I didn't need Mike telling me about it, especially not after he'd fucked Billy more recently than I had. I wanted to scream at him.

But all I said was, "That means Billy's not enjoying it."

"Tell me about it," Mike said sarcastically as if it were all my fault. "He just lies there and takes what anyone dishes out. The more he does that the more frustrated Jerry is getting. You have to do something."

"I'm not quite sure why this is my responsibility," I said. "To make Billy a better screw for other guys."

Mike got hot under the collar at my accusation but I could see it hit its target. "That's not what I meant. What I meant is..." he paused to work out exactly what it was he did mean. "You two were made for each other. I know you still love him." I did but I wasn't about to confess those feelings to Mike. "And I know Billy still loves you."

That was a cheap tactic. "How do you know?"

"He told me last time I fucked him."

"Last time?"

Mike could see the look of horror on my face which gave away my secret more than any words I might have used. He had the good graces to look sheepish. "Well, you know. Jerry is free with the invitations and I couldn't turn down that ass."

"If you're so concerned about Billy's welfare, why don't you rescue him?"

"I would, except..."

I waited. Mike's brow creased his brain clearly running through a myriad possibilities for a plausible response. I got sick of waiting.

"You're happy to reap the benefits of the best ass in the city, hell, in the whole country for all I know, but you're not prepared to put in the hard yards maintaining it?"

Bullseye! Mike sighed. What he said next would help me decide whether to throw the bastard out or listen some more. "Okay, you got me. You know I've got a soft spot for Billy. But, yeah, I prefer to visit than to take care of the upkeep."

"Jerry's your man now."

Mike threw his arm across my shoulder. I left it there although I felt far from matey. I recognised the gesture for what it was. "He's not up to the task. Billy needs you. You give him that inner spark."

I had come to the same conclusion myself in the months I'd had to ruminate over it, something I'd done incessantly since that fateful night.

I shrugged my powerlessness. "He's shown no interest in returning home. He won't even answer my calls to his cell phone."

"Jerry won't let him."

"He's not being held prisoner."

"No. Not exactly. He's a prisoner to his feelings for you." Nice touch, I thought. "He's so ashamed of what he did at the theatre, he can't forgive himself."

"I told him I forgave him. It made no difference."

Mike was getting increasingly frustrated. "He thinks he humiliated you."

"It can't be any worse than the night he did it with you and Jerry and Raoul."

"Much, much worse."

I was playing with him. "What did he do?" I knew what Billy did; I'd been there and witnessed most of it. I had my own guilt that I hadn't stepped in to prevent the gang fuck. The only person who knew that was Matt, currently in the spare bedroom listening to our conversation.

How much anyone knew apart from those involved was a matter of conjecture, but as Mike's version unfolded, I knew someone had been trumpeting Billy's sexual submission to sympathetic listeners, and that person would be Jerry. Mike began hesitantly, obviously censoring the more outrageous elements of Billy's degradation, but as he trod carefully through the minefield of misdemeanors that had been related to him I heard his breath becoming more shallow and saw his cock hardening in his jeans. He was being turned on just telling me the story. No wonder he wanted the old Billy back again.

I interrupted. "That's enough." Mike had a quiet smile of triumph curling around his lips. He'd noticed I was hard, too. Just as I was hard every time Matt and I watched the video footage of the dub-con gangbang caught in high definition digital from the theatre's camera used to archive productions. I'd had the good sense to switch it on in the manager's office before witnessing the whole sorry event. And Matt had retrieved it after Billy had walked out on me.

"I told him before this shit even happened, that I forgave him in advance for anything he ever did. He has no need to feel shame. Or that he humiliated me."

"Come on, Steve. This is Jerry we're talking about who's boning him ten times a day. Your fuck ugly boss who's telling anyone who'll listen that he's the best top in the world because he managed to steal Billy right out from under you."

"Sure, Jerry's a piece of slime, but he's Billy's choice and all I care about is his happiness." Mike was exasperated. "Besides, I'm seeing someone else at the moment."

"What?" That had come as something of a surprise. I'd guessed that Mike was in league with Jerry to get me to take Billy back so they could continue fucking him on the sly and rub my nose in it. In fact, I was seeing someone. I was fucking Matt on a regular basis. He was hot. He was a slut. And he took cock almost as well as Billy. But he wasn't Billy. Try as he might he could not turn me on like Billy did. And, boy, did he try. Matt allowed me to watch him being fucked by gangs of men, either openly or secretly. Sure it was a good show but it just wasn't the same.

It had taken me a while but eventually it had penetrated even my thick brain that I loved Billy despite his failure at monogamy, struggling against his unacknowledged natural propensity to be a slut bottom. Because he sublimated his desire to be fucked by stray cock, he unintentionally put himself in situations where he was taken against his will and, more often than not, in full view of me. Usually with people I despised or who despised me. That made it doubly exciting to him. Like being fucked by Jerry and, even more, enjoying it. He was subconsciously punishing me.

I'd attempted to have this conversation with him after the first incident with Jerry. It was why I had told him I forgave everything he ever did that hurt me, past, present and future. He was the man for me. But he would have to come back to me of his own volition when he was ready. If he ever was.

"One of the guys who saw the show. Came over to apologise for what went on. Hadn't realised they were really fucking him." I just prayed Mike wouldn't have the sense to check to see if I was telling the truth.

"Is it serious?" Mike asked.

"We're taking it easy. But, you know what; I think it might work out."

"Poor Billy."

"Fuck Billy. It's his own fault,"

I could see that I'd shocked Mike; his visit hadn't gone at all well. "But, for old time's sake. If you really think Billy needs a friend. Why don't you take him over to Vince and Andy? They run Second Skin, the leather fetish warehouse. They reckon they're good mates to Billy. They'll look after him." Mike smiled for the first time since the conversation had taken a wrong turn.

"You'll be able to drop in and see him." Mike was clutching at straws.

"Nah, I don't think so, they're not my sort of people. And vice versa. They never thought I was good enough for Billy. Always trying to split us up. Now they've got their wish."

I could almost hear the cogs grinding in Mike's brain. Jerry could offload Billy but still tap that magnificent ass every now and then. Mike's money and influence would ensure he got a share of the spoils as well. Billy could get back to his old self and I would be out of the picture.

He must have thought I was the world's biggest fuckwit. My only regret was that Billy was the meat in the sandwich. Literally. I had to subject him to further degradation to win him back. He would hate me before we were through but the stakes were so high I had to go through with it. I did want him back, desperately, even if it meant sacrificing him to people I despised and who would use every sexual weapon in their arsenal to humiliate and ridicule me.

After Mike left, Matt came out of the bedroom. "Great fuckin' performance. You got me so hot for it just talking like that. You want to pork me now?"

"I'm a bit raw. Okay?"

"Yeah, I understand. You up for watching those two pricks from upstairs, do me?"

I smiled. Those two pricks from upstairs were a gay couple who had moved into the building about six months before. They had seen Billy and me walking around the area and made themselves known. Their apartment was ultra chic and minimalist, they'd been together a number of years and they had two kids, fathered by in vitro with a woman friend of theirs. Alice was nine and Philip was around 18 months older. They were the sort of prissy queens who travelled overseas every year to escape the winter cold, always going somewhere summery, they subscribed to the opera and ballet although they never seemed to actually attend, and they had important friends in high places. Plus they had money. Rumor had it, their exorbitant lifestyle was subsidised by their access to large quantities of party drugs which they sold on through a network of discrete party queers. They had once asked Billy, albeit indirectly, if we were interested when they'd found out about our precarious financial state. We'd refused politely.

They said their very generous offer was always open. They had, of course, also made very generous offers to Billy to give up his ass to them even going so far as to throw a party at which they and their friends had tried to get Billy drunk and pliable. They had spiked his drink but Billy's tolerance to such stimulants is quite low and they'd over-estimated. It was one of those occasions on which I was more amused than horny, so when Billy began acting ridiculously over the top I took him home, leaving them seething.

They seemed to have come to terms with it, and remained friends although upon learning of the sordid details of our split they had turned up at the door with fudge brownies and champagne to cheer me up. Their concept of cheer was to make an insultingly low offer on the apartment, because they knew I could no longer afford to stay there. Or they thought that and I was not about to discourage them in their assumption. In fact, Matt and I were surviving. He had a steady stream of work as a professional photographer, but mainly because Matt had 'confiscated' the takings, foolishly left unattended, for Billy's special gangbang show. The pirate chorus had cursed their bad fortune while secretly blaming one another or a member of the participating audience. They had no choice but to write it off.

I knew the real reason for Nigel's and Jason's visit when they began pumping me for information on Billy's current whereabouts so they could also ply him with their particular brand of comfort and care.

"We owe him money and we'd like to pay it back."

Yeah, right. Guys with cash to throw around owe Billy money. Didn't they plan their lies in advance to make them more plausible?

"I know what you're going through," Nigel said, flapping his arms in the air as he poured more champagne into my glass in an attempt to loosen me up enough to spill the beans on Billy's whereabouts. "When my first boyfriend left me, I was desolate. Simply desolate." He attempted his impression of desolation but it came across more like constipation. "Until I met Jason here. He turned my life around." Jason reached out and clutched his hand. On the surface it looked the picture of gay romance and fidelity. I wasn't buying it.

I leaned over and rubbed my hand along Nigel's thigh in sympathy. He flinched at my touch but I pretended not to notice and kept rubbing toward to his crotch. Eventually he slapped my hand and squealed, "Naughty."

Chastised, I hoped I looked my part more convincingly than they did, I apologised. "Sorry, Nigel, I thought you both had a more, shall we say 'open' relationship than most."

"Silly boy," Jason chuckled. "What on earth gave you that idea? Nigel and I are devoted to each other."

I blustered a little. "Something Billy told me once. That you two guys were always trying to get him alone together."

"Well," Jason said snidely. "Now you know better. Now you know what a slut and a liar Billy is."

I could have covered the gap between us lightning fast and had my hands around his throat before he'd even taken another breath, his last, but I just added his insult to the tab I kept in my mind for payback one day. Then I lowered my gaze so they would not see the anger and resentment I harbored and shook my head sadly. "It just goes to show you can't trust anyone."

At the door, Nigel touched me briefly. "It must be devastating to find out what a whore your boyfriend is in such a public manner and have the whole world snickering behind your back."

"I can't begin to tell you what it's like," I said, feigning sadness.

"If there's ever anything..." Nigel didn't finish the sentence.

Jason had the final word. "Fags like that give us all a bad name."

As they swished down the hallway I heard them guffaw.

"Nigel would be hot if he wasn't such a two-bit screamer," Matt said coming out of the bedroom in just a pair of tight briefs. He had certainly improved since we'd both been working out at a gym together. His body was so fuckin' ripped it was hard to keep my cock to myself when he paraded around nude. I'd let myself go a little while in my relationship with Billy and I was determined to get rid of the love handles and bulk up. As well as that, I was working as a casual on various building sites around town, lugging bricks and other manual labor, work I'd picked up through a union mate. It was good to come home exhausted at the end of a day. My body was getting into such shape that Matt could scarcely keep his hands off me. Car detailing positions had all but dried up with Jerry's badmouthing me to anyone who would listen.

"They're very keen to find Billy."

"Perhaps he owes them money," Matt suggested.

"Or maybe it's Billy asshole they're after." I smiled at the memory of it.

"I'll have to sample this famous ass for myself one day just to see what everyone is raving about."

"In your dreams, bottom boy," I ruffled his hair. "Don't underestimate your own powers."

He dropped his briefs and bent over an armchair spreading his cheeks so I could see his inviting pink hole. I smacked his butt teasingly.

"Yes, sir," he groaned in encouragement.

"Good boy." I slapped him harder as a reward and then ran my finger down his crack until I reached the lips of his puckered hole. "Get that juicy ass of yours greased up and be in position before I strip or you'll be mincemeat."

"Yes, sir." Matt snapped to attention, grinning broadly. In the few months he'd been sharing the apartment and my bed, I'd grown fond of him. As much as he tried, though, he was no replacement for Billy. Close, but no cigar. He helped enormously keeping me sane and focused. If he helped me get Billy back I wasn't sure how I could repay him, so slipping my rampant cock into his smooth tight hole every now and then was no big imposition on me.

Matt bent double over the chair, lube glistening on his ass lips while he held his cheeks apart. Sure, he enjoyed the lovey-dovey stuff we got up to late at night but nothing suited Matt more than a short sharp fuck. He liked it to hurt so he'd greased his chute with just enough for me to slip in easily but not enough to make it painless for him.

I pushed a finger into the warm slimy hole which closed around it like some anal sea anemone. We had to be careful though. I didn't want anyone to know of our association. Not that I wasn't proud to be with him, but my plan necessitated deception. Matt understood and, apart from the gangbangs I set up for him with guys from out of town, overnighting or conferencing for a few days before going back to the wife or the boyfriend, which I watched with great excitement although only granite hard, not the diamond hardness Billy induced, Matt played away from the apartment.

I replaced my finger with the head of my cock and felt the muscle part to give me entrance, sinking down to my balls in one fluid motion.

"Oh fuck, Jesus," Matt gasped as I withdrew only to batter at his asshole again. He didn't like me to allow time for him to adjust to the burning sensation before I started pummelling him. I was happy to oblige and many's the time when I shot my spunk into his tight, clutching ass tube, I was also expelling my anger and frustration.

I squeezed his balls hard making him wince in pain as I worked up a smooth rhythm that I knew would bring me off quickly. Wrapping my fist around Matt's pole I increased the speed of my fuck strokes all the while matching them with my hand. I wanted Matt to come first so I could experience that incredible clutching spasm the ass muscles perform on your prick. The pulse in his cock signalled his release. As he squirted over the back of the arm chair, his sphincter tightened enough that, with one mighty shove that almost toppled us, I spewed my juice deep inside him.

That brief activity flushed the pipes and my anger at Nigel and Jason for their catty remarks. I slapped Matt's ass extra hard so that he rubbed the sting proudly.

I was in no such mood for quick sex after Mike had left me despondent over Billy's emotional health, although I believed he would take my advice and bring in Vince and Andy. Within the week I was proved correct, Billy newly installed at the Second Skin warehouse which acted as their workshop, retail outlet, play room, and living quarters. Vince could not contain his glee and rang me with the news although he attempted a subtlety that was beyond him.

"We know how concerned you must be about Billy so we felt it incumbent upon our friendship." Incumbent? Who spoke like that? Friendship? Not likely! He repeated himself as if savouring his own pomposity. "Incumbent upon our friendship to let you know he's all right. He's come home to us and we're taking good care of him." If I had a dollar for every barb he twisted into those few words I'd be wealthy. I could just imagine Andy listening to the conversation snickering at Vince's fake concern.

"I'm pleased. I'd heard he was having a terrible time at Jerry's and suggested to Mike you might be able to take him in," I was as much mock sincerity as Vince. "Is he okay?"

"Terribly worn out. But he'll survive."

My next question was worth a try. "Can I speak to him?"

The answer was predictable. "Oh, I'm sorry, he's sleeping right now. When he gets his strength back, we'll have you over."

"I look forward to it," I lied.

"Any message for Billy?"

"Just tell him to get better quickly and..." I hesitated just long enough that Vince would believe I'd blurt out something so banal and blithering they could live on the telling of it for weeks to come. "Tell him he's lucky to have two such good friends as you and Andy."

I could imagine his disappointment that I hadn't said I missed Billy and wanted him back. It took every ounce of my willpower not to scream it down the phone.

"Okay, will do," the obviously deflated Vince said. "Don't forget we'll be in touch soon about that visit."

Soon turned out to be six weeks; and it arrived engraved. A sit-down dinner at their headquarters, to be catered by Billy at his first social outing since our break-up, to show his friends and admirers that he was on the road to recovery, eager to join the workforce again. They made it sound like he'd been suffering a terminal illness instead of merely needing a retread on his overused elastic sphincter muscles. But I was pleased to hear about his 'recovery' although I was sure Vince and Andy had taken every opportunity to test that recovery for themselves.

On the night of the dinner I arrived punctually at 8.30pm as specified to find everyone else already there. Call me paranoid but I smelled a plot afoot. I was bundled into the dining room where the others were seated impatiently waiting to eat. It was no use telling them my invitation specifically requested me for the time at which I'd arrived when everyone else's had said 7.30pm.

"Billy's entrée will be ruined and he put so much effort into it," Andy tutted. I mumbled my apologies and said something about the traffic as I took my place at one end of the table, picked by Vince so that everyone had a perfect view of me as the night progressed.

The introductions began. I already knew Andy, Vince, Mike, and, of course Jerry had managed to inveigle an invitation. "I don't think you know Matt here," Vince said.

I looked at my secret flat mate and said, "I think we may have met somewhere… Yes, weren't you the designer on that production of The Pirates of Penzance?"

Jerry smirked.

"Yes, I was. Did you enjoy it?" he asked.

Vince jumped in, all concern. "We hoped the subject wouldn't arise tonight, Matt. I'm so sorry, I should have warned you. That's where the, um, unfortunate incident occurred that led to Steve and Billy calling it a day."

"Oh, please do forgive me. I didn't mean to open old wounds," Matt said. He was developing into a good little actor.

I shrugged. "There's nothing to forgive really. I discovered my boyfriend was a faithless slut who would open his legs for any cock going, no matter how stunted and ugly." All eyes turned to Jerry. "Best I find out sooner rather than later."

Vince interrupted before the conversation became too barbed too early. That initial foray was but a warning shot. "Matt is a photographer and he's currently taking the pictures for our new line and I must say it's going to cause quite a stir."

"Quite a stir," Andy agreed.

"I look forward to it," I smiled.

"You'll have an opportunity to see some of it this evening and even sample some of the wares," Vince beamed. "In fact, all of you will."

There was a murmur of excitement.

The remaining two people at the table were strangers to me.

"This is Gideon." I nodded to the rough looking man in his fifties seated to my left. He was dressed, or should I say undressed, in a leather harness that could scarcely contain his massive chest, and his arms which were covered with intricate dragon tattoos from his wrists to his shoulders. Yes, you could improve on perfection. His nipples were pierced with gold bars, his hair shaven back until it was just stubble on top of his head. For a man of his age he looked spectacular and filled his leather trousers to perfection showing a rather impressive tubular lump in his crotch.

"And this young man is Clive. He's a party organiser."

I stared at Clive. He was as unprepossessing as it's possible to get before disappearing up his own fundament. About twenty-one or twenty-two he was thin, sallow of complexion; he didn't look healthy at all. His hair was long but hung limply from his head. His eyes were sunken, his lips thin and pale. His eyebrows were pierced and his earlobes plugged in the latest fashion. He nodded brusquely without really looking at me.

"Shall we begin before even more of Billy's meal is ruined?"

There was mumbled assent and Vince clapped his hands. I took a deep breath as Matt shot me a sympathetic glance. Billy wheeled in the entrée. There were loud gasps not least from myself which did not go unnoticed. Billy acknowledged the gasps as signs of approval and smiled. His eyes were downcast so he hadn't seen me. I had steeled myself for this moment but my resolve wavered. I suspected he had not been told of my attendance at the dinner party and that's why I had been invited to arrive later than the others.

Vince called Billy over to display the new Power Bottom because that is what he'd created. Billy was strapped into a harness that bit into his muscles, obviously manufactured with steroids and a regimen of extreme exercise. Reluctantly I had to admit it made my cock twitch. But it was his ass that had undergone a mammoth transformation. He had always had a bubble butt but now it was as if it had been carved in Italian marble by no less than Michelangelo. He was costumed only in his chest harness, a leather strap around his swollen cock and balls, his legs shod in leather sandals laced up to his thighs. It was as if he'd stepped out of one of those old Italian sword and sandal movie epics. Except for the spiked dog collar he wore around his neck. That was a nice touch.

What wasn't a nice touch was the tattoo on his ass cheek. It had the appearance of one of those stamps on meat carcasses. But even at a distance I could read, contained in the red boxed outline, the words 100% Pure Slut.

"Fuckin' nasty," Jerry cackled.

"The perfect finish to a work of art," Mike added.

"Much better than the old Billy." Jerry's glee was hard to contain.

"You may serve," Vince commanded.

Billy, keeping his eyes cast downward as he'd obviously been instructed, slid the plate of soup from the trolley in front of Vince silently.

"Bend over. Part your cheeks."

Billy splayed so Vince could push his fingers into that glorious asshole, extracting a small plastic bag that contained his soup spoon, one of those small bent plastic scoops the Chinese use. I was horrified that Billy would allow himself to be used like this but he seemed totally under Vince's control. Matt looked at me horrified. Andy, next, took an inordinate amount of time to retrieve his spoon and then Jerry took even longer, finally extracting two, which he held aloft.

"I think you'll find you need only one spoon, Jerry. Perhaps you would like to return the other to where you found it," Vince instructed.

Jerry did like and made a show of plunging it back inside Billy who had made no sound during the ritual humiliation. Matt was the quickest to find his spoon, although not so fast as to raise suspicion he wasn't enjoying the experience.

Finally, it was my turn. Billy placed the soup in front of me and bent obediently beside me. All eyes were on me, not a breath could be heard, so I slid my fingers into his easy but still remarkably tight hole and knew immediately I'd been set up.

"There doesn't seem to be another spoon," I said calmly.

I felt Billy twitch in recognition of my voice. I did a little trick with my fingers inside his asshole which I knew he loved and I was rewarded with the first sound he'd made all evening: a sharp gasp heard by everyone at the table.

"How stupid of me," Vince said, slapping his forehead theatrically. "When you didn't turn up on time we thought you weren't coming. A spoon for our guest, Billy."

He left the room without looking at me, returning moments later with my spoon which he placed in front of me.

"Enjoy, gentlemen, please. You may eat with us, Billy."

I looked about but there was no place at the table for him to sit. From the trolley, Billy took a dog bowl, placing it on the floor. He kneeled down and began to lap his food as if he were a dog. Vince leaned over to pat him. "Good boy."

Turning to the assembled guests, Vince proclaimed proudly," It took us a while to house train him but we got him in the end." There were smiles and snickers all round. "All it takes is discipline. And a good home where people know how to really take care of a pet."

It was going to be a long night. The only consolation was that the food was delicious. Billy had surpassed himself. "This is better nosh than we get at that shithouse restaurant of yours, Gideon," Jerry claimed.

I saw Gideon struggle to keep his temper in check. "Yes, it is very good indeed," he agreed finally, thus sidelining any further discussion.

Tension was so thick you could have carved it and served it as a main course. Conversation kept to trivialities for the most part, restrained there by Vince who only lost control of the situation whenever Jerry offered crass comments which, I noticed, repelled most of those at the dinner. He was obviously at the gathering under sufferance, his main task being to annoy and humiliate me.

Billy gathered up the plates and wheeled them to the kitchen reappearing to pour wine for the guests before disappearing again.

"I must say that really was delicious," making sure the full import of the word 'delicious' encompassed not only the food but the performance as well. I knew worse was to come and was grateful I had practiced my smile. To leave now, even pleading an emergency would mean they had triumphed. I had to stand my ground.

The main course was wheeled in. Billy placed the most succulent Apple Brandy Chicken in front of each of us before doing the rounds with a cos lettuce salad as accompaniment. He stood beside Vince awaiting instruction. "You must try the salad dressing. It's Andy's own recipe, and if I might be allowed to boast a little, it has its own unique flavor because...well, you will see soon enough. Billy."

With one fluid movement Billy crouched directly over a small glass jug and, with a control I had never seen before, squirted into it just the right amount of dressing. From his asshole! The ingredients must have been more oil than lemon juice otherwise Billy's ass chute would be too raw for the games I assumed would be the highlight of the evening. "Just a little more, please Billy," Vince said and a further spurt was added.

It was unremarkable how many people around the table passed on the dressing although Vince and Andy made liberal use of it as did Matt and Clive. I had a double helping much to Jerry's horror, screwing his face up in disgust. Billy again dropped to the floor and was fed morsels by Vince and Andy.

The small jug of vinaigrette sat in the centre of the table like a time bomb. When Vince finally spoke again it was with steel in his voice. "I do hope, gentlemen, that you won't be as ungallant as to refuse Andy's hard work preparing such a fine vinaigrette."

"Fuckin' shit mate, that's gross," Jerry said.

"Indeed, Jerry. A remarkable observation considering you have not tried it." It seemed Vince was determined to humiliate each and every one of the guests before the night was out. He leaned across the table and drizzled a liberal amount on Jerry's salad. "Don't be so hasty in making up your mind. If you are not the man of discernment we believe you to be then our special dessert will not be to your liking either."

Jerry knew a threat when he heard one and sheepishly nibbled at the dripping lettuce, attempting not to screw up his face. I'd already tasted mine and had to agree it was far superior to store bought varieties, but I may have been biased. Eventually taste overcame Jerry's reticence and he ate his salad with gusto. I marvelled that the prospect of getting into Billy's ass could precipitate such huge behavioural change.

So far I had been let off lightly so I knew the coup de grâce must lie in waiting. The conversation centered around Second Skin's new designs which Andy was keeping very close to his chest. All he would reveal was that the line was called 100% Pure Slut and that the launch party would be the talk of the town, as would Matt's photos for the brochure which would be for sale on the night.

I think I was the only one at the table who dreaded it, everyone else seemed extraordinarily keen on the idea.

"Clive here is organising the event and those of you who know him will relish the idea of something totally kinky and outrageous. It will push the envelope on what is considered good taste in fetish design."

"Billy will obviously be the centre point of the campaign. With his reputation blanket publicity is guaranteed." It was the first time Clive had spoken all night.

"What reputation is that?" I questioned.

Jerry snorted. "That he's a total fuckin' slut who can't get enough cock."

"And what do you base that on?"

"Well, um, you know. That night at the theatre."

"All I've heard is rumor and innuendo. You seem to be the only person who has inside knowledge."

"Me and Billy the slut boy here."

He was baiting me.

Billy looked up quickly. If I read the signs right he wondered why I was humiliating myself further by attending this function.

Andy saw his momentary lapse. "Naughty boy!" Suddenly a switch descended on Billy's back. I hoped the infraction was worth the punishment.

Vince sighed. "All that training. What a pity." Vince whipped him once again. "Bad boy!"

Matt looked on helplessly wanting to intervene as much as I did but we kept our place.

"Fucking hot the way he takes a beating." Mike was panting and had slipped his hands under the table.

Vince obliged with a few more strokes just to show that he could, then stood up and announced that we would adjourn to the living room where it would be far more comfortable to 'partake of a very special delicacy for dessert.' As we moved farther into the warehouse Matt came over to me and made some loud comment as if taunting me, then whispered, "This is utterly barbaric."

The concrete floor living area was comfortably furnished with leather lounges and chairs and a number of accoutrements were scattered within easy reach in case the action became hardcore. I noticed the rugs had been rolled up and stored in a corner. Billy took orders for tea and coffee without raising his eyes again and disappeared to the kitchen. Matt enquired as to whether he needed any assistance but Vince told him 'the boy' was trained to do everything he was told.

The conversation turned to the forthcoming leather fashion line and Clive again became animated. He explained that he and Gideon were also models for the catalogue; in his case only body parts because he realised he was not really model material. I'd already taken a wild guess as to which body part as his trousers were hard pressed to restrain it.

Billy had served the refreshments and was standing silently awaiting orders. Vince beamed then asked, "Who's for dessert?" Hmm, a double meaning. Everyone shouted their appetite for whatever it was except for me and Matt. "Matt, I think you should try the specialty of the house. It will help you in your work." Matt nodded. "Steve?"

"No thanks, I'm trying to cut down." I patted my stomach.

Andy was quick off the mark. "I hope you don't mind me saying so, but you are not looking your best this evening. You've let yourself go. Such a pity. You'd be quite a catch if you looked after yourself."

"If you change your mind later, there's plenty to go around," Vince chuckled at his little joke. "Boy! Dessert!"

Billy's body language told the story that he was none too pleased to be performing this duty. He lay down on his back on one of the padded leather benches in the centre of the room and hoisted his legs in the air holding them in place. Vince lathered his hole with lubrication and sawed his fingers in and out to open Billy up further. "Tonight's dessert gentlemen is home-made cream pie, our own special recipe. I do hope you will all help with the ingredients for this spectacular dish."

There was much laughter and a smattering of applause as we all made ourselves comfortable. Gideon stepped forward to begin the action, flexing his muscles like a pro bodybuilder to the delight of those watching, and stripped off his leather shorts. He was a clumsy strip tease but once his cock was revealed, all was forgiven. He lowered his balls over Billy's face, demanding he lick them. Billy's tongue snaked out to obey, sucking them into his mouth, bathing them in his spit. It reminded me that Billy's mouth ran a very close second to his ass in giving pleasure, followed by his substantial, but to my mind under-utilised, cock. It was now engorged, obviously enjoying the attention.

He prised Gideon's muscle-bound asscheeks apart and dove into the crack. We stood to get a better view as he tongue fucked the big bodybuilder, sucking and chewing his virgin asshole. The hunk moaned his satisfaction before sliding his prick into Billy's hot throat. His head was hanging over the edge of the bench, the thick weapon so far down his gullet we could see his Adam's apple bobbing as he tried to swallow.

Vince, after checking to ensure I was watching, slid out of his leather chaps and squeezing his cock at the base rammed full force into Billy's hot ass, sighing with satisfaction as he sank in. Clothes were shucked so the audience could sit naked, jerking, awaiting their turn. I remained resolutely fully dressed and because of the sloppy clothes I was wearing, it was not obvious that I was turned on by the display. I grabbed another glass of wine as if I were watching a favourite television program instead of my ex-boyfriend, whom I still loved and wanted back, copping an anal battering.

Andy had gone to the home theatre set-up and the large screen TV was now showing the home-made footage of Billy's training. His favorite band, Nine Inch Nails, was spitting out his favorite hymn to slutdom which had the thumping refrain 'I want to fuck you like an animal.' The beat and the repetition of the lyrics were hypnotic and Vince speeded up, he didn't want to hog the limelight, he wanted all the others to have a turn, particularly in front of me. He wanted to legitimise his possession of Billy.

On the screen I watched him being birched and abused by Vince and Andy in their efforts to train him as their slave slut and house dog. Billy's natural exuberance was at odds with what he was being asked to do and his punishment was all the greater for it. My heart bled for his pain, and the expression of hopelessness that they'd captured in graphic close-up. They had fucked him repeatedly, using his ass as their come dump, never giving him a moment's rest until they wore him down and he was the pliant fuck toy on the bench in front of me.

There seemed little joy in what Billy was feeling. Even during his worst slutty behavior in front of me there was always a cheerful shame to what he was doing. Here his body seemed bored. Yes, he was allowing these men to do what they desired to him, but he was totally passive. Vince let us all know he was coming by screaming out the fact before pulling out. A small trickle of sperm oozed from Billy's ass. Gideon disengaged from his mouth, waving his thick uncut cock like a baton for all to admire before poking it into the sub's guts. Jerry was not about to go last and quickly elbowed his way to the gaping mouth but pulled up short, swearing. "Oh shit, all that coffee's gone straight through me. I gotta take a piss."

Vince's voice broke through the cacophony of sex sounds on the screen and on the concrete floor of the warehouse. "Slut! Open your mouth." Billy did as he was told. "There you go, Jerry. No need to lose your place in the queue."

Jerry looked amazed. "You mean, you want me to..."

Vince nodded. "Be my guest."

Jerry's stream of hot piss hit Billy square on the face. "This is so fuckin' nasty," Jerry gloated. "Drink it, slut. Go on, drink my piss. Don't waste a drop."

Billy slurped it into his mouth as best he could, we heard his throat contract as it went down, but the flow was too strong and a lot of it went into his hair and over his chest. Gideon didn't seem to mind that he was being splashed and was not put off his stroke. In fact, the warm piss against his body seemed to excite him to the extent that he roared like a wounded elephant and sank into the asshole and grunted. Jerry pushed him aside as soon as it looked as if he'd dumped his load and smashed his own stumpy cock in Billy's ass. Mike and Andy were now at Billy's head aiming their straining pricks at his mouth until two jets of hot piss scalded Billy's eyes and nose. He choked as he attempted to take it all down but they just laughed trying to push their still pissing cocks into his open gob making it even more difficult to breathe. Piss gushed out his nostrils and I thought they'd end up drowning him.

When they finished Billy was awash with the stench of manpiss as Jerry got stuck into his ass. Everyone stood back to watch the show because no one wanted to get in Jerry's way. "So slut boy, did you miss me, huh?" He grabbed Billy by the throat to make him look in his eyes. "You miss daddy's cock, baby. The only cock that makes you happy. Tell me who's got the best cock in the world, slut boy?"

"You have, Jerry," Billy said, but it sounded hollow. To anyone but the egotistical Jerry it sounded totally insincere. "Boy can't get enough of my great big cock, can you slut? You love the feel of it in your mancunt. You want daddy to fuck you like the whore you are, don't you baby?"

Jerry tightened his grip around Billy's throat, squeezing it to encourage him to parrot the words about his sexual superiority, his skill as a cocksman. Jerry spat in Billy's face, calling him a slut cunt whore and any combination of names he could conjure. Billy was smeared with saliva and piss and Jerry rammed like a machine. Mike, almost sympathetically pushed his cock into Billy's mouth making Jerry release his grip on his throat. Billy could at least breathe now but it gave Jerry something else to turn his foul mouth to. "Suck that cock, slut boy. Take it down your throat while I pound your fuckin' asshole."

Mike started to join the chorus. "You're just a fuck toy, Billy. For us to use any way we like. Suck my cock. Use your mouth like a cunt. That's it, take me down your throat." Mike slammed in and stayed there. I could hear Billy gulping for air, his eyes watering, until he looked as if he were about to pass out when Mike pulled his cock free, strings of drool hanging off it. Billy gasped for air, his face slimy and smeared. "Open your throat, slut," Mike commanded. "I want to really fuck your face." Mike barely gave him time before he drove his prick right into Billy's craw then increased the pace so he was pile driving to the sound of choking and near puking. It was music to Jerry and Mike. They high fived as they dumped their spunk in Billy's body.

Andy stepped up and took a turn at 'stirring the porridge' as he called it and Gideon decided he needed to unload his piss in Billy's vulnerable mouth. The others were resting to get their second wind or, in the case of three of us, our first.

Vince turned to Matt. "Your turn, mate. Don't be all day about it." Matt looked at me in distress. "Don't look at poor old Steve there. He's a sorry excuse for a cuckold. Hell, not even that any more because Billy belongs to us. You can do what you like to him. He'll be all shagged out by the end of the night and no good to anyone for a week or more."

"I'd really like to," Matt said meekly, "But I'm a bottom."

The room laughed.

Vince was encouraging. "No disgrace in that mate, but Billy will make a believer of you. Once you fuck his asshole you'll never go back. It's addictive. Feel free to curse him any which way you like. Billy loves the abuse. See." He pointed to the big screen where he and Andy were skewering him at each end.

Matt may have been a bottom psychologically but his cock was certainly top material. It was a nice length and thickness and it stayed hard forever, especially while he was being fucked aggressively. Now he was going to be doing the fucking. Not only that, he was taking on an insatiable bottom and doing it in front of a highly critical group of his peers. It was a big ask of anyone. Especially as there was no life left in Billy, none of that spark that made him great. He was merely going through the motions.

I was watching Matt in a new light. The guy was young, eager, and horny as a rabbit. I enjoyed watching him cop it from a group of men, now he was about to impale the love of my life. His body had great definition, his pecs and abs were firm as stone, and he was a good-looking kid. That was the problem. Although he was in his mid twenties, almost the same age as me and Billy, he acted like a kid, making him seem years younger and much less experienced than he really was. I crossed my fingers hoping he would make good.

Matt slid into open-all-hours Billy and started on the long climb to orgasm. It was a lacklustre effort and Matt knew it. Billy was bored. Everyone who'd fucked him so far was acutely aware they hadn't managed to hit the spot that took him to another plane so that his body cried out for penetration and his eyes rolled back in his head. If experts like Mike, Vince or Jerry couldn't achieve it I held out little hope for Matt.

But he'd obviously been taking notes. As his cock rutted in and out of Billy's ass he leaned in and grabbed

Billy by the pecs. You could see Billy wake up. He punched Billy's chest hard. Really twisting the nipples then slapping the tits. Grabbing Billy by the throat with one hand, he slapped his face. Not viciously, but enough to awaken Billy's latent interest. Leaning in, he kissed Billy square on the lips before licking his way down to Billy's ear and nibbling on the lobe, poking his tongue in his ear hole.

Then Matt drew back to his full height and rammed his cock so hard Billy's body was shoved along the bench. "Holy Jesus fucking Christ," Matt screamed. "Fuckin' whore. I bet I know what you want, eh slut. You want to feel the best cock in the world? To go with the best ass in the world. That's what you are, fuck slut. An assdump just waiting for huge cock slamming your cunt, eh, Billy. You want to feel me inside your ass while your boyfriend is watching."

Billy looked over at me for a moment sadly before Matt wrenched his head back. "Fuck, Billy, I could plug your ass all night. We're just minding your sweet ass, Billy. Opening you up for your real master. Fuckin' Satan himself. Feel the devil's prick in your bowels, slut? Filling you with hot red cock. Sizzling cock in your ass." Billy got a wild look in his eyes, beginning to moan at the fantasy. Matt pulled out and beckoned Clive over, while keeping up his dirty talk about devil fucks and Satan "You want Satan's cock inside you, Billy? He's the only master who will ever satisfy you. He understands you, Billy, and what you need. Your ass filled permanently with hard cock. You want Satan's seed inside your belly breeding you."

As Billy groaned his acquiescence, Clive pistoned his huge uncircumcised cock right into Billy's guts, stretching his ass lips almost beyond human endurance. Clive was rough. If he had little in the way of personality in his everyday life he made up for it in sexual prowess. He was a demon when he fucked. He didn't care at all about his partner; all he cared about was sinking his cock into a warm tight hole. He now had one of the best impaled on his ass splitter. Matt moved to Billy's head, cradling it as he continued his verbal onslaught. Billy was really into it now, the fantasy and the reality meshing in his mind. Jerry could no longer contain himself and jerked off over Billy whose eyes were already sinking back in his head. Mike joined him then Andy and Vince until Billy's face dripped man slime. It was a total slut bukkake.

There was a roar from Clive and his entire body shook as he blew his spunk inside Billy's battered asshole. He could barely stand after he'd blown his load and stumbled backwards leaving Billy's asshole gaping for a moment before it began to shrink back to its normal size.

Matt turned him over so he was kneeling with his ass in the air and told him we all wanted to see the devil's sperm that was inside his ass. Suddenly come began to bubble out like a volcano that has lain dormant for too long. Matt held his hands cupped to catch the slimy libation. When he'd collected a handful, he presented the juice to Billy to lick up, and then rubbed the residue on his cock so Billy could finish him off. He finally blew his load in Billy's mouth.

The gaping slime hole was too much for Gideon who went for his third or fourth round, I'd lost count, while Vince drew the party's attention back to me. Billy was getting into it now and they would all enjoy the remainder of the evening.

"Well, Steve, are you going to join us for dessert or are you going to be a party pooper?"

"I'm afraid I have to be off shortly, but thanks for the offer. I have a new boyfriend and I don't think he'd appreciate it if I came home smelling of someone's slut, do you?"

There was a kind of strangled sob from Billy and I knew he'd heard and that my barb had hit home. I felt bad but it had to be done. Matt would be there to comfort him if he needed it.

I said my thanks and my goodbyes. They were reluctant to see me go only because their target of humiliation was leaving. Jerry had already dismissed me and had replaced Gideon at Billy's ass, already his foul language turning the air blue with his 'sluts' and 'whores'. At the door I turned to face Billy, Jerry still puffing away on top of him. "By the way, Jerry." He listened, but he didn't slow his stride. "You may want to go a bit easy on the slut talk when you're referring to Billy. I got a DVD in the mail last week, no sender details or return address. Pity, I'd like to thank him personally. You'd love it. In fact, you're one of the stars. It seems that theatre where Pirates was performed has a digital camera set up in the front of the balcony to archive their shows. Seems they not only got the musical, they captured all the action afterwards." Now everyone was paying attention. "Contrary to rumours going around, Billy was actually the victim of a vicious assault and a far from consensual gangbang afterwards, liquor was forced down his throat until he was too drunk to give his consent. Billy is totally blameless."

Okay, I was gilding the lily a bit, maybe a lot, but it had the desired effect. I suspect Jerry shrivelled in fear. Vince and Andy looked to the big screen and I thought I saw panic there as well. Matt smiled behind their backs. Poor Billy looked grief stricken, possibly at the thought that his life had gone off the rails when he made the wrong decision and walked out on me. His knees gave out on him on the bench and he collapsed. I didn't think there'd be much joy left in the remainder of the dinner party that night.

There wasn't a lot of joy anywhere for a week or so. Matt came home about an hour after I'd got in to say that my little revelation had rather dampened spirits even though only Jerry had anything to do with Billy's theatre fuck but they had begun to question their own borderline activity that night. Matt jumped on the bed naked and grabbed my cock. I still hadn't blown my load. I lay back with my hands behind my head as Matt filled me in on what I'd missed including the first hour before my arrival in which they'd planned the evening's events right down to my humiliation. I was right, Billy had no idea I would be in attendance. Matt had spoken to him briefly and he was as miserable with Vince and Andy as he had been with Jerry. He missed me but was still too ashamed to return to our apartment for fear he would poison people's opinions of me.

There was still work to do.

Matt was to follow up on the outcome of my startling revelation about the illicit DVD on Billy's resolve but that would have to wait for the first photo shoot in three day's time. Matt would have Billy alone and they would be able to talk freely. "Hell, he's such a power bottom, I may even fuck him," Matt laughed. I slapped his ass hard as I slipped inside him and rode him as I fantasised Billy beneath me.

There wasn't much joy to report when Matt came back from the first two photo shoots either. He ran the pics he'd taken from his digital camera through the wide screen TV and Billy appeared vacant and lifeless, a zombie. "He does everything I ask of him, but there's no enthusiasm, no spark. There's that word again."

"You gave him his spark back the night of the dinner party, you can do it again."

Matt laughed. "It had nothing to do with me. You told me what to say. I told him he should be the best he'd ever been to make you jealous and want him so badly that you would just carry him away from all the bad times. And it worked like a charm. Then you managed to kill it again."

"As I intended," I said smugly. "Why should I help Vince sell stuff using Billy. I bet they're not paying him anything."

"Only in sex that he doesn't want. He did admit in a moment of weakness that you were right about Vince and

Andy. They don't care about him. They see him as one of their trophies and an easy lay but mostly as a way to get back at you. They were really pissed off when that part of it didn't work." Matt thought for a moment. "Billy's suffering badly. They're taking it out on him because the photos are not turning out as they want and they're thinking of cancelling the show. Or at least postponing it."

"They can't do that; it'll ruin all my planning."

"And Clive is pulling his hair out over the party he's planning because okay, he's got Billy's co-operation but not his enthusiasm so it's all falling apart as well. The worst part is Vince has taken to beating him. It's so bad that when he turned up for the photo shoot today there are some pics I couldn't take because he's too battered." He found the photo and ran it on the screen. Billy's back was covered in scars that had barely healed from constant birching by the looks of it and the blue green splotches of bruising stood out on the pale skin of his lower back. "He doesn't complain but he's hurting. And he thinks he's hurting you. He thinks you looked like shit at the dinner because of those baggy clothes you wore. He thinks you've let yourself go and blames himself for it."

I sighed. I gave in and told Matt how to salvage it.

After their next meeting Matt could hardly wait to show me the photos. He was more excited than I'd seen him in ages. "Billy really is the perfect model," he raved. "The camera loves him. Especially when he's up like he was today."

The camera may have loved him but I wasn't sure that I did. Yes, the photographs were stunning but I didn't know that I wanted people to see Billy lying in a public urinal with Gideon pissing in his face. Billy looked angelic, his entire body awash in piss wearing a half singlet emblazoned with the words 100% Piss Slut. I didn't like it but I got hard in an instant. There was another of Billy down on his knees about to engulf a huge cock, obviously Clive's, poking through a glory hole in the same toilet: 100% Cock Sucker. Matt had done an amazing job and over the following weeks the pics began to appear on the net and pop up in gay bar rags that dared to run such provocative ads, as well as posters that disappeared almost as soon as they went up. My favorite was of Billy standing smiling at the camera a small dribble of come running down his chin as he smiled: 100% Come Slut.

"And whose is it?" I asked.

"It's yoghurt. But it was mine originally. He sucked me off for authenticity's sake but almost swallowed before he realised what we were shooting. The genuine stuff just doesn't look real in photographs. You're right. I could be a top for Billy. In fact, just thinking about it makes me horny."

"Don't even think about it tonight. I'm still sore."

"You got it done then?"

"Yep."

"You must really love him. I hope I meet someone one day who'll love me like that."

I ruffled his hair. "You will. But, just for a change, how about you top me? See if you can make my eyes roll back in my head."

The buzz around town was gathering momentum and Billy's reputation underwent something of a rehabilitation. People began to believe the stories of his outrageous behaviour at Pirates of Penzance were all fake; spread as a prelude to all the publicity of Second Skin's 100% Slut range. Tickets to the launch party were changing hands for vast sums of money on eBay, especially as the party entertainment was advertised with Billy totally naked in a blasphemous pose with a muscular horned Satan, in a half leather hood, towering over him, about to ravage his body. It's amazing what you can achieve with Photoshop. Under the mask, in fact, it was me. I had shaved all the hair off my head, as well as my pubes, and most of my body hair, I'd bulked up tremendously although only Matt knew about it, and I'd tanned to a nice toasty brown. With my body oiled and my biceps pumped so they swelled on my arms like giant walnuts, I was a pretty impressive sight.

Matt convinced them to use my photo because it was superior to Gideon's. He'd made sure of that. Vince didn't recognise me so he had no objections. And Billy gave it his seal of approval by taking a copy of the ad away to jerk off. I already had a large print of it framed and hanging above our bed. 100% Satan's Slut promised to be the party of the year.

Matt continued to bring home a never-ending variety of the new range, tight half-singlets that covered only Billy's pecs and then so tightly you could make out his nipples and the color of the aureoles through the fabric. He looked so hot in them I wanted a lifetime supply. So did the public as the advance orders far outstripped the manufacture. They covered just about every permutation of slut sex that Andy could think of – and that was quite a few. I thought the most appropriate was Billy, lying on his stomach facing the camera, his back arched so the viewer could see his amazing sculpted butt, a group of horny men behind him their eyes fixed on that magic spot between his asscheeks. 100% Insatiable.

As was the public's appetite for info on the big event. Nigel and Jason even took to popping in for an update on Billy, having the decency to apologise for their previous outrageous slurs. Again, I didn't believe a word of it. It was interesting that Nigel seemed to be more interested in the model behind the muscular Satan figure. I made sure I was wearing my baggiest clothes so my new body would not give me away and I always wore a cap or a beanie to disguise my shaven head.

The only person I didn't hear from was Jerry, not even to taunt me. He'd left town not long after the dinner party leaving his business in the capable hands of his manager, Earl, who, once the ads for Second Skin began appearing rang to see if I wanted my old job back. What he wanted was another go at Billy's ass. He was a sleazy bastard just like his boss. I declined politely and told him I'd come back to work for Jerry when hell froze over.

I already had my invitation to the launch which, because of its explicit nature, was invitation only and closed to the general public. A private post-launch party had been organised at which Billy would be tail tagged by the guests. I had not been invited to that one and only knew about it because Matt had been hired as official photographer to take very graphic happy snaps.

Matt had inveigled Clive and Vince into using me, or rather the hooded man in the advertising, for the actual show. Buzz around the traps had been almost as positive for me as for Billy. I didn't want my cover blown so I turned up for the briefing in costume hoping Billy wouldn't recognise me. As Vince was present, Billy was supposed to keep his eyes downcast, especially as Vince had sussed out our attraction. Our performance was to be simplicity itself. Billy would be wheeled out amid smoke and to a thumping soundtrack, distorted to make it sound more satanic. I was to enter through the audience. We would do our stuff, it was entirely up to us what that consisted of but it had to include penetrative sex and lots of fingering of Billy's immortal asshole. I nodded that would be no problem. Billy readily agreed. We had thirty minutes of music but once we'd blown we could signal to shut it off or continue for the duration. Then I was to exit through the audience carrying Billy over my shoulder. We were not to come back under any circumstances. Once we'd doubled back to the dressing room I could join the party as a guest either in or out of my costume. I'm glad they hadn't asked to inspect the merchandise as it would have given the game away.

As the big event approached I was a bundle of nerves, only keeping the lid on it with Matt's help. But something peculiar was also occurring. Word got out about why Jerry had left town and more than a few married gay men were walking around town glancing over their shoulders lest a divorce lawyer be on their tail. Others in relationships were just as jittery and began to examine their prenups in greater detail. A number of them cancelled their attendance at the Second Skin launch or, at the very least, the after-party sexathon. Matt was told his services were no longer required at that event although his invitation was still valid. They'd even offered me one in the guise of the hunky Satan. It threatened to be a forlorn affair until Vince upped the ante by getting Billy to sign a waiver that he agreed to any and everything that occurred. Then rumour got around that it would be a down and dirty kink party and sleazebags began lining up for tickets.

It meant my plan had to work.

Matt let me in via the back door as I was already in costume apart from my elevated leather boots which gave me extra inches to be more imposing. They were shaped as much like hooves as possible while retaining sufficient comfort to allow me to walk normally. I could hear the buzz of the crowd who had been waiting patiently, guzzling free alcohol, and feeling up the semi-nude waiters who distributed finger food as well as their phone number -- when requested. They were on the make and this crowd was in the serious money. The parade of fashion was about to start and I stayed hidden from the models, mainly cute twinks and muscle boys from the local gym, doing this in exchange for free clothing. Vince and Andy were cheap bastards.

The PA system crackled into life, Vince going on and on with his spiel that gave absolutely no credit to Billy either as inspiration or model. He singled out Andy, then himself, and finally Matt's photos, as the most important elements of the launch's success. Matt had already told me there were red sales dots all over the warehouse for pictures that had been sold, and he had a pocket of business cards from people who were very interested in any forthcoming exhibitions he might be having, with or without all the hoopla of this one.

I heard Billy taking deep breaths and muttering to himself as if praying. I thought I heard my name mentioned. "Please let Steve be here. Please let him like me again."

I could have put a stop to it all right here but Billy deserved his success and he was safe now. The lights in the warehouse dimmed and Billy disappeared to take up his position on stage. They'd rehearsed it over and over until it was drilled into Billy's head. The music would begin with the theme from Jesus Christ Superstar and at the appropriate spot in the music a spotlight would hit his butt at exactly the tattoo. It must have worked because the audience went wild. The whistling and the stomping and the good-natured catcalls continued for so long it threatened the smooth running of the show. I saw the video footage later that Matt shot and after the spot expanded to reveal Billy in his entirety, wearing only his form-hugging 100% Pure Slut T-shirt to match his tattoo, he just beamed although you could see his eyes darting around the darkened party area looking for me as he admitted afterwards.

As he stood there his cock began to harden and Vince interrupted the ovation to get the show started. Billy acknowledged his fans and strode confidently backstage where he changed into his next outfit. He was pumped. I psst at him from my hiding spot as he got into his next costume, time was of the essence. He turned and smiled when he saw me, his cock twitching making it difficult to tuck into his leather shorts. I hoped the metal teeth of the zipper were well away from his dick. I gave him the thumbs up and he mouthed 'Thanks.'

The show ran smoothly and Vince and Andy took their bows at the completion of the twenty-minute catwalk parade. To Vince's chagrin the audience called for Billy and he was hauled out to acknowledge another ovation.

Vince made the announcement that the 100% Satan's Slut show would be starting in five minutes and now was a good time to leave if you were of a sensitive moral disposition. There was much laughter and I suspect not a little trepidation. The audience was asked to keep the marked area free for the performance and I heard a noisy shuffle as people moved. Matt came to find me and ushered me along a passageway cut off from the party so I could enter without being seen beforehand. I'd actually taken Cialis to ensure my rampancy and it had already kicked in although that may have had something to do with the fact I was about to bone Billy for the first time in five or six months. And in public.

Matt had toyed with covering my body in red paint but it didn't work well enough and, in the end, we'd settled for my all-over tan and all-over oil. My muscles glistened. I felt so hot, even more so when Matt pulled my head down and sank his tongue in my mouth. I would be sorry to lose my playmate; we'd already moved his gear into the spare bedroom at the apartment in expectation of Billy's return.

He got me all hot and bothered, his intention, and my cock throbbed with excitement. Would I be able keep my sanity if I lived with two such accommodating bottoms? That was a problem too far at the moment. The lights dimmed, a voice boomed over the PA announcing the imminent start of the show and the music, something from Aida, pumped through the room. I smelled the odour of poppers and joints and, from experience, I knew there would be harder drugs consumed as well.

I found my mark. Matt got his digital camera ready to record my triumph. We hoped. The lights came up on a group of semi-naked slave boys, all wearing 100% Pure Slut tank tops in various colors and slogan permutations. Held on their shoulders was a human-scale crucifix to which a naked Billy was roped and bound. Alongside the parade walked two Romans in leather briefs and tank tops proclaiming 100% Pure Domination. Every few steps they flogged Billy with birches. He wriggled convincingly, although I discovered later they really were flogging the shit out of him because he wouldn't give up his ass to them before the show. By the time the cross was lowered to the front of the stage, Billy was bleeding.

They leaned the cross at a sharp angle, locking it in place against a bracket in the wall. Billy was strung upside down his head at crotch level, his arms and legs rope bound to the beams. While one Roman soldier herded the slaves to the side of the stage where they kneeled in mock terror, Gideon as the other soldier, pulled his limp cock from his costume and aimed at Billy's mouth, letting fly with a stream of piss. He attempted to guzzle it down but, because of his position, it was difficult to swallow and the acrid liquid was seeping down his nostrils. Billy struggled, the piss stinging his cuts. When Gideon had finished he poked his wet prick in Billy's vulnerable mouth until he grunted loudly, pulled his cock free and squirted on Billy's face, all in wide-screen color close-up on the wall monitors for those who did not have a good vantage point.

The second Roman took Gideon's place and repeated the action until Billy's body glistened with drying piss and strings of spunk. The Romans untied Billy and turned him over so he was face down on the cross, his ass exposed and tied him down again. Gideon took a crucifix from his waistband and the two soldiers spat on it and then on Billy's asshole. I knew he'd been lubed well before his appearance on stage. They began to slowly insert the cross in his ass. Billy screamed as it disappeared to the cross bar. Leaving their last gobs of saliva on his face they strode from the stage to stunned silence. This was outside the comfort zone of some of the audience. The lights dimmed even further. It was time for my entrance. The sound was increased in volume to almost ear-splitting level, there was a violin shriek approaching, at which point the warehouse would be plunged into total silent darkness, a red spot would pinpoint me standing at the back of the room, and I would stride forward.

I tensed, ready for my cue as the timing was all-important. I had to be spot on for the music to work. I ripped the leather hood off my head, I wanted everyone to know it was me coming to claim Billy. It would be too late for Vince to stop the show now. I made sure the two horns Matt had glued to my shaved head were firm, adjusted the leather harness that showed my pecs and abs off to good effect, and ripped off my leather shorts, leaving me in only my boots. My cock was kept hard by the sheer excitement for what was to come and by the leather band wrapped tightly around my balls and my erection.

The red spot hit me. I snarled. I towered at six-feet-five inches in my heels as I strode through the crowd. I must have been a daunting sight. By the time I reached the elevated platform that was the stage, the new soundtrack kicked in. It wasn't part of the original plan; this was a little added extra by Matt and I. We'd created a compilation of heavy duty songs by Billy's favorite band, Nine Inch Nails, overlaying it with the sounds of Billy's assault and subsequent gangbang. The voices were quite recognisable and a few members of the audience sneaked away quietly. Jerry's voice, in particular, stood out.

Billy's body had jerked when he heard Nine Inch Nails screaming 'I want to fuck you like an animal' and he tried to lift his head to look at me. He wriggled against his ropes in frustration. Good. Let him suffer a few moments longer. A few people recognised me and whispers ran round the audience. The frisson of expectation increased when Vince and Andy caught on and I heard them cursing off to the side. There was little they could do short of blacking out the stage and disrupting their own launch.

Billy must have known something had changed because of the whispers and the change to the soundtrack. I dragged two of the slaves over, commanding them to rub their cocks against my leather boots and then jerk off. I forced them look up at me while they stroked their cocks hitting them in the face with my own to hurry their orgasm. The slaves played their parts to perfection, dumping big loads on my boots. Dismissing them to scramble back to their slave mates, I strode to Billy, grabbed his hair, and pushed his face on to the slime.

"Lick it clean, come boy!" I hissed in his ear. "I want it to shine. Use your tongue. That's it. Good boy. Swallow all that juicy slut come."

Billy was still trying to work out my identity but I kept my face out of his sightline. He didn't recognise my body because it had changed so much since he'd last seen it naked and he had assumed I'd gone to fat from my appearance at the dinner party. I squashed his face against my boot until it was spotless. Then gave him the other to clean. For the sheer hell of it, I jammed the crucifix brutally in and out of his asshole a few times before removing it. I leaned in close to his ear.

"Are you a slut, boy?" Matt has set up a radio chest mike for me so my voice thundered through the room.

I reached up and fingered his ass. I inserted three fingers slowly, seeking the far reaches of his bowels. Billy bucked to get free.

"Are you Satan's fuck slut, boy? Are you my slave? Will you devote your life to me, boy?"

Billy was not responding, merely attempting to wriggle free. I delivered the coup de grâce; I flicked that switch inside Billy's asshole. He bucked violently, cried out, and fell still.

More quietly I asked. "Are you my slut, Billy?"

He groaned almost inaudibly. "Yes."

"Will you be my slut alone?"

"Oh, yes."

"Louder, Billy. Are you my total slut?'

"Yes, sir!" he screamed.

I signalled to the slaves to blindfold Billy and untie him. I grabbed a handful of his hair forcing him to his knees in front of me. Holding him securely, I commanded a slave to remove the blindfold. It took seconds for his eyes to adjust but the first thing he would have seen was the unmistakable message tattooed just above my cock: 100% Slut Lover. I felt him struggle when he saw it. I yanked his head back until he was staring into my eyes. He grunted with surprise and pleasure, closed his eyes, and shot his load all over the stage without anyone touching his cock.

I pushed his face down to lick it up while I kneeled behind that glorious ass that I had missed over the months we had been apart and sank my cock to the hilt.

"You're my slut, Billy. Mine alone. You will give me your ass whenever I command it. You will give it to anyone I tell you to. Your asshole is my domain. You want that Billy?"

"Fuck, yeah." His voice was raspy with desire.

"Tell them, Billy."

"I want to be your slut. I need your cock inside me. Fuck me hard. Fuck my slutty asshole. I'm begging you to fuck me like the come dump I am. I want to serve you. My asshole is yours. My mouth is yours. My cock is yours. Command me."

Billy was breathless. I took my time, sliding in and out, reaching parts that others hadn't managed in a while.

I pulled out and turned him over roughly, shoving his legs in the air. Matt moved in for a close up and I wished

I could have had him in on the action too. Ah well, there was plenty of time now.

I looked into Billy's eyes and there were tears forming. I had to continue, I could not give in now much as I wanted to just sweep him into my arms and hold him.

"You like what you see, slut?"

"Hell, yeah."

I shoved my cock back into his ass roughly. I wanted it to hurt.

"You like what you feel?"

"Fuck, yeah!" he screamed. I rammed my cock in so hard I knocked the breath out of him, his eyes rolled back in his head, and then I pulled my prick free. I spun him around on his back so the audience could see his gaping asshole. I signaled to the slaves and they held him in position. I stepped down into the audience and grabbed two guys who seemed as turned on by the experience as Billy. I whispered to them and they didn't hesitate to get in on the action. One of them was wearing a tank top that proclaimed 100% Pure Top and the other 100% Oral Top. There was no squabbling over holes for these two and they assumed their positions gratefully, spending no time on preliminaries and rammed their cocks home. They worked well together verbalizing their excitement. It would have been a boring performance indeed if they hadn't.

They blew minutes apart and then faded back into the crowd to the backslapping of their mates. I gave the slaves permission to take their turn and they descended on Billy like a tribe of locusts ready to devour human prey. I singled out the cutest twink for myself and had him worship my cock and balls. While I watched, I leaned back against the cross and opened my legs to give the slave plenty of access. His mouth felt good and he ran his hands across my six-pack closing his eyes to go into his fantasy.

Billy was awash with spunk, it dripped from his bruised holes, by the time the slaves had finished working him over. I had one last favour I could do for Matt. I inserted a butt plug in Billy's ass. That would hold long enough to get him home. There Matt could feast to his stomach's content while I reamed him. I didn't think Billy would begrudge the man who helped bring us back together.

As the music ground to a halt, Billy whispered, "Take me home." It reverberated through the warehouse. I wanted everyone to hear it.

I lifted his exhausted body over my shoulder, carrying him through the crowd to thunderous applause, out through the front door and to my car. Billy was back.

NEVER TAKE CANDY FROM STRANGERS

He was the Trick as well as the Treat.

Steve and Billy are out trick or treating with a neighbour's kids on Halloween in the gay area of town because, as one of the youngsters says, "They have better candy", when they stumble across a costume party where Billy becomes an instant success in his skimpy Tarzan loin cloth. The kids are tired and want to go home but Steve is reluctant to leave Billy alone at the bacchanalia because he can guess where the partygoers want to sink their Halloweenies.

$\mathcal{I}$ knew something was up the moment I walked through the front door of our apartment. Not because I'm psychic or anything even remotely supernatural but because I heard Billy groaning, "Fuck me, hard." My heart sank. Nigel laughed, "You are such a total slut, Billy." Jason was there as well, "I could fuck that ass of yours all night." Then a strange voice broke in, "You'd like that, wouldn't you, Billy?" I didn't recognise it at first until he added. "Jerry said to say 'hello' and tell you he hopes to be back soon to take up where he left off." Fuckin' Earl, Jerry's second-in-command. Jerry was my former boss who'd not only fucked my boyfriend twice – in front of me – but also taken him away from me.

Billy had only been back about nine weeks from our six-month separation and already the buzzards were circling. Out of my jurisdiction Billy was a slut, but a passive slut who just lay there and took whatever was dished out like a zombie. Sure, the ass was hot but not as sizzling as when the two of us were in a relationship and the guys fucking him did it right under my nose either secretly or not-so-secretly. That added an extra frisson giving Billy's ass the heat of a furnace.

I crept down the hallway to catch them at it because I loathed all three and would delight in throwing them bodily out of our home. I was annoyed that Billy had even let them through the front door. They had to be really working Billy over to make him moan in pleasure like he was doing.

"Fuck, that is so hot." Jason was breathing hard. "I don't know if I can stand it for much longer."

It wasn't really Billy's fault. He was so cute and innocent, and he had an ass with a world-wide reputation for being one of the best and, if you got it at the right time, almost insatiable. I could have pimped him out and retired wealthy within twelve months, but I loved the fucker and I didn't like to see advantage taken of him. I didn't mind him taking advantage of extra cock, I knew he loved me, it's just that he took on all the bastards who wanted to see me humiliated. Hell, he took on anybody when he was in the mood. Fortunately, those moods did not strike all that often unless they were lubricated with alcohol or enthusiastic praise. The easiest route to Billy's ass was via his ego.

"You know you've got the best ass in the entire world, don't you Billy?" Earl had obviously learned the lesson well.

I ducked into the kitchen after first peeking around the door to check the shutters over the breakfast bar were closed. Fortunately, too, the blades were at an angle that gave me an almost perfect view of the living room without anyone being able to see me unless they were lying on the floor.

Relief! My initial interpretation of what was occurring in the apartment was wrong. The sounds of Billy in full sexual flight were coming from our TV. He was screening the DVD of his assault at the hands of the pirate chorus on the closing night of The Pirates of Penzance. It was his behaviour at that event that led to the fracture in our relationship. Not from my side, but his. He believed he had brought disgrace upon me and ruined my reputation. I didn't give a shit about reputation, just him.

Since his return Billy and I couldn't have been closer. The night I carried him from the opening launch of Vince and Andy's 100% Pure Slut range of leatherwear and tank tops to the thunderous applause of the audience we became the celebrity couple to go to: for opinions on anything from human rights violations in countries we'd never heard of, through the right of same-sex couples to marry, to more intimate and personal opinions on open relationships and how Billy kept his ass tunnel clean as a whistle. I don't intend detailing any secrets here because Billy is in the process of writing his own book of sex tips. I hope it takes forever because he's currently running his experiments on me.

Matt had been waiting in the car park outside the Second Skin warehouse with the motor running on my escape vehicle. I didn't really expect trouble but with bastards like Vince and Andy you could never be too sure. Matt had the back door open and I dumped Billy's come-stained body on the seat and joined him, covering him with a blanket. "Home, James," I teased Matt.

The car took off. "How you feeling, Billy?" Matt called over his shoulder.

Billy squeezed my hand. "Just great, now."

"I gotta say, that was the most amazing fuckin' thing I've ever seen. You two would clean up in porn. I'm so fuckin' hard, I can barely drive," I caught Matt's eye in the rear vision mirror.

"I think you should pull over and let me drive if you're that easily distracted," I said.

Billy looked at me still trying to understand. "Has Matt been in on this the whole time?"

"Yep, since day one," Matt acknowledged.

"How long have you been planning this?"

"Since the night you left me," I said simply. "We've been scheming since then."

"And fucking, too, I bet."

"You should talk." I leaned over to kiss him eagerly.

He managed to say, "But I wasn't enjoying it," before my lips met his and my tongue was welcomed into his mouth. We only broke our lip lock because we had to separate to breathe.

"Whose fault is it that you didn't enjoy it?" I said slightly annoyed.

"Now, guys, let's just be grateful everything has turned out so well," Matt said, and I knew he was right.

Billy looked suitably chastised.

We rode the rest of the way back to our apartment in silence, me realizing how fragile this new realignment of Billy's affections was. Once inside, Billy's spirits soared and he danced around seemingly pleased to be in the old familiar surroundings. He ran to the bedroom and was awed by the huge blow-up photograph above the bed of the two of us as Satan and his adoring demon slut. He looked sheepish on his return to the living room where Matt and I had collapsed after the tension of the evening, a tension that seemed to have bypassed Billy.

"Do you really have a DVD of that night?"

"Sure do." On Matt's answer Billy got rock hard.

"Someone's pleased about that," I said, squeezing his prick.

"So you know it was my fault," Billy said. "I let it happen."

I hadn't intended having this conversation so soon, and definitely not in front of Matt. "Look, Billy. Okay, you let yourself get into the situation where it was easy for them to take advantage of you. You're too trusting. You have to promise me, if it ever happens again—" He went to interrupt obviously to tell me it never would happen again, "If you ever find yourself in a situation where it may happen and you give in to it or it's forced on you, you can come to me if you need absolution or revenge or anything else."

"I hurt you."

I nodded. "It wasn't what you did..."

"It's what I said?" I nodded again. "The fact I said that Jerry was better than you."

He sighed. "I don't know what gets into me. I don't know why I do these things. Or say things that I know will hurt you. My body acts without connecting to my brain. My mouth says things without going through the filter. All I knew was that Jerry wanted to hear me say that and I wanted to say it and while it was happening it was true. But it's not true except for that moment. For that situation. Does that make sense?"

"Yes," I said. "But it doesn't make it easier."

"It was what I said, more than what I did that made it too hard for me to come home that night."

"Still, you should have told me. We could have worked it out."

"What? And miss all the fun I'm having?" Yep, his mouth did a complete detour of his brain. He saw my face cloud. "No, silly. I mean you rescuing me. Most guys would kill to have a boyfriend who went to the lengths you did. And what about that body? When did you get to be like this?" That was a neat deflection.

"It's for you," I said simply.

He tugged at the Satan horns still attached to my head. "These are such a fuckin' turn on. Did you know it was my fantasy?"

"Matt and I went through your stuff and we found lots of devil artwork and comics in your private papers.

Plus things you've said over the years suddenly fell into place."

"Promise me something," Billy pleaded. "Don't throw the horns away. You might like to use them every now and then. Deal?

"Deal."

"Have you two lovebirds finished, so I can claim my reward?" Matt was impatient.

"I promised Matt your ass."

"What are you waiting for?" Billy yelled in delight. "I loved it when you fucked me. You were different. Now I know why. But I thought you were a bottom, like me."

"I am, but when I'm presented with an ass like yours I just gotta fuck it. But first." I watched as Matt pushed Billy's legs in the air and gently removed the butt plug, handing it to me. Billy's mouth cried out for a pacifier, so I obliged, while Matt, fascinated by the oozing sperm, licked the sloppy opening as it dribbled, then lay back and opened his mouth. Billy lowered his body until it was just above Matt's face and his ass gaped as a huge wad of man sludge glopped on to his face and into his mouth.

"Sit and spread that slime, fuck boy."

Billy looked at me in surprise. Apart from our playacting as devil and worshipper at the 100% Pure Slut product launch, I had never ordered him around.

Billy parted his cheeks and sat on Matt's eager face, grinding against his nose and mouth, smearing the spunk all over both of them. I grabbed Matt by the hair and pulled his face into Billy's creamy hole. "Eat it out, fucker!" Matt didn't have to be asked again and I could hear his tongue slurping any leftover stale come. Billy squirmed in enjoyment.

"Okay, slut. Your turn. Suck my cock." I saw him about to remonstrate that he wasn't a slut but then realised it was me, for a change, ordering him about. He grinned wickedly, probably remembering he'd promised to be my slut during our demonstration fuck at the party launch. "Yes, sir!" he said with an enthusiasm that would probably earn him a stinging rebuke from a less lenient master.

Billy opened up to take me, tonguing my knob and down the underside of the shaft where it was most sensitive. It was good to have his mouth and throat back where they belonged. I grabbed his head, holding him firmly as my cock penetrated the back of his throat almost choking him. I'd seen how much he kicked against it when others had tried the same thing on him but I had also seen the secret grin of pleasure now that I was dominating him.

I wanted our first night back together to be memorable. "Hey, Matt. You told me how much you enjoyed the little slut's ass, how about you show me."

I pulled out and held Billy's chin up so our eyes met. "Right, slut fuck boy. You're gonna give your ass up to Matt. I want you to treat him like you'd treat my cock if it was inside you. Understand?"

Billy shuddered. "Yes, sir!"

"I want to hear you enjoying it. I want you tell me how much you love Matt's cock, understand?"

"Yes, sir."

Matt slithered out from under Billy to kneel behind him, poking his cock at the slippery hole, sinking his full length without any resistance. He gasped as Billy clenched his ass around the invading prick and I took the opportunity to pull his face toward me and sink my cock between his teeth. His body began jerking back and forth, buffeted by the two hard bodies slamming his holes. We fell into an easy natural rhythm but I had other plans for this little trio. I pulled out; moving to kneel behind Matt, fingering his hole with grease I'd retrieved from our play drawer. It was the slightest of smears but enough that he took my prick easily.

I remained in position as Matt moved his pelvis to thrust into Billy and then ram back against me. "Oh, fuck. Does it get any better than this? You guys are so fuckin' hot; I want to be like this forever."

Billy wasn't about to be outdone. "Fuck the shit outa me, Matt. I love your hard thick cock ramming my guts. Make my fuckin' asshole bleed!"

"Right, slut boy. I'm gonna breed you. Make you beg for my cock like a fuck slut."

Call me sleazy, call me hypocritical, but there was a reason for this role play exercise for me. They were getting off on it. Maybe the verbal abuse was a little too friendly because they knew each other too well for it to work totally, but Matt became a different person when he was topping Billy. I'd learned to be more perceptive, to be more aware around Billy. Part of me had to step back and evaluate. Our relationship was for keeps and I wanted it to be the same for him. The only way that would happen was to be sensitive to his needs. It didn't hurt that I was learning a helluva lot about myself as well.

For instance: their dirty talk just wasn't doing it for me. Sure, it was fun but it didn't have that edge. When Billy was being fucked in front of me, especially by one of our friends, it was just so much role playing. When he was being fucked openly, or even secretly, by my enemies and they were cursing either Billy or me to hell and back, that was real. That was a ball breaker. I loved watching Billy and Matt fucked by gangs of men. However, what I really loved most was watching Billy being totally humiliated by sleazy bastards who were out to humiliate me. Makes a strange sort of sense to me. But I know it's fucked and it does my head in – almost.

Because I had learned this about myself I knew I just had to keep it secret. Not for Billy's sake; I didn't think he would mind in the least, but because if he knew it wouldn't work any more. The danger was that one day Billy would go too far and I would no longer be able to look at him in the same way but, as yet, I couldn't anticipate what that step too far would be.

I guess I could go to a shrink and have him or her explain it to me, same as Billy could with his dilemma, but I figured we were a match made in heaven and, fuck it, life is too short and much too sparse on the intense sexual experiences the two of us were getting off on to change our ways.

So, in part it was psychological experimentation that led me to pair off Billy and Matt, but also because I wanted them to enjoy each other and get their rocks off. I owed them that. And I didn't hear anyone complaining. All I heard was lots of gasps, fucks, moans and a heap load of 'holy shit.' I pulled out of Matt because I was too close to the edge but helped him by jamming three fingers into his asshole, cork-screwing them as he plunged back. Feeling for the little nut of his prostate as he rammed harder into Billy, I massaged it as best I could so that with one almighty shudder I felt his sphincter grip my fingers like a tightened band as his spunk skidded up Billy's receptive ass.

"Lie on your back, fucker," I commanded Matt. "Watch my cock flooding the slut's asshole. Your reward will be a face full of fresh juice."

He didn't have to be told again for I knew what pressed Matt's buttons. I should after all these months. Billy squeezed his ass ring to welcome me. There was no frantic need now and I began at a pace so leisurely it gave me time to appreciate what I had impaled on my prick. You didn't have to go at it like a bull at a gate;

this was so enticing you just wanted to be inside him forever. There was something different between the two of us. It was like Billy was welcoming me back, telling me that this was the cock he always wanted no matter what happened in the future. Whether it was rough or smooth, my cock was what satisfied him for the long haul.

Acknowledging it with a little flick of my cock inside him, I picked up the pace. I wanted to come so badly, even after all the sex I'd been involved in that night, that I didn't hold back. Matt was helping by licking my balls as they scraped across his nose and chin on their journey to Billy's ass. Suddenly, my spunk was shooting inside him as I pressed my body tightly against his butt in a futile attempt to get more cock inside him. His muscles squeezed, milking every drop out of me.

I stayed inside his ass as my cock shrank. I concentrated. Billy and Matt both must have sensed I had something else in mind because they remained still. With intense self control, I began to piss in Billy's ass. It began as a trickle, and then became a flood, the hot piss oozing out around my prick and on to Matt's face. He lifted his head to lick the underside of my cock and balls and lap up the warm liquid.

My bladder relieved I told Billy to squeeze his ass together as tight as he could while my limp cock popped out. A squirt of piss came with it and Matt drank it greedily. God, I loved these two guys.

"Okay, sluts. Do it!"

Billy lowered his ass, slowly dribbling the piss and come into Matt's open mouth. As the trickle became a flood he pushed his mouth against Billy's leaking asshole and attempted to control the flow. He managed for a while until the pressure of the fluid forced its way out and Matt's handsome face was covered in spunk and piss. He gasped for air.

"Lick his face, Billy."

Billy turned, the two of them licking and sucking each other's lips, nose, chin, eyes, and cheeks. I was so hard watching their beauty defiled like this.

"Lift his legs, Billy. I want to watch you fuck him while you lick him clean."

Billy hadn't come as yet and I was keen for him to blow his load otherwise he would be horny all night. This was something unusual in his sexual vocabulary, but I knew Matt would be hot for cock and it was a treat for Billy who didn't get to top me nearly enough.

The catch in Billy's breath as he slid in revealed he was far from reluctant in this endeavour. That pleased me. I didn't want to force him against his natural inclination. I knew Matt would enjoy it because Billy had a nice thick cock that was just a little above average length. On the odd occasion he'd used it on me, he had shown an unexpected aptitude. Matt obviously agreed.

"Billy, boy, you're wasting your time as a bottom. The world needs more tops as good as you."

That pleased him and he leaned in to lap at Matt's wet and slimy face. The two of them clung together as I lay back and fell asleep. When I awoke late the next morning all three of us were wrapped in one another's arms across our queen-size bed. It was the most peaceful slumber I had managed since Billy's departure. From the angelic look on his face, it was the same with him. Even Matt, who thought he would be banished to his own room, looked content.

I scrambled over them and went to the kitchen to make coffee. The smell must have woken them because I was surprised when I felt a pair of strong arms circle my waist and Billy nuzzled my neck. "Morning, gorgeous," he said giving my cock a gentle tug.

"Yes, it is a gorgeous morning now." I turned to take him in my arms and kiss his wonderful morning sour mouth. Matt stood scratching his balls and yawning while watching us. I beckoned him over and put my arm around him.

"As long as Billy is agreeable, you're part of the family now," I said.

Billy pouted. "Do I get to fuck his sweet ass or is it only for you?"

As Billy made a scrumptious breakfast for three, we began talking. It lasted all day. It didn't matter; we were all too fucked to go out. We talked through Billy's six months 'in the wilderness' as we decided to call it to avoid opening up old wounds. He pledged his fidelity to me once again, and I again accepted his troth knowing full well he meant what he said but most of our so-called friends and all of our enemies would do everything in their ability to make him break it. No matter, that's what kept me on my toes.

We decided on the rules governing our relationships. Matt had no desire to be trapped in a monogamous household – is there such a word as trigamous? He wanted to retain his independence while fucking either or both of us. Neither Billy nor I had a problem with that. Now that our relationship had stabilised, we were secure enough that a third person could easily be accommodated, especially one that lived with us, because we wanted Matt to stay. We both enjoyed his company, he enjoyed our bodies, and it was a comfortable home for him. Importantly, it helped pay our mortgage. Billy, fortunately, was beside himself with glee when he learned his fuck show had paid for his half the mortgage during his absence, especially when we told him the charity for which it had been earmarked was the pockets of his tormentors.

That brought us around to the DVD of his debauchery. He was nervous about my having seen it but I assured him that, although some of the things he said had wounded me there was no lasting damage and, that, over-all I found watching it a real turn on, especially now that he'd returned home. No point telling him I'd found it even hotter watching it in real life. He asked to view it and Matt and I adjourned to the bedroom to give him privacy to come to terms with his debasement. It took a mere ten minutes before he was banging on our door begging, "For god's sake both of you, get out here and fuck me now!"

The little slut was so proud of it he began showing it to close friends, although I'm not sure that the three people in our living room fitted into that category. I tried to warn him that people might get the wrong impression and think he was easy. He vehemently denied he was any such thing and looked at me with his puppy dog eyes so I just gave in and let him do what he wanted. I think my call was the correct one and hearing these so-called friends in the living room calling him a slut merely confirmed it.

"I can see you miss it, Billy," Earl said. "Otherwise you wouldn't be watching this DVD. Jerry said you'd miss it eventually."

Billy was adamant. "I don't miss it. I've got more than I can handle right now."

Earl laughed at such an obvious half-truth. "Your cock says otherwise." He was massaging Billy's cock through his shorts.

Jason looked over with interest from the drama unfolding on the flat screen TV to the drama unfolding in front of him.

"Cut it out," Billy said.

"I know you don't mean it," Earl said. "You're just saying it for the benefit of these guys here because you're scared they'll tell your boyfriend." I didn't like the sarcastic way he emphasised the word boyfriend.

Jason nodded at the screen. "I'd say from the looks of this, he's right about you. But don't mind us, Billy. We can keep a secret."

"I'm not sure we should be doing this," Nigel whined.

"Oh, I'm quite sure that we really should." Earl forced Billy down on his knees.

"No," Billy said. "I told Steve I wouldn't do it anymore."

Earl kept him down and was joined by Jason who held Billy by his shoulders.

"What he doesn't know," Earl said sarcastically.

"And we won't be telling any time soon," Jason guaranteed.

"He'll be pissed off if he finds out we've had sex," Billy was floundering.

"But we're not having sex," Earl said. "Not real sex, at any rate."

Billy relaxed. "That's okay then. I thought—" Suddenly Billy's voice was cut off when Earl rammed his cock in his mouth.

"Real sex is when we get to fuck your ass. A blow job is just a blow job. No harm done, Billy boy. Just relax and go with it. Steve couldn't possibly be upset with a little blow job between friends. Right, Jason."

"Nah, a blow job is nothing. These days it's just like a handshake. Only friendlier."

"We want to bone you, Billy, really we do," Earl's voice came in bursts as he fucked Billy's face mercilessly. "But I gotta get back to the office. Pity I'll miss Steve. Would have been good to catch up with the bastard but, maybe some other time."

Billy was gagging but Earl didn't care. "Hey, Billy boy, your throat is almost as fine as your ass. I'm so sorry Jerry dumped you. He is too. That's why he sent me over. Told me not to lay a finger on you but why should I let that bastard have all the fun, eh, Billy? Anyway it's not my finger you're sucking, is it?"

Jason peeled back his foreskin and spat in his hand while he watched, stroking slowly until the head of his prick glistened. Nigel seemed to be nervously weighing up the odds of getting caught.

It wasn't until Earl starting zipping up his fly that I realised he'd come. Billy was wiping his lips as Jason stepped up to take his place. "Oh, I've been hanging out for this day, Billy. Suck my fuckin' cock."

Earl looked over admiringly as Jason's weapon choked off Billy's windpipe. "He's gonna love feeling that up his ass one day, Jason." Silently, I agreed. Jason had one beautiful cock. And he knew how to use it. He allowed Billy to do the work, standing still and enjoying it. Earl clapped him on the back in admiration. "If you love his throat just wait until you slide that prick of yours right into his bowels. Sheer fuckin' heaven, mate. Don't you forget it." he turned to go. "Don't forget, Billy boy, that offer won't be open forever. Why don't you pop over to the showroom some day when Steve's not around. Me and the boys sure would love to catch up with that cute ass of yours."

Suddenly the TV screen went blank as Earl removed the disc from the player tray. Had that been the only copy, I would have been on to the thieving bastard in no time flat. He was a fool if he thought I didn't have the original well hidden.

As he left he called, "Thanks for the DVD. Jerry will be very pleased I got it for him. No evidence means he can come back to town. Looks like your ass is gonna be pounded sooner than you hoped. Ciao!"

I heard the front door close.

"Asshole," I heard Nigel spit.

"Come over here, Nigel. Get your cock out and let him suck it. You might learn something."

Nigel looked ready to kill at the reference to his poor oral skills.

"Don't get me wrong, you're great at giving head, but Billy here, Billy is in a class of his own. This is fuckin' amazing."

Curiosity got the better of him and Nigel slid his cock out of his jeans. He had a nice sized cock, not as long as Jason's but nothing to disgrace him either. Jason moved aside and Billy wrapped his lips around Nigel's dick. "Oh. My. God."

"Told you, sweetheart. I've never had a blow job like that ever. Billy's a natural. If that's his blow job just imagine what his ass must be like. Outa this fuckin' world! We gotta get us a bit."

From the way Nigel was responding he wouldn't last long. I suspected that Jason didn't do a lot of reciprocation in their relationship. Nigel held Billy's head and fucked his face in short sharp stabbing motions. It would have been painful if it hadn't been over quickly. Nigel was flushed in the face and went to sit down while Jason finished off. I crept back down the hallway and when I heard the tell-tale sounds of Jason shooting a load in Billy's gullet I opened the door and called out. "Hey, sweetheart, I'm home."

I fumbled with the lock to give Jason time to straighten himself up before going into the living room.

"We've got visitors, Steve," Billy called, and then cleared his throat as if it were full of phlegm.

"You coming down with something?" I said as I leaned in to kiss him.

"Just something caught in my throat."

I saw Jason and Nigel exchange nervous glances.

Instead of the peck on the cheek I normally gave Billy, I stuck my tongue into his startled mouth. He attempted to push me off but I wasn't about to let that happen.

"Steve, we've got visitors. What's gotten into you?" He was embarrassed.

"Maybe they'd like to watch you and me make out," I said.

"Gross," Jason said.

I licked my lips. "Mmmm, what have you been eating, Billy? Tastes great."

"I had a banana smoothie earlier, must be that," he lied.

First time banana smoothie tasted like spunk, I thought to myself. What I said was, "Coffee anyone?"

They all placed an order and Nigel came into the kitchen to help me. He was nervous as I filled the coffee percolator. "Come on, Nigel, what is it?" I said kindly.

"It's none of my business," he began.

"Go on," I encouraged. If it's none of anybody's business then why bother raising the matter?

"Well, you know Earl, that guy you used to work with?"

"Ugly bastard, rough as guts, sewer mouth. All the personality of a poisonous puffer fish?"

"Um, if you say so."

"What about him?"

"Look, I think he's a bad influence on Billy."

"Why do you say that?"

He hadn't thought this through because he didn't have an answer ready apart from telling the truth which would incriminate himself.

"Just a feeling from what I've heard around the traps," Nigel said.

I squeezed his butt cheeks suggestively before draping my arm around his shoulder. "I heard on the grape vine you thought I was hot in those ads with Billy."

He swallowed hard. "Uh, yeah, but I didn't know it was you."

I squeezed his cock. It was hard. "Does that make a difference?"

"I couldn't do it with a friend," he said and removed my arm.

"What about Billy then?"

He panicked. "What about Billy?"

"Could you do it with him?"

"Why, what have you heard?"

I ruffled his hair playfully. "Just joshing you, Nigel. Of course, you couldn't do it with us. That would almost be incest."

He breathed easier and by the time we went back to the living room with coffee he had relaxed.

There was general chit chat for a while and Billy came and sat at my feet so I could play with his hair. He was like a cat in that way: purring with satisfaction. Nigel looked jealous.

"We did drop in for a reason," Jason said finally when all the trivial conversation had dried up.

"Yeah?" I said.

"Well, you may or may not know that our anniversary is coming up." Jason beamed as he looked at Nigel. And yes we did know; they'd both been annoying the shit out of us for weeks now hinting what sort of a gift they'd like.

"And you want to know if I'll let you fuck Billy for the night as a present?" All three of them looked at me.

Two of them expectantly. Then I laughed. "Sorry. Just my little joke. I know not everyone wants to get into Billy's pants. Why would you when you two are so obviously in love?"

"Exactly." Jason smiled but moments before he had gone quite pale. It was fun toying with these amateurs.

"You know we have no privacy with the kids home and we can never find babysitters."

Fuck, no. Not the babysitting gig again. We'd done it a few times before and even though Alice and Philip, their son and daughter via in vitro, were good kids it sure put a dampener on their lives. I marveled that Jason and Nigel had any sort of a life at all. Perhaps that was the root of their problem.

"We were hoping to have a quiet night alone for a change," Nigel said, and him I believed. He looked so adoringly at Jason it would be hard to turn them down.

"When is it?" Billy asked, always the practical one.

"Halloween," Jason said.

"Won't they want to go out trick or treating?" I asked scarcely able to conceal my distaste.

"Yes, that's the really big favour," Jason said. "We'd need you to take them out and get them home at a reasonable hour."

"Sounds great," Billy enthused. I'd hit him about the head later. He got on well with their kids whereas I'd be quite happy to feed them chocolate brownies with arsenic frosting. I hate kids. They should all be sent away to a desert island when they're born and only be allowed to come to the mainland when they turned eighteen. A lot of the world's problems would be solved that way.

"Can we, Steve? Can we? It's been years since we celebrated Halloween. It would be so cool to go round with the kids. We can get dressed up..." Billy had already made up his mind.

I had to come up with plausible excuses. "It's all apartment buildings around here."

"Not to worry about that," Jason said. "The kids want to go over to the east side to that new yuppie suburb all the upwardly mobile gays are moving to. Philip said 'Gay guys have better candy.' Isn't that just delicious?"

Yeah, so cute I want to puke.

"That's adorable," Billy squealed.

The moment he wants to adopt or have kids via a surrogate, I'm outa here.

"Adorable." I gritted my teeth as I said it.

"We'll pay for your time," Nigel said quickly, although I saw Jason give him a dirty look.

"Of course, well look after them. No need for payment. You might be able to do us a favour some time," Billy said.

Yes, like stop trying to fuck my boyfriend.

Nigel helped me with the dirty mugs and while in the kitchen I spun him around and plunged my tongue into his mouth. He sank into it until he remembered where he was and who it was coming on to him. He struggled free and as he glared at me and left I ran my finger up the crevice in his ass. He squealed and Jason looked over, unamused.

After they left, I said as casually, "You've become very pally with the upstairs neighbors."

"What does that mean?" Billy snapped.

Ah, if I hadn't known because I saw it, I'd know from Billy's response that something had happened. "I just meant I'm glad to see you're getting on well with them and you have friends of your own. And I think it will be fun taking the kids out. You can dress up in something sexy and turn on all the dads."

That idea got him in a good mood again.

"Did something happen today I should know about?" I wanted to see how truthful he'd be.

He admitted reluctantly, "Well, Earl came over today."

"What did that bastard want?"

"Don't be so hard on him, Steve. He wants you to take your old job back. They need you. The place is going bad. Now that you're not there as a detailer on the cars the customers are going elsewhere."

"It would be a bit daunting going back knowing that the staff there have all had you especially, if my memory serves me correctly, Earl. Why would you want me in an atmosphere like that?"

He looked at the floor. "That job you've got now. All that manual labor."

"Look at the body it's given me. I thought you liked that."

"I love it," Billy said snuggling up to me. "But you're always so tired. You come home exhausted. It's great you've got such a hot body but I want to do more than just look at it while you sleep."

It was true. Billy and I weren't fucking like rabbits but between me and Matt I thought we were keeping him happy. I said so.

"Yeah, but..."

He left it hanging and I realised now why he'd put up so little resistance to the three men who'd used his mouth earlier that afternoon. I was neglecting him.

"Okay," I said. "I'll think about it, but I don't give a shit if Jerry goes to the wall or not. I didn't think you'd care either—"

"I don't, Steve, really I don't."

"Earl's not trying to fuck you again, is he?"

"I think he might like to, but I couldn't. He's a bastard. The things he called you while he was fucking me. He humiliated you, Steve. I couldn't let him touch me again. I'd be physically ill."

Okay, so most guys at this stage would have exposed their treacherous lover and shown him the door. I knew that Billy was lying. I knew that Billy was lying to spare my feelings. I knew Billy was lying because the idea turned him on. I just had to make sure to keep the two of them apart. It wouldn't be too difficult.

I thought another reason Billy might like me in a more regular job was that being a manual labourer on a building site my hours were erratic and, even worse, I was currently working just a few blocks away and was prone to drop in unexpectedly. I didn't believe Billy was playing around but it was too easy when you had animals like Jason or Earl or Jerry tempting him.

The silence that followed his lie must have made him guilty because he blurted out quickly. "He wanted me to suck his dick, Steve."

"Did you?"

"I wanted to," he admitted. He was ashamed.

"Why didn't you?" I thought reverse psychology might work. If I gave him permission he might not want to do it in future.

"Because of what you would think of me."

I grabbed him and threw him down on the lounge, pulling down his shorts and smacking his muscular ass. "That you're a gorgeous insatiable slut boy? But I know that already. So if you want to, go ahead and suck his dick."

"Really?" He was wide eyed.

"But don't let him fuck you."

"I wouldn't. My ass is exclusively for you. And Matt."

I'd lubed my fingers while we were talking and gently pushed them between Billy's legs. "Did you suck him off, slut?"

"Will you hate me if I said I did? After all he's done to you."

"Hate you. Hell, no. It makes me hard thinking about it. If you tell me he'll have no power over us. So, tell me what it was like, Billy. All the details."

His eyes lit up and he described the texture, the taste, the thickness of Earl's cock as it ploughed his throat. And while he did, I ploughed his ass. It was an intense workout and as we lay side by side afterwards, he confessed. "Earl offered me a job, Steve."

"Something nasty, I expect."

"When I was with Jerry he made me sleep with his customers if they spent a lot of money with him. It kept a lot of them coming back. They liked me."

"I'll bet they did, sugar."

"Since I left his sales have dropped off and Jerry wants me to come back. No, not as his lover—"

"Still, he'll want your ass every opportunity he gets and he'll rub my nose in it."

"I'm sorry, Steve. I never meant for that to happen. He wants to set me up in an apartment near the showroom and I'd go there for special clients and he'd pay me ten percent commission on each sale."

"That's very generous. If you can trust him. But I bet in no time you'd be expected to service Jerry and Earl and the rest of the staff for free."

"I turned him down, even though we could use the money."

"We don't need it that badly."

Should I ask about Jason and Nigel? He wouldn't volunteer the information but, if I asked he would tell me. Then I would have to do something about the situation. I kept mum.

"If it's just a fuck you're after I think I could persuade some of the guys from the building site to work you over."

"Really? Some of those guys are hot."

"Hot as me?"

"No one is as hot as you but, um, maybe you could wear your hard hat next time."

The following few weeks were mainly uneventful, except for two incidents. The first was that I rang Earl the day after my conversation with Billy and told him I would consider coming back to the car yard but I would give him my definitive answer after Halloween. I had committed to jobs up until then and I couldn't let the company down. I made it sound as if I were keen to return. I wasn't. But the money was good. I also told him that I had only just discovered that someone had stolen a DVD of the night Billy was fucked. I could hear him take a deep breath ready to launch into a denial but I got in first. "I don't know who it was, we've had a heap of visitors over lately, but best warn Jerry in case it was stolen by some unscrupulous person who is going to upload it to the net. Billy and I aren't too concerned because we've got multiple copies of it. Billy loves showing it to his friends." I heard a curse even though Earl had his hand over the mouthpiece. And on the offer you made Billy..." I paused long enough for him to worry. "The one about setting him up in an apartment so he can service your wealthy clients. Billy's thinking about it."

"He told you?" Earl was incredulous. "You'd let him?"

"Of course I won't fuckin' let him. What do you think I am?" I stayed calm.

"What if he wants to?"

"He won't. Anyway, if the offer is still open for my job in three weeks I'll let you know."

"Great," Earl lied. I could hear him grinding his teeth. "It would be good to have you back on board."

The second incident was of much more consequence. Billy, Matt and I were having a leisurely evening at home. Billy lay on the lounge between the two of us as I massaged his feet while we watched some police procedural on TV. When the intercom buzzed we all cursed. This was the first opportunity we'd had to be together like this in days.

It was Gideon, an older guy who'd played the Roman soldier who fucked and whipped Billy at the Pure Slut launch. Unless he was stupidly brazen he obviously wasn't here to fuck Billy again. I hadn't seen him since that night and Billy seemed just as surprised at his visit so nothing untoward was going on there.

When I let him in he looked a little uncomfortable but greeted Billy like an old friend.

"You're looking good, Billy."

"Thanks. You too," Billy said, as puzzled as I was.

"Good to see you, Matt. Great video of the launch. You made me look great."

"I didn't do anything. You always look great." Matt wasn't stretching the truth. For a fifty-year-old Gideon was a super daddy. But he couldn't look me in the eye.

"Gideon, you were paid to do a job. You did it. You did it well. You fucked and beat my ex-boyfriend. And you pissed in his mouth which got me all hot and bothered. You're a true professional. So just relax, mate."

He sank more comfortably into his chair. "When you work with someone like Billy it's a pleasure to do him." He looked grief stricken, probably thinking he'd gone too far.

I laughed.

Billy smiled. "I'll take that as a compliment, Gideon."

"Look, I'm not good at small talk so I'll get to the point. You know I run a restaurant." We nodded. "Well, it's going downhill faster than Jack and fuckin' Jill. I can't cook for shit and neither can any of the staff I got. Not on the wages I can afford to pay them. Oh, they're good enough guys but they couldn't tell a julienne from a filibuster."

We all got the giggles from Gideon's colorful turns of phrase and even he got a lopsided grin on his face. It broke the ice.

"Hell, no use lollygagging. Billy, we need your help otherwise we're fucked," he said.

I couldn't help myself. "Makes a nice change from Billy being fucked."

Gideon ignored my sarcasm, probably because he didn't understand it. His involvement with Billy had been on a purely professional level, even at Vince and Andy's dinner party.

"Billy, I thought you were a bit of a flake, especially when you lived with those two leather fuckwits. I couldn't understand how you didn't see right through them, but," he shrugged, "that's no concern of mine. When I got to talk to you though I could see you were an intelligent guy with his head screwed on the right way. And now you're back where you shoulda been all along with Steve. Fuck me, if I knew what was going down I wouldn't have joined the gangbang. I didn't understand. Sorry."

I was hoping he'd get to the point sometime soon.

"What I'm trying to say is I'd like for you to come and take a look at my restaurant and see if there's any advice you can give me which might help save the old place. Otherwise it's gonna go under." There was dead silence. "Oh, I'll pay you, of course. I brought a cheque over in case you said yes and to show you it's all on the level. Considering what's been done to you these last months I would understand if you were sceptical."

"Gideon, I'm really flattered," Billy said. "But I'm just an unemployed sous chef. I don't have any experience in what you're after."

"Yeah, but you got a good eye. I noticed that about you right off. Please, Billy. I'm desperate."

"Of course, I will. But as a friend. I don't expect payment. I'll only be giving you my opinion, you can take it or leave it. But don't expect miracles."

Okay, call me a cynic, call me paranoid, but my first thought was that this was another elaborate ploy to get Billy and fuck him. I chastised myself for being that way but the morning Billy went off to inspect the restaurant I expected to find him back in our apartment covered in spunk. Instead, Billy turned up at the building site where his tightly clad ass attracted the attention of all but the exclusively homophobic tradies. Unfortunately, there were all too many of them. He got wolf whistled and propositioned as Gil, the foreman, brought him up to where I was working. He was flushed with excitement.

"I came up to show you it was legit and all above board because I knew you were worried it was just another trap," he said. "I guess I did for a while, too. But it wasn't. The restaurant has great potential. I'm going to go in and keep an eye on things for a week and see what advice I can give. I'm excited, Steve. It's the best opportunity I've had for a while."

And so it proved. Billy suggested a few cosmetic changes, a few menu changes and soon business picked up – a little. The most important thing though, Billy had a purpose and he came home excited. Matt and I both gave silent thanks to whichever god it was looking out for him.

That settled, now all I had to dread was Halloween, especially after Billy modelled his costume for me. Naturally he rejected any of the ghouls, witches or fairies. He had gone for Tarzan of the Apes. And Tarzan of the tiniest loin cloth I had ever seen. It was essentially two flaps of leather, one to cover his cock and balls, barely, and one to cover his ass crack, only if a stiff breeze didn't blow up the Khyber Pass. I could not persuade him to choose a less suggestive costume but did manage to get him into a pair of leopard skin briefs so he could at least retain his modesty. Not that he had any. He knew he looked hot, he knew he'd turn on a lot of closeted dads, give them a thrill, but that they'd be unable to do anything about it. I was just grateful his 100% Pure Slut tattoo was covered.

We hadn't seen Jason and Nigel in the interim, whether because they were guilty or just busy, I wasn't sure. Nigel popped in once, briefly, to remind us of the arrangements and give us more detailed instructions.

We arrived at their apartment at the allotted time to collect nine-year-old Alice, a ghastly pink concoction of tulle and fairy wands, and eleven-year-old Philip, who had gone for the traditional vampire. Me? Jeans and a tank top with absolutely no reference to sluts stencilled anywhere near it. I thought at least one of us should look less like an escapee from a clinic for sex addicts and more like a regular dad.

Jason and Nigel were dressed to impress in expensive top brand suits. They were a stunning couple if you could divorce them from their personalities. Their destination was an up-market restaurant where just the cost of the antipasto could have paid for the Sydney Opera House.

"It's going to be so romantic," Nigel gushed, clutching Jason's arm like a 1930s' starlet.

"I've promised Nigel something extraordinary, and I'll deliver. He'll never forget the experience." Jason was so cocky. We took Philip and Alice by the hand after they kissed their dads good night and headed for our big adventure, as the kids called it, among the landed gentry who could afford a house and a quarter acre block in a suburb that had been gentrified by the influx of gay men with ready renovation money.

Billy's Tarzan costume, or non-costume there was so little of it, attracted a lot of comment. The kids we ran into loved it and knew his character right away and wanted their photos taken with him. Children of all ages loved Billy because he was such a big kid himself. Some of the cheekier adults wanted to see what was under Billy's loincloth and would lift it up for a better view. Because they believed either Alice or Philip, or both, was his child, quite a few mums thought they had a chance with him, as did a few dad's whose eyes were taken with Billy's scarcely concealed ass.

A number of people recognised him as the face and body of the Second Skin range and invited him to come back without the kids and without me. A few more thrust business cards into the waist band of his loin cloth. He could have made a small fortune as a stripper or, uh, companion to some of the men who answered the door. If none of them were recipients of Billy's largesse, Alice and Philip were certainly showered with goodies most of the men and a few women would have liked to have showered on Billy.

Right now the kids were getting cranky, from the exhausting pace they had set, and from the soporific effect of sugar overload. Inexplicably, Philip was determined there was always one more house to go. "I know it's around here somewhere," he said as he took my hand and dragged me down another street. I was about to call it a day when he shouted "There it is, next to the park. I knew it." He hauled me along at a blistering pace, Billy piggy-backing a very tired Alice in his wake.

At the door, I said mock sternly, "Righto, this is the last one, and then we're going home."

"Daddy said you have to take us out for something to eat first."

"Yes, we'll get takeaway."

"Can I have pizza?" Philip asked.

The door opened and Billy was about to say something when a chocolate was popped into his open mouth. Billy loves chocolate but once he starts he can't stop so we never have it in the house. He sucked it with considerable pleasure.

"Oh, I am sorry," the man at the door said when he noticed us. "I was expecting someone else and that's an old

Halloween ritual. Do forgive me. Hello, what have we here?"

Alice and Philip, impatient at being ignored, chorused, "Trick or treat." The guy retrieved a bag from a stand near the door and dumped handfuls of candy into both kids' sacks so that Alice and Philip looked as if all their Christmases had come at once. Billy thanked the kind gentlemen. As we turned to go, he said, "This may be a strange question but did you go to Redmount High?" He was talking to Billy who nodded that he had. "I thought so, you're Billy —" They both roared each other's names at the same time. His name was Guy and they had been in the same class together.

Like all such reunions they began talking shop and have you seen such and such lately, and whatever became of whosits, and my god, you're gay too. "Come in, come in, won't you. Join us. We're having a little sedate Halloween do. We have one every year."

"I think it's time I got the kids something to eat and then to bed."

"Yours?" Guy enquired.

"No, they belong to friends of ours who are out celebrating their anniversary tonight," I said, eager to leave. Philip was getting fidgety.

"What a shame," Guy said. "Here, I'll write down my phone number and maybe we can catch up in the near future." Guy left the door open and I glanced inside. There were men in quiet conversation dotted around the room that I could see. Classical music was playing softly for ambience rather than listening.

"Steve?" Billy's tone managed to make my name sound as if it consisted of three syllables instead of one. I knew what that meant.

"You owe me," I said. "I'll take Alice and Philip for their meal and back to our place to wait for Jason and Nigel, and then I'll come back and pick you up."

Billy hugged me and kissed my neck.

"Here we go," Guy said presenting Billy with his address and phone number. Billy passed it on to me.

"If the offer is still open, I'd like to come in for a bit. Steve will drop the kids off and come back for me. Is that okay? I mean I'm not dressed for a party and I didn't bring anything."

"Of course, you're more than welcome. You all are. And that includes the kiddies. We've got computer games, everything to keep them amused."

"No, I think I should be getting them back. You stay and enjoy the party, Billy. Have you got your cell phone?" Billy took it from his waist band and flourished it in my face as if I were worrying too much. "What time does your party finish?"

"Goodness, there's no official time. Sometimes they go all night. There's plenty of room to crash if necessary," Guy said.

"No, I should be back in about two hours. Two and a half at the most."

"That will give us plenty of time," Guy said, ushering Billy into the house.

"Okay, you two, let's go." I bundled them into the back seat and buckled them up. I had to admit they hadn't been much trouble at all, but I was keen to get them home and then come back for Billy.

The two kids squabbled over who had the best collection, swapped candy, and spat out what they didn't like, until Alice fell asleep. Philip was a precocious young kid and started on the why, why, why? I gave him the answers on the few occasions that I knew I was correct, but his next question floored me.

"Why didn't daddy come out and say hello?" he asked.

"Come out where?" I asked puzzled.

"At that last house. That's where he said the two of them were going to a party."

"The house where we dropped off Uncle Billy, you mean?"

"Yes. That's what I just said."

"Jason and Nigel are at that party?"

Philip was getting exasperated. "Am I not making myself clear or something?"

"I thought they were going out to dinner for their anniversary?"

"Yes, but then they were going to Uncle Guy's party. I heard them say."

I had a sinking feeling. "So they could drive Uncle Billy home to save me going back out?"

"Oh no, they said they would be staying all night and wouldn't be home until lunch time tomorrow."

"But they are supposed to be picking you up later tonight." I didn't understand.

"I heard daddy Jason tell daddy Nigel that they would ring you later and say they had too much to drink and were going to take a hotel room and for you to take care of us."

I would never hate children again. "And did they know Uncle Billy would be at the party?"

"Yes. They were very clever, you see. Alice and me, I had to make sure we took you to that house so Uncle Guy would see Uncle Billy and invite him in. And then you would drive us home and you would have to look after us." Philip seemed pleased that I was paying so much attention. I suspected he was somewhat neglected by his dads in the conversation department.

"Did they say why they wanted Uncle Billy at the party without me?"

"I didn't understand that part of it. They wanted to do something to Uncle Billy but they couldn't while you were around. What would that be?"

"Probably they wanted to surprise him. We'll have to ask him tomorrow."

I felt sick. I could not believe that Jason and Nigel could be so treacherous. They had it planned down to the last detail. I could turn the car around and drag Billy back home. I'd only left the sedate party, obviously staged for my benefit, about ten minutes before. I had to think. Billy was now so loquacious I could barely concentrate on the roadway let alone formulate a plan. I blocked him out and let his babble become background noise but subconsciously listened out for any further clues.

Stopping the car on the side of the roadway, I told Philip I had to take a piss. He giggled at the swear word but it gave me an opportunity to get out to make a call on my cell phone and not be overheard. First, I rang Billy to ensure he was all right. From the background noise, the sedate party camouflage had been dropped as soon as I'd left to be replaced by loud rock music at full bore. He sounded fine and said everyone was well behaved and had kept their hands to themselves. I warned him to be on his guard. I asked him if Nigel and Jason were there and he said he hadn't seen them. He thought it strange I would ask that but I mentioned that Philip had let slip they might end up there. He didn't find that suspicion so I let him get back to his mingling.

Next I rang Matt to explain the situation. "I can be there in twenty minutes with a baseball bat or a gang of street vigilantes. It's your call." I knew he wasn't kidding.

He knew the pizza joint where I was taking the kids and, with speed, he could be there in fifteen, twenty max. In the end it took him twelve. I'd settled Alice and Philip in to one of the tables and told them to order what they liked. To the kindly waitress who had gushed over them, I explained that I was having a problem with my car and I was waiting for help, and asked her to keep an eye on them while I was outside. I slipped her twenty dollars and she became an instant mum. I could see them through the glass in the brightly lit family restaurant so I could be back at their side in seconds if need be.

Matt had agreed eagerly to help me. I'd already received a friendly call from Jason to check up that everything was all right. He'd sounded pleased that I was taking the two kids out for a meal and seemed uninterested in the fact I'd left Billy at a party. He was playing at being the concerned father, but it was that call that precipitated Philip to spill his guts. Bad timing. You could never totally account for bad timing in your plans.

I didn't hurry Alice or Philip. Matt came and sat down with us. I explained that my car had broken down, something I couldn't fix and that I had called for road service and they had informed me there would be a two-hour wait. Meanwhile, Uncle Matt would take them home and look after them until their dads arrived. As I treat, I said they could sit up and watch television as long as they liked provided they didn't tell Jason. They solemnly promised.

I rang Jason on his mobile. He took a while to answer and when he did there was the muffled thump of a bass line and the echo as if he was talking in the toilet at the party. So Philip was correct. He certainly wasn't at a restaurant. I told him I'd broken down in the middle of nowhere and was waiting for a service truck and that I'd been told of a long delay. Realizing I couldn't keep the kids out for such a long time I'd rung Matt to come and pick them up and take them back so Nigel and he wouldn't worry.

"You heading back to the party?" Jason seemed a little panicked at the thought.

"No, much too far away and it serves no purpose. When I finish talking to you I'll ring Billy and tell him he'll either have to hitch a ride back to the apartment with another guest if any are going that way, or else he'll have to stay the night and Matt or I will pick him up tomorrow some time. Unless you're early and Matt can go back and get him."

"It looks as if we may be later than expected. I'm sure Billy will be okay."

"I'm not worried about Billy; I'm more worried about my car. Billy can take care of himself. He's a big boy. Here, I'll put Philip on." I handed him the phone and, from his conversation, Jason was giving him the third degree. Obviously satisfied, Jason spoke to me again commiserating, totally insincerely, before seeking confirmation on how long I was likely to be stuck where I was. "About two hours," I repeated. "And that's only if the car doesn't have to be towed."

"I hope it's sooner," he said.

"No chance of that. They're busy tonight and chances are it could be even longer."

"Bugger that. Sorry you're having such a miserable night when ours promises to be one of the best ever."

I put Matt on so they could discuss the details and they exchanged cell phone numbers. Then Jason hung up. I helped Matt strap two very tired kids into the back seat of his car and he took off. I knew Jason would be ringing him at regular intervals and would ring me for an update in about an hour to suss out my whereabouts. I programmed my phone to vibrate and headed back to the party. I drove past the party house which seemed remarkably quiet in this suburban neighbourhood for the amount of noise that came through the phone. I hoped I wasn't making a fool of myself and hadn't fallen into a trap.

The property was bordered along one side and at the back by woodland which afforded me ample cover. I crept up to the wooden fence and could hear the thump of dance music and the indistinct babble of voices. It was dark now although the moon cast a silvery light over the landscape on the balmy spring night. I loosened a few palings in the fence, grazing my knee as I climbed through, and dropped behind bushes in the garden. An ornamental hedge hugged both sides of a gravel pathway that meandered through the foliage and the shrubs. It was a well planned garden and fortunately offered me plenty of protection. I could get right to the edge of the lawn behind the hedge without being seen.

A strong halogen light illuminated the grass area where people were seated chatting and drinking. A hot tub bubbled away under an awning at the back of the house, adjacent to an old dilapidated shed. If I could get inside that shed from the back, for the front of it was padlocked, I would have a view of the entire back yard and was within easy listening of most of the conversations. I had not seen Billy or Nigel and Jason as yet.

A few people were dancing on an elevated wooden platform abutting the verandah a short distance from the tub. Scattered around the back lawn were carved pumpkins containing the ubiquitous red candle that cast an eerie glow over the proceedings.

Then I saw it. If I'd had a sense of humour at that moment I would have slapped my head. I scrambled quickly back through the fence and ran to my car. I rifled through the boot and found an old shirt, now little more than a rag I used to wipe the windshield, alongside a pair of daggy shorts that I wore when I washed the car or worked on the engine. Next, a mixture of oil and dirt smeared on my face and along with my leg and arms. A baseball cap topped it all off, and I was ready.

I clambered back through the fence and made my way along the gravel path to the edge of the lawn. A few people looked up. I ostentatiously played with the zipper on my shorts as if I'd just taken a piss and waved to a pretend friend out of sight. The partygoers were in costume, some of them even in masks. My brawny arms and legs attracted a few leers and one guy even sidled up to me asking what time the entertainment was to start. I shrugged and he seemed satisfied with that.

Grabbing the nearest unattended glass of alcohol I entered the house. The lights had been kept low otherwise I would not have dared. "What are you supposed to be?" a drunken man accosted me in the hallway."

"A zombie," I said softly.

"Sexiest fuckin' zombie I've ever seen," he spluttered and moved on.

I thought the kitchen would be the best place to start and walked along the hallway when Billy suddenly came out of a doorway. He saw me. He stared at me blankly, and then he smiled. He grabbed me by the hand and pulled me back into the bathroom. He had his tongue in my mouth groping me before I had time to breathe.

"Hey, Billy, give me a chance to catch my breath." All I had to do was explain the situation and we could walk out of there.

He backed off and looked at me again. "Do I know you?"

"What the fuck? Of course you know me." I looked into his eyes and they were dilated. "Come on, let's get out of here."

"Where to?"

"Home," I said.

"It'll have to be your place, my boyfriend is at mine. But not just yet. Guy says they've got a surprise for me after I do my dance, and I'll really love it."

"Your boyfriend lets you carry on like this?"

Billy smiled. "What he doesn't know. Besides, it's not real sex. I won't let anyone fuck me."

Not unless you're so off your face you can't stop them, I thought.

"You're cute," Billy said, reaching for my lips. "I might even let you fuck me. Come and get me later."

He opened the door and disappeared. I heard whistles and realised he must have gone out into the yard. I found the kitchen in which Guy, Jason, Nigel, and a fourth who had his back turned, were huddled in a corner. I busied myself getting a drink but they continued as if I didn't matter. Obviously the whole party was an open secret to all but Billy.

"His boyfriend will be gone for hours," Jason whispered.

"That's the hottest ass I think I've ever seen." Guy turned to the fourth man. "You set this up, didn't you?"

"You bet. I'm sick of those two fuckers parading around as if butter wouldn't melt." I froze. It was fuckin' Earl. "Billy's ass was born to be fucked and he loves it. Hard and as many as possible."

Guy still wasn't convinced. "What about his boyfriend?"

"The stupid bastard can't expect to keep an ass like that to himself. The kid's insatiable. He wants more cock than his boyfriend can give him."

Jason interrupted. "I thought he'd be into it by now. That chocolate you gave him at the door was powerful enough to make sluts of the whole party. So, we'll have to give him some more then, pow, he'll be begging for it."

Nigel was worried. "What if Steve comes back?"

"The whole army could go through him by the time Steve gets his car repaired. But, I'll check in a minute to see what's happening on that front if it will set your mind at ease," Jason wasn't going to let this opportunity escape.

"But won't he know what's happened when he sees Billy?" Nigel was a worry wart.

Earl sighed. "Who gives a fuck? We just tell him he's married to a total slut and we were just doing what Billy begged us to do."

Jason added, "With the amount of stuff I put in the chocolate, I can guarantee he will be begging."

Guy was practical. "What if he accuses us of rape?"

"The word of a known slut against the cream of this city's business and culture. Who'd believe him?" Earl had all the bases covered.

Jason added. "Until we find out what the fuck is going on with his boyfriend's car we've persuaded Billy to put on a show with no touching." He did that irritating thing with his fingers to signify no touching was in inverted commas.

"But blow jobs don't count because they're not touching." Earl was a bastard.

They all laughed although I noticed Nigel looked uncomfortable.

"With any luck Steve's car will be fucked and have to be towed, then we double dope Billy and he'll open his ass for everyone. And just so we can enjoy over and over again…" Jason handed around some little blue pills which they all swallowed with their drink before heading outside.

Earl clapped me on the shoulder as he passed, whispering conspiratorially. "Come on, mate, you don't want to miss this. The town slut is about to give a show. And with any luck, you'll get a chance to fuck him after."

They changed the music to something suggestive and sleazy and Billy was standing on the makeshift platform grinding his hips, his mind in a world all his own. He was the centre of attention – his favorite position. I looked at him. Muscular, but slim now that the steroids used to inflate his body for the Second Skin launch had leached from his body, his abs a solid six-pack verging on eight, his biceps with the sort of definition you just wanted to lick, his thighs smooth and hairless, his eyes Pacific lagoon blue, and his short spiky hair a genuine blond verified by his same-colored pubes that he sculpted into a tidy bush. His perky mouth screamed cocksucker and his ass was a transcendental experience. Perhaps that's why I was throbbing in my shorts.

I sat at the back of the crowd to watch. The audience was rowdy, some of them already drunk, many already horny on the promise that Guy had made for the party.

"Take your briefs off, Billy. Give us a real show," someone shouted.

He smiled sheepishly, but others took up the chant. "Billy! Billy!"

He glanced at his watch, obviously to see if he had time before my return, shrugged as if to say, what the fuck! Then hooked his fingers in the waistband of his leopard skin briefs and they hit the floor. He tossed them at the crowd. Earl caught them, holding them to his nose to sniff.

The front of his lap-lap still covered his groin although, as he gyrated, it lifted to give a great view of his balls and his hard cock. He turned and wiggled his ass, slowly teasing by lifting the leather that covered his tattoo. As it was revealed there were cheers and applause.

"Take it off! Take it off! Take it off!" The chant got louder and Billy grinned wickedly at the approval of his display. He bent over, poking his ass at the audience and slid down his loin cloth until he was totally naked. Then he rotated his ass slowly, the most blatant invitation I had ever witnessed.

"Don't just show us, Billy. Do something with that amazing ass." It was Earl. "Show us why it's the best fuckin' ass in the world."

That did it! Billy looked about for a prop and found an empty beer bottle on a nearby table. He grabbed it and held it aloft. The audience went wild. I saw Earl and Jason high five as Billy placed the bottle on the stage and then lowered his asshole over it. The long thin neck slid in easily but it wasn't that much of a show because of sightlines.

"We can't see, Billy. Lie on your back." Earl was almost directing the show.

Billy appealed for a table from the garden be brought up, and then whispered to the two men carrying it, one of whom was Guy. The other was an older man of indeterminate age who had a hairy beer gut and a beard. Billy hopped up on the table and the two men held his legs over his body with one hand and pulled his cheeks apart so his asshole was on view. Guy handed him the bottle and Billy began to insert it slowly between his ass lips. It was a beautiful sight as it disappeared down to the shoulder. The hairy man moved to push his thick cock between Billy's lips but he was stopped. Billy looked at his watch.

"Do I have time?" he pleaded to Earl.

"Sure, Billy. All the time in the world."

I heard Nigel complain. "Steve could be back any minute. What if he catches us?"

Earl laughed. "There are more of us than there are of him. He can watch. He can join in if he likes. Or maybe Nigel you'd like to spend some time getting to know Steve better."

"He'd love to," Jason said viciously.

"Just like you want to get to know Billy better," Nigel spat. "So we're even."

"I wish he was here to watch this," Earl said. "It would make it that much better. Fucking his boyfriend in front of him."

"Mmmm," Jason was excited by the idea. "Maybe after this, the three of us can be gangbanging Billy in their apartment when Steve gets home. It would be worth it for the priceless look on his face."

"I'd better take charge of this," Earl said, striding to the stage.

"Gentlemen. Young Billy here has kindly consented to allow you access to his body but there's to be strictly no touching. By that he means his ass is out of bounds." There was a general moan of disappointment. "But, gentlemen, we are hoping with a little gentle persuasion," and Earl held aloft a handful of chocolates to a roar of approval, "to get him to change his mind. So, in short gentlemen, you can fuck his mouth, you can blow down his throat or we can all cover his face with our come until he almost drowns in it."

I doubt Billy heard because he was too busy having his mouth widened in a rictus grin as the bear's cock stretched him wider than I had seen before.

"And, gentlemen, we're hoping this will be an all-night affair and so our good friend Jason has a supply of helpful supplements to keep your stamina up. Originals and generics. Please have your money ready. A few men dug into their pockets to extract their wallets and Jason did a profitable trade.

Some stayed in their seats or on the grass watching the activity but most mingled around the supine Billy on the table. I was one of them although I kept to the back of Earl and his cronies. After the bear dumped in Billy's throat Guy attacked his mouth with his cock as another partygoer tried it at the same time. Billy opened to take the heads of both pricks at once. There was nothing gentle about any of the men milling around him and they stabbed at his mouth like he was just a hole for their pleasure, dumping their spunk on his tongue or all over his face. A couple, too eager to wait for his mouth, was content to blow over his hard cock as well as his flat stomach and abs.

There was an air of haste to the activity and Earl repeatedly consulted his watch. I disengaged from the group and went inside where a few men were seated talking in the living room, others topping up their drinks in the kitchen. I found an empty bedroom and shut the door, locking it behind me.

I could text but if Earl or Jason were suspicious they might believe someone else had sent the message, or that I suspected something was amiss and was on my way back. No, I would have to speak to him. I didn't want to hear him lie, that tore my guts out.

Pressing speed dial, I heard Billy's phone ring in the kitchen. I quickly disconnected. I dialed Jason and heard it ring in the backyard. There was sudden quiet.

I kept my voice steady and cheerful. "Hi, Jason."

"Hi Steve. Good news or bad?"

"I can't seem to raise Billy. He's not answering his phone."

"Perhaps he just didn't hear it. Didn't you say he was at a party?"

"I'm worried. I'm thinking of catching a cab back to check he's all right."

"Why don't you just leave it five minutes and try again. I'm sure he'll pick up. I think you're worrying about nothing."

"You're probably right. I'll do that. Thanks."

I heard a scramble out on the verandah.

"Where the fuck is Billy's cell phone? We gotta find it before his boyfriend rings back," Earl shouted.

I heard people searching everywhere; I held my breath while someone tried the door to the room I was hiding in. Then a shout of, "I've found it, it was in the kitchen."

Sexual activity continued apace for I could hear Billy slurping on cock, blithely unaware of the frenzied activity going on around him. Earl attempted to get Billy in some sort of state that he could speak to me sensibly. I let them sweat for ten minutes before I rang back. They were cursing my tardiness because I had put a dampener on their free-for-all with Billy.

"Quiet everyone," Earl commanded. "I'm putting it on speaker so we can all hear what's said."

"What's my boyfriend's name?" Billy said.

Jason hissed. "Steve."

Billy really was off his face. It would be interesting to see how he handled this call.

"Hi, Steve," he said as he answered.

"Hi, Billy. How's the party?"

"Fantastic. I'm having a great time."

"You didn't answer when I rang before."

"Sorry. I left my phone in the kitchen and didn't hear it. But I got it now."

"I just rang to tell you the road service guy is about ten minutes away from here and provided everything is okay, I should be back to pick you up in about half an hour. Will you be ready?"

"I think so. Might be a bit rushed but it should be all right."

"Okay. Gotta run, I can see the van coming now so it may even be twenty minutes. Love you, Billy."

"Yeah."

"Shit, we've got twenty minutes with Billy's mouth here so let's not waste any time."

Back outside, I noticed Earl fossicking near the old shed. He found what he was after and held up an old plastic funnel.

"Okay, gents, we're still hoping that Steve's car will be beyond repair and that he won't make it back here. In which case we'll have an entire night to get to know slut Billy better. Failing that, we can all dump a load in Billy's gullet to stake a claim for the next time we get him alone like this. And make no mistake, gentlemen, there will be a next time. Because Billy is like a drug. You gotta keep going back for more. Everything else pales in comparison. So step up gents, try his throat, his mouth, his lips. Give the cocksucker what he craves."

Billy started sucking like a wild thing and I joined a few of the men who were content to watch rather than join in. There were always a few in every crowd. No one took any notice of us, they were all too concerned with their own pleasure. A few of them were taking too long; they were tapped on the shoulder and asked to step aside. Eventually, with time ticking away there were still too many to be taken care of.

Earl picked up the funnel and placed it in Billy's mouth. "Step up gentlemen, two or three at a time and dump your load, that way we can give the filthy cocksucker what he wants most, enough come to drown in."

Guys were jerking their cocks to beat the curfew, stepping forward to dump their loads in the gaping funnel which Earl held above Billy. I watched in awe as spunk slid from the narrow neck and into his open mouth where he rolled it around on his tongue to get the full taste before swallowing as fast as it was delivered, without spilling a drop. It was so fuckin' hot I blew a load in my shorts as I watched. I counted sixteen men step up to the plate and make a deposit in the Bank of Billy.

Earl had yet to come and he waited until after Jason and a reluctant Nigel jerked off into the funnel. He presented it to Billy to lick clean, slapping him across the face with his savage purple prick before pulling his lips apart with his thumbs. He pushed his cock in roughly and shouted, "It's like fucking a spooge pie. Shit, it's so warm and slimy." He held Billy's face down with his hands and ground his cock into his mouth. He glanced at his watch and picked up speed. I wondered what it would be like to sink your prick into his mouth and throat slicked with all those loads of man slime. I envied Earl.

It didn't take long before he swore like a porn actor and blew his load.

"Good boy, Billy." He patted him on the head like a dog. "Here's your reward. It will get rid of that ugly taste in your mouth as well."

"I love the taste of come," Billy said. "But I like chocolate even more."

He opened up and Earl popped the drugged chocolate inside. Billy was the picture of satisfaction.

It was decision time. I could put an end to it right now by slipping out the back and pretending to arrive at the front door. Or…

Jason whispered to Guy, "There's enough in that piece to fell a horse. He'll be a fuckin' sexual insatiable in no time."

My decision was made for me. There was no way I could control Billy once whatever drug it was hit his system. He would just have to ride it out.

I walked to the back fence for a little privacy and dialled. I could hear Billy's phone ring a short distance away.

"Hi, honey," he said.

They didn't bother with speaker this time.

"You sound like you're enjoying yourself," I said.

"I am." I could hear the grin in his voice.

"I've got bad news. The car has to be towed so I won't get back there tonight to pick you up. I could get Matt to drop over if you want."

"Nah, it's cool here. There's plenty of room to crash."

"I'll be over first thing in the morning to get you. Okay?"

"That's fantastic because the fun has just started here. I got my second wind."

"Hey, don't overdo it. But have a good time."

"Oh, I will. I sure will."

"Love ya."

"Me, too." He said.

With that phone call, I sealed his fate.

I walked back to join the party. Billy was wild eyed; the drugs had really kicked in this time. "Okay, guys," he yelled. "You heard. My boyfriend's not coming back tonight so come and get a piece of the best ass in the country."

He grabbed Jason and Nigel out of the crowd and hungrily kissed them, like a starving man "You two are so fuckin' hot. I wanted you to fuck me ever since we met. I wanted you throw me down in front of Steve and fill my ass and my throat with your hot fuckin' cocks until I couldn't breathe." Billy lay back on the table and raised one leg so he could finger his ass while he stared at Jason. "You want this hole. This tight little ass chute. You want to stick your cock in my guts and blow your nasty spunk inside me."

Jason appeared mesmerised. Billy picked up the bottle and inserted it roughly in his rear. "I wish this was your cock, Jason, pounding my asshole. Come and fuck me rough. Like you want to. I've seen you staring at my hole when Steve is not around. Come and feel it. Feel my slimy asshole." Billy removed the bottle as Jason walked over and slowly pushed three fingers against his ass, staring as they disappeared in Billy's hole.

Billy now turned his attention to Nigel. "While you're waiting Nigel come and try my mouth; I know you like it. You dumped a load of your sweet spunk in it before. I love the taste of your juice. Come and fuck my mouth." Nigel was stroking his cock to the sound of Billy's hypnotic appeal. He moved toward his target and slid his prick down Billy's throat. Jason snapped out of his trance and battered his cock against the gate to Billy's sluthole. He pushed and Billy engulfed him. He just had time to cry out before Billy went to work milking that beautiful prick inside him.

"This is the best ass I've ever fucked," Jason whimpered.

Billy's voice had calmed the rabid crowd. Nigel and Jason were fucking him slowly and sensually, taking their time to enjoy the experience. This was their anniversary fuck and I knew if the drug had kicked in Billy would be wanting it hot and nasty shortly. The crowd watched patiently, there was no crowding or shoving, they had all the time in the world now.

Jason had great technique, moving his hips about each time he plunged inside Billy, a look of wonderment on his face. Even Nigel was enjoying Billy's lips vacuuming along his shaft.

"Your turn," he said to Nigel as he nudged Jason gently to make way. Nigel fumbled his first attempt until Billy guided him inside. Jason watched impatiently as his lover fucked my lover's ass. You could tell Nigel lacked experience as a top but you could also tell from the wonder in his eyes he had never experienced anything like this before. A look of disappointment clouded his face as he grunted briefly, an obvious sign he was dumping his load prematurely.

Billy was sympathetic. "Your cock felt as good as I always thought it would. We've got plenty of time to do it again. And again. And again."

Jason was back inside his ass before Billy had even finished his sentence. This time, there was no pretence at civility. He battered like he was attempting to knock down a door.

"You fuckin' ugly slut cunt," Jason sneered. "Your ass was born to be fucked by my cock. Can you feel it right up inside you, cunt boy? Your ass is the only thing I've wanted since I saw you. I knew your ass would belong to me one day. You've always craved my cock, haven't you slut?"

"I want to worship your cock, Jason. I want to feel it in me, while I suck your boyfriend's cock. You like to watch me blow him, don't you Jason?"

"I want to see you covered in come, Billy. I want to see your face a huge wad of slime and then watch as you swallow it all down. Nothing is too nasty for you, Billy. And I'll see that you get it."

This was a new side to Jason and Nigel didn't look as if he liked it. The dirty talk continued for a while longer until the other men, tired of being excluded, descended on Billy. Jason increased his pace because he knew he would be pulled from Billy's ass if he took much longer. With a loud explosion of foul talk he shot his load and pulled out, his cock shaft glistening.

That was the signal for Billy to be done over like a piece of meat. At one moment he was on his stomach, cock pushing into his ass while others shot into his throat. He had no way of controlling it. Another time a rough fucker pushed Billy's cheek against the wooden table, crushing down on his head as he viciously fucked Billy's mouth until he puked up the litres of manslime he'd swallowed earlier. The mouth fucker did not let up until he blew his load then pushed Billy's face down in the puke. Others used the slime as lube to jerk their cocks and another as extra lube to slip his larger than normal cock into Billy's ass ring.

They all dumped inside him at least once before there was a break in the action. I had never seen anyone so brutalised and still beg for more since I'd witnessed a meth gangbang years before. If that's what Billy was on he'd welcome this mob fucking him to death before he'd be satisfied. That made me angry. Sure, I was fuckin' turned on and wanted to join in but I was afraid I'd be recognised. Perhaps later when the participants were fading.

But they didn't fade. They went back for more and more. Some left thoroughly sated after dropping one or two loads while others seemed to have cocks that never got flaccid although they were longer achieving orgasm each time. Billy must have been incredibly sore, or else had lost all feelings along with his sense.

While I was caught up in the excess of the moment I was also an objective observer. Billy was being battered but he held his own against the constant stream of cock that was merely looking for a come dump. They weren't fucking a human being; they were fucking a reputation so they could boast to their mates. They might remember Billy, although even that was debatable, but Billy wouldn't remember most of them, if any at all. They were drones to Billy's Queen Bee. Only Jason had made an impression.

Billy wouldn't remember much about tonight and I regretted that. He loved watching himself in action although usually in a much more structured event than this. This was mayhem. And, reluctantly, I had to admit most of it did not excite me. My cock throbbed when Jason was fucking Billy with his nasty talk an added bonus, and one or two of the others, the guy who crushed his head for a skull fuck, for example, were connoisseurs, but the remainder…forget it.

I heard Billy say, "Have you come to fuck me, mate? I missed that cock of yours. I got an itch and only you can scratch it. You told me I was your favorite fuckin' boy cunt."

I watched with interest because there was the hint of consciousness in Billy's eyes, the first time I had seen it tonight. "You want to fuck me until I can't stand up. Treat me like the scum sucking boy cunt I was meant to be."

A smile curled Earl's lips. "You got it Billy. I'm one nasty motherfucker and you're the only guy can match me."

Billy licked his lips. "I've been waiting for you. See, my ass is all creamed up just the way you like it. You watched didn't you? You watched them fuck me like I wish Steve would watch me."

"Steve's a fuckin' wimp. He can't feed your hunger like I can. He hasn't learned the only way to control you, Billy, is to set you free. He's so into the nice suburban home and the appearance of normality. You'll never be normal Billy. Don't try to be. There's evil in you. Let it free. Only then will you be happy."

"Rip my ass open, Earl. I want to be your ass cunt."

They circled each other like wary animals. It was a fascinating ritual. It was another side of Billy I hadn't seen. It made me wonder if there were two Billy's. If there were, where had my Billy gone?

The party had thinned out by this time and men were lying exhausted and sleeping in the house and on the back lawn. I pretended to be among them but was watching from under my cap. They were taking no notice of us anyway.

Earl searched among the carved pumpkins and chose a large one with a startled expression. He threw out the candle which had long since burnt down. He lowered it over Billy's head and positioned it carefully. It looked as if it had been deliberately carved. He pressed his cock to the O-shaped mouth and it slid through impaling Billy on the other side. Grabbing the pumpkin and holding it firm, Earl rammed his cock in and out spearing Billy in the process. I could hear Billy gasping to breathe, attempting to ward off choking.

It was bizarre, Earl fucking a pumpkin head on Billy's shoulders. But it was also fuckin' hot watching the thorough mouth fuck Billy was copping. He gurgled, coughing and choking, in an attempt to swallow all Earl's sperm when he blew his load.

Earl brandished a baseball bat that he'd found leaning against the old shed. He prodded Billy so that he fell back on the table. Earl batted his legs in the air and told him to show his asshole.

"You're fucked, Billy," Earl said. "If you keep this up your asshole will be loose as some old two-bit whore. You'll be Tarzan of the Gapes."

Billy response was muffled by his pumpkin helmet.

"I'm a dangerous man, Billy." He thumped the baseball bat down close enough to Billy's head to smash open the pumpkin. Billy didn't flinch.

"Not half as dangerous as me, Earl." Billy grabbed the end of the baseball bat and lined it up against his asshole. With a superhuman effort he pressed down on it, his face contorted in pain until three or four inches slid inside him.

"Come with me, Billy. I'll take you places you never dreamed of."

Earl was slowly sliding the bat further and further into Billy's guts. Every now and then Billy would grab it to stop penetration, pause for a deep breath and then the relentless pressure would continue.

"Why do you stick with that ineffectual boyfriend of yours?" Earl rotated the bat and Billy grimaced.

"Love?"

"Don't give me that shit."

"Believe it or not, he understands me better than you."

"You're right, I don't believe you."

"He knows how to get me off."

"But you treat him like shit."

Billy smiled. "He loves it.

"I think he does."

Earl leaned in, kissing Billy on the lips. "Goodbye, sweet prince. I'll come back for you one day." He pulled the bat from Billy's ass and walked away without looking back.

When he'd gone, I stumbled over. Billy looked up at me. "You're the cute guy I met earlier. Come to fuck me? I need it. My ass is itching like fuck."

God help me because I couldn't help myself. I wanted the taste of the countless loads and the strong, pungent taste of Earl that Billy had swallowed. I wanted to slide my raging cock in among the spunk from a dozen or more strangers stewing in his ass. I rode him slowly, licking and biting his neck, twisting his nipples until he cried out in pain. I spat in his face and in his mouth but still he begged for more. They had drugged him well. If I left him here he would be totally fucked out by the morning.

I lifted him off the table and carried him, still embedded on my prick, to the hot tub.

"Where are you taking me, cute man?"

"Home, Billy."

"I have a boyfriend."

I dumped him in the swirling water and climbed in after him, seating him back on my cock.

"Why do you do this?" I asked.

"To see if he really loves me."

"A slut?"

"I don't want to be. Oh, part of me does; the bad part."

"What if your boyfriend loves you because you're a slut, not despite it?"

He stopped, and looked at me. "You think that's possible?"

I nodded.

I put my hand around his cock and worked it slowly so he barely even noticed at first. As I built up speed he began to flex his pelvis against my cock and squeeze his sagging ass muscles. The hot tub was having a revitalizing effect and soon I pushed extra hard to jettison my come to mix with all the strangers' before me. Billy followed soon after and the strings of his sperm floated to the surface. He collapsed against my chest and fell asleep.

It was getting late and a few men, still horny and priapic, wandered out to have another round with the drug fucked bottom only to find him missing. It was only a matter of time before they found him and the slut fuck began again. I could not protect him against all of them.

I woke him gently and he stared at me.

"Steve? Steve!" He hugged me tightly and kissed me hard. "You came back for me."

"Of course I did."

"I thought you may have left me here to teach me a lesson."

"Why would I do that?"

"Because I was nasty. Insisting you take your old job back. And because I sucked off Earl."

"Don't forget Jason and Nigel."

He blushed.

"You let them fuck you in the ass, as well."

"When?"

"Tonight."

"I can't remember. Did I like it?"

I nodded.

"Did you see them do it?"

"Uh huh."

"Did you like what you saw?"

"Shit, yeah, love. It was sizzling."

I helped him out of the tub.

"I bet Nigel was a dud, right?"

"You were very kind to him, though."

"Jason?"

"Oh, man. He was sooooo hot for you."

By this time we were at the back fence, after I'd gathered his loin cloth, Earl had his briefs, and his mobile phone. I helped him through.

"Fuck. I wish I could remember it."

On the journey home, Billy settled for my graphic description of his fuck with Jason, often asking me to repeat certain moments. By the time we were back at our apartment he was ready for more.

"Can I have him again, Steve. Please may I? I want to be conscious next time. Especially if he's as hot as you say."

"On one condition," I said.

"Name it."

"Provided I can watch."

"Openly watch or hiding watch?"

I turned out the light and Billy snuggled up to me. "Your choice."

He mulled it over for a moment or two. "If you're hiding he has to think that you'd be upset if you caught us. And if it's in front of you then he can't think it's with your consent, otherwise it's boring." He was learning.

"That's why we get on so well together, we think along the same lines."

"You'd really do that for me?"

"Just don't make a habit of it, Billy."

He never did get to try Jason again. The shit hit the fan the following morning when no one could find Billy at the party and no one admitted to taking him home. There was talk of drug-fucked Billy wandering away from the party to be attacked or worse, killed. Recriminations were shouted down phone lines and, in the apartment upstairs there were ugly scenes between Jason and Nigel, which we all heard about later. Billy encouraged it by dropping out of sight for a few days while Matt and I swore we had no idea where he was and expressed alarm and concern.

We milked it for what it was worth but at the end of three days Billy made a 'miraculous' reappearance minus his memory of the previous four days and the world slipped back into its routine. Except for our neighbors upstairs who called it a day. I think that was wise on Nigel's side. He even shamefacedly apologised to Billy for his part in the gangbang. Billy pleaded ignorance, which was the truth. By way of a consolation prize Billy did find shaky cell phone footage of Jason banging him on a pay-per-view website which he still treasures, a little too much to my liking.

Within a month of the infamous party, Nigel and Jason were gone. Jason threatened to return one day to claim Billy's ass as his own, rather anti-climactically making it on voicemail rather than in person, otherwise Billy would have forced him to make good on his threat there and then.

The upstairs apartment was eventually rented but we didn't take much notice as I was at work all day and Billy's time was more and more consumed by Gideon's restaurant where he was working some evenings as chef.

It was one such evening when I was interrupted in my sit-ups by a knock at the door. I was in shorts, dripping perspiration from the exercise, when I opened to be confronted by what looked like a schoolboy with a loosened tie around his neck and his only other article of clothing being a pair of snug South Park briefs that did nothing to hide his rather substantial schlong. I'm afraid I stared.

He smiled politely. "Hi, I'm your new neighbor from the fifth floor. I'm afraid I've locked myself out. Do you mind if I use your phone?"

DONE LIKE A DINNER

They threatened to spread his boyfriend like a tablecloth at the banquet!

Steve gets wind of a plot by his co-workers to publicly humiliate him at the company piss up which is being held at the restaurant where his boyfriend, Billy, works. The night passes pleasantly enough until the wives and girlfriend's go home after which Billy is forced to service the remaining diners under the table. The sexual free-for-all threatens to get out of hand when Steve finds himself locked in the men's toilet, unable to go to the aid of his hapless boyfriend.

"So the restaurant where Billy works is doing okay?" Gil was uncharacteristically full of bonhomie as we ate sandwiches on the building site where I was a day labourer. It was a change from my job as a car detailer, an industry in which I could no longer get work because of the spiteful references of Jerry, my former boss.

"He seems to be thriving there. He's gone from offering casual suggestions on how to improve the place through part-time chef to now essentially running the kitchen. That's always been his dream." I was proud of Billy, my cuter than fuck boyfriend, although our differing hours meant we were like ships passing in the night. Fortunately, I usually managed to throw a quick fuck into him before I left for work in the morning and drain his balls so he wouldn't be horny all day.

Our flatmate and third partner, Matt, usually there to fill in when I wasn't, currently resided in Europe where he was on assignment – he's a top-notch photographer – and sent back sizzling accounts of his adventures. So sizzling, in fact, I'd caught Billy jerking off feverishly while he read them on a number of occasions. Times like that, Billy was hot for cock and I was glad to give it to him.

"I thought maybe it would be a good place to have our piss up," Gil said. "It's not too, um, dress up, is it?"

"Shit, no! It's an old diner that's been done up. Good old fashioned home cooking. Bit too large for its own good. Built when there were a lot of factory workers in the area who had half an hour for lunch. A coupla steps above a greasy spoon cafe but well below the pretentious places that get reviewed in the paper."

"Sounds ideal. Will you talk to Billy about it?"

"Sure. If it's what you want."

The company always gave the guys a piss up when a job was complete and the low-rise apartment building on which we'd been working was almost concluded. They were selling fast off the plan and the display apartment had just been set up. We were finishing off and it would be a couple of weeks, a month max, and we'd be out of there.

I was hoping they would employ me on their next job site. Okay, it wasn't my area of expertise but I enjoyed the hard, physical labour and it was doing wonders for my body. I'd even been able to give up my gym membership, which was a substantial saving. And my new muscles were a total turn on for Billy.

So why wasn't I totally happy about Gil's news? Don't get me wrong, I was pleased they'd chosen Billy's restaurant, it was a shot in the arm it needed. It wasn't even that I knew an all-out assault was to be made on Billy's delectable ass at the piss up. It was the way in which they were going about it, and the reason they were going about it. It would make it impossible for them to employ me for future jobs. That was the aim of one of the labourers in particular. He was much more important on site than me, so if it came to a showdown...

I found out by accident. A series of coincidences that so seem to guide my life and keep me one step ahead of Billy. I'd borrowed some of the site's work tools over the weekend to repair a few problems I'd neglected in the apartment; nothing serious which is why they'd been overlooked for so long. Trouble is, I forgot to take them back the following Monday and they were needed. And I was needed for an important pick-up on the other side of the city. The solution was simple. As Billy would have already left for his job in the restaurant I gave Gil my keys and told him where to find them. I headed out for the pick-up which took close on ninety minutes round trip.

The area around the worksite was a disaster area meaning I had to park some distance away and walk back to get the fork lift to handle the deliveries. Most of the men were working on the upper floors while the trailer loader was in the basement car park. The roller-door was propped open to save us the infernal squeak each time it lifted and closed, so I ducked inside. I heard whispered voices which tended to echo around the vast deserted area. I was about to call out that I was back as one of the voices was Gil's. The other I recognised as belonging to Jameel, self-appointed head cocky of the Arab tradesmen on the building site.

What stopped me was that I heard the word 'Billy' and my interest piqued. There are no Billy's on the work site; Gil had been to my apartment earlier that morning, so chances are the Billy to whom he was referring was my Billy. I crept closer to where they were chatting on the upper level, hidden by the concrete support pillars on my level. Pallets of tiles, boxes of electrical appliances, and crated bathtubs waiting to be installed meant I could creep quite close to their position. Gil was having his usual smoko while Jameel cradled a coffee.

"I didn't bother to knock," Gil said, obviously in the middle of his story. "Steve, stupid bastard, gave me the key. He said Billy would be at work. Steve's always bragging about how hot Billy's ass is but I never expected to see it in action."

Jameel spat. "Faggot stuff."

Gil ignored him.

"Anyway, I let myself in. I'm in the hallway and I hear all this groaning and moaning. I didn't know if somehow I got the wrong apartment so I checked. Nah, it was the right one. Pretty stupid really as the key fit the lock. So, I went in further, quiet like, I didn't want to scare anyone if they were home."

Jameel laughed like he didn't believe him.

Gil was not going to be deflected from his story. "I couldn't believe my eyes when I walked into the lounge room. He was on all fours, like a dog, and this guy was ramming his cock into his ass like he was working over a whore."

I heard the disgust in Jameel's voice. "Oh, mate, I woulda puked."

"Yeah," Gil agreed. "I thought that woulda been my reaction too. But..."

"Tell me you beat the shit outa the both of 'em"

"I couldn't do that. The one being fucked musta been Billy." Gil's voice got all dreamy. "He had this really cute ass. I couldn't take my eyes off this huge dick, I never seen one so big except in porn, fucking it like there was never gonna be another chance. The guy was cursin', slappin' Billy's ass as he fucked him stupid."

"You watched them? You sick fuck."

"Couldn't help it. I never seen two guys doing the dirty before, not even in movies. You know, it's no different to watching a guy do a chick in the ass. But no chick's ass was as hot as Billy's. He musta been doing something to the guy who was up him because the fucker's eyes were glazing over and he was mumbling about the hottest ass he ever fucked and that sorta shit.

"I stood there watching for a few minutes then the one on top noticed me. He smiled and said, 'You come to join in? His mouth's not busy.' I shook my head and mumbled about coming to pick up some tools. They both laughed, I sorta went red. 'Don't be embarrassed. Go get your tools and not a word to Steve about this, mind.' That would explain why Steve said Billy wouldn't be home."

"Let me be there when you tell him his boyfriend's a slut. I wanna see him cry for myself," Jameel crowed.

Gil was adamant. "I can't tell him!"

"Why not?" Jameel was desperate for the revelation to come out.

Gil took a deep breath. "Because...because of what happened next."

I smiled to myself. I could guess what was coming. No one could resist Billy when he turned on the charm. Even a married guy like Gil, especially as I knew his marriage had gone a bit stale in the sex department. His wife was doling out missionary position for special occasions although even those were becoming less frequent. The way it was progressing Gil would be lucky to get his end in at the next appearance of Halley's Comet. So, faced with Billy's wicked cocksucking mouth and seductive come-milking ass, two areas strictly off-limits in his wife, well...Gil was only human.

"You got what?" Jameel screamed in disbelief.

"Hard. Harder than I have been in years. Harder than when I took Viagra once."

"Aw, sick shit."

"Yeah, easy enough for you to talk. This Billy guy is sex on legs. I'm no fag but I swear he'd get Jesus hard if he walked in on what I saw. Seems the other guy was a regular who lived upstairs and drops in whenever Steve's out and the fancy takes him which seems to be daily. This Billy character likes it hard as fuck and on a regular basis. So I grab the tools and I'm about to leave when they call me back into the living room. I go in and this Billy is facing me, smiling, a real cocksucking smile, licking his lips. 'You work with Steve?' he asks. 'Gil,' I mumbled. 'Shit, you're his boss?' I nod, Billy smiles, 'Steve never told me you were so hot. Speaking of hot, you look all sweaty. There's a beer in the fridge. Help yourself.' Sounded good, so I got a beer. They didn't stop what they were doing. Not embarrassed a bit. I perched on one of them bar stool things. Yeah, I watched. Not often you get that close to a live sex show, even if it is faggots. Billy was getting a right hard banging. I hadn't seen anyone fucked like that since four of us did a slut at college. I guess it was the memory of that, but I got hard."

I could tell Jameel was about to sneer but Gil got in first.

"Just listen, mate. I'm no faggot but, well, it's been a while, so when Billy offered to blow me, I wasn't about to turn him down. I thought I'd close my eyes and think of some sexy chick but once he wrapped his lips round my prick, well, there was no way. I never had a blow job like it. Used his lips, his tongue, sucked my balls, licked my knob, and took me right down his throat. Like velvet. Like sticking my cock in velvet. I held his head; he took the battering I gave his face. All the while the other guy is ramming his ass. Really ramming.

Billy is taking everything the two of us dish out. Then, fuck me, I shoot in his mouth and he fuckin' swallows it."

I heard Gil groaning, like he was reliving the experience.

"Shit, mate," Jameel said. "You almost make it sound okay. I ain't never had no blow job like that. Nasty." There was a long pause before he added. "So, you ain't gonna tell Steve?"

"Fuck, no! He'd kill me. Besides, I promised while I was zipping up that I wouldn't tell Billy's secret. He invited me back any time I wanted to fuck him again. Gave me his mobile number."

"You gonna go?" Jameel sounded more than curious.

"Thinking about it. That ass of his sure was pretty."

"Gross!"

"Besides," Gil added. "I like the idea of putting one over on Steve. All the trouble he's caused. I like the idea of feeding my cock to his boyfriend in secret."

"Shit, yeah. Not faggot stuff, just pure revenge!" Jameel was warming to the idea. "My girlfriend won't blow me, all she does is a hand job but only after I get really shitty with her. Not much satisfaction there. I guess it would be great revenge to get Billy to suck my cock while Steve's out. Laugh behind his back."

"You think the other guys would be up for a revenge fuck?" Gil asked.

"Long as it's not faggot stuff. They hate Steve; they'd do just about anything to get even with the fucker."

"Like fucking his boyfriend?"

"I think I could talk them round."

Jameel and Gil were in full plotting mode.

"Doesn't Billy run some sorta bar and grill?"

"Uh huh."

"What if I can persuade the powers that be to have our drinks night at Billy's place? We can start flirting with him in front of Steve. I think Billy gets turned on if guys show him a bit of attention," Gil said.

"I heard that he goes off with a few drinks in him," Jameel agreed. "Hell, maybe he'd even do it in front of Steve."

Gil backtracked a little. "Hey, I don't want any trouble. Nothing that's likely to get the cops involved."

"But maximum humiliation is the aim, right?" Jameel sounded excited by the idea.

"As long as I get to fuck Billy again. I don't even care if it's in public."

I crept back to the car park entrance where I called out as if I'd just arrived. Gil came to help and when we'd finished unloading the boxes, we took a lunch break. That's when he passed the idea of the piss up by me. I'd severely over-estimated the strength of my friendship with Gil. I thought he liked me. I knew Jameel, and the other members of the Arab crew, didn't. They kept pretty much to themselves. They were good workers; each did the job of two men with no complaining, to make up for the time they took off during the day for prayers. There were five of them: Jameel, Omar, Fadi, Hakeem and Wazir. They were hot as fuck. Jameel was so sizzling he'd been a finalist in the Tradies Tools competition, run by a major chain of hardware stores.

The finalists appeared, one a month, on a special calendar, posed so close to naked there was only a tool belt in it, to raise money for charity. The public got a chance to vote online for their favourite who would walk away with $10,000 first prize. Plus a chance at a modelling contract. Jameel's body was so ripped there wasn't an ounce of body fat on it. He was a wall of solid muscle, tanned to perfection, his hairless torso the colour and shine of hot buttered toast, a smile like a warm summer's evening, dark short-cropped hair that framed his incredibly handsome features, and a small, neat goatee. It helped that he filled out his jeans to mouth watering effect and, if the pics in the calendar and on the web site were anything to go by, had buns of steel.

Jameel was one for the ladies, and they lavished their attention on him. He lapped it up as if it were his Allah-given right. Then, particularly after the calendar appeared, he suddenly found himself a pin-up boy for the gay community. He copped shit from his mates and others in the building industry who thought it was all a bit 'gay' posing 'like that.' Jameel was not noted for his tolerance of gay men, lesbians were another matter altogether, and he'd often regale his mates at work on Monday with tales of the faggots he'd smacked in the mouth who wouldn't leave him alone.

We'd been friendly enough up to that point; I'd accepted the good natured ragging about being gay but suddenly gay became faggot and his mates turned on me. So, tit-for-tat, I turned on them. It culminated in Jameel grabbing me by the throat, almost choking me the day I asked him to sign a copy of Billy's calendar that took pride of place in his bedside table drawer where it would be retrieved for a late-night wank if he felt the need for visual stimulation.

Jameel had flung the calendar at me, unsigned, and spat in my face, telling me he was no faggot and no faggot lover. I reminded him that gay men were amongst his biggest admirers and that if he wanted their votes he'd better cool it. "Why, faggot?" he asked. "You gonna run to your queer mates to snitch?"

The head butt caught me by surprise. I went down. I was off work for a couple of days. The union took Jameel's side in the dispute, there were no witnesses to the supposed assault even though there had been a number of tradesmen milling about watching, and I was told my worker's compensation would be less than forthcoming if I persisted. I retreated and from that moment I was a source of irritation to Jameel and his backers. But I'd believed Gil was on my side.

Of course, I went to the gay papers with my story and they wrote inflammatory headlines such as 'Tradie Favourite Slugs Gay Builder, Calls Him Faggot!' That almost did it for me on the building site. Most of the tradies refused to speak to me, particularly after Jameel's odds to win the contest plummeted from 2/1 with the bookies to 12/1. In a show of solidarity Billy said he would tear out

Jameel's page from the calendar and destroy it, although days later I found it hidden in the bottom of his sock drawer, under some old newspapers.

In the end, Jameel lost by a landslide. His popular vote had near enough gone backwards from the day the gay bar rags ran their stories. He'd been counting on the win to help pay for his honeymoon and to get him out of the building trade and into more lucrative modelling.

I confess, I didn't help matters by turning up for work the day after his humiliating loss with the biggest smirk plastered across my face. Jameel and his gang advanced on me and only the timely intervention of Gil, who sent me home on full pay, prevented the crap being beaten out of me. It would have been worth it. A fragile peace came into force on the site but I found myself virtually ostracised, not exactly conducive to good working conditions but I was determined they would not force me off the job.

Now I discovered that Gil, the foreman, the one friend I thought I had, was as venal as any of them. In fact, he was worse. He was plotting my downfall while proffering the trappings of mateship. The others at least had the decency to be nasty to my face. I wasn't pissed that he fucked Billy. Not at first when I believed it was merely sexual frustration that led him to cuckold me secretly. It was a different matter when I learned of his treachery in planning my total downfall with the complicity of my work mates.

There was no way I could tell Billy of their plan. I didn't want him to turn down the lucrative booking that would help keep the restaurant afloat and thus keep him in work. I would feed him just enough information that he would give Gil, Jameel and the others a wide berth at the restaurant thus avoiding any conflict or temptation. It would also keep him on his guard against drinking on the night in question because a couple of alcoholic beverages and Billy was anyone's for the asking – even my enemies. Especially my enemies.

What did amuse me was Billy's involvement with Kurt, the 'guy from upstairs' in Gil's tale of sexual skulduggery. He hadn't named him but he was obviously the young twink who had turned up on our doorstep one evening when I was home alone engaged in strenuous exercise. His only articles of clothing, if you could call them that, were a loosened tie and a pair of South Park briefs that did little to hide an impressive erection. He told me he had just moved into the vacant apartment on the fifth floor and he'd locked himself out. He wanted to call a friend.

More than happy to invite in such an attractive young man, his slim body and youthful good looks a powerful aphrodisiac, I pointed him to the landline then went to make a coffee for the two of us after he'd accepted my invitation to stay.

His phone conversation was colourful but no amount of cajoling, begging or threats seemed to move the unknown party on the other end of the line. He slammed it down after telling the recipient of the call sarcastically, "Okay then, if you want me to wait until you get home, I'll be in the hallway in my underpants. If I'm not there just knock on a few doors to see if anyone has picked me up to suck on my big juicy cock."

He scratched his balls lasciviously, for my benefit I was sure, and sighed deeply. It had to be an act. I'd wager it was his routine, wandering about the building dressed to please the inhabitants of the mostly gay apartments, in an effort to snare sex. Perhaps he expected to be paid; maybe he did it for the sheer love of cock. Either way, I was surprised Billy hadn't thought of it, but then we were both too well known for him to get away with it.

I brought him his coffee, and then sat in the armchair opposite his display which was as inviting as it's possible to be without him actually being naked.

"Nice flat you've got here," he smiled glancing around in a perfunctory manner, giving the lie to his interest. "You live alone?"

"Nah, my boyfriend Billy is at work."

He glanced at the clock on the wall. "What time is he due home?"

"Not until early tomorrow morning. He's a chef."

His face lit up. "That gives us hours."

I pretended naiveté. "For what? I thought you were going to parade around the fifth floor in your undies until someone took you back to his apartment and fucked that snug little ass of yours."

"You think my ass is snug?" He stood, pretending to examine his butt from every angle, before he grabbed a handful of his crotch. "It's usually my cock most people admire."

"I did notice. That's quite a pistol you're packin'. Between the two of them you must keep your boyfriend very happy indeed."

He smirked. "I don't have a boyfriend."

I sure hoped he wasn't going to insist he was straight. "Oh?"

"I have a sugar daddy." He was watching for my reaction as he said it.

"You're barking up the wrong tree. I don't need to pay for sex."

He wasn't offended. "What makes you think I'm asking?"

"For sex? Or for money?"

"Either."

"Simple mathematics," I replied. "One, no-one goes around an apartment building, especially a gay apartment building, dressed like you are unless they're advertising. Plus, you dialled only seven digits when you were supposedly calling someone for help. The imaginary sugar daddy? There are no seven digit numbers so the call was a fake."

He didn't seem non-plussed that I had caught him out. "I thought you'd be too distracted making coffee to take any notice of the phone call, except the bits I wanted you to hear."

"Does it usually work?"

"Always. Guys can't wait to wrap their lips round my meat."

"I can believe that," I said. "It's a very impressive looking weapon."

"Why don't you come and examine the merchandise up close?" he suggested.

"Even for merchandise as choice as you, I don't pay."

He stood up and shucked off his undies, his thick cock pointing skywards, then approached me, sitting in my lap. "For you, it's on the house."

I'm not one to turn down a freebie. He snuggled against my bare chest and played with my hardening cock through my shorts while I tugged his mammoth weapon thinking how much Billy would enjoy it sliding into his well-greased ass. That's about where our negotiations broke down. I didn't mind chowing down on his cock, ditto with him on mine, but neither of us was prepared to allow the other to penetrate his ass. Impasse. It was resolved with an enjoyable but hardly earth shattering mutual oral session. Had I not had a boyfriend of the calibre of Billy, I probably would have made more of an effort over Kurt. When we'd both brought each other to orgasm - I swallowed, he spat – I suggested that if he wanted to sink his sausage into some prime ass then he could do no better than call on Billy during office hours while I was at work. He smiled at my imprimatur. "I might do just that," he said as he went back to his apartment, the pretence of locking himself out well and truly over.

I'd not given Kurt much more thought from that day. I was pleased he'd obviously boffed Billy, not so pleased he seemed to be doing it on a daily basis. There was something about the twink I didn't trust. I couldn't blame Billy for taking advantage of readily available cock, especially one as succulent as Kurt's, as our overlapping hours didn't leave us much time for the more intimate displays of our relationship. I worked days, he worked nights. On the occasions our schedules coincided we took advantage to renew our passion and it was as delicious and exhausting as ever. Neither of us had any complaints in that department. So, if Billy got the itch and needed a little extra on the side, I wasn't going to begrudge him that. I just wished he wouldn't keep it secret. I hate being the last to know what's going on.

I was lucky, therefore, to be in on the ground floor with Gil and Jameel's planning for revenge. Billy took on board my warning, reiterating his disgust at Jameel's behaviour toward me, but, at the same time, I could see he was excited at the prospect of a major function at the restaurant. He was putting in a lot of extra unpaid hours in the hope they would take him on permanently, he was on call at present, paid only for the nights Gideon's had choice bookings. If he could make an impression with our piss up, word of mouth would help them limp along.

When the booking was made official, he went into full chef mode, poring over menu options, liaising with suppliers, ensuring the waiters were employed for the night. Billy was at his best when he had a project, and this was a biggie. He sought my advice because of my knowledge of my workmates, albeit limited and hostile, and researched Muslim options. He left nothing to chance. So the weeks slipped by until we wound up our work on the apartment block and handed it over to the realtors to do their part.

If Gil and Jameel were still planning something they kept very quiet about it. I heard nothing further even when eavesdropping on their whispered conversations. It was hard to believe they would attempt anything at the dinner because the entire company would be there, from architects to the CEO of the company, from tradies through to suppliers.

The big night rolled around all too quickly, meaning I was out of work once again and heavily reliant on the goodwill of the company to employ me on one of their next jobs. I was tense over my prospects because Billy and I, like the restaurant, were barely making ends meet. I spent the day at Gideon's helping set the place up, spreading the newly cleaned linen tablecloths, much too nice for the laminate crowd that was coming that night, setting out the cutlery, folding napkins, cleaning glasses, any little job to help and settle the butterflies in my stomach. They were the portent of disaster.

In the late afternoon, as the staff all took a well-earned break, I told Billy how proud I was of his achievement. He nuzzled my neck as we sat at one of the semi-circular booths that lined the walls of the restaurant, the more intimate tables scattered in geometric patterns around the dance floor. The stage was festooned with flowers as management was prone to give out novelty awards to its workers who ate up the small appreciation, as well as long self-important speeches on the value of property development. The menu was set but there were four or five choices in each course. There had to be once you allowed for vegetarian, halal and Kosher meals.

Billy was exhausted but also elated. "Gideon has some big news he wants to talk to me about after the dinner tonight." I could see he had his hopes up. "If it all goes well, I think he might be going to employ me full time."

I hugged him reassuringly. "It's okay, Billy. I won't let anything spoil your night. If Jameel and his mob are mongrels, I'll turn the other cheek. Just don't let them use you to get at me."

"No way," he said adamantly.

I presented him a special gift for the occasion in a small satin lined box: a chef's hat pin with his name engraved in it. He blubbered when I gave it to him and insisted I pin it to his apron. I left to shower and change for the big event. It would be a lonely enough night for me, putting on a brave face in front of Gil and Jameel, pretending I didn't realise the depth of their hatred, mixing with management who were all essentially strangers. At least I would be seated at the same booth as Gideon who was keeping an eye on the proceedings ready to jump in any time that Billy needed help. But conversation with the man whose name adorned the restaurant would not be exactly scintillating. He had limited small talk plus there was the added taint that he'd been one of several guests at a notorious dinner party who'd all taken turns with Billy in front of me. It made no difference that we'd been going through a separation at that stage.

Surprisingly, the restaurant meal went off without a hitch. When I'd returned, showered and shaved, the place was abuzz with activity. I knew better than to stick my face in the kitchen, there would be plenty of time after the event to congratulate Billy. The subdued lighting and array of flowers and ornate decoration that appeared so gaudy in daylight took on an atmosphere of simple elegance under subdued lighting and classy tableware.

People were standing around in small groups as I made my way to the table I'd been assigned. Gil introduced me to his wife, a sour-faced harridan who nagged him most of the meal, usually about trivialities. Gideon was fluttering around like an expectant father until I dragged him to the bar for a double of whatever it was he was drinking and he started to mellow. The worst aspect of the evening was that Jameel and his mates were in the two booths on either side of ours. They had brought their wives and girlfriends. Jameel's fiancée, I assume it was as I was never introduced, sat glowering at me most of the meal, no doubt blaming me for her future husband's loss of prize money and modelling opportunity. Every time I caught her, I nodded my head politely, smiling my widest smile.

I thought they may have attempted to disrupt the meal by claiming problems with the halal dishes but Billy had anticipated that and employed a Muslim chef, sidestepping any complaints. Despite my misgivings, everyone seemed to be enjoying themselves immensely. I asked Gil's wife to dance between the main course and dessert, the music pumped out over the restaurant's old PA system, the company too stingy to fork out for a live band. She thawed enough that she was almost pleasant but I was grateful when the music ended and I could lead her back to the table. I'd done my duty by her for the night. After that she became positively loquacious, with an opinion on every subject that came up for discussion, usually the opposite of the case anyone else was putting.

Also before dessert, the 'entertainment' if such it can be called, bored me rigid. Patronising novelty awards to keep the workers happy and platitudes about the growth of the company and its concern for the environment. I took the opportunity to slip outside for fresh air. The night was humid, fortunately the restaurant was air conditioned, smokers forced into the car park if they wanted to indulge in their addiction. When I came out the side door there was a scramble among the on-site workers to stub out their butt ends and race back inside. I was left alone with a few of the management team who looked at me askance and made no effort to include me in their conversation.

I walked around the car park, chancing upon a couple going at it in the back seat of their Holden Commodore. I thought I recognised Fadi's girlfriend but it certainly wasn't Fadi with her. By the time I did one complete circuit, snickering at the utter stupidity of life, and went back in to take my seat, the presentations were coming to a close. The desserts were a triumph; some people asking for seconds after which coffee or a selection of caffeine-laced or herbal teas were available to those who wanted them.

An hour or so later, the main pressure of the night over, Billy began to circulate in his apron on which the pin I'd given him was proudly displayed. He visited each table and spent time conversing with the diners. His face was flushed with success, as well it should have been. He'd managed to prepare meals that were the equal of most major eateries in the city at a modicum of the cost and with much less pretention.

Wives and sweethearts packed off to a hen's do they'd been champing at the bit to attend all night, the Arab boys were now getting boisterous. My internal radar was on alert, especially when Billy reached Jameel's booth. There was a stilted conversation about the quality of the food and the enjoyment level of the evening. I was beginning to relax by the time Billy started to move on. Then it happened.

Jameel knocked his coffee spoon on to the floor, a deliberate act. He turned to Billy, smiling. "Oops! Do you mind?"

Billy was mortified. "I'll get you a new one." Jameel stopped him. "Nah, don't worry. Just see if you can find the one under the table. I'll clean it off."

Billy looked uncertain. "You sure?"

"Isn't the customer always right?" He laughed. Billy kneeled down, disappearing under the table. Gil attempted to distract my attention by asking how I enjoyed working for the company. I bullshitted as best I could, not bothering too much about what I was saying as he had no intention of employing me again, and watched the next booth without letting on I was doing so. The men were nervous, often glancing my way as if checking on my apparent ignorance of their plan. I should have known they'd wait until their women had been dismissed for the night.

Billy was nowhere to be seen. I noticed Jameel slumping in the booth, his hands hidden beneath the table, his head thrown back, and a grin a mile wide on his lips. His mates were watching him nervously, but enviously. Something bumped the underside of their table, followed by the distinct sounds of gagging. Jameel suddenly opened his eyes, staring straight at me, totally unembarrassed, his lips parted in a silent groan and his body juddered almost imperceptibly. Suddenly Billy appeared from under the table and handed Jameel his spoon. 'Thanks, Billy. Great service. I'll have to recommend this place to a couple of buddies of mine."

Billy glanced at me sheepishly. "Great. We need all the business we can get."

"Oh, they'll give you the business all right." Jameel looked at me. "Billy has certainly spiced up this place, Steve."

"Yeah, I'm proud of him," I replied.

"Really. Surprised to hear you say that, man," he said, "Why's that?"

"Just thinking that all the servicing he's doing here, can't leave much time for you."

Billy looked as if he was pleading with me not to cause any trouble.

Just then, Fadi's spoon slipped to the floor.

"Ah, Billy, you mind, mate? It's easier for you."

"Sure," Billy glanced at me, guilt all over his features, and then bobbed under the table.

Jameel dug the knife in. "Billy sure is eager to please, Steve. A regular little service whore."

Fadi didn't last long. He gave a loud gasp that had people on the dance floor turn in his direction, before he sort of collapsed in a heap.

Billy duly scrambled out from under the table and handed the spoon to him.

Omar didn't even bother disguising what was going on, just tossing his spoon in the air. It landed on the edge of the table. "Hey, Billy," Omar said. "Spoon." Billy looked at it. I could tell he was agonising over whether he should keep up the charade and knock it onto the floor or just slip under the table and blow his tormentor. He looked at me, guilty as hell, saw how disappointed I was that he would humiliate the two of us by sucking off my sworn enemies in public, then got on with the task at hand, leaving the spoon where it lay.

Gil had given up any pretence of trying to keep me occupied and away from what was occurring in the adjacent dining booth. Indeed he was obviously eager to join in. His trousers were bulging and his breathing was shallow.

While Omar made little peeping noises every time Billy obviously sank down on his prick, Jameel called across to Gil. "You weren't wrong mate, about Billy's mouth. Pure velvet, though it'll be slimy velvet by the time the night's over. I'm sure gonna go for seconds.

"In your dreams," I said standing up ready to take them on.

Jameel smiled evilly. "I suggest you sit down, Steve. It's not a case of what you want any more. It's what we want. What Billy wants."

"He doesn't want this!" Even as the words left my mouth I knew I was wrong.

"Why don't we ask him then?" Jameel suggested. As if on cue, Billy bobbed up from beneath the table. "Go ahead. Ask him."

My heart sank. Billy was still licking his lips and swallowing. I couldn't do it. I knew what his answer would be.

Jameel spoke for me. "Hey Billy boy, Steve wants to know if you enjoy sucking Arab cock?"

"What's not to like?" It was a half answer, even Jameel could see through that ruse.

Jameel said, "I didn't hear you, Billy. What was that answer you gave?"

"I love Arab cock. I'm gonna suck it all night until your balls are empty." He was so embarrassed he disappeared under the table without waiting for instruction. It wasn't until Wazir gave a little start that we knew who the next subject of his oral ministrations was to be.

Our little corner was attracting more and more unwanted attention so that even Jameel was becoming concerned. It wouldn't do for other partygoers to report back to his fiancée. "Is there any way of dimming the lights along this wall so it's not so obvious what's up?"

I couldn't help the sarcasm. "I thought the whole idea was to make my humiliation as public as possible."

"But not ours," Jameel said. He made no further comment. He didn't need to.

I slid out of the booth, went to the power board next to the maitre d's desk and dimmed the lights along the one wall. They hadn't been bright to begin with, unlike on the dance floor. I toyed with the idea of walking out, leaving Billy to his fate, pleasurable as it would be to him. But I had to see it through. When I got back, Wazir was buckling up and Hakeem was thrashing about gasping.

"Ah, much better," Jameel said about the lighting. "It brings out the slut in Billy's features."

He beckoned to someone on the other side of the room. Tommy, the union rep who'd been less than helpful to me, ambled over.

"Join us," Jameel suggested, moving along the vinyl seat to make room. Tommy squeezed his large frame into the space. "I think Steve's mate Billy, the guy who runs this restaurant, wants to thank you for your personal intervention in Steve's little problems on the site."

Kareem must have exploded at that point as he gasped out a few words in Persian.

"Ah, that sort of thanks. Well, he can be my guest. I heard the rumours. I didn't believe them but I've been watching you guys and... Holy fuck!"

Tommy didn't even attempt to keep up his end of the conversation as Billy obviously sucked his dick; instead he gripped the table and grunted. He didn't last long. He was the most vocal of the lot of them. No one took much notice because Tommy was noted for his bluster. When he sank back into the padded bench Billy crawled out from under the table. He had a string of spunk across his cheek.

"I think you better clean him up, Steve."

I got a tissue out of my pocket.

"Nah, too easy. How about you lick it off, eh?"

The idea of eating the repulsive Tommy's come off my boyfriend's fucked face for some inexplicable reason turned me on. I pulled Billy's toward me, running my tongue along the slime path on his cheek until I'd suctioned it all up. Rolling it around in my mouth, allowing everyone to see what I was doing, I swallowed.

"You faggots really are nasty fuckers," Jameel shuddered, although I saw him adjust his crotch.

"If you'll excuse me," Billy said forlornly, "I'm needed back in the kitchen."

"Oi, Billy. What about our boss?" When Billy looked confused, Jameel added, "Gil. You haven't taken care of Gil."

It was my turn. "He's already been there, done that," I said.

Jameel didn't turn a hair. "Well, he can do it again." He snapped his fingers, Billy fell to his knees. I felt him brush against me under the table. Gil appeared embarrassed. He was seated right next to me while my boyfriend sucked his cock. It must have been a daunting prospect, but once Billy wrapped his lips around his cock, Gil lost all reticence.

"Oh, fuck, Billy, yours is the best mouth I ever had round my dick. I missed that mouth, Billy. Suck me, slut!"

The others crowded around to watch my reaction. I sat frozen with humiliation, not by Billy sucking cock in public, he'd done that often enough before, but by the fact I was hard from watching him suck my worst enemies, especially the gross union rep, Tommy. As I'd swallowed Tommy's putrid slime from Billy's cheek, I'd come in my own trousers. But still I was hard. Billy squeezed my leg as he worked his magic on Gil's cock, I could hear the saliva as Gil pushed into Billy's mouth. I lifted up the flap of the tablecloth. Billy had unzipped me and was stroking my slimy prick. He looked up at me, Gil's cock buried to the hilt in his throat, his eyes begging for forgiveness at the same time questioning why I was hard and slick with ejaculation.

Gil grabbed my arm as he shot into Billy's mouth. I shoved him away, dislodging Billy from his cock in the process. Gobs of come shot over Billy's apron before he could get his mouth back where it belonged. When he stood up again, he had Gil's juice dripping all over his chef's hat pin. Without looking at any of us, he strode off to the kitchen.

The crowd was thinning out by now; only the most devoted dancers were still on the floor, most had wandered off into groups or were getting their coats for the journey home. Gideon came back from congratulating the kitchen staff, telling us Billy would be out shortly. I was thankful Gideon was here because he wouldn't allow the shit that had been going down previously to reoccur and ruin his restaurant's reputation.

"I've got some great news about the restaurant," Gideon said, after he'd silenced the rowdy group by tapping a spoon against his wine glass. That was the signal for a waiter to enter with champagne flutes for all, followed by Billy with bottles of what looked like expensive French champagne. The remaining twenty or so revellers watched us with envy. Billy dismissed the waiter, sending him home, volunteering that he'd tidy up. He filled the glasses of the non-drinkers with Edenvale cuvée, a non-alcoholic bubbling wine. He let Jameel examine the label before he consented to drink. Even after what they'd done to him, he wasn't about to play tricks on them. The other bottle was the imported French variety.

Gideon proposed a toast. "To Billy, and the great job he did tonight."

There was a loud guffaw from most around the tables, before they repeated "To Billy, and the great blow job he did tonight," much to Gideon's consternation.

There was no room in my booth for Billy so he was forced into Jameel's. Wanting to speak to Gideon he kneeled on the banquette and leaned over the ledge between the booths. Simultaneously, Omar stood up to get past Billy to go to the men's room.

"I'm bursting," he declared. "Hey, Billy, move that sweet ass of yours so I can get to the men's otherwise there might be an accident."

What happened next was so quick it was hard to tell if it was deliberate or not. In moving aside to let Omar through, Billy dislodged the champagne, splattering it all over his trousers, thoroughly soaking them.

"Oh, shit, man. I'm so sorry. Here, let me." Omar grabbed a few paper napkins, attempting to mop up the liquid, but making it worse.

"Aw, shit, Billy, take your pants off and I'll wash them while I'm in the men's room and dry them under that hand machine."

"Thanks, man," Billy said. "But I can do that."

"Hey, no problem, dude. You haven't spent any time with Steve tonight so this is a great opportunity."

"Yeah, I guess," he said.

"It's all settled then," Jameel said, fumbling with Billy's belt. He had his trousers down round his ankles before Billy could object. "Aw, man, your nice jockey's are soaked through as well. Here, we'll get them done at the same time."

Billy was still kneeling, now butt naked. "Just as well I'm wearing my apron," he laughed.

"It's not covering your ass." I gritted my teeth because I knew I was playing into their hands.

"No problem, Steve," Jameel said. "I'll just stand here behind Billy until Omar gets back with his nice dry clothes."

Because of the narrow space between the seating and the table, Jameel was pressed right up against Billy's ass, but he was correct, no one could see his naked butt. Billy listened while Gideon went on at length about the huge success the night was and how it was only through Billy's perseverance the eatery had stayed open as long as it had. It sounded more like a wake than a testimonial.

I heard the sound of metal teeth unzipping just before I saw the startled look on Billy's face. Jameel was gripping Billy tightly around the waist and rocking back and forth against him. He obviously had his cock buried to the hilt up Billy's ass.

Wedged against the back of the seat, his ass vulnerable to anyone who stood behind him, Billy's face clouded in anger. He could get hurt if he didn't relax. I handed him another champagne and clinked glasses, looking him in the eye as I said, "Here's to the future, come what may." He got my drift and smiled. If Billy was not enjoying being degraded, there had to be a reason. In my toast I was telling him I forgave him, that he might as well enjoy it. He guzzled the drink straight down and asked for another which I gave him. He raised the glass and shouted "Come one, come all!"

The sound attracted the attention of the company CEO who came over to the group. Jameel was obviously too close to orgasm to stop.

"There you are Billy; I've been looking for you everywhere. I want to thank you for a wonderful—"

He was interrupted by Jameel, unable to control himself. "Shit, fuck. Oh. Sweet ass. Sweet fuckin' ass."

"What's going on here?" the CEO demanded.

Omar took that moment to return.

"Where's Billy's trousers?" I demanded.

"I'm such a dipshit; I left them in the men's room."

I growled as I pushed my way out of the booth. I would get them myself and I'd drag Billy home. Clean up could wait until tomorrow. As I stormed off, I heard the CEO say, "I want a piece of that. Hold on, while I get someone to drive the wife home."

I slammed the men's room door open but there were no trousers to be seen anywhere. "Hey," I called, "Where did you put them?"

I heard the door click shut and knew it had been a trap. I banged on the door and yelled but the toilets were so far away from the dance area no one would hear me. I would be stuck until someone needed to use the facilities and unlocked the door from the outside. Or I would have if I hadn't taken the precaution of getting duplicate keys to all doors in the restaurant. Okay, so I'm paranoid when it comes to Billy. But hey, they came in handy.

I banged on the door, screamed, "Let me out you bastards!" I waited for a reaction. None! I was hoping they wouldn't leave anyone posted at the door, that they'd all be too keen to get their cocks into Billy. Nervously, I unlocked the door from the inside, grateful they hadn't left the key in the outside lock. I opened it a sliver but there was no guard. I slipped out into the shadows at the back of the establishment, scrambled under one long table that went almost to the dance floor, the cloth draped over the edges keeping me hidden from view. I crawled as fast as I dared until I reached the limit. There were two smaller tables in front of me; Jameel was dragging one of them on to the dance floor, stripping it off in preparation for a sacrifice.

I heard the CEO wishing people a good night and then the front door slammed shut and bolts drawn. He strode back to Billy who was being handed a rather full glass of champagne.

"To the party of the year," the CEO declared and they all raised their glasses. Billy was the only one to quaff his in one gulp.

"Which has only just started to get interesting," Gil added and they drank again, Billy taking a second equally large draft.

"Where's the boyfriend?" the CEO asked.

"Locked in the lavatory." Jameel said.

"Good. Fucking troublemaker." The CEO slapped his hands together. "Let's get this show on the road."

By lying on my stomach I could peek out from under the hem of the tablecloth without being seen. Everyone was visible from their chest down.

"Gentlemen, the sacrifice," the CEO said.

Two of them grabbed Billy and began to yank his shirt off. They were in a hurry and took no care. Billy was slightly under the weather but struggled. The CEO who had been removing his trousers slapped Billy hard across the face. "It won't do to struggle, my pretty. I will have your ass." He pushed Billy, now totally naked, face down across the table, telling two of the others to hold his arms. He began to slap Billy's butt cheeks, the sounds echoing off the walls. Billy yelled but his cries became whimpers as he got used to the pain, his ass cheeks reddening. He would be enjoying it by now. He was not one to turn down well executed corporal punishment.

The CEO was sweating, his arms beginning to tire. "Right, let's have him up on the table on his back."

Billy was manhandled so that his legs were held in the air, his asshole vulnerable. The CEO ran his hand across Billy's bright red butt, along the crevice of his ass flicking the hole with his thumb, before squeezing his balls and running a finger up his very erect shaft.

"You like it, Billy?"

Billy nodded.

"Let's see just how much you like it after we've all finished with you. You scared, boy?"

Billy shook his head, the alcohol lulling him into a false sense of security.

The CEO looked around, grabbing a small glass olive oil pourer that had not been removed from one of the adjacent tables, dribbling the contents over Billy's balls and down his ass crack. He prodded his finger into Billy's hot hole before wrapping his oiled hand around his own prick. It was a CEO's cock, well above average, hard, purple and angry. He shoved. Billy bucked against it, even though the drink should have partially anaesthetised him.

"Holy mother of God," the CEO sighed. "Oh, fuck. I've fucked a lot of cunts and asss in my career but this; this is one of the very best. This is vintage ass." He plunged in and out, gasping as he sank in to his balls. "Guys, hold his ass cheeks apart. Yeah, like that." The CEO pulled his cock all the way out, held it level with Billy's hole, then rammed back in again. He battered against the sphincter each and every push, spewing out a litany of expletives that turned the air blue. Billy would be hurting tomorrow. The other guys were in various stages of undress, unabashedly stroking their meat as they watched the battering ram against Billy's anal gate.

"Fuck, Billy. If your asshole is always this hot, and your mouth is as good as they all reckon, then I might have a job for you."

Billy smiled. "Tempting as you make it sound, I already have a job. I couldn't let the boss down. He's been good to me."

"What job is that?" the CEO was panting now.

"Running this restaurant. That was your good news wasn't it, Gideon?"

The CEO roared with laughter. "Is that what you think this little celebration is all about?"

Billy sounded bewildered. "What is it then?"

"I was gonna tell you, Billy. Honest." Gideon sounded apologetic, even though he was stroking his cock in preparation for fucking his chef.

"He sold the restaurant tonight, Billy. That was part of the plan. Gideon used you to get the place looking successful. He always intended selling, but he held out for a higher price. He managed to get it thanks to your skill. The development company was in tonight as our guests and they signed on the dotted line. Gideon convinced them there were a lot more bookings like tonight's. They upped their offer. Gideon signed the place over. They're going to tear it down to make way for a shopping mall which we're going to design and build for them. So you have no job. Though you could earn a good living flat on your back if you weren't so keen to give it away."

Billy struggled but it was useless against all the hands that held him down. "You cunt, Gideon."

"Someone shut his slut mouth," the CEO commanded.

It was Gil did the honours. Billy's head was pulled back sharply over the edge of the table, Gil sinking his cock in deep, cutting off his air so that when he pulled out Billy coughed up phlegm.

"I wish Steve could see the way we're using his slut of a boyfriend. That'd wipe the smirk off his fuckin' superior face." Jameel had a real mean streak.

"No need for that," the CEO said. "He'll see the results of our efforts. His boyfriend covered in our spunk, all over his face and hair, in his eyes, oozing out of his gaping asshole, slicking the lining of his throat. We'll leave him here on the table when we leave. He'll be so fucked no one will want him after we're through with him."

"By the way, Billy," Jameel said, bending close to his face. "We never had any intention of working with Steve again so when I told you that if you sucked us off we'd let him come on board the next job, it may have been a bit of a lie."

The CEO laughed and high fived Jameel.

Billy struggled for all he was worth but to no avail. I should have jumped out from my hiding place and taken them all on, but it would have been useless. Call me a coward if you like but I know who else's ass would have been on the line. I needed to send Billy a message so he could relax, to enjoy as much as possible rather than fight it. I crawled back under the table until I reached the maitre d's desk again. I shuffled through the CDs that were scattered through one of the drawers. It had to be here somewhere because I knew Billy used it late at night when he was cleaning up. It was his favourite.

I found it jammed in its plastic case at the bottom of the pile, and then slipped it into the CD player which I hoisted on to the top of the desk, turning it up loud. Nine Inch Nails blared through the restaurant. I heard a voice call "Who's there?" but by that time I was scurrying back to the toilet to lock myself in. A few seconds later someone knocked on the door. I pounded from my side, "Let me out, you bastards!"

Whoever was checking up on me called out, "He's still locked in."

The music had stopped. I hoped it gave Billy courage.

I left it a while before I unlocked the door to step out into the restaurant, now eerily quiet except for the grunts and groans from the dance floor. "Open up, Billy, I don't want to have to hurt you."

Sneaking back to the CD player I took note of the track before I clambered back under the table. Using the remote control I fast forwarded the CD to the anthemic track then pressed play. I moved quietly back to my position. The CEO was having a problem keeping his cock in Billy's ass; the consensual fuck had turned to non. Billy was cursing his tormentors until the CEO backhanded him across the mouth. In the pause, waiting for his reaction, Billy's brain must have registered the music.

"Go and turn that shit off. Pull the plug out of the wall if you have to," the CEO blustered.

Suddenly Billy's ass was backing up, wedging the cock tight inside him. He clenched as he mouthed the words in time to the CD: "I want to fuck you like an animal!"

"That's more like it, Billy. Glad we see eye to eye."

The music stopped and Billy flopped back on the table limp. The CEO fucked his unresponsive body. Hoping they hadn't unplugged the system totally, I pressed the remote control. The song started up again, Billy snapped back to 'life' grinding his ass against the CEO's balls. "You like this song, Billy? Is that it? It turns you on?"

"Fuck, yeah." For emphasis Billy grabbed the nearest cock and sank his mouth around it.

"Leave the music on. It's an aphrodisiac for the slut."

I managed to loop the song, its lyrics thrumming in the gang's brains, turning them into sex zombies. I heard the CEO cursing and grunting, as he shot into Billy's hole. "He should be wide open by now, boys. This will really fuck him over."

They lifted Billy off the table and the CEO lay down on his back, his prick still hard. "Okay, lower him onto my cock, facing me. Yeah, that way. So his asshole is at groin level. How's that, Billy?"

"Fuckin' awesome!" he said.

"How would you like my cock every day?"

"Shit, yeah."

"All right, Jameel. You first."

Jameel greased his cock with the olive oil, pressing against Billy's tight full hole, attempting to slide in on top of the CEO's considerable cock. They were really going to open him up, the two largest pricks filling his chute.

Billy screamed as he was double penetrated, Nine Inch Nails spitting out their animal desire, the only thing that kept Billy from collapsing. Eventually Jameel was in as far as he could go, the CEO telling him to begin slowly. "Let the slut get used to it, then we can bang his brains out until he can't stand up."

He must have liked the sound of his own voice because he continued, "Fuck, Billy, your asshole is meant to be double penetrated. You like two cocks up your ass, slut? Feel Jameel's Muslim prick invade your hole. Steve's hole. You want Steve to taste our juice when he eats you out? Taste all the hard cock that's invaded your hole? You can't stop us, Billy. Lie back and enjoy it. Feel the two cocks rubbing together inside your gaping sluthole."

Billy screamed. "Fuck my mancunt!"

"Oh, we will, boy," the CEO said. "No one will want to look at you by the time we've finished. You be like some old two-bit whore who sucks men off in public lavatories for the price of a cup of coffee. You like that idea, boy?"

"Fuck, yeah," Billy moaned. "Make me your cock slut. Feed me all the spooge you got. Drown me in your man juice. Fuck my asshole until it splits wide open."

I love it when Billy talks like this. I had to take my cock out for relief.

Jameel let out a wail as he sank his cock into Billy one last time, obviously blowing his wad. When he pulled out his deflating cock spunk oozed out as well, running down over the CEO's balls.

"Don't waste it, feed it to him."

Jameel scooped it up, feeding it to Billy who sucked the fingers clean.

Gideon lined up behind Billy next, his cock almost as large as Jameel's, and pushed, a little less slowly this time because there was less resistance. As there was as each and every man took his turn in Billy's incredible double penetration.

Billy howled like a banshee as each new cock invaded his guts and his string of obscenities made the gangbang even more charged. Some of the guys lined up for seconds, while others dumped a load in his mouth or over his face.

It was about two hours before they'd all had enough. Two hours that the CEO had kept his cock wedged in Billy's ass. When the last of the fuckers had finished, he flipped him over, ramming his cock hard into the sloppy hole. "My god, you're a magnificent fuck. I hope we can do this again sometime, Billy."

In your dreams, I thought.

While the CEO was grunting to get traction, the others were dressing hurriedly, eager to escape. Billy kept up the pace, milking the embedded cock as best he could with a slack sphincter until the man in his ass shot his final load. The CEO patted Billy on the head. "Tell Steve when you let him out of the toilet where we locked him, not to fuck with us. There's a lot more where this came from. And a lot worse."

He smacked Billy's savagely on the ass, slamming the door on his way out as if to give his threat emphasis.

I crept from my hiding place and buried my face in Billy's butthole, kissing it better, sucking out the cream which was like poison. I swallowed, and then took Billy's face in my hands, kissing him until he came round. He was limp as a rag. I carried him to the car, grabbing his CD and his clothes as we left. It wasn't the first time things had ended like this.

I went back inside to salvage anything of value, including a crate of unopened French champagne. I also trashed the maitre d's desk in an effort to find what I was after. Then we made our way back home, Billy barely conscious. I ran the bath for him, filling it with sweet smelling salts, welcoming him into my arms as we lay together soaking the night's experiences away. I was still hard even after coming twice.

The next morning I listened to our voicemail messages. There was one from my brother who lived five hundred kilometres away begging Billy and me to come and stay with him because his wife was expecting her first child. How's that for serendipity? Billy and I were both unemployed so we had ample time to spare.

Plus, I really wanted to be out of the state when I put the CCTV footage of Billy's gangbang on the net where I just knew it would go viral.

IN THE FAMILY WAY

It was one father of a holiday!

Steve's sister-in-law is about to make him an uncle so he and Billy head to redneck central, the family nest, to help out Steve's patronising brother Ed. But there are ulterior motives at work: Steve's parents want more than anything to split up the relationship and welcome Steve back into the family, while Ed wants Billy to help out a mate – or else!

It was good to get out of the city, and take a break from all the traumas of the past few months. The invitation to 'come home' for the birth of my sister-in-law's first child, making me an uncle, could not have come at a more timely moment, albeit an unexpected overture from my brother, not noted for his affection for me or for Billy. We were rapidly running out of friends, real friends, whose liking for us was not in direct ratio to their liking for Billy's ass. Billy's behaviour had become something of a scandal, and his reputation, well deserved I might add, had catapulted him to the top ten of people you should get to know intimately before you die.

Katie, my younger brother's wife, had a soft spot for me and Billy, accepting us much more readily than my own blood relatives. Ed was dad's favourite. Understandable, I guess, because he was a big fucker, like dad, who followed the old man into the police force, eventually settling for a job with Police Rescue where his career had blossomed. Dad had been happy to spend his years as a general dogsbody cop, basking in the reflected glory of one of his sons – the only one he readily acknowledged. The other one he didn't talk about much. Not the fag son with the way-too-faggy boyfriend who earned his living as a chef. What sort of job was that for a real man? Even my mum was not enamoured of my boyfriend which, apart from the distance between us in kilometres, was the main reason we didn't visit all that often.

Katie was the driving force behind the mini-reconciliation by getting Ed to invite us back for the birth of the newest addition to the family. We would be staying at their house, in the spare bedroom. Together. I had insisted on that as part of the arrangement. The simple reason we were invited, was that Ed is a slob. Never cleans up after himself, has no idea how to cook or clean, nor any of the domestic skills needed for day-to-day living.

In exchange for bed and board, and turning a blind eye to the fact that we were adult consenting fags, we were expected to fetch and carry for him, the job the long-suffering Katie would be unable to perform. She had already warned him that when the baby came home she expected Ed to start pulling his own weight around the house, particularly when it came to domestic chores. His only response to the request was, "In your dreams."

Nothing, it seems, not even a new heir, could deflect him from his daily ritual of keeping the body beautiful. He, of course, looked at it differently. He worked out to keep his body in peak physical condition for those dangerous cliff rescues, crawling through the ruins of earthquakes, and, most importantly, getting kittens out of trees.

He once confided to me in a moment of weakness that trapped pets were the jobs he enjoyed most because "the chicks are always so grateful afterwards."

We took our time driving to the small industrial city they called home now. I had never called that particular city home, but my brother had moved there for the 'lifestyle' – meaning the proximity to the beach, to the rainforest, and a steady supply of choice women to fuck on the sly. My parents had moved to the area a year or so later when dad got a cushy promotion to the local constabulary. He could see out the years till his retirement in relative comfort and far from the life-threatening policing problems of a capital city. I declined to follow their example, preferring the anonymity and larger gene pool from which to choose in a large cosmopolitan city.

"No one in your family likes me so I don't know why I was invited," Billy complained.

"Perhaps they're warming to you," I suggested.

"Mmmm, and pigs might fly, too."

"The invitation was from Ed."

"At Katie's instigation, no doubt."

I sighed. "Look, we've got to make the best of it. Welcome the new baby. Then we're out of there."

"I'm out of there sooner if they treat me like they normally do."

It was true, they treated Billy abominably and I had no great expectations for this trip either, although Ed was very specific about bringing him.

"It's not just you, Billy. They treat me badly as well."

"Why do you let them?"

It was a fair question. I'm not sure I had an answer.

"Habit, I guess. They've always been that way. Dad dotes on Ed. I can't do anything right in his eyes. I'm an abject failure."

Billy snuggled up to me in the front seat. "Not at relationships."

"Any time I was successful at anything, Dad and Ed would try to belittle the achievement, or me. If that didn't work, whatever it was I achieved, they'd try to take it away. Spoil it. Wreck it."

"Didn't your mother try and stop them?"

"She's always played second fiddle to my dad."

"Thank god we're arriving without any great successes or achievements," Billy said.

"Except us."

"And that they could never ruin."

"Doesn't mean they won't try."

We did the trip in a few hours, taking turns at the wheel and stopping regularly for coffee and toilet breaks. Billy was on his best behaviour and I didn't have to rescue him from any embarrassing situations. His libido seemed subdued. Of course, he had scratched the notorious itch recently, very recently, and it lay dormant for the moment.

I may have given the impression in the past that Billy was continually on the lookout for sex. Far from it. Most of the time he was a happy homebody who enjoyed nothing more than a warm cuddle and leisurely lovemaking.

He would break out of his normal routine through boredom, alcohol and drugs, or a misplaced desire to please: everyone else in the world but me. I was grateful for small mercies. The last thing I needed among a decidedly antagonistic family was to have Billy break out, like an attack of measles, especially in a city which was small enough that word would get around.

We had left our apartment in the early hours of the morning to avoid the peak hour traffic and made good progress even allowing for our dawdling, so we pulled up in front of Ed and Katie's mid-morning. Ed and my dad were at their respective jobs so the welcoming committee consisted of Katie and my not-so-welcoming mum.

Katie was all over both of us, or as much as she could being essentially nine months pregnant and ready to drop the sprog any second, let alone any day, while my mother whispered in my ear as she hugged me, "Couldn't you have left him at home?" I gritted my teeth and hissed back, "No. And don't start."

"Hello, mum," Billy said, fully aware he was the subject of our little whispered exchange.

She couldn't let it be. "Why don't you call me Vanessa, it's much friendlier."

If Billy was upset by the fact Katie was encouraged to call her mum but she seemed chagrined if he did likewise, he didn't show it. "Okay, Ness, will do."

One up for Billy. If he wasn't allowed to call her mum, because she didn't want to legitimise our relationship even though we had been together for years, he would use her name, but on his own terms. He would contract it to a diminutive that he knew she detested. This was not an auspicious start to our stay. And we knew worse was to come. There would be pressure to look at real estate in the town because it was 'so much cheaper than where you are' and 'it's a great place to bring up a family.' They never gave up but I'd long ago become inured to their attempt at guilt blackmail.

Katie showed us to the spare bedroom where we dumped our bags, mum wrinkling her nose in distaste that Billy and I were sharing a bed. It wasn't ideal staying in such an antagonistic atmosphere, particularly as Ed is one huge stud who, if anything, has got better looking and better built with age, thanks mainly to his basement gym. I was hoping Billy knew better than to even go there. First, he was a cop who barely tolerated gay men, let alone his own faggot brother. But most of all, he was my brother. That was real barbed wire out of limits.

Something niggled about the invitation. I didn't like it. I had little time to concern myself with it as Ed returned home not long after we'd unpacked and made ourselves comfortable. He seemed genuinely pleased to see us or else was a more consummate actor than I'd given him credit for. We didn't go in for that brotherly rough housing that seems so prevalent in Hollywood movies, instead settling for the brisk handshake and the clap on the shoulder. I must admit he looked one helluva man in his police rescue gear. I could tell Billy was as impressed as I was.

He wandered off to change and returned in shorts and a singlet, telling us this was the time for his exercise regimen and, if we cared to, we could join him in the basement which he'd converted into a gym. I'd heard stories about the Men Only basement. It was where Ed went to chill out, sacrosanct to him and his mates. It was his refuge, particularly after intense or emotionally draining call-outs. I'd never been invited into its hallowed embrace before and took this as an opportunity to have a look. What a disappointment! I'd expected lots of things, including walls adorned with porn calendars and a floor strewn with beer cans and pizza boxes, instead it was a cosy but nondescript room with his gym equipment in the corner farthest from the stairs, a small bar and two old three-seater lounges and an armchair, well used if its flattened seat was anything to go by, positioned in front of a small flat screen TV.

Billy whistled and made a bee-line for the gym.

"Look at all your equipment," Billy gushed.

I stopped myself from snickering at the double entendre by turning it into a cough.

Ed was a little surprised. "You know about weights and shit?"

"Are you kidding?" I said. "He spends every waking moment at the gym. He'd live there if he could."

He looked sceptical, as if the concept of gay gym culture hadn't penetrated this far north. I suppose it was linked in with his belief gay men are effeminate and can't hold a candle to a 'real' man such as himself. They got nattering about training, protein shakes, the best method of crunching or some such, all technical gym shit that bored the proverbial off me. I told them I was going upstairs and was dismissed without even a moment's notice by both as they helped themselves to a beer from the bar fridge. I didn't know which was worse, being stuck with two obsessive gym bunnies in the basement, or my whingeing mum, up top.

Time with Katie and mum won. I sat quietly, listening to women's problems until I'd heard enough about the possibility of complications, and the necessary accessories for any successful child rearing. That got boring quickly and I went to lie down, exhausted from the journey. I must have napped because when I awoke, the house was quiet. I went to the kitchen to get a drink for my dry mouth. Katie was asleep on her bed and mum had gone, probably to pick up my dad from work. It had only been forty minutes or so and Ed and Billy were still in the basement.

I wandered down the stairs and heard them deep in conversation, plus the clink of weights. It was all very generic, the sort of getting-to-know you small talk straight men are famous for, made slightly uncomfortable in this case because only one of the men was straight. I was about to walk in on them when I head Ed attempt a sort of embarrassed back-handed compliment. "I guess with a body like that you must be the man of the relationship."

I had to hand it to Billy, he didn't fudge his reply. "Hell, no. Steve fucks me in the ass every chance he gets. I'm a total bottom. Can't get enough of his cock."

"So you guys are, like, married?"

"Not officially, but if you mean are we in a relationship, you bet!"

"No way would I let some dude stick his wiener in my butt."

Billy sounded unconcerned by Ed's admission. "Not everyone likes cock in their ass, like not everyone wants to stick their dick in a chick."

That seemed to set Ed thinking. "Billy, mate. You mind if I ask you some personal shit?"

"Nah, go right ahead."

"You won't get sore?"

I peaked around the door which was hidden sufficiently that they would not see me. Billy had stripped to his boxers and Ed had been spotting him while he lifted weights.

Billy smirked. "It takes something mighty big to make me sore."

His joke fell on deaf ears. Sexual double entendre was not Ed's strong suit.

"This is, um, strictly private like?"

"That works both ways. Anything I tell you doesn't get back to Steve."

"You guys have secrets?"

"Yeah. I thought all couples did."

"No shit, even fags?"

I thought Billy would tear his throat out for using that word. I was wrong. "Even fags."

Ed leaned in conspiratorially. "I got a mate, real ladies man, wife, three kids, fucks pussy like there's no tomorrow. Had business in the city a few months back. Ended up with an invite to one of them American pumpkin carving thingies."

"You mean Halloween?"

"That's it. The company he works for invited him. He said he didn't realise until he got there, it was all fags. He don't do that shit but the grog was free and there was lots of it and no one made a pass at him..."

He's either butt ugly or he's lying, I thought. From the look on Billy's face, he was thinking something similar.

"This guy is a member of a bowling team me and dad belong to and he was telling us that this gay slut turns up dressed like Tarzan, bugger all on, and, well, you can guess the rest."

I didn't have to guess, I'd seen it firsthand.

"No, tell me what happened."

"Seth, that's our bowling mate, he says this fag couldn't hold his grog and soon he was propositioning everything with a dick which meant everyone at the party. Begging to be fucked, he was. Now, we're used to slags who are ugly as fuck and sloppy to go with it, but he reckons this fag was a real chick magnet, movie star material, with a hot body like he worked out regular."

I couldn't see where this was leading and Billy appeared equally as puzzled.

"He was so fuckin' horny he shoved a bottle up his Khyber Pass to show what he wanted. Well, seems most of the party took the hint and went through him at least once. Seth watched, said he'd never seen anything like it. The guy is begging for more and all the fuckers are raving, really raving about how great his ass is. Now, don't get me wrong, Seth is as straight as they come. Straighter. But with all this fucking and groaning going on around him, and all these dudes giving his ass and his mouth ten out of ten, Seth's getting blue balls. Okay, Seth's let some fags blow him when he's real horny and there's no chicks about, haven't we all? But he's never fucked a bloke in the ass. But he's tempted."

Billy shrugged. "He's only human."

"So, anyway, he gets in line and long story short, he fucks the slut. Says it was the best ass fuck he's ever had, bar none. Better than any chick, better than anything you can name. And Seth would know. He's a connoisseur. Says this fag did things with his ass that he never knew you could do. And he was still tight even after all the cocks that had gone through him."

Billy cut to the chase. "Did he go back for seconds?"

Ed did too. "He wants to."

"What do you mean?"

"Just that. He's become obsessed with this guy's ass. He doesn't want to marry him or anything, but it's all he can talk about. It's driving us nuts. We think he needs a second go at it and that'll help him get over it. What do you think?"

"If the guy's as good as he says, maybe he'll want it even more."

"But he won't be as good the second time, will he?"

"Why not?"

Ed suddenly turned. He dropped the bullshit pose he'd been putting on. "Because if he is, his precious boyfriend might find out about what he does behind his back. Because the slut freak is gonna be terrible sex, on purpose, so we can get our mate back."

Billy's only response was 'Oh."

"You got him so fucked in the head he thinks your ass is better than cunt. How fucked is that? We keep telling him a hole is a hole. Keep it in perspective."

"Wish I could help you out here..."

Ed grabbed him by the neck. "Oh, I think you'll help us out. Otherwise we tell Steve about your extracurricular activity. We let it slip to mum and dad just what a piece of trash you are. We can make your life hell, mate. Got it?"

"I don't think your parents could think worse of me than they already do."

Ed tossed him aside.

"All this new comradeship was to lure me back here to fuck your mate?"

"Yeah," Ed spat, scarcely containing his contempt.

"You want me to be a dud fuck and that's gonna cure him on the spot?"

"That's the plan."

"Ha!"

Ed glared at him.

"That would work if a fuck hole was just a fuck hole. But that's so far from the truth your plan is doomed from the start."

"Oh, yeah? What's so different about your slut hole?"

I shook my head in admiration. Billy had hooked him, turned him around. Got him curious.

"Ask your mate."

"We did."

"And?"

"He said you were a freak of nature. Your ass and your mouth were born to be fucked. And he'd never felt anything like it in his life before. What did you do, drug him or some other sick shit?"

"Look, I don't even know who your mate is. A whole party load of guys went through me."

"Sick fuck."

"Yeah, like you and your mates don't all pile onto any chick who'll open her legs?"

"That's natural."

"I bet you fuck 'em in the butt every chance you get, as well."

"Yeah."

"Well, I just happen to have the best, most fuckable ass, not forgetting my mouth, in the country."

"Who says?"

"Your mate for one."

"So what makes your ass so special?"

That was like a red rag to a bull. Billy had his shorts off and was lying on the bench pulling his butt cheeks apart.

Ed picked up Billy's shorts and flung them at him, fearful that anyone might catch them. "Put them back on. Cover yourself up."

"What? You don't want to inspect the goods before your mate does the dirty."

"I'm no fag."

"We've established that already. But you did ask what makes my hole so special."

While pretending not to look, Ed did in fact cast a glance at Billy's rump.

"Yeah, well, you got muscle in all the right places. It's a good butt. But the hole looks just like any other hole."

"It's like a house, you live on the inside. Well, my ass is the same. Doesn't matter what it looks like on the outside, it's what it feels like once you're inside."

That seemed to make sense to Ed.

"Go on, try it," Billy encouraged.

Hold on a minute, a little voice in my head screamed. This is my homophobic brother you're asking to play with your butthole. Don't even think about going there.

"I told you, I'm no fag."

"I know that, so just use your finger. That'll give you some idea and there's nothing gay about it."

"You sure."

"Of course, I'm sure. In fact it'll help me convert your mate back to normal."

"How?"

"Well, I've never been in my own ass, much as I'd like to try it for myself. So if you can tell me what's so good about it that'll help me bugger it up when your mate has another go." Ed shifted uncomfortably. "Come on, it's to help your mate."

Ed hesitated. "What have I got to do?"

"Lick your fingers till they're all slick and then just push it in my hole and saw it back and forward like it's your cock."

"Won't it hurt?"

"Nah, I'm used to it. Which fingers do you use on Katie?"

Ed held up two fingers.

"Use those then so you've got a comparison."

"I'm only doing this 'cause it'll help Seth." Ed put his fingers in his mouth, slicking them with his spit. He hesitated before he moved his hand toward Billy's butthole. I was fascinated to see if he would follow through because he looked decidedly queasy about the whole thing. He withdrew his hand a number of times, not able to complete the docking.

"Come on, Ed. You said it, it's just a hole."

"Yeah, but it's a guy's butthole."

"Here, line your hand up, close your eyes and just pretend it's some chick's hole you've been wanting to get into. That's it. Feel how silky it is. Yeah, push your fingers in. That's it. Feel it opening up. So tight. So juicy. Now push your fingers in and out."

I couldn't believe it. My brother was fucking Billy's asshole with his fingers.

"Can you feel it, Ed?"

"Fuck, yeah." His breathing was ragged.

Billy went to work on Ed's fingers, muscle milking them like they were the best cock in the world. I could see the concentration in his face, the same look he got when he was working my cock over.

"Oh shit!" Ed panted.

"If that's what it's like on your fingers, now imagine what it would be like on your cock."

Ed must have been imagining because I saw the front of his shorts begin to tent. Realising he had got too carried away, Ed pulled his fingers out roughly.

Billy wasn't about to let up. "Don't forget my mouth."

He saw an opportunity and went for it. Ed, totally confused in such a sexual situation, hesitated and Billy had my brother's shorts down and, by the time he realised he had a faggot attached leech-like to his cock, it was too late, his body had gone into automatic and was thrusting into the warm wet throat desperate to reach orgasm. I couldn't believe that after all my warnings Billy was giving my abhorrent brother a blow job. The surprise on Ed's face revealed he couldn't believe he had a faggot sucking his cock, giving him feelings he didn't know existed.

I watched, totally pissed off that Billy was giving my brother what by rights was mine alone. Okay, it wasn't incest, but it was betrayal of the worst kind. I cursed myself for my indecision and my body's disloyalty for giving me a steaming erection.

Ed wouldn't last long and, sure enough, I soon heard the sort of grunts that indicated he was shooting a load into Billy's mouth. Few people could withstand my boyfriend's technique, once he turned it on you.

I wondered where the situation would go from here. It would be awkward, certainly, violent, perhaps. I could see Billy tense, probably anticipating the same thing. I was ready to step in now. Far too late. I was beating myself up over allowing it to happen. I could have intervened.

As it turned out, mum called down the stairs, "Your dad's here." She left it at that but it was enough for Ed and Billy to scramble back into their clothes, slightly embarrassed in each other's company. Ed grabbed Billy forcefully by the neck, drawing his face close to his own, gritting his teeth. "Not a word to anyone or I'll fuckin' kill you." It did not sound like an idle threat.

He pushed Billy back down on the bench as he strode toward the stairs. "Billy," he paused without turning around. "Tonight. Down here. Midnight. Got it?"

Billy mumbled "Yes," while continuing to dress. I backtracked, running into Ed as I pretended to be coming down the stairs to get them.

"Dad's home," I said, scarcely daring to look him in

the eye, because I could read the contempt he had for me.

He brushed past without saying a word. By the time I got back to the basement, Billy was dressed.

"Have a good time with Ed?" I asked casually.

"Could have been better," Billy replied.

I left it at that, powerless to do otherwise.

Fortunately, my father's overt sneers at my relationship, my faggotry, my everything, in fact, pointing out what a disappointment I was, and pointedly ignoring Billy, even when he directly addressed him, kept my mind off the troubling activity to which I had been witness. Katie was the only one who admonished my dad over his cavalier treatment of us, stressing how glad she was to have help around the house, but Ed told her not to take dad's remarks so seriously, apart from the fact she wasn't blood family so didn't understand. I saw that stung her.

Billy prepared the evening meal, which mum and dad had stayed for, from the ingredients to hand, managing to make something so special it almost made Katie cry at her lack of skill. I could tell even mum was silently impressed, although my dad managed to find fault with so much of it mum had to squeeze his arm because he was making a fool of himself. Subsequently he went off into a huff muttering about nobody being able to make good Aussie tucker any more.

I suppose to dad's mind the fact Billy and I sat there and endured the belittlement meant we were weak, but I didn't want to precipitate a vengeful argument that would wreck the fragile family harmony. It was getting late when dad made a miscalculation. He turned to Billy, smiling. That should have been a dead giveaway. "So, Billy," he said the name as if it belonged to a child of ten, "I hear the fags are demanding the right to get married now."

I gave Billy a warning glare.

"Looks that way," he answered.

You could have cut the tension in the living room with a knife.

"I guess you and my son won't be tying the knot any time soon," dad smirked.

We could have left it hanging, but his statement cried out for a follow up and, after an interminable pause, during which dad looked supremely pleased with himself, Billy sighed and asked, "Why's that?"

"Correct me if I'm wrong," he said, pausing for effect, "but the marriage vows include something about fidelity and honouring your loved one."

My stomach was tied in knots, but Billy seemed quite calm when he said, "I haven't looked at them recently but I'll take your word for it."

"So that makes you," dad was positively crowing with triumph, "a well known sex slut, ineligible for the ceremony."

Even Ed was wary. With good reason. But Billy was not the vindictive type. He laughed loudly, but it rang false to me, and replied, "Someone should have told Tiger Woods then."

That wiped the look of superiority from my dad's face, and my mum, obviously sensing his belligerence, jumped in. "That's enough politics. My old mum always said never discuss politics or religion in company."

Thwarted in his attempt to start an argument which he was sure he'd win, dad turned on her. "Your old mum was a cunt," he spat.

That did it. The night broke up quickly after that. Billy and I said we'd do the washing up, mum suddenly developed a splitting headache and wanted to be taken home, Katie pleaded exhaustion, helped to the bedroom by a concerned Ed who still had time to motion to Billy, miming 'downstairs' and 'midnight' to which Billy nodded. I had my back turned but had seen the communication reflected in the kitchen window.

I was exhausted from the tension during the evening, Billy's betrayal, and his further traitorous behaviour threatened for later that night. I had to think. When we finally flopped into bed, I made a half-hearted play for Billy but was rejected. Staying awake was not an option, even with my mind analysing all that was going on. I woke up with a start around 1am. I was alone in bed. My heart beating fit to burst through my chest, I got up and made my way groggily to the stairs to the basement. At the bottom I made out a single lamp illuminating the lounge. Ed was on top of Billy, pounding roughly into his ass. They were being quiet about it, even though no one would hear a sound upstairs, restraining themselves to grunts and gasps and whispered obscenities.

I had to admire my brother in all his sexual glory; he was a magnificent sight, even though he was ploughing my boyfriend's faithless ass. I felt myself getting turned on and knew it was time to leave. I asked little of Billy and forgave most things, but fucking with my brother was absolutely verboten. He'd crossed the line. I'd have to give the relationship some serious thought. I sneaked back to bed, realising there was no point in breaking up the coupling in the basement, meaning I could at least retain a shred of dignity, and fell fast asleep.

Much as he tried not to, Billy woke me when he crawled back into bed about an hour later, smelling of spunk and sweat. He'd obviously decided a shower was not an option at that time of the night. I mumbled, "What have you been up to?"

"Couldn't sleep," was his perfunctory reply as he turned his back on me. Normally, he would have been naked in bed. I noticed he was wearing his jockeys, in case I was tempted to invade his hole myself and feel the evidence of his treachery. I lay awake for ages thinking it through. The infidelity did not concern me, that was a given with Billy, it was the choice of partner. There was no future to their relationship, it would not be repeated after we left my brother's house, and if they kept silent about it, the repercussions for my humiliation were slight. I fell asleep mulling over these points.

I woke up the next morning having come to no conclusion during the night. Billy seemed keen to avoid being alone with me, spending considerable time chatting with Katie, offering to run errands for her, massage her feet, any task no matter how menial. I spent time trawling the net looking for work, because we would eventually have to return home to pay our mortgage, if for no other reason.

Over the following days, mum dropped in every chance she got to lecture me on my choice of partner. Dad must have filled her in on stories he'd heard, no doubt embellishing for major disgust, although most of Billy's escapades defied embellishment. Dad didn't make an appearance at all, for which I was grateful. Billy deserted the bed each night for a liaison with Ed. I stopped checking after the second night and lay awake until he returned in the early hours of the morning, becoming more and more careless with his sexual hygiene so that on one occasion I went to caress his back and traced my fingers through sticky come that had not yet dried. He also continued to wear his briefs to bed, denying me any conjugal intimacy.

All hell broke loose early Saturday morning, the sounds of frantic activity waking us both. We quickly dressed and rushed downstairs where Ed was helping Katie into the car. Ed asked me to ring mum and dad and get them to meet him at the hospital. I smiled at Katie, wishing her well, reminding her we'd be at the hospital as soon as the baby was born.

The car took off at breakneck speed. I went inside, the aroma of brewing coffee wafting through the open front door. Billy was in the process of making breakfast, my stomach rumbling its assent.

"What have you got planned for today?" I asked.

"I thought I might just relax, swim in the pool. Haven't had a chance to do that since we arrived. You?"

"I was going to lounge around, maybe read a book, or get some sleep. It must be the different bed, but I don't seem to be getting restful sleep here. You look pretty ragged, too."

Billy had his back to me. He stopped what he was doing but did not turn around. Out of nowhere, he said, "Steve. You know I love you, don't you?"

What could I say? If Billy was leading up to a confession I could wait for it, although I had no idea what my reaction would be. I could condemn him with what I'd witnessed. In the end, I settled for "Of course I do."

He seemed to relax, immediately going back to his cooking. I did end up lying out on the sun lounge, topping up my tan, reading while Billy frolicked in the pool. He got bored quickly; splashing me to get my attention, so I dive bombed him causing an enormous splash of water to drench him. Swimming under water I pulled down his Speedos, and bit his cute butt cheeks.

I felt him tense, struggling to pull up his swimming costume. I broke the surface and noticed the reason. My father was standing at the edge of the pool, watching us closely. His face gave away nothing of his feelings. He was still a remarkably handsome man, just fifty years old, kept in good shape by his job and the occasional use of Ed's gym equipment. He still had his hair and, as yet, there were no streaks of grey. He was wearing shorts and a loose shirt.

"I hope the neighbours aren't watching your shenanigans," he said tersely.

"Dad, you know as well as I do, they can't see anything over the boundary fence or through the tall shrubs. Ed planned it that way," I replied.

"Just saying, that's all," dad muttered.

I had a terrible thought. "What's happened?"

"Nothing yet. I've come back to pick up Katie's medication. In the rush she left it behind." He patted his pocket. It was a hot day, so dad sat down fanning himself with his hand. "How about a cold beer before I head back to your mother?"

"Sounds good," Billy said.

I mumbled agreement.

I got out of the pool, dried myself superficially, before settling back down on the sun lounge. Dad brought out three beers and we toasted the health of the, as yet, unborn baby. The beer was bitter, more bitter than I liked usually, but it was cold and that's what counted. Dad sat quietly on the lounge beside me while Billy did laps, rewarding himself with a gulp of beer as he retrieved the can at the shallow end nearest to where I lay.

It was so relaxing in comparison to how most of the week had passed my body began to feel heavy.

"I think I might have a nap. I'll see you later, dad. Let us know how Katie is when you have some news." I pulled down my sunglasses, propping myself up comfortably.

"I'll head back as soon as I finish my beer," he said.

That was the last thing I heard until the loud sounds of horseplay startled me. Someone had jumped in the pool and the spray had spattered across my body, the cool water rousing me. I tried to move but my limbs felt like lead. I could not raise my arms or my legs. I panicked, lest I'd had a stroke. I attempted to cry out but no sound came from my throat.

I could see perfectly clearly, I could hear and feel everything around me, I just couldn't move or speak.

"See, I told you he was asleep," my dad said, chuckling.

I could see them, both leaning on the tiled edge of the pool, directly in front of me.

"Steve! Are you awake?" Billy said loudly enough to rouse someone napping.

"He's dead to the world. I slipped some pills into his beer," dad said, explaining the bitterness I'd tasted as well as the reason my beer had been opened before he handed it to me. "We get lots of drugs down at the station and, well, me and the boys like to experiment. The one I fed Steve will knock him out so he won't remember a thing when he wakes up. Just that he's had a very relaxing sleep. We sometimes use them on chicks, who don't want to come across."

I could see the shock on Billy's face.

"Why would you want to give something like that to Steve?"

Dad moved in behind Billy, pinning him between his arms. Billy tensed.

"Ed told me what the two of you get up to in the basement."

If I hadn't already known what was going on between my brother and Billy I would have been shocked senseless by that statement.

Billy struggled to get away.

"Billy, Billy, Billy." My dad tried to calm him down. "Relax."

"If Steve finds out he'll kill me."

"He won't find out, unless you tell him."

"No chance of that."

Dad's breathing was erratic. He was standing much closer to Billy now, pressing right up against him.

"Ed reckons you've got the hottest ass he's ever sunk his cock in. And a mouth that takes cock like no woman he's ever met."

The pride in Billy's voice when he spoke was unmistakable. "Well, he'd know, he's a connoisseur."

"That boy knows hot ass when he finds it. That's why when Ed says something is hot; I know for sure it's fuckin' hot. And you, Billy, are top of the fuckin' hot pile it seems. I am a bit surprised though that Ed has gone all faggy suddenly."

"I guess he was just horny, that's all, what with Katie not being able to give him any."

"He's always hot for it. Like his old man."

"You're not so old. Plus you're a good-looking guy. You must get a lot on the side, Mr. —."

"Call me Stan. Or dad. Whichever you like."

Billy looked shocked. "I didn't think you liked me."

"Oh, yeah, Billy. I like you. And I really like what you're doing with that ass of yours, rubbing it against my cock."

"Now I know where Steve and Ed get theirs from."

"Steve's got a big one, has he?"

"You bet."

"Does he treat you right, Billy? Look after your needs?"

"Not enough, dad. He's never got enough time or cock for me."

Dad moaned. "That's right, son, grind your ass against my prick. Get me nice and hard. We got a team of guys here, Billy, we live to fuck. I'm sure we could satisfy you."

I could see Billy leaning against the concrete edge of the pool grinding back against dad.

"Oh, baby, you are such a slut."

Billy suddenly disappeared. He must have ducked into the water because I saw a look of surprise on dad's face. He stood motionless for a few minutes before he could no longer contain himself.

"Oh shit! You can take me further down your throat than any chick I know. The guys on the team would love a mouth like yours. A fuck mouth to fill with spunk." Billy broke the surface to gulp in air. "We love to watch a slut swallow us, Billy."

I couldn't believe my dad was coming on to my boyfriend. My dad who hates gays, or so he keeps telling everybody who will listen. Now he was jabbing his cock into my boyfriend's mouth. They had totally forgotten about me it seems, so caught up in their own horniness. It was revolting, gross, and disloyal, that Billy would put out for my dad who constantly belittled me.

Billy came up again for air.

"No more fucking around, son. Bend over."

Dad pushed Billy hard, slamming his face into the tiles and concrete edging the pool. Billy didn't look happy.

"Hey," he shouted. "Quit shoving."

He said it loudly enough that for an instant they must have remembered me. They looked in my direction, and froze.

"Steve." Billy said tentatively. Then slightly louder, "Steve." Then he called a third time.

I wanted to answer, to punch my dad in the face, but my body would not obey any commands.

"See, I told you he was dead to the world. That stuff knocks you out good and proper. I slip it in Ness's hot milk whenever I want to go out tom catting. I know the exact dose to work. I'm always home before she wakes up."

They watched for a few moment's longer but I couldn't budge. Of course, they weren't to know I was awake under my dark glasses.

Dad was getting impatient. "Now get your ass around my cock. Ed tells me you're a slut for cock. Can't get enough, and you fuck like there's gonna be a cock drought tomorrow."

I heard Billy grunt, the sound he makes when someone has a hard part of their body inside his. His hole is the centre of the universe, a black hole his enemies would suggest. Everything in Billy's life is secondary to his ass.

"This is so gross," Billy panted, sounding anything but turned off. "You're Steve's dad."

"That's what makes it so fuckin' nasty. Don't tell me the idea doesn't excite you, Billy, your cock is rock hard."

Billy was fighting him unsuccessfully. "It's just too nasty. If Steve ever found out, our relationship would be history."

Dad got mean. "I don't give a shit about your relationship, you stupid little fag. You're exactly what Steve deserves. A cock slut that everyone's been through. Just like poor stupid Steve to hook up with trash like you. You were born to be used, son, there's no escaping it. You're a slut and we love sluts. They'll do anything for cock. Like you, eh, Billy? Even if it means getting fucked nasty by your boyfriend's dad right in front of him while he's asleep. Makes you feel dirty, eh, son? The fact he could wake up at any moment and catch you? But that's the chance you'll take for nasty cock, isn't it, Billy?"

The cock in his ass and the filthy talk from dad were all the aphrodisiac he needed. Billy was on a high, and for all the reasons dad had listed.

"Wouldn't it be really nasty, son, if I dumped a load of daddy spunk in your ass and you got Steve to eat it out, swallow every drop of it. Eat his daddy's spooge. How hot would that be?"

Billy was squirming. "No way!"

"Yeah, way, fag. Unless you want me to tell your boyfriend what's been going on here. How you made a play for me and Ed. I'll tell his mother and Katie as well. Not only will it ruin your relationship, it'll ruin his standing with the family as well. But if you do what I tell you, then it's our little secret and everything will be okay."

"That's not just nasty, it's perverted."

"And you're hard just thinking about it." Dad was obviously playing with Billy's cock while he fucked his ass. "Face it; we're two sides of the same coin. I want to watch you humiliate my fag son."

"He won't know, so where's the humiliation?"

"You'll know, and you'll feel like a fuckin' tramp. As for him. Oh, I can wait; wait for the day I tell him I fucked his precious little Billy in the cunt."

Billy was moaning like he was in exquisite pain. I had never heard him so turned on.

"You like it dirty and twisted don't you, son?"

"Yes, daddy."

"Make him tell you what it tasted like. Watch him savour it, swirl it around on his tongue."

Billy screamed, "Breed me, daddy! Make me your total ass cunt."

"Fuck, son. Feel me squirt my load deep inside your guts. Take that load. Feel my fuck juice right up inside you."

They both collapsed over the edge of the pool to get their breath back. Then dad hoisted Billy onto the concrete. "Go on, do it."

I could see Billy take tentative steps toward me. I was revolted at what he was about to do. I wanted to scream but I couldn't move. Dad got out of the pool to join him. He pulled my head back so Billy could squat his asshole over my face, pressing it to my lips. Dad held my mouth open with his thumbs. I wanted to bite them off but had no power.

"I want to see everything, Billy," dad said. "My spunk oozing out of your asshole into my son's mouth. Rub it into his face; make him swallow that perverted slime."

I prayed I would sink into unconsciousness so I wouldn't be awake for this humiliation but it wasn't to be. The slime began as a dribble then cascaded onto my tongue. I tasted my dad's spooge and swallowed as fast as I could to blot it from my memory. My dad was hard again, but he looked at his watch, shaking his head.

"Would have loved another go, but gotta get back to the hospital." He patted Billy on the butt. "Save yourself for the big night."

"What big night?"

"When Ed's baby is born. There'll be champagne and cigars and lots of Billy butt fucking."

"What if I don't want to?"

"But you do. It's written all over your face. You're panting for it."

Sadly, it was true. Billy was already looking forward to it.

"And Steve?"

"He can join in if he wants. Otherwise, there's my little herbal remedy."

"What if he finds out?"

"You gonna tell him, Billy. I sure won't."

My mouth tasted of dadspunk, my body refused to obey me, and I just wanted to die. I was not about to get my wish but it was about forty-five minutes before I could get feeling back into my limbs. I cursed my luck that my cock was the one extremity that came back harder and brighter than ever. Billy saw it bulging in my shorts.

"Steve?"

I had to clear my throat a few times before I could speak. Billy rushed off to get me some water. When he returned he held the glass to my lips, then squeezed his fingers around my erection. "Someone must have been having a good dream," he smiled. "Hope it was about me."

"That hard on is all about you," I said truthfully.

He sat in my lap.

"What did you and dad get up to while I was asleep."

"He was showing me how to improve my technique," he said.

"I thought he would have liked your technique just the way it is."

He looked concerned. "What do you mean?"

"Just a very weak joke," I replied.

I couldn't stand him touching me, so I stood up, still a little woozy, and headed for the shower, where I wanted to wash the last few hours from my body if not my memory. I knew better than to bring up what I'd seem straight away. I was too raw and likely to make matters worse. I'd bide my time.

The rest of the afternoon and evening were strained. We generally avoided each other as much as possible, Billy spending an inordinate amount of time in Ed's basement. That, at least, gave me the run of the house. That night after watching one of Ed's numerous action adventure movies on DVD starring Dolph Lundgren, to whom we'd both usually jerk off, we went to bed, both wearing our briefs. About 3am there were sounds of activity in the kitchen. Billy, as usual, was gone, but I doubted he and Ed would be fucking so brazenly. Still I tiptoed down the stairs. I heard Ed whispering to Billy. "Some of the guys will be over tonight to celebrate. You know; cigars and that shit. Just a small group. They know what's going down. Two of the guys pulled out. Not interested, so there'll be five of us."

"Only five?" Billy said.

Ed laughed. "We gotta get rid of Steve somehow."

"Dad said he'd use the pills again," Billy said.

"I guess that'll work. You said Steve's not suspicious at all."

"He's been acting a bit odd but I think that has to do with the strain he's under."

"Come here, you," Ed said.

I peeked around the door and saw Billy bounding to Ed, who took his face in his hand and planted a big sloppy kiss on Billy's lips. I blew in my briefs. I hadn't even realised I was hard. I went back to the bedroom to change. Billy came up a short time later.

"I thought I heard voices," I said.

Billy yawned. "Ed is back. Katie had the baby about an hour ago. He's come home to get some sleep and he'll go back to the hospital tomorrow. Big day for him. He's got his mates coming over tomorrow evening to celebrate. I said I'd cater."

"That's good, love. Glad you're getting on so well with the family."

I pulled the blankets up around my chin and hugged myself, fearful I might cry.

We spent the next day visiting the hospital in the morning where the proud mum showed off the little bundle that was my nephew. Billy was careful not to claim any familial link to the child lest he raise the ire of my mum and dad. Dad treated us both worse than he had before. Even though he'd enjoy the hospitality of Billy's butthole, it did not leaven his homophobic outbursts. I wondered at Billy's pride in allowing the man to fuck him and then take his abuse. We only stayed an hour before driving back to Ed's place to begin preparations for the booze up later that evening.

While I ferried alcohol and groceries for Billy's catering back from the mall, he was cleaning the basement so that it sparkled like never before. Happy with the results he set about prepping the ingredients for the snacks. He'd gone to a lot of trouble to make it special, so special I was jealous. I told him so. He rather flippant reply pleased me not at all, "Well, when you have a baby, I'll do a special party for you, too."

His casual attitude steamed me up and I'm afraid I snapped back, "If I have a baby with you there's no way we'd be able to tell who the real father is."

He looked at me strangely but, because he was so preoccupied, he shrugged and went on with his work. By the time the first guests arrived, there was enough snacks and booze to feed an army. Billy had already volunteered to play cater waiter and, as I knew no one at the party, I volunteered to do the bar. I was heavy handed with the drinks because I thought if I got them pissed enough, their planned excursion into Billy might falter. But these guys could hold their liquor.

There were about twenty to thirty people coming and going in the first few hours but as it got later, because people had to work the next day, something Ed had no intention of doing, the crowd thinned. I did notice the occasional pat or squeeze to Billy's butt, not always by the men. Billy and I were never introduced as a couple, when Ed bothered to introduce us at all.

I was introduced to Seth, the guy so totally addicted to Billy's ass after sampling it at the Halloween party, he'd threatened to give up cunt, but I didn't remember him. Ed took him over to Billy whose face lit up as if in recognition. It was a good performance because Billy had little or no recollection of that particular night.

I was still without a plan of action. I wished I'd been able to get my hands on the powder that dad had used on me. I'd have no hesitation in knocking out the entire party if I could. I avoided drinking anything I hadn't opened myself in a new bottle or can. I thought it strange that dad made no effort to come near me, except to replenish his drinks. He was boozing hard, I suppose because he was now a grandfather.

Billy brought me a plate of sandwiches which I kept under the counter where no one could interfere with them. The evening passed noisily but uneventfully. About 11pm there were only a handful of guests remaining. I began to carry the empties out to the garbage so there would be less to clear up in the morning. As I leaned over to pick up a bottle or two I felt very dizzy. I grasped the bar, but fell on my ass on the floor.

People surrounded me, making no attempt to pick me up. I heard voices as if from the end of a tunnel.

"Looks like it's finally working," someone said.

"Took long enough," said another.

Dad looked me over. "Takes longer to work in food. Much faster in alcohol."

The fuckin' sandwiches. Billy was in on it.

It was his face down at my level that I saw next. "How you feeling, love?"

I felt my mouth open and close like a goldfish but no sound came out. Then my head fell forward.

I heard Ed say, "Dump him in the bedroom then we can get this party started."

I was manhandled toward the stairs when Billy intervened, "Better idea. Makes it much more exciting. Prop him up in that armchair over there so he's watching the whole thing."

"Sick," Ed said, but I could tell from his voice he liked the idea.

I was manhandled across the room and unceremoniously dumped in the arm chair.

"Yeah, like that," Billy said from what sounded like the bottom of a barrel. "Ugh, put his sunglasses on. I don't want to see his eyes staring at me."

That was the last thing I heard until I woke up I don't know how much later. My head felt fuzzy. They'd set me up as if I were some royal character watching his minions perform for him.

Billy was still serving food to the half dozen people remaining - except he was now butt naked. He finds it hard enough to keep his clothes on at the best of times, let alone the worst of times, like this.

The guys were standing around drinking and smoking foul smelling cigars. No Cubans these.

Seth was nervous. I guess he wondered if he'd oversold Billy's expertise. He wasn't to know my dad and Ed had already sampled the goods, finding them very much to their liking.

Ed encouraged him. "Go on, Seth. What are you waiting for?"

"I don't know if I can do faggot stuff in front of you guys."

"That is one hot ass, eh, dad?"

Dad winked. "Better than hot."

Seth looked from Ed to dad, saw them grinning, and got the picture. "You bastards. You tested him out, didn't you?"

"After the wrap you gave him, there was no way we couldn't," Ed said.

"You fuckers. Now he's spoilt goods." Seth didn't sound as if he were serious.

"Like you care," Ed laughed.

"Come here, baby," Seth ordered Billy. "Get down on your knees." He obeyed instantly. "Look at that mouth." So saying, Seth hooked his thumb in Billy's mouth forcing it wide open. "Fuck, look at those lips. That fuckin' hot throat."

They had all gathered around the victim.

"I'd rather look at his tight ass," dad said. "It was born to be fucked."

"How long we got here?" Seth enquired.

"As long as it takes," dad told him. "We want to bust his asshole so his faggot boyfriend won't ever fuck him again."

"We hate the fucker," Ed sneered.

"Hey," Billy objected from the floor.

"Shut it, freak," Ed commanded.

Billy did as he was told. There was no way he would be able to control the situation so the best move was to go with it. That must have been Billy's strategy, though why he said what he did next was beyond my comprehension. Perhaps it was the drugs in my system fogging my brain.

"You guys gonna stand around all night talkin' about it like women or are you gonna bust my cunt like you said?"

Dad's voice was poisonous with ridicule. "Listen to the freak. As if he has a say in the matter."

"You think you can take us all on, Billy," a guy called Tim asked. "We've had some of the best sluts in the country and they can't stand up after we've teamed them."

"I can vouch for him," Seth said. "He can take on an army and still beg for more."

"I hear lots of braggin' but don't feel no taggin'," Billy was being deliberately provocative.

Oscar, who had been quietly listening stepped up to the plate and unzipped, hauling out his meat, thrusting it in Billy's greedy face.

"About fuckin' time," Billy said before gulping Oscar's entire prick down his throat in one go.

"Holy shittin' fuck," Oscar screamed.

I thought for a moment Billy had bitten his cock off.

Ed was quick to shoosh him. "Hey, tone it down, Oscar. Neighbours."

Seth was looking smug. "Didn't I tell you guys?" He high-fived the other men

"Sorry we didn't believe you mate," Oscar wheezed as Billy kept his mouth around his shaft refusing to relinquish it.

"What if his boyfriend wakes up?" Tim asked.

Dad was adamant. "He won't. Billy fed him enough to knock out an elephant. But if it even remotely looks like he's gonna wake up, I'll feed him another dose."

"Weird the slut wants his boyfriend propped up in the corner like that." Seth said.

Ed shrugged. "Some sort of kinky shit. He likes the idea that the boyfriend could catch him at it."

Tim lowered his voice. "I thought that's what you guy's wanted. Have the boyfriend catch you working him over to split them up."

"Yeah, we will, that's the next step," Ed admitted. "Have him walk in on dad and me double dipping. Double whammy. Totally blows him out of the water that we're fucking his little twinky, plus we get the pleasure of seeing him lose it and throw his boyfriend out. No sense him having a good relationship when we don't."

Tim was impressed. "Cool."

Seth complained to Oscar, "Don't take all day, mate, give others a turn."

Oscar was having none of it. "His ass is free so don't hassle me. I'm gonna facefuck this freak all night. Ride his lips till they split open."

"Does he swallow?" Tim asked.

"Fuck, yeah! He does all sorts of sick shit," Ed admitted.

"Oh, man, like what?" Oscar pleaded.

"He'll lick your ass, drink your piss, eat come off the floor, and shove a bottle up his cunt. I don't think he's got any limits."

"No more, you'll make me come," Oscar said.

"How rough can I treat the whore?" Tim asked.

"Rough as you like, but don't injure him or go leaving permanent marks." I don't know where Ed got off making up the rules.

Billy obviously was unhappy not being the centre of attention. He grabbed the cigar from Oscar's hand, put it in his mouth and drew back on it. Without exhaling, he wrapped his lips around Oscar's prick again.

Oscar shuddered. "Guys, get a load of this."

Billy demonstrated again and, of course, the focus was back on him

They stood in a semi circle, their cocks hanging out of their pants, or else naked from the waist down. Each man had his turn as Billy took a draw on the cigar, and then clamped his lips around the guy's cock while holding the smoke in his mouth.

"Fuck, that feels good. Never thought cigars would come in handy for cocksucking," Tim said.

Seth agreed. "So warm. Shit, Billy, think I'll knock my wife up again just so I can get you to come celebrate with us again."

Dad thought the more dirty and rank he got the more humiliated Billy would feel. It was having the opposite effect. The more humiliating the language the more turned on Billy became. "That's it freak; suck your old man's prick. Never seen one like it have you, son? Big fuckin cock. It's all you're good for, freak. You and your fag boyfriend. We're gonna bust your cunt and throw you out on the street where you belong. Get my faggot son the cure."

I watched as one by one they took turns blowing their load in Billy's mouth or over his face. He was thriving on the attention. He took the abuse and came back for more, ignoring what they were saying in his insatiable pursuit of cock. I doubt he would have noticed or even cared if they said they were going to snuff him out.

I was dumbstruck as Billy ate out Ed's and dad's assholes, then came and plunged his tongue into my mouth. I could taste their funky buttholes on Billy's lips. He repeated it with Tim and Seth, only Oscar refusing the experience.

When it came to Billy's asshole, they jostled for position. Some liked it tight and dry, others wet and sloppy. As they intended doing him over and over there was a chance that everyone would get a sloppy turn. They positioned him every which way: on the floor, over the bar, on the lounge suite, on the gym bench, even on my lap so I could watch in close up, even though they believed I was unconscious. I was sometimes as the drug worked its way through my system but I always awoke to witness some new atrocity being perpetrated on Billy, even though he seemed to welcome the abuse, especially when meted out by my dad.

It was early morning by the clock in the basement by the time they'd all had their last turn at Billy's gaping hole. There can have been little traction left, Billy himself as limp as my paralysed dick, covered in cock snot, saliva and perspiration.

When Ed approached him to help him take a shower, Billy opened his legs in response. "Five not enough for you,

Billy? You need more cock. We'll remember that for next time."

Next time? They were already planning a repeat. Nah, it wasn't gonna happen.

Ed had installed a shower in the basement, because Katie always complained he stank after a workout. They tossed Billy in the stall and turned on the water. While he was scrubbing himself clean they carried me up to the bedroom and lay me on the bed. It would be up to Billy to undress me and pull the blankets over me in an attempt to make it look as if everything was above board.

It was mid-morning before the drug finally wore off and I was in any fit condition to put my plan into action. Billy was asleep in bed, only his asshole showing any sign of the night's activities. I know, because I examined it. I packed our suitcases and carried them out to the car while Ed was at the hospital.

Sure, I could confront Ed and my dad, but that would mean that I knew what they'd done. They would have succeeded in their humiliation of both Billy and myself. Best to leave before they could do any further damage. I carried Billy to the car and lay him on the back seat where he continued to sleep the sleep of the thoroughly fucked. Just before I pulled away from the kerb for the drive home, I rang Ed on his mobile and asked to speak to Katie. I wished her all the best and told her we had to leave because I'd been offered a hugely important job with a major international company, provided I could start before the week was out.

I don't think she believed me but she was also not surprised that I wanted out. The atmosphere was toxic. I was sure that eventually she and her son would also leave the family nest. I assured her she was welcome to come and stay any time she was in our neighbourhood and she said, "I just may take you up on that," before handing the phone to Ed. He didn't take too kindly to our running out, suspecting that Billy may have blabbed. He must have walked out into the hospital corridor to question me further but I kept my voice calm and perky, in keeping with my news and that eventually convinced him of the truth of my story.

I said a quick goodbye to dad, whose voice was as sour as the spunk in Billy's ass, and to mum who complained that she would have to do all the work now that we were deserting the family. I terminated the call quickly after that, issuing the general invitation to pop in any time, knowing full well they all hated the city.

The expressway was flowing freely that Monday midday and I made good progress. We'd be back home before the sun had set. My only problem now was what I would say to Billy when he woke up.

RIGHT UP HIS ALLEY

The team is in town, and Billy wants to be more than just ball boy.

Their relationship at an all-time low, Billy pushes the wrong buttons when Steve's brother and dad turn up with their bowling team and want to take Billy along to the tournament as their mascot. They're none-too-pleased when Steve tags along on the bus trip and stumbles across their real plan, to split up the crumbling relationship. Will he decide Billy is not worth the effort and walk away or will he make one last ditch effort for the man he loves?

Billy was anything but pleased to wake up and find himself in our car driving home. He let me know how less than happy he was by screeching at me for the next few hours telling me in no uncertain terms I could have left him at my brother's place and come back for him on completion of my business, that my sister-in-law needed help, that my family was counting on me, etc. The subtext was that he wanted my dad and my brother to fuck him into oblivion. I wasn't supposed to know that as I'd been drugged, inadequately as it happened and should have been unconscious throughout.

I was obliged to keep up my pretence of an important job interview, otherwise he may have realised I knew of his flagrant infidelity and his lamentation would have risen several notches in an attempt to justify himself. Accusations would fly, taunting cruelty would lead to further estrangement and suddenly our relationship would be on the rocks.

I can tolerate a lot of what Billy does because it excites me. Although Billy is the best fuck this side of Uranus, our life is rather mundane so a little sexy cuckolding, especially if I can witness it, gets us both hard. It's a cat-and-mouse game we both play with expert precision. However, I have to be prepared to forgive unbelievable lapses of taste from my partner.

A lot of people think Billy is shallow. Well, put it this way, if he were a creek, you wouldn't get your feet wet paddling in him. But we have great times together. I'm not sure that in a lover I need an ability to discuss the philosophical ambiguity of existentialism in the works of Jean-Paul Sartre or even the paradoxical chromatic scale of 1970s disco music, but put him in front of a David DeCoteau movie or an interview conducted by Joan Rivers and the man is a minefield of gossip and waspish critical acumen. They say sex is not everything in a relationship, and I agree wholeheartedly, but to think you need to discuss the latest political upheavals in Bhutan is elitist claptrap. Billy and I know where our interests coincide and that's what we talk about around the TV on a cold-winter's night sipping hot chocolate while he plays with my balls.

And Billy has balls in abundance. He would take on the world for me single-handed in an instant, especially if it meant taking the male half of that world up his ass. I just wish it hadn't included my dad and my brother, members of the evil empire who would do everything in their power to bring me down, to humiliate me in my success, beginning with my relationship. Their marriages are cemented but only superficially, the cracks gaping just below the surface.

The next few weeks were a fragile truce although Billy became suddenly secretive about his emails. He would only read them when I was out of the room and would slam his laptop shut if I came in as he was typing. I ignored the provocation but if he thought I hadn't noticed his erection as he typed, he was dreaming. If he thought I didn't notice him disconnect calls on his mobile when I was within earshot, he was in major denial. He was obviously hatching a plan. If it were with men other than those in my immediate family, I would be well pleased, but I suspected they weren't.

That my dad and obnoxious brother were so preoccupied with Billy surprised me, unless they, like so many before them, had fallen prey to his inviting anal canal. I suspected it was a little of that plus a lot of the need for revenge. Fucking Billy was the icing on the cake.

It was confirmed when Billy rushed out one morning, late for a casual job he had in a lunch-time cafe, leaving his laptop logged on. I noticed it flashing on his desk in the spare room. He was always one click shy of shutting it down properly and it was in sleep mode. I wondered briefly if he'd set it up as a trap to see if I would attempt to read his emails. I searched for hidden strands of cotton thread which would break as I opened the lid, or small explosive devices that would shoot green dye or talcum powder over my face as I clicked the keys. I was paranoid, concluding that Billy didn't have the nouse to set up such an elaborate trap. If he wanted to catch me out he would merely leave the laptop open on the table and hide in a cupboard to watch.

The correspondence was not all that revealing except insofar as it confirmed my suspicions it was my dad with whom he was corresponding, with an occasional note from my younger brother, Ed. They were careful to avoid anything incriminating merely bemoaning the fact that he, I was never included, left so abruptly and they hoped to catch up again soon, inviting him to come and stay any time he liked, with or without his current encumbrance - that would be me.

There was an oblique mention of organising a get-together so the fun could take up where it left off. No mention was made of how that would be achieved but I was well prepared when Billy mentioned he'd heard from my dad that the police bowling team was coming to town for the national amateur championships.

I may have jumped the gun. "They're not staying here."

"They're not asking to," he said. I didn't like the condemnatory edge he had to his voice.

"Then what do they want?" I knew there had to be a trap somewhere.

"It's a real honour," Billy squealed with delight. "They want me to be their good luck mascot."

"What exactly does that entail?"

"Apart from attending the games, I don't know."

I had a fair idea of what it involved but I wasn't about to say it out loud.

"I thought you hated bowling."

"Yeah, but it's in support of a good cause," Billy said.

"What, driving a wedge between the two of us,' I sneered.

"There you go again. You can be such a cynic sometimes."

"When it comes to my dad and my brother, I'm a realist."

"Well I found them both real charmers," Billy said. "Maybe you don't know them like I do."

"Thank god for that," I muttered. "I suppose you intend to accept?"

"Why not?"

"What if I ask you not to?" I was becoming whiny.

"Then you'd be disappointed."

"That's what I thought." Pushing my luck, I added. "I suppose a weekend of ten pin bowling to support the family won't be all bad. I can catch up with mum, and Katie's new baby."

"Um, they're not coming. It's just Stan and Ed. And you're not invited. They, um, find your attitude too negative."

I let that one pass. "You'd be home each night, of course."

"Ah, they thought it would be a good idea if I stayed at the hotel with them. Saves all that travel back and forth. It will only be two nights. Not like you'll have a chance to miss me."

They'd planned it right down to the smallest contingency. Billy was to be more than a mascot; he was their after-hours entertainment as well. And there had to be a sting in the tail, meant to bring me down a peg or two. Better yet, something to destroy our relationship. It was rocky enough already, it didn't need much help to finish it off.

Once Billy had emailed his commitment to the enterprise my dad took to ringing and asking to speak to Billy or, as he would whisper down the phone to get my temper flaring, 'that little hot-assed slut you call your boyfriend.' I ignored the bait and merely passed the phone over. Billy took it into the bedroom and closed the door. I could hear laughter and what I thought was groaning. Later, I found a scrunched up tissue pushed under the bed. It was still damp and smelled of Billy's come.

Dad tired of hectoring calls on the landline trying to bait me and began calling Billy direct on his mobile. He liked to time it so that he interrupted our meal, our one sacrosanct alone time. It was another wedging tactic because the first time it happened Billy told him to ring back after dinner. He didn't call back. From then on Billy jumped to attention no matter what time of the day or night he called. It caused numerous arguments between the two of us. Billy was not circumspect enough to keep that to himself and I often heard him repeating the gist of our heated arguments as he went into the bedroom to close the door. Sometimes the phone calls went for hours.

I was stressed anticipating their moves, but in the end I was forced to concede, for my own sanity. Billy could go and I'd be ready to pick up what pieces were left once he returned. Assuming he did.

That would have worked had it not been for an unfortunate accident, a fire at the bowling alley where the tournament was to take place, the largest in the city and the only one capable of handling the logistics of the championships. With three weeks to go it appeared the whole thing was in jeopardy. Billy became a snarling ball of frustration hitting out at every perceived slight, making life so unbearable I was about ready to let them use our living room as a bowling alley if it would bring me a little peace.

I was almost relieved when he received a phone call late one night with what was obviously good news. After a brief call he rushed out to the kitchen and hugged me, something he hadn't done for months.

"The tournament's back on," he said. "They've found a venue that can host but it's out west. They can't cancel the plane tickets so the team is flying in here. A bus will be waiting to drive us to the venue."

I calculated it would be a six-hour plus bus trip, driving all night to get there in time. Billy suddenly became extremely affectionate and led me by the cock into the bedroom where he proceeded to fuck me into the bed with his ass. I made the most of it because there'd been something of a Billy drought for me of late. It did us both a lot of good but I knew there was a price to be paid.

"You wouldn't mind driving me to the airport, would you, on the night they arrive, because they can't divert the bus to pick me up here?"

I didn't much fancy delivering my boy friend into the hands of a gang of men who intended fucking him with scant regard for me, but I had little choice. So, on the night in question I dropped Billy at the terminal to wait for the team's arrival. I parked the car near what seemed most likely to be their bus, confirming it with the driver who was smoking and reading a newspaper in the front seat. I went back to the Arrivals hall to find Billy pacing impatiently but the flight was on time and soon the eight cops, obvious even in their civvies, strode out of the baggage area.

Billy charged forward and I thought he was about to fling his arms around my dad but a severe look stopped him in his tracks. My dad and brother waved to me as the team checked everything was in order. Billy essentially dismissed me without so much as a kiss.

"Haven't you forgotten something?" I said.

He looked angry that I was insisting and gave me a quick peck on the cheek.

"I meant that your bag is in the car. You'll want to collect it unless you intend getting around naked the entire weekend."

Billy turned beet red, indicating that was precisely what he intended. We walked to the car park, me leading the way, while Billy hung back with my dad and the other team members. There was no use making a stand at this point, it would only lead to further ructions in our partnership and maximum humiliation for me.

I retrieved Billy's bag from the car boot, carrying it across to the bus, Billy already on board jumping up and down like a child in the long back seat. I accounted for so little he didn't even bother to check that I stowed his bag. I'd had enough. I was angry. My dad was about to board when I strode over. He barred my way.

"Where are you going?" he asked, none too friendly.

"I'm coming with you," I said.

"There's no room," he lied.

"Yeah, right," I said, roughly shoving him aside.

As I climbed on board, he grabbed my arm, restraining me.

"What about those seats back there?" I asked, pointing to the row in front of Billy.

"That's for our bowling balls. Much too fragile to trust to the luggage compartment. They need a seat of their own."

When it looked as if I wouldn't back down, my dad called one of the other team members who'd stretched out to sleep. "Hey, Bud, can you shift over for my son. He needs a seat."

Dad made his way to the back of the bus and I heard Billy whisper, "What's he doing on board?"

"He's coming with us," dad said.

"Shit!" was Billy's only response.

I remained where I was, fearing a public confrontation if I approached Billy now. The bus nosed through the suburbs until the burble of excited voices waned, the team and its support crew all settling down for the night. They'd need to be as rested as possible for the next morning's Meet and Greet and, of course, the tournament in the afternoon.

The driver turned out the lights. I rested my head to get some sleep but it wasn't long before the sounds of giggling from the back of the vehicle woke me. My brain was on alert. Billy's whispers eventually turned to the sound of gagging, followed by low groans. I surreptitiously leaned over the arm rest to gaze down the bus's darkened aisle. Street lights illuminated the interior briefly as we passed them, enabling me to catch a glimpse of Billy, his mouth suctioned to my dad's prick. Sickened by his treacherous behaviour, none the less I was hard in my jeans.

I dared not watch for long or else they would discover my voyeurism. Timing my glances to the darkest moments in the bus, I witnessed, horrified, Billy seated on dad's lap impaling himself on his cock, riding it like a man possessed. I heard the slurping sound of cock banging Billy's lubed asshole. He'd obviously come prepared. I turned away to stop myself from becoming so angry I would attempt something foolish but the gagging sound of cock in Billy's throat made me look again. One of the team members was standing blocking my view. He obviously had his cock in Billy's craw.

Over the next half hour, different team members took their turn at Billy's mouth, my dad still buried up to his balls in Billy's butt.

I heard loud gasps from dad and then there was total silence. I suspected no one had thought to take care of Billy's needs which meant major frustration for him which, in turn, meant he would be more likely to indulge in dangerous behaviour. I gave it ten minutes before chancing another look. The back seat seemed quiet. Billy had his head resting in my dad's lap, the others having returned to their seats to sleep. I could hear the soft buzz of snoring.

The bus had left the city limits so the halogen lights along the expressway did not illuminate the interior of the bus as they had on suburban streets. I chanced it, creeping along the aisle to the seats where the bowling balls took up space. Moving some of them aside quietly I squeezed in, scrunching low so I was hidden from view, throwing a blanket over myself and lowering my seat back slightly so I could watch anything that went on behind me through the space between the two seats.

The whispering woke me.

"Shit, dad, you think we oughta go through with this? Some of the guys really like Billy and are happy just to fuck him all weekend like we planned. They're not so keen on doing it in front of Steve."

"You want your brother to come out on top?"

I could see Ed thinking about it for a minute. "Nah. I suppose we can always waylay the slut somewhere if we want to use him at a later date."

"No need for that. We'll be using him until his asshole wears out. Anyway, you don't think Steve will want him after we've all dumped in his holes, do you? Filling him full of spooge?"

I saw Ed pull a face.

"But I'll drop a hint he's always welcome to be team mascot. We might even set him up in a cheap flat so we can all drop in any time we want to get our balls drained. I sort of mentioned it, pretending it was a joke, but if we all chip in it would be easy."

"What did he say?" I could see Ed was warming to the idea.

"You know Billy. He just said, 'Wow, that's a dream of mine. My own flat where guys just come in any time and take me.' He got hard at the idea."

"What a whore."

"He already is, son. Steve just doesn't know it yet and I think it behoves us as his family to let him in on the secret."

"Hold him up, dad. I need to drain my balls."

"Try his ass, son. Hardly been touched. Just my spunk inside him. Make it a family affair."

Dad manoeuvred Billy so Ed could slide in behind him on the vacant seat. He pulled Billy's shorts down, had his cock out, spat on it perfunctorily and yanked my yawning boyfriend to his knees before sinking his cock in without any warm up. That woke Billy big time.

"Stop wriggling, slut, you know you want it," Ed whispered.

Dad had his dick out, pushing it in Billy's face.

"Stop fuckin' wriggling." Ed whacked Billy over the back of the head.

"What if Steve catches us?"

"He hasn't so far," dad said. "Anyway, isn't that part of the fun? Getting brother-in-law cock up your ass while your boyfriend is asleep at the front of the bus. Just think about it."

Billy must have and decided he liked the idea because he was soon sucking dad's cock that had been buried up his butt a few hours earlier, pushing back against my brother's prick invading his hole.

My cock oozed its appreciation as I watched through the space between the seats.

They rode him rough and hard, caring little for his comfort, just bludgeoning his holes with their blunt cocks until they spewed inside him.

"Fuck, son," Dad wheezed. "I dunno which I like best, your cunt or your mouth." He shook his prick to dislodge the last drools of spunk, Billy licking them eagerly from his hand.

Ed pulled out slowly. "Shit, I could fuck his ass all night."

"Don't worry, you'll get the chance once we work out what to do with Steve at the hotel," dad said.

"As long as you don't hurt him," Billy said. "That knock-out stuff was great last time."

"We've got something even better lined up this time, Billy. Something special for you."

The sound of that worried me.

"You guys are fuckin' awesome," Billy said. "And to think, if I'd believed Steve I would never have got to meet you."

I heard Ed snicker as he returned to his seat.

I waited patiently, my dick uncomfortably hard at the memory of what it had just seen, until I heard snoring from the back seat and then fumbled my way back to the front of the bus. I didn't wake until we pulled up in front of the hotel in the early hours of the morning.

Not expecting me to tag along, dad had obviously booked a triple room for the three of them, and now had to extemporise. He eventually managed to book two rooms side by side with a connecting door. "Got to have ready access to our mascot," he said, leering at Billy.

The remainder of the night passed peacefully enough, no attempt being made to infiltrate our room from the other side, which meant Billy was so horny he attacked me once we'd gone to bed. There was none of the snuggling and kissing, just raw unfettered fucking as Billy manipulated me to full mast and rammed his ass down on it, grinding in a manner that made me realise just how hungry he was for release. I held him by the waist, for I know how to push his buttons, sinking my prick into his ass canal that squelched with the juice deposits of my dad and brother. I didn't care. I wanted him badly, to show how much he needed me to bring him off.

His eyes shot open in surprise as my cock did the little tricks I use to excite him, he moaned as I put pressure on his balls, and he screamed my name as I poured inside him and his cock shot its load all over my stomach. I knew they would have heard us in their adjoining bedroom and I was well satisfied. Even more so when Billy snuggled against me and muttered, "I love you, Steve," before he fell asleep. Now I could survive anything that my dad decided to throw at me this weekend.

We ate breakfast with the team next morning in the hotel restaurant before they headed off to the welcome party at the venue, a huge barn of a bowling alley across town. I decided to catch up on my sleep – and to search my dad's hotel room. In the end it was to no avail as I found nothing that gave away any plan he might have been fomenting.

I wandered across to the bowling alley in the afternoon to watch the elimination rounds of the competition. Nothing untoward seemed to be taking place except that dad's team would pat Billy's ass for good luck, which it seemed to bring them. I watched from the back of the alleys for a while before making my presence known. Dad attempted to show Billy the finer points of bowling, perhaps far too intimately for my liking, but there was little enough he could do in the open. Billy disappeared to the men's room at one stage, taking an inordinate amount of time in there, smacking his lips as he returned, but as it was not a member of my dad's bowling team he'd serviced I was content.

I stayed to chat for a while but I was obviously a distraction, besides which I was bored, and decided to watch the action through the two-way window in the bar.

I could see the activity on the floor but remain unseen by them, a precaution by management to separate the bar area for the over-18s from the remainder of the child-friendly establishment.

There were a few women hanging about, equally as bored as I was, obviously wives or girlfriends of the other teams' members. Dad and his mates always travelled female free to enable them to get up to all kinds of mischief once away from home. I ordered my favourite Scotch and sat on one of the high stools staring at the men knocking down pins. I felt a presence beside me before he spoke.

"You with one of the teams?" he said.

I turned. He was an average looking Joe with a sportsman's body. The tell-tale bowling team patch adorned his jacket.

I nodded toward my dad's team. "You not playing?"

"Injured my hand this morning," he said. "Stupid accident. Gotta sit the whole weekend out. Could be worse, they could have had no bar."

I commiserated with him. We swapped names. His was Vic.

"That gangbang you guys are throwing tonight. What's the big secret?" Vic asked.

I looked at him.

"Yeah, we're not supposed to know about it, but Stan is promising the best piece of ass ever. Says the slut will take on all comers."

It didn't take much to guess who that was.

I tapped the side of my nose. "Let me tell you, it's no exaggeration."

"Jesus. Stan's parties are always the best so she's gonna be fuckin' sore by the end of the weekend. I hope she's charging heaps."

"I hear the slut does it for love," I said maliciously.

"She's some old scrubber, looks like a gorgon?"

"No way, this slut is gorgeous," I said.

"You're only saying that because Stan's put the price up. Wants to make a killing."

"What's he charging?"

"Two hundred bucks. It sure better be worth it."

"I'll tell you what, Vic. If you're not totally satisfied by the end of the weekend then I'll suck your fuckin' dick, that's how confident I am."

He thumped me on the shoulder good naturedly. "Good enough for me, mate." He took off to tell the other members of his team.

Word must have got around because by eight o'clock that night we had about twenty guests crowding the two rooms. Grog was flowing, libidos were pumping, and the animals were getting impatient. Billy had no idea what he was in for and was prancing around the room, acting as waiter as a favour to dad. He was wearing fuck all except for a copy of the Tarzan loin cloth that had proven so popular at the Halloween party at which our upstairs neighbours had laid a trap to capture Billy's delectable ass, until then decidedly off limits.

Dad's party was exclusively male and rampant at that. To these hormonal sex starved walking pricks even Billy was starting to look good, little realising that he was the surprise. The lights had been lowered, a few of the more brazen men fondling Billy's butt cheeks, a few even going so far as to rub their finger down his crevice, or else rubbing up against him as he served drinks. Dad's team mates, in particular, were champing at the bit having already experienced Billy or having been told of his prowess.

I thought I saw party drugs being passed around, the alcohol was flowing freely and I wondered when dad would attempt to slip me a Mickey Finn. I was on guard but in case he managed to slip it past my guard I was taking the smallest sips possible. So far, nothing!

The music was raucous, the atmosphere heady with testosterone. I could see it was affecting Billy, making him jittery, ready to explode sexually at any moment. I didn't have long to wait. There was a hush as dad ushered this stunning blonde into the room. All attention turned to her. Her tits strained the flimsy t-shirt she almost wore but which had the habit of slipping off her shoulder revealing a nipple. She wore heels that were so outrageous I wondered how she walked without toppling over. Her shorts were so tight they left nothing to the imagination. She was obviously the night's entertainment. I glanced at Billy who looked far from pleased to be upstaged like this.

The crowd hushed so Chelsea could introduce herself and lay down a few rules. She was there for two hours. It didn't take long for most of the participants to calculate that left them with a maximum six minutes to do their business and hop off if they were all to get a turn. A lot of people were going to miss out. Chelsea didn't muck around, peeling off her clothes, before spreading herself over our bed, welcoming all comers. There was a rush for her services.

One of the men who'd been unsuccessful in the crush, complained. "What's this big surprise you told us about, Stan?"

I was still conscious so I wondered about that myself. It couldn't be Billy because I'd be able to intervene unless dad thought I would be too cowardly to interrupt their gangbang. I soon discovered the plan when Ed and a fellow team member named Lonnie sidled up to me. Before I had a chance to react or cry out they gagged me and wrestled me to the floor. No one bothered to look as they were crowded around the door into our room, watching the action on the bed, or else hanging on dad's announcement. They gave me no chance to get free, fastening my wrists in cuffs and locking them in place to the metal radiator. I struggled but apart from making a lot of clanging noise, I was securely fastened.

Dad grabbed Billy, tearing off his loin cloth, pushing him toward the suitcase rack which he'd dragged to the centre of the room. Billy was naked as a jaybird as he kneeled on the wooden rack.

"Show us, Billy," dad said.

There was muttering about 'faggot shit,' but that didn't prevent the men from watching fascinated as dad parted Billy's cheeks to finger his tight butt hole, enabling everyone to see what was on offer. Dad unzipped and hauled out his cock, already hard in anticipation, poising it at Billy's mouth. Billy tongued it lasciviously. They were performing, attempting to sell Billy's expertise. Dad let out with a few expletives, a few 'Jesus,' and an equal number of 'Holy fucks.'

Dad addressed his audience. "You guys know I'm no queer but let me tell you, this slut's asshole and his mouth are superior to anything I've ever had before. Even better than any female whore. If you don't believe me, just try him. He'll be here all weekend. And he'll be wanting cock all that time, I guarantee it."

To show he was as good as his word, dad pulled out of Billy's throat, snapped his fingers and took possession of a syringe that Ed handed him. It had no needle which meant they were about to inject the liquid into Billy's ass.

"This gents is one of the constabulary's highest grade confiscated butt rockets, means Billy, who is nigh on insatiable, will feel no pain as the weekend unfolds but will need a continual feed of cock, in fact will be begging for it like an addict. It's up to you gentlemen, between games, to keep him fulfilled. Let's bust his hole."

The contents of the syringe were squirted into Billy's butt, making him wriggle as it stung the membrane in his bowels. It would produce a meth rush to his brain so his ass and mouth could withstand any pounding the men gave him. I was thankful for the small mercy that Billy would likely as not, remember little of the actual weekend except for the feeling of euphoric sex.

It wasn't long before his eyes dilated and he began moaning, grinding his ass, begging to be fucked. Dad was the first to oblige, staring at me as he inserted his cock, no pretence this time, slamming him mercilessly, genuine in his curses. Dad's position as alpha male meant that if it was good enough for him to stick his cock in Billy's mouth or ass it was sure good enough for those men way down the pecking order who weren't likely to get a go at Chelsea until she'd been run ragged, if at all.

They fucked Billy with total disregard to me. He must have believed they'd already drugged me otherwise he would not have been as eager in his infidelity. Obviously their intention had been to fuck Billy for enjoyment while humiliating me by making me watch his degradation.

Ed took his position at Billy's head and so began the frenzied family fuck of my lover. They didn't care for Billy as a person, just as two fuck holes that brought them maximum pleasure as well as maximum shame to me. I glared defiantly as they high fived while sinking their cocks into a pliant body.

There was no use struggling, it merely made the cuffs eat into my wrists more severely. I couldn't call out because of the gag. My feet were free but, apart from tripping someone up, they were useless. It was best to preserve my strength for later in the weekend when they would have to free me. My one regret was that my cock was hard as granite and I had no way to relieve myself.

I had to give dad credit, he knew exquisite methods of torture. He dragged the rack closer to me now that I was confined, in order that I could watch Billy's penetration in close up. He sank his cock into Billy's hole so that I could watch the sphincter expand and contract as his prick pounded the muscle. Ed grinned as he choked Billy's airway with his prick and I heard every whimper as Billy begged to be fucked like an animal, felt every shudder as their rough treatment battered his drug fucked body, smelled the perspiration from the exertion, and tasted the bitter fruits of defeat.

Dad and Ed finished up and shook the sweat and semen off their cocks across my face as two more took their place. I lost count of the men who took advantage of Billy's yielding nature, many of them taking seconds with his body because there was little chance of a return bout with Chelsea. She was no nonsense about her whole schedule. She wasn't in it for the love like Billy, she was in it for the cash, and at the end of two hours, on the dot, she stopped. I heard one poor fucker complain that he hadn't come yet as she pushed him aside, and got off the bed.

She came naked into the room, her body dripping saliva and sweat, come crusting to her body, her hair a graveyard of dead sperm. It ran down her leg from her well used back passage and her cunt. She approached dad who whispered in her ear before she nodded enthusiastically, a bundle of notes changing hands. She disappeared into the bedroom to re-emerge about ten minutes later still naked except for a large black strap-on dildo.

Chelsea shoved aside the two men who had been working over Billy's holes, determined to have him for herself.

"Here, Billy," she cooed. "Suck my rubber cock, boy. Get it nice and slick for when I stick it up your asshole."

He was too out of it to care it wasn't real, as long he had something filling the void in his bowels he was happy.

He slurped at the black rubber, deep throating it expertly treating it as if it were the real McCoy.

"I'm gonna bury this big black rubber cock up your ass, Billy. Make you beg for it, until your hole bleeds."

Billy was soon screaming to be fucked so Chelsea withdrew from his mouth and buggered the strap-on right into his butt. I saw him struggle as the full impact of the dildo in his chute hit home. The pain passed, as it always does, and Chelsea rode him better than most of the men had. Billy was so far gone he didn't care as long as he had cock, real or rubber, embedded in his body. None of the men had made Billy come as yet but Chelsea was pounding him like an expert and I noticed the tell-tale signs of approaching orgasm as he arched his back, gasped in breath and finally let out those little 'ungh' sounds he always makes. He collapsed against the rack, his spunk dripping onto the carpet.

She pulled out of his butt and unstrapped the apparatus. She sashayed to where his head was resting, not far from me, and pulled her cunt lips apart so he could see pearls of come oozing from her slit.

"You want it, Billy, don't you?" she soothed, her voice seductive and hypnotic. "Real woman's cunt. Eat it, Billy. Lick it out."

Billy has an insatiable hunger for man juice but I knew he would never have sex with a woman, oral or otherwise, to get it. But his eyes were glazed, and he was not in control of his senses. I had reckoned without that.

"Eat it, son," dad encouraged. "Think how Steve would react if he was here now. Think how perverted the whole scene would look to him. He'd feel totally betrayed, wouldn't he, son, if you cheated on him with cunt."

Ed mounted Billy's ass, gently pushing him closer to the oozing pussy with every thrust. I wanted to turn away but it was too compelling to miss. Billy's face moved imperceptibly closer to her cunt. It seemed to fascinate him, like watching a cobra at close quarters. Chelsea opened wider and a glop of spunk dripped out. She caught it on her fingers, rubbing it over Billy's lips. He couldn't help himself, his tongue snaking out to taste the jizz, finally sucking the fingers into his mouth, licking until they were free of all slime.

Dad held a small bottle of poppers under Billy's nose. By the time the buzz hit him Chelsea's cunt was almost in his face. Ed was pushing him subtlety toward the treasure house of spooge, until a second bout of poppers buzzed Billy enough that he tentatively poked out his tongue and, finally, there was contact. He licked the spunk around her cunt, swallowing it hungrily. He looked to dad for approval.

"Taste a real cunt, son," dad whispered. "Lovely cunt hole full of spunk. Daddy's spunk, your brother's juice. Lap it up, son. You love cunt, son. Eat it."

Billy dived right in nuzzling and sucking Chelsea's pussy, suctioning every drop of semen from her. She lay back to give him better access. Billy pulled her lips apart.

"Eat it, son," dad intoned. "Eat her pussy, boy."

She laughed, throwing her head back, then clamped her legs around his head forcing his tongue inside her, Billy oblivious to everything except the spunk-filled hole in front of him.

"Come on, bro," Ed said smugly. "Be a man. Eat her cunt. Eat it. Eat it."

The chant was taken up by a few of the men in the room who were fascinated to watch a gay man eating pussy for the first time.

"Look, boy. Spunk oozing down her thigh. What would Stevie boy say if he saw you eating a whore's runny cunt hole? He'd puke, wouldn't he, son?"

Billy nodded his head, obviously turned on by the idea.

Dad indicated me. "What's say we pretend this bastard over here is Steve. What you say, son?"

"Uh huh" Billy mumbled, glancing in my direction without recognising me.

"Show him how much you like cunt now, Billy. Why don't you fuck her, son? Put your cock inside her, feel how good it is to fuck a real woman, not a faggot."

Dad was jerking off, turned on by the depravity of what he was skilfully controlling. Turning to me, he snarled viciously. "Even your boyfriend prefers pussy to your cock. What do you say to that, loser? Who's the real man in the relationship now?"

Billy kneeled. Chelsea grabbed his cock, milking it a couple of times to get it nice and slippery, then aimed it at her cunt. I watched as his prick slid into her fucked mound. Chelsea cackled in triumph as Billy pumped, screaming "I'm fucking cunt. Look at me, Steve. I've got my cock in her cunt hole."

Dad could take no more. He ripped the gag from my mouth and I was about to protest loudly when he held my nose, forcing me to open my mouth, the signal for him to squirt his spunk inside. Expecting me to spit it on the floor he replaced the gag forcing his daddy sperm down my throat, the ultimate indignity. Although Billy fucked Chelsea like a man possessed, it lasted just moments before he scrunched his face up and withdrew his cock. I thought at first he'd come but his cock had withered, no longer able to penetrate her.

"Come on, son," dad encouraged. "You can do it."

But Billy just sat there shaking his head. It was as if he was actually seeing things clearly for the first time. Then it passed as quickly as it appeared.

Dad led him over to where I was handcuffed.

"If this was Steve, son. What would you do?"

"If this was Steve," he said staring at me as he grabbed a handful of my hair pulling it backwards. I saw no spark of recognition there.

"Fuck you, Steve!" He spat in my face. "Guess what? I just fucked my first cunt. You can still taste it on my prick."

Dad removed the gag quickly. "Make him taste it for himself."

Billy pushed his cock in my direction as I struggled to move my mouth away, but he held my hair until I thought he'd tear it out by the roots. "Open up, Steve, let me feed you my cunt-flavoured prick. You'll love it."

Dad repeated his earlier trick, pinching my nose until I had to open my mouth to breathe again. Billy took that opportunity to slide his cock over my tongue.

"Suck it, Steve. Suck it clean of cunt juice. Taste good, eh?"

He fucked my face, not allowing me to breathe. I gagged, tasting bile as it rose in my throat. Billy had no concern for anything other than his own pleasure. It wasn't long before I tasted his warm salty come as it hit the back of my mouth and slithered down my throat. Dad re-inserted the gag, the men cheering Billy like some triumphal Roman soldier returning from the battlefield.

Chelsea slipped out unnoticed, the men having turned their attention to Billy. Vic, the guy I'd met in the bar, was working him over, giving me the thumbs up that I'd been right all along. They took turns fucking him in the ass and the throat till the early hours of the morning, treating him like a piece of meat with holes in which to dump their loads. I was grateful that Billy's body had been numbed to the abuse it was suffering even while his brain was sending out endorphins of pleasure.

Eventually, they were all fucked out. Ed carried Billy into our room and dumped him, slimy as a snail's trail, on our bed. They uncuffed me and manhandled me into the room, securing me to the bed. I was forced to lay alongside my depleted lover, my cock desperate for relief. Billy woke during the night, horny as buggery, and me being the only cock within arm's length, rode my poor weapon until I thought it would break off with the strain. I came twice while shackled to the bed, still unable to speak because of the gag, and Billy still senseless to my identity.

In the morning they allowed me breakfast and the use of the bathroom before they bound and gagged me again. Billy was confined to the other bedroom. I could hear him through the door, begging for cock. Dad told him to sit tight, that there would be a steady stream of men, the losing teams who would drop in to entertain him. It was my unenviable task to sit listening to him being abused while I could do nothing to prevent it.

In the afternoon, dad and Ed returned with another group of men eager to try the slut they'd heard so much about at the bowling alley that day. They injected another dose of crystal meth into Billy's ass and he became even more rampantly horny than the previous night. With no Chelsea to halve the activity on his body, Billy took them all on and still begged for more.

Dad ensured I got a close-up view as both he and Ed pummelled Billy's fuck holes, taking bucket loads of spunk until I thought he would throw up. At the end of the night there were just the four of us remaining.

Dad was in my face, his mouth contorted in hatred.

"What do you think of your precious boyfriend now? He's just a used cunt hole. Doesn't give a shit whose cock is in his mouth or in his ass. Doesn't care that you're watching him used as a come dump. Doesn't even recognise you. Some love affair eh?"

As if to confirm the diagnosis Billy crawled across the floor toward me, his face dripping with slime, his tongue licking across his lips trying to taste the spunk that was almost drowning him.

"Open up, son."

My dad blew a wad into Billy's mouth and I saw it puddle under his tongue before he swallowed it down.

"Thank you, daddy," Billy said, seconds before keeling over on the floor exhausted.

"There's your bride, son. Filthy, freak slut. Don't say we didn't warn you. Took a real man to show him what a fuck is really all about. Had him begging for a real man's cock, not some faggot dick. And your slut boyfriend prefers cunt to your fuckin' asshole. Your relationship is dead, son. Totally fuckin' dead."

My body ached from its confinement, my mouth dry and chaffed, still they cuffed me to the bed, keeping Billy for their own pleasure for one last night. I heard him begging and whimpering throughout the long hours before morning, as they treated themselves to one last fuck before they packed and left on the team bus. They took the cuffs off me because they were regulation police issue and there would have been hell to pay if they'd gone missing, but I was tied me to the bed with cord found in the linen press in the hotel hallway.

They left Billy in their room, covered with sperm crust and bruises. It was hours later that he staggered into our room, bleary eyed and smelling of the sewer. He was disoriented and it startled him to find me bound and gagged on our bed.

"I made a terrible mistake, Steve."

He fumbled with the knots as he began the litany of begging forgiveness. He wasn't sure what had happened but with the amount of come dribbling from his ass he knew it was major. He also knew that I had witnessed the whole episode and must by now have seen my dad and my brother work him over.

"I'll get help," he sobbed. "Please forgive me. I didn't mean to betray you. Honestly."

I had to remove the gag myself; he seemed too timid in case I attacked him verbally.

I didn't trust myself to address his treachery here and now. It would have to wait.

"Come on, love," I said, prodding Billy toward the bathroom. "Let's get you freshened up, have some breakfast, and find out how to get back home."

GROUP THERAPY

The only cure for his sex addiction is to bang it out of him!

After giving up his body to his brother-in-law as well as his father-in-law and the members of their bowling team in front of his boyfriend Steve, Billy realises he has a problem and sets out to find a cure. But sometimes the cure is worse than the 'disease' as he discovers when he joins the shadowy cult organisation, Gay Sex Addickts Anonymous.

I don't know which was worse, Billy begging forgiveness every five minutes or Billy giving me the best sex I'd ever had in my life. And giving it to me frequently. Much too frequently. Perfection can become very boring indeed. But for sheer fingernails-down-the-chalkboard screechiness, Billy pleading for one more chance is unsurpassed.

"I'm sorry," he sobbed, not for the first time. "I don't know what got into me."

I was withering in my reply. "My dad and my brother for starters."

That set him off wailing even louder. If he kept it up I would be forced to leave him, he was doing my head in.

"Billy!" I snapped to get his attention. "I said I've forgiven you, now give it a rest."

He whimpered. "I'll get help. I won't do it again."

"Don't promise something that's outside your control."

"You're the most important thing in my life," he said, sidling up to me suggestively. "It's just sometimes I forget."

"Then tie a string around your finger so you don't."

Billy held his hand up. "A ring would look better."

I sighed. "We can't afford it. I'm trying my damnedest to make our finances stretch as far as I can. We're both only working part-time; it's a squeeze, Billy."

Billy pouted. "I'll go and work in a factory, that should help."

I shuffled the paperwork aside and held his hands. "No, you're too good a chef to do that and I'd hate for these magic hands of yours to suffer any damage. Don't take any notice of me. I'm just grumpy."

He sank to his knees, a bright smile on his face. "I know just the thing to fix that."

To get any peace, I would have to allow him to have his way for just a few moments. If I make it sound like a chore I don't mean to. He had my trousers and underwear around my ankles in record time, my prick straining in the cool morning air after having been brought to full awakening by Billy's incorrigible mouth. He stripped so expertly I'm sure his clothes are held together with Velcro so he can shuck them quickly. He had lubed his fabulous ass from one of the various tubes and bottles placed strategically around our apartment so he was never more than an arm's length away before I could refuse him.

He squatted on my chair, positioning my prick before jamming himself down on top of me. A small amount of pain made him gasp while I shuddered at the exquisite feeling of his ass muscles stretching to allow me entry.

He squeezed on each upward and each downward thrust so that my cock was held firmly by a sphinctral glove. I had never experienced such anal finesse from any other lover and I wondered how I could ever grow tired of this. But I did sometimes. It must have been a flaw in my character.

This particular morning, though, I went through the motions more easily than on other occasions because Billy hurried as he knew I would be late for work if he prolonged my ecstasy. This was to be a quickie. I massaged his throbbing dick as he ground himself against my groin. I wanted him to come as well otherwise he would be horny all day and get up to all sorts of mischief.

Seems my ruse was not successful because when I came home that evening Billy had, indeed, been up to all sorts of mischief although, surprisingly for him, not of the sexual kind. As the employment agency with which he was registered did not call that morning with a casual job at a restaurant or café, he'd spent the day at the computer and was eager to share his news when I came home.

I feared the worst because he'd plied me with a glass of our best Cabernet Sauvignon from the few remaining bottles in our wine 'cellar', a darkened recess at the bottom of our built-in wardrobe. His behaviour was so devoted I began to suspect he'd not only fucked my dad and brother but had somehow managed to involve my grandparents and my mum as well, so it was with a sense of relief that I accepted the print-outs of his Google search on the net.

He paced nervously as I glanced over them, finding they all had one subject in common – sex addiction. Billy had gone to the trouble of highlighting certain passages in canary yellow so I could follow his thought processes. He was obviously convinced he had an obsession bordering on, if not downright embracing, addiction. I found this self diagnosis somewhat dubious as Billy could go for long periods without seeking sex from strangers even when it was openly presented to him. Granted, occasionally he had an itch that needed scratching, which usually involved numerous cocks in his ass and those usually belonged to pricks who knew me and detested me. Billy could home in on them like a pigeon returning to nest. But sex addiction? I didn't think so.

But how to tell him?

He stopped pacing. "What do you think?"

He was so eager I hesitated to deflate his confidence. He took my silence for acquiescence.

"You won't hurt my feelings, Steve," he said proudly. "I've owned up to my problem and you have no idea how liberating it is. I feel like a new man."

My eyebrow rose at his statement and I couldn't help snickering. He glared at me then realising what he'd said he began to giggle. "If I'm looking for a cure I shouldn't say things like that. People will take it the wrong way."

"Come here, sweetie," I sat, patting my lap.

He put his arms around my neck and I kissed him gently. He was frisky but wanted to discuss his Road to Damascus moment.

"As soon as I read a definition of sex addiction, and all the symptoms, I knew they fit me like a glove," he said seriously. "Who would have thought you can have too much sex?"

"People who aren't getting enough," I said to lighten the mood. "Look, Billy—"

"I know it's expensive..."

I glanced through the sheets of paper again because I hadn't taken the cost on board and, sure enough, he wasn't kidding about cost.

"But in order to get the cure I can do without a few luxuries."

I'm not sure to which luxuries he was referring as we were already close to the bone, unless, of course, he meant eating and paying utility bills.

My answer was totally sincere. "You don't have to do this for me, Billy. I love you just the way you are. Sure you push me too far sometimes, like your latest escapade."

"And I want to make sure it never happens again."

I sighed. There was going to be no deflecting him from his course of action.

I smiled encouragingly, even though my heart sank at yet another screwball plan. "Okay, what's the deal?"

He salvaged one sheet of print-out and tapped it with his finger. It had copious highlights and some indecipherable scribbles in the margin.

"I rang around," Billy said. "Chatted to a few people. After all, I don't want to go into this with my eyes closed. Some of them are only in it for the money."

He took a few sheets from me and crumpled them before tossing them in the bin.

"A few of them are Fundamentalist whackos."

More sheets bit the dust.

"Which leaves us with this one."

With a flourish meant to impress, Billy presented me with a brochure on the cover of which was the smiling face of The Reverend Hedley Buckling, as the caption beneath the picture informed me, proclaiming he could "break the debilitating illness that is sex addiction." All you had to do it seems was turn up at Gay Sex Addickts Anonymous.

"It doesn't say how much it costs to get the cure," I said sarcastically.

Billy grinned from ear to ear. "That's the good news. For me it costs nothing. Zero. Nada. Zilch."

That should have set alarm bells ringing, I thought.

"In case you think I'm stupid, I did check. GAYSAA meets at the Gay Community Centre and they wouldn't allow just anyone to use their premises, now would they?"

Just anyone who had the rent, I thought ungraciously. What I said was, "That's great, Billy. So you're committed to this thing?"

"I thought you'd be pleased. I am doing it for you." Billy was getting sulky.

"Don't do it for me, Billy. If you want it to succeed, you have to do it for yourself."

"I guess." He was still pouting.

I hugged him. "I do appreciate that you're doing this for us. Any support you need just let me know."

"I can do anything with a good man behind me."

That line had so many possible rejoinders to it I had to struggle to let it lie. I had rarely seen Billy so determined except, of course, when it came to the pursuit of sex. Not the curtailment of it.

I guess I believed it would all be a flash in the pan. He'd go to a few meetings, check out the sods who were sex addicts, or wished they were, and fall off the wagon when the first cute guy unfurled his zip. Then we'd be back to normal. Still, I'm the sort of person who always likes insurance.

I rang the Gay Community Centre the next morning from work and spoke to some guy who ran the joint. He was pleasant enough but refused to confirm more than the basic facts that the Rev. Hedley Buckling did run a sex addict clinic on the premises, that it usually cost eight hundred bucks to join and that the reverend's credentials checked out and that he'd received his degree in religious studies from some southern US university that awarded academic titles based on ability to pay rather than on scholastic achievement. He invited me to drop in any time to have a look at the centre for further information about the reverend's program.

During my lunch break I headed across town to the warehouse district. The Gay Community Centre was like a lot of those found in major cities: neglected, depressing, catering to a forlorn collection of political and social groups that hung on to members by the skin of their teeth, staffed by idealistic volunteers and one or two paid members. This one was no exception, except that when I was buzzed through the well-protected front entrance, only a small white card bearing the letters GCC near the security pad declaring its function, and climbed the stairs to the first floor office, I was met by a beaming face.

"Sleazy Peasley," I hollered when I recognised the man I'd known at college. "What the fuck are you doing here?"

"Obviously running a centre that caters to fuckers like you," he smiled.

We shook hands warmly and he guided me into the reception which was peppered with flyers for long defunct lesbian defence classes, gay men's anal health clinics and how to classes in bondage and discipline. The white board affixed to the wall gave a more up-to-the-minute picture of the premises' activism, the week split up into a number of squares with a room number adjoining such activities as Marriage Equality Committee, Homeless Gay Teens, and Transgender Rights. Among all the political groups were scattered the occasional social club for older lesbians, sporting groups and, twice weekly, on Tuesdays and Fridays, Gay Sex Addickts Anonymous.

I tapped the board at that spot.

"Ah, so you're the inquisitive fucker who rang this morning pumping me for info?"

Ted was filling the coffee maker he produced from a locked cupboard. "I keep this for special guests," he admitted. "That urn coffee is muck. Good to pave highways but not fit to put in your belly."

He swished out two mugs that were sitting on the sink. Signs were posted everywhere about leaving the area tidy after the meetings and that all mugs should be washed after use, all those tedious housekeeping rules that were more abused than adhered to. He prised open a tin of biscuits that warned on the lid, "This is the property of the Gay & Lesbian Drama Co-operative. Open at your own peril." Obviously Ted had opened it many times before to no ill-effect.

"Come in to my office, we can chat there without interruption. Any phone messages will go to voicemail."

His private fiefdom was in marked contrast to the spartan facilities elsewhere. A simple plate affixed to the door read Ted Peasley, Administrator. Someone had obviously heard of his prior reputation and had scrawled 'Sleazy' above his name on the door in black marker pen. The attempts to scrub it off had merely highlighted it.

"You reputation precedes you," I said, nodding toward the addition to his name plate.

He managed a weak smile. "There's no escaping your past."

Kicking the door closed, he put our coffee and biscuits on a desk littered with schedules and pamphlets, and drew up a dilapidated arm chair for me. He sat on the more comfortable divan opposite, while I wondered at the use to which it was put as it had more of the appearances of a 'casting couch' than of practical office furniture.

"Look, Steve. Not to put too fine a point on it. Lay off the Sleazy, will you. Doesn't go down too well with the politically correct types around here."

I made a joke of it. "They're usually the ones who are the worst offenders."

"No, seriously."

I waited for the smug smile and the catch phrase, "Gotcha!" but it didn't arrive. He was serious then.

"Sure." I was embarrassed and eager to change the mood. "How the fuck are you? Long time, no see."

"You didn't go to the college reunion this year?" he queried.

"Haven't been for years," I said.

"You really should come to the next one. Catch up with the old crowd. They'd be pleased to see you."

"Yeah, right," I said sarcastically. "They weren't very pleased to see me at school back then, not sure why they would be now."

"All water under the bridge. Anyway, what are you up to?"

I filled him in briefly about my work as a car detailer and my lack of opportunity because of the Global Financial Crisis. I kept it all strictly business.

"No sweet toy boy in your life?"

I don't know whether it was his leer or some little voice in my head telling me to remain mum about Billy. "I'm...um...seeing someone at the moment but who knows how it'll turn out. You?"

"Me?" He roared with laughter. Looking about as if to check no one was listening in, he leaned forward and whispered, "That nickname wasn't given to me for no reason. Just between you and me it's an understatement." For emphasis he tapped the side of his nose.

"Your secret's safe with me." I was glad I'd kept my own counsel.

He relaxed, spreading his legs wide as if in invitation. I couldn't help but gaze at the prominent bulge in his jeans. Casual seemed to be the mode of dress for working hours. He saw me looking and licked his lips.

"You sure are looking fine, Steve. What say you and I..."

He was attractive in that harsh way Hollywood thugs have. Not ugly exactly but average looks that had the edges rubbed off through hard living if not hard liquor. Late at night, in a darkened back room, with a hint of desperation...

I looked at my watch. "Tempting as the offer is, Ted, can I take a rain check? I'm on my lunch break and have to get back. Employment prospects aren't good if I lose this position."

He took his hand away from the fly of his jeans. "Sure." His disappointment was apparent.

"What can I do you for?"

That was Ted all over. A walking, talking cliché. I never liked the guy at college and I didn't like him now but I could pretend friendship in order to get the information I need.

"That call earlier about the sex addict's group."

"Run by the Rev Hed."

"Pardon?"

"That's what we all call him around here. The Rev Hed. The Reverend Hedley Buckling. Clever, eh?" He roared at his own joke.

I joined in half-heartedly.

"I have a friend..." I knew it was the wrong way to begin the conversation as soon as I'd said it. Ted winked at me. "He thinks he's a sex addict and wants to be cured for the sake of a relationship."

"Okay, I get it. This...um...friend. Is he good looking?"

"Is that important?" I asked, wondering where it was leading.

"Fuck, yeah."

"I guess so," I stammered.

"On a scale of one to ten, say, is he as good looking as...well...you?"

I thought it best to let him go on believing it was me rather than reveal Billy's interest, considering on a scale of one to ten Billy is a twelve.

"About the same."

"Hmm," he pretended to be weighing up a score. "So, about a nine."

If Ted was being complimentary he wanted something. I smiled at his appraisal to show my appreciation.

"Top or bottom?"

Where was this leading?

"Bottom. Mainly bottom."

"I would have picked you, I mean your friend, as a top." His slip was deliberate. "But makes it easier for me."

I wanted to scream that I was a top but it didn't seem the most opportune thing to say. I just glanced at the floor. Ted walked over and squeezed my shoulder supportively.

"Hey, mate, don't sweat it. Nothing wrong with being a cock slut. Some of my best friends and all that bullshit." He adjusted his crotch in my face. "You sure you haven't..."

I stood quickly, almost knocking him over. I squeezed his cock affectionately then consulted my watch again.

"I'm already late. What can you tell me about the group?"

He wrapped his arm around me as he walked me to the door.

"Better than tell you, why don't you come along for a meeting tonight?"

I froze on the spot. Billy's first meeting was this evening and there was no way I wanted to be seen as part of it. He would never forgive me.

Ted brushed aside my hesitation. "Not as a participant. Look." He pulled up the shades on his internal windows and it gave a clear view of the main area, smaller offices off to the sides. "We can hide ourselves in one of the side rooms and watch what goes on. You can hear everything because they use the main hall. They won't even know we're there. Unless you make a noise when you come."

I shivered at the thought but I could sacrifice my mouth or ass for a ringside seat at Billy's initiation. Ted patted my ass appreciatively.

"What time?"

"The meeting's at eight. Get here at seven. I don't unlock the doors until half hour before."

To seal our deal, I leaned in and pecked Ted on the cheek. He made a grab for me but I managed to escape his grip. "Uh huh. Tonight at seven."

He grabbed a handful of his crotch. "We'll be waiting for you."

I rang Billy from work, explaining that I wouldn't be home before he headed off to his first meeting. I could tell he was nervous, but also a little excited. Our life had settled into a bit of a rut, although I wasn't convinced this was the right way to go about revitalising it. I didn't believe Billy was a sex addict any more than I believed the Reverend Hedley ran a legit sex addict's clinic. Ted told me he charged up to $800 a quarter to the men in his 'advanced' group which met on a Friday. It was for the hard-core sex addicts and the recidivists.

I wished Billy all the best at his meeting. "You must tell me all about it when you come home," I said.

"We have to sign a code of secrecy," he said. "But I suspect it'll be just a lot of gay men sitting around talking about their sex lives. Just so long as I don't get excited."

I knew what happened when Billy got excited in a group of gay men. That was one of the reasons I was back at the Community Centre, seated in one of the few comfortable chairs in a side room, obviously the domain of Gays for Vegetarianism if the brochures and whiteboard scribbling were anything to go by. I thought it very remiss of them to leave the plans for their political activity in open view. I guess the meat industry didn't see them as much of a threat.

The room was in darkness but between the slats of the Venetian blinds I could witness any activity in the large central area in front of me. Ted was helping the Rev Hed set up the chairs, probably closer to where I was hiding than was usual. The man himself was an unprepossessing gent in his fifties who had indulged too frequently and had become portly rather than obese. He would have been attractive in his youth, though never a great beauty, but that youth was long since passed. If it hadn't been for the dog collar he would not have warranted a second glance, but his clerical choker was bright pink, throwing his florid cheeks into sharp relief.

I heard them conversing. "There's a new lad turning up tonight," Hedley told Ted. "We might have to test his bona fides in case he's the press or someone trying to cause trouble."

"You can't be too careful," Ted agreed. "Anyway, you go set up the coffee and biscuits and I'll finish off here. Then I'll lock up the small rooms, you won't be needing any of those tonight, will you?"

"Not tonight."

"I'll let myself out. If you don't mind just locking up when you leave."

"Thanks for trusting us, Ted. It's appreciated. Not many would." The reverend had a nice line in sincerity.

"Hey, don't sweat it. Gives me an early night."

Ted quickly set up the remainder of the chairs, about twenty in all, and set about opening and slamming the doors to the adjacent rooms. When he reached my hiding place he called, "Night, reverend, see you later."

Hedley popped his head around the door and wished him a good night. When the leader of the sex addicts' group disappeared back into the small kitchen Ted joined me and slammed the door.

"Now, you just wait," he whispered.

"What goes on in the advanced group?" I asked. "How much worse are they than this lot?"

"Can't tell you much about them except they're a lot of old fucks. Not cute like some of the guys you get at the beginners' classes."

"What was that business about the press?"

"Seems the Rev Hed has a few serious enemies who'd like nothing better than to expose him as a fraud. Always trying to sneak in, take photographs, that sort of shit. Usually likes to test them out before allowing them to join."

"I see."

"Hey, don't worry," he said, groping my ass, a gesture I really detest. "Sit tight and enjoy the show. Who knows, next week you...or your friend might be a newbie."

In the half hour lead up to the meeting men drifted in, most of them seemed to know one another as there was an enormous amount of air kissing as well as good natured banter, most of it around the subject of sex. They were all the shapes and sizes and colours of the rainbow although there was one common denominator: they were all under about forty. I suppose it made sense to separate the older men from the younger as their mix may have led to sexual tension.

Billy made an entrance about ten minutes before the starting time. I noticed he'd worn his tightest jeans which showed off his butt to great effect. Most eyes turned in his direction and more than a few of the men licked their lips. He'd also worn his tightest t-shirt which hugged his torso like a second skin revealing every outline of his abs and his pecs, barely containing his biceps.

One of the men talking around the urn stepped forward to introduce himself, holding Billy's hand for much longer than was necessary before introducing him to the group.

"That's Howard, Hed's right-hand man and, most of us suspect, his little bum boy."

Buckling came out of the kitchen, beaming at Billy, shaking his hand warmly with both of his own, and welcoming him in a most effusive manner. I saw Billy visibly relax. When everyone had a coffee or a tea and one or two biscuits, the reverend led his flock to the seats. He sat at the head of a semi-circle that was at an angle to our position. Hedley was turned away from us but we could see all the other attendees. Billy was given pride of place in the centre of the ring next to Howard.

"Gentlemen we have a first timer in our ranks tonight so would you all like to introduce yourselves."

One by one, they stood and announced their name, informing us they were a sex addict. Billy seemed eager to hop up and join the confessional but Howard restrained him. At the conclusion, Hedley turned to Billy. "Now young man, what is it we can do for you?"

Billy stood, albeit much too proudly for what was here considered a disease, and announced. "Hi, my name is Billy. And I'm a sex addict."

His admission was greeted with hoots and hollers, foot stamping and whistles, as if he'd just given a flawless rendition of the most difficult opera aria imaginable instead of just admitting he couldn't control his sexual appetite. I wondered how many of the group were mentally calculating their chances.

"Fuck, he's hot!" Ted whispered, sucking in his breath while adjusting his crotch. "What I wouldn't give to fuck him to paradise and back."

I don't think Ted even registered I was in the room he was so focused on Billy.

"Dear God, let him be a bottom."

"What difference does it make?" I asked. "He's out there, you're in here."

Ted looked at me as if I was a moron. "I just ring up any I fancy and tell them their membership is suspect and to drop by and see me so I can take care of it. I always do. And my cock always gets its reward." He stared at Billy. "Oh, baby, come to poppa."

I certainly didn't want Billy having anything to do with Sleazy Peasley if I could help it even if I had to suck his fetid dick for the privilege of spying on my lover.

Billy sat down looking well satisfied at the reaction to his confession. Hedley called for quiet.

"Well, Billy, we welcome you to our meeting and we're glad to have you join us but at the same time saddened that you have this debilitating affliction that makes life miserable for each of here tonight."

The group looked far from miserable to me.

"But what is it that makes you think you are a sex addict?" Billy went to answer but Buckling put his hand up to silence him. "We sometimes get people here who are not genuine." There was a mumbled assent from the group. Billy went to interject. "No, Billy. I don't believe for one minute you might be one of those venal bloodsuckers from the press. But you may be here under false pretences through no fault of your own. We are not against sex per se. Sex is god-given and therefore wonderful. But too much of anything is not good for you."

Amen to that, I thought. *Even perfection.*

"When you become obsessed with something it becomes a problem. And we here have become obsessed with sex. Are you obsessed with sex, Billy?"

"Oh, yes," he admitted. "I can't stop thinking about it."

"Are you thinking about it right now?" Howard asked.

Stupid question, it would be hard to be thinking of anything else as they were talking about it.

"Hell, yes." Billy was breathing deeply.

"What are you thinking, Billy?"

"How much I'd like to fuck some of you guys."

"Oh, shit. I don't know if I can hold on," Ted croaked. He'd whipped out his dick and was caressing it as he watched.

"That's not unusual, Billy, and it certainly doesn't make you a sex addict. Thinking about sex is okay, it's when you turn those thoughts into action that it can become an addiction. After all, it would be perfectly normal for you to admire one or two men in the group."

"No," Billy whispered.

"No, what, Billy?"

"No, it's more than one or two."

"How many, Billy?" Howard asked.

"All of you," he admitted.

"What a slut," someone blurted out, although he sounded far from condemnatory.

"All fifteen of us?" Hedley asked.

"Mmmm."

"Are you in a relationship, Billy?"

"I'm seeing someone," he said. I could hardly condemn him for his answer as I'd used the same line. I hoped Ted wouldn't get suspicious but he was too turned on to notice.

"Does he know where you are tonight?" Hedley enquired.

"No, I told him I was doing overtime at work."

"Good boy." Buckling was patronising.

"Are you a top or a bottom, Billy?"

"I mainly bottom."

There was a groan of appreciation from the group. I guessed that more than a few of them were already hard.

"I think you sound admirably qualified to join our select group. We just need one more little confirmation. Remove your clothes, Billy."

Without question, Billy stood and stripped until he stood naked in front of the group, his cock rigid.

"Come here, Billy." Buckling ran his fingers over Billy's butt cheeks before parting them to get a better look at his puckered hole.

"Very nice, Billy. I bet men line up to fuck that hole of yours."

"Yes, sir," Billy said, his voice thick with desire.

"And you'd like each and every one of us here tonight to sample that anal button?"

"Oh, please, yes."

Two of the group dragged an old two-seater lounge over to the thick of the action as the men quickly attempted to outdo each other in their attempts to disrobe. Hedley, as befitted his status, took his time revealing his hairy belly and the large appendage that dangled beneath it. He sat in the lounge, dragging Billy's head down over the arm rest until his face was in his crotch, obviously to arouse him by licking and sucking the minister's balls and long, thick prick.

Howard was lathering Billy's luscious butt from a jar of lube he'd taken from his bag, thrusting his fingers into Billy's hole with a pincer movement to open him up for what was to come. Once Buckling was fully erect, he rammed his cock savagely in Billy's throat, skull-fucking him for a few moments, the sound of choking and gagging echoing around the room. The other men stroked their cocks or else helped out their neighbour while they watched.

Ted forced my hand onto his already slimy prick. I would have to go through with it if I wanted to witness one of the Reverend Hedley Buckling's Gay Sex Addickts Anonymous meetings. I squeezed as I ran my closed fist up Ted's shaft, flicking my thumb across the oozing head as I reached the peak.

"Is this what normally happens to a new member?" I asked.

"Occasionally, if the new guy is hot. They all try to take turns at him. Doesn't work if he's a top. But if he's a slut bottom like this guy seems to be, then pow! It can go for hours. Keep doing that thing with your thumb."

Satisfied that Billy was sufficiently greased up, Howard released him and Billy kneeled on the lounge above Hedley's cock, lowering himself to swallow the reverend's swollen weapon in one go.

"Holy fuck, did you see that?" one of the onlookers asked.

Howard admonished him for the blasphemy because Buckling was far too busy buried in Billy's hole to do anything other than gape at the pleasure radiating through his body from his cock. Billy slid up and down the minister's slick pole belying his desire to be cured of his so-called sex addiction. Howard stood next to the action and guided Billy's mouth over his hard dick as the others moved in for the kill. I had a perfect view of Buckling's cock punishing Billy's asshole. It was a glorious sight, obviously one enjoyed equally by Ted whose cock was pulsing fit to burst forth over my hand.

"That fuckin' slut has the best ass ever," Ted moaned. "I want to get my hands on him; I'll fuck him to death. What a way to go." He mumbled a few more sexual inanities before he grabbed my head and pulled me down onto his spewing prick. I wanted to spit it out on the floor but I knew better than to rile Sleazy Peasley. The best thing was to deep throat him so his spunk bypassed my taste buds and slithered, phlegm-like, down the back of my throat. I have to say he blew a copious load that from someone else may have been pleasurable.

I wiped my mouth as I sat up, Ted leaving his dripping cock hanging out of his fly. I hoped he wasn't expecting a repeat.

"Look at that slut take it," he said admiringly. During my preoccupation with bringing Ted to climax, Hedley and his assistant had obviously dumped a load because Billy was being fucked by two different men now, one over the arm rest while his head was forced down onto the prick of the guy sitting in the lounge. The reverend and Howard were on their knees, somewhat incongruously as they were naked, their dicks dribbling tardy sperm, their heads bowed as they recited a litany of religious mumbo jumbo for Billy's salvation.

The subject of their ministrations was at that very moment milking two men of their slimy juices, and then screaming for more cock as he changed partners once again.

I was rock hard in my trousers watching Billy being worked over by a bunch of sex addicts who had the willpower of a gnat, and a paper minister whose practises were highly suspect. Ted began to harden again as well so I feared for my ass, but he tucked it back into his jeans and zipped up.

"Sorry, Steve. That ass out there is so good it would be a shame to waste spunk on anyone else. I'm saving it for my meeting with that new kid so I can show him what a real fuck is all about. He needs a real man to hold him down and fuck him into the ground. Not the pathetic panty waist thrusting these guys are giving him."

I couldn't disagree with that diagnosis but I wasn't sure Ted was the man for the job.

One by one they took turns at his ass or mouth until they'd all come at least once, a couple of them going back for seconds. Billy collapsed on the lounge, his holes rimmed with slime. Howard presented him with his clothes and told him to get dressed. Hedley had already composed himself and disappeared into the kitchen from whence he emerged when he heard Howard's voice.

"Coffee's ready," he announced cheerfully. As they all congregated around the trestle table set up for the event because the kitchen was too small to accommodate the crush, he announced, "I have no hesitation in declaring Billy one of us. No doubt about it, but in seeking proof enough to satisfy even the most sceptical, we've all taken a backward step." There was a murmur of agreement although no one sounded particularly upset. "In acknowledging that fact we take our first step toward the cure. Our treatment starts now."

They all bowed their heads as Buckling mumbled a few religious platitudes before declaring the meeting closed. Some of the men wandered away calling their farewell as they headed for the stairs while others huddled around the coffee urn obviously hoping to take Billy home with them. Hedley dragged Billy toward where Ted and I were hiding in order to speak privately.

"Are you okay, Billy?"

"Uh huh."

"We didn't overstep the mark with you?"

"Fuck, no!"

"Some new members don't understand our unorthodox methods..."

Billy replied dreamily. "I really appreciate your unorthodox methods. I'm looking forward to learning more. And soon."

Hedley smiled indulgently. "That's my boy. Howard and I have discussed your treatment and we believe you'd achieve more going straight into our advanced class. It's a little more intensive and rigorous than tonight but we're sure you could handle it. What do you say?"

"More intense and more rigorous than tonight? Hmmm." Billy paused but there was no doubt in my mind which way he was leaning. "I like the sound of that."

"We thought you might. Welcome to our little group, Billy. By the way, you said you were seeing someone at present?"

Billy nodded his head.

"It goes without saying that anything that occurs here, stays here. If our methodology got out there may be some in authority who would question its efficacy."

"No need to worry about that. I won't breathe a word. But you do think I can be cured?"

I was taken aback. For all his enjoyment of the night's gangbang, he was serious about a cure.

"Definitely, Billy. One thousand per cent guaranteed."

Ted and I managed to duck out not long after the last stragglers left the building, Ted swearing he was going to sample that ass himself before the next meeting and me rushing to get home before Billy. Fortunately, he was standing talking to two of the guys trying to get him to come out for a drink although he continued to refuse politely. When they discovered he was going to hail a cab to get home they offered him a lift. I knew that would delay him for a while because they both intended getting their cocks into him again.

They must have blown quickly or else Billy didn't come across because I beat him in the front door by a scant five minutes.

"Evening, love," I called from the lounge room, pretending I had been watching television. "How did it go?"

He stuck his head around the door. "If you don't mind, I'm gonna take a shower to get the smell off me and then I'll come and tell you everything."

I made him a snack and watched as he devoured it while seated in his dressing gown. When he pushed the plate aside, he sighed and asked for a hug and a kiss. To my surprise, he did tell me everything that had taken place at the meeting.

"Did you enjoy it?" I asked as he snuggled into me.

"Yes and no," he admitted.

We were on the same wavelength.

"You know I always enjoy getting a lot of cock and loads of come but, well, maybe I am a real sex addict, jaded and in search of something more perverse. Tonight was enjoyable and I'm glad it happened but I wasn't excited by it."

"You didn't get off?"

"Yeah, twice. But it wasn't like when I do it with you or..." He stopped himself just in time but I wasn't about to let it rest.

"Or?"

"You know."

I did know. He meant the times he humiliated me in public. It was a turn on for both of us although neither would admit it to the other.

"You're not upset about what I did, are you?"

"If you feel you have to do it then you have my blessing."

"Hedley is talking about me joining the advanced class. Is that all right?"

"What's it cost?"

"He didn't mention a charge."

"If you need it," I said.

In the end he did need it, although he was pleased with himself when he took Sleazy Peasley's call on his mobile but refused to come in to discuss the so-called anomalies in his application. Billy immediately contacted Buckling who told him it was a scam, either for money or, more probably because of his nick name, for sex. Once upon a time Billy would have jumped at the opportunity to swap body fluids with someone called Sleazy Peasley. Maybe GAYSAA was working. What were the odds?

Ted was less than pleased when I called in the next day. He told me about the chewing out he'd got from Buckling after Billy had dobbed him in.

"Probably inadvertent on the young guy's part," I said. Billy didn't need Peasley as an enemy.

"Fuckin' slut!" Ted spat.

I changed the subject. "What's this advanced class the Rev Hed was talking about last night?"

"Don't know much about them. I never stay back. They're all old geezers. The over forties. Real hard cases. Ugly as fuck. I prefer the younger guys at the beginners meeting. More my style."

"Mind if I sit in?"

"I dunno," he said. "You sure you're not checking this out for some scandal sheet?"

"You knew me at school Sleazy, couldn't write my way out of a paper bag. Nothing's changed."

"Long as you don't expect me to feed you a load to make it worth your while. I got better things to do than sit around listening to pensioners go on about their sex life. Ewww!"

"I owe you," I said.

"And I intend to collect," he said fingering my butt crack. "Just not tonight. I got a hot date."

"Not with..." I nodded toward the seats already set up for the Friday meeting.

"I wish," he sighed. "Mind you, the little slut was fascinated when I told him I was called Sleazy Peasley. Seems he must like a bit of the rough stuff or the more outrageous things two men can get up to."

"I dread to ask," I said.

"Oh, you'll find out soon enough when I plug that fuck hole of yours."

He tossed me a sheet of paper with a code scribbled on it.

"Just program that into the security pad at the bottom of the stairs. You have thirty seconds to get out before the alarm goes off. All you need to know is that they use the small room over there on Fridays as well as the main hall. It's unlocked. Make sure you turn the bolt on the inside of the room you're in. Don't want anyone catching you unawares. I wait downstairs for the Rev to arrive and then piss off so you better get yourself a coffee and a bucket to piss in because it could be a long night."

"I'll ring you and let you know what happens," I said.

"I'm not expecting it to be anything like Tuesday night."

"Have fun on your date," I said.

"Hope this has all been worth it. I'll enjoy watching you, I mean your friend, being initiated when you join."

"Makes me wet just thinking about it." I hoped he couldn't detect the sarcasm in my voice.

I made myself a coffee and took a few biscuits to tide me over. I did get a bucket in case I needed to piss during the night then I locked myself in the room and waited. I'd adjusted the slats so that I could see into the room next door but in such a way it was unlikely anyone would see me. Howard and Buckling arrived, setting up the trestle table with mugs, instant coffee, tea bags, sugar and milk, adding a plate of forlorn biscuits covered with plastic wrap to keep them fresh.

They spoke so quietly I could not make out what they were saying although I heard Billy's name mentioned more than once. Howard came over to the room next door;

moving the table and most of the chairs against the far wall so there was more open space in front of the cheap vinyl divan that dominated the pocket-sized cubicle. He left a carry bag on the table.

Billy arrived early, dressed in sweet fuck all. He must have driven because there was no way he could have worn that outfit on public transport and no taxi driver, other than a pervert, would have stopped for him.

"Now, Billy," Buckling said conspiratorially. "You know I said tonight was more intensive therapy than the last meeting."

"Uh huh."

"One of my unusual methods, and it's scientifically proven that it does get results, is to confront your addiction."

"What do you mean?"

"Say, for example, if it's chocolate that you're addicted to, then you eat more and more until you make yourself sick of it and can't face another slab of the stuff."

"Oh, yeah, I've heard of that method," Billy said.

I wondered how it worked with heroin addicts.

"You think you could stand that?"

"You mean you want to fuck the addiction out of me?" Billy was incredulous at the idea.

He wasn't the only one.

"Basically. But by making it a bit more and more repulsive each time."

I could see Billy getting hard in his skin tight shorts. The idea appealed to him greatly.

"Will it work?"

"Eventually."

"It won't turn me off sex with the guy I'm seeing?"

"Not at all," Hedley assured him. "Now, how about you wait in here because I want you to make a grand entrance."

Billy did as he was told and paced about the small room as a few men joined Buckling and Howard at the coffee urn. Ted was not wrong: the men were well over the forty mark. Rough looking buggers, the worse for wear. Dissipated, drug fucked, true addict material. These men looked as if they really did need Buckling's help, not like the wankers on the Tuesday night who were play acting at addiction, using the group for pick-ups and sexual partners.

Nine men turned up in all, ranging in age I would guess between fifty and seventy-five. Ted had not laid out as many chairs tonight although they were in the usual semi circle.

"I guess it's time to begin," Howard announced. "Gents, if you'd take your seats."

Billy emerged from his hiding place and was somewhat non-plussed when he first saw his new group, older and more battered than he expected. Still, he smiled at them and took his seat in their midst.

Hedley greeted the group. "Good evening, gentlemen, I hope you've all been well and managed to win the battle against the evils of sex addiction since our last meeting."

From the grumbles and curses it seemed most had lost the battle and had long since lost the war.

"This is our new member, please introduce yourselves."

They went through the rigmarole of name, rank and serial number as I called it. Then Billy stood up proudly to give his name and declare his sex addiction. There was none of the hoopla that accompanied his Tuesday night admission. These men were restless. It was, after all, Friday night, one of the busiest sex nights of the week and they were missing out.

"Now, Billy, tell us one of your sex addict adventures. One of your really nasty adventures. Can you think of a one particularly perverse event?"

If anything, Billy would have problems narrowing it down to just one. But he did, and he chose the very adventure I would have gone with. His pack gangbang at the hands of a chorus of pirates during a production of Gilbert and Sullivan's *Pirates of Penzance*.

The men paid little attention as Billy began the story, stumbling over words, retracing his steps to impart facts he'd previously forgotten until eventually his tale began to weave a spell on them and they stopped fidgeting and whispering behind their hands. By the time he'd finished three of the men were jerking their cocks while another two had small phials of poppers stuck to their nose as they listened to the story, groaning their appreciation. Buckling did nothing to stop them. In fact, he seemed pleased by their overt show of appreciation.

There was enthusiastic applause when Billy wrapped up his story.

"Thank you, Billy, for your most edifying example about the evils of sex addiction."

I doubted anyone at all in the room found anything evil in the story Billy had told. Quite the opposite.

"If you would be so kind as to show these gentlemen what it is that gets you into so much trouble?"

Billy pulled off his singlet and peeled his shorts down over his perky butt. He was naked as the day he was born. He lay back in one of the chairs, opening his legs wide and holding them apart to display his hole. A few of the men whistled.

"Please gentlemen, inspect for yourselves. It's not often you get to see in graphic close-up what has brought about a young man's downfall."

The men didn't have to be told twice and milled around Billy, prodding his butt and squeezing his prick.

"Billy's is a sad, sad case and only the most extreme measures are likely to prove efficacious. We begin his therapy tonight and we hope you will all help this poor creature recover his ability to say no to sex addiction."

The age, physical deterioration, or the ugliness of the men was no barrier to Billy, in fact it seemed to spur him on to more perverse pleasure as they fingered his hole or else slobbered over his nipples and his balls.

"Billy, if you would like to go into that room we've prepared and make yourself comfortable, we'll begin your therapy. I must warn you that once begun we won't stop until your first session is complete. Is that understood?"

"Completely," Billy said dreamily as he walked to the room next door to me. I watched as he spread himself on the vinyl divan and greased up his ass from a tube in the bag Howard had left earlier. He also extracted one of the small brown bottles and took a tentative sniff, sighing loudly as he sank back on the lounge.

"Fuck, this is so hot. I wish Steve could see me now," he groaned.

I turned my attention to the floor proper and noticed the men were all placing large denomination notes into a tin that Howard was taking around. In return each man got a small chit. After all nine of them had taken a turn, one man whom I'd heard admit to the name Bull, held up the slip of paper which had a black ink '1' marked on it. His mates clapped him on the back before he strode toward the room where Billy was waiting. He would have been in his sixties and his name was not misplaced. He was a huge man, covered in a thick mat of black fur, his cock poking from beneath his large belly.

As he entered Billy's room, I heard my boyfriend moan "Oh, fuck," and take another hit. Bull was a take-no-prisoners sort of guy. Finding the lube on the edge of the table he scooped a large gob onto his fingers and worked it into his cock which seemed to just keep on growing the more he played with it. Billy's eyes bulged out of his head as he saw the mammoth prick aimed at his asshole. He had just time to grit his teeth as Bull plugged him dead centre. I could feel his pain from my vantage point.

"Shit, you're so tight, son." Bull sighed as his balls hit Billy's butt. "So fuckin' tight. But you won't be by the end of the night, that's for sure. By the time we've finished with you'll need about a dozen fuckin' cushions to sit down."

Watching this hairy ape of a man plugging Billy was so hot I shucked my clothes in order to wank in time to his thrusts that made Billy grimace. I wondered just how far into Billy's guts Bull had his cock.

"Take it, son. Take daddy's cock up that tight ass of yours," Bull droned like a badly scripted porn movie. "You can feel daddy's prick pushing against your insides."

"Fuck me, daddy," Billy whimpered. "Ride my boy butt, daddy. Fill me with your juice."

Bull obliged, knocking Billy's head against the back of the divan, threatening him with concussion.

"I'm gonna blow my seed inside you, son. Breed you like a prize bitch. You like that?"

"Yes, daddy," Billy whined.

Bull leaned in and placed his mouth over Billy's as he pumped his cock harder and harder into Billy's pliable asshole. The only sound of his orgasm was a loud piggy grunt followed by a shudder and then his body relaxed. I thought Bull would crush him but Billy wrapped his arms around the man and held him in place.

"Fuck, your ass is good. I hope I can get me some more of that."

"Any time," Billy sighed, obviously satisfied.

Bull shook his cock, flicking the last remnants of sperm on the floor. He patted Billy on the head and thanked him before he went back to the group. "He's hot," was all he said of Billy's expertise.

Next was Sam, who I estimated was the youngster of the group, in his fifties. He had a goatee and a moustache which gave him an evil appearance. He removed his clothes to reveal a rather scrawny body which made his average sized cock appear larger than it was. It was still a good mouthful as Billy discovered when Sam unceremoniously shoved it down his throat and held Billy's head in place so that he choked on it.

"That's it you little fucker, choke on my cock. I want to watch you gasp for air, you little punk. I want to watch your lips hanging off my cock, boy. Look at me when I talk to you. Yeah, don't try to move your head. I've got it steady, boy. Just look up at me. What do you see, boy? Eh? I like to watch my boys chewing on my dick. Makes me feel like a big man. You know I'm a big man, boy, don't you?"

Sam pulled his cock out of Billy's slime caked mouth, strings of gag coming with it. He grabbed Billy by the throat forcing his head up before rubbing his slimy cock all over his face. Forcing Billy up on to the divan he reached between his legs and plunged his fingers deep inside his asshole, stirring like it was porridge. When he pulled out they were covered in the slick slime that Bull had left behind.

"Open up, boy. Clean my fingers. That's it, suck it all off."

Billy opened his mouth and Sam fed him his spunk covered fingers. Billy sucked the finger, licking the webbing as he watched the skinny addict towering above him.

"On your knees, boy."

Billy scrambled in position, Sam wasting no time in impaling Billy on his scrawny prick, fucking him like a dog, bellowing his foul expletives as he buggered my boyfriend. I jerked my cock, spraying my load against the wall, stifling my cries of pleasure, matching those coming from the next room.

One by one the men entered the room using and abusing Billy's ass and mouth. At least I had discovered Reverend Hedley Buckling's perfidy. His beginners sex addicts' meeting was to recruit young, insatiable bottoms who became the fodder for his Friday night meetings, little more than prostitution, in which the recipient was blissfully unaware and received no remuneration. Nice work if you could get it.

Bluey, number three, was a red-head, over six feet tall, his chest covered with a mat of fine red fur. His ass was fire red and when he squatted over Billy's face, it looked as if Billy believed he'd died and gone to heaven.

Bluey straddled the whole of Billy's face, threatening to suffocate him. The giant of a man ground his ass until I thought Billy would get butt burn all over his face.

"Eat it. Taste good? Chew my hole. Push your tongue right up my asshole, mate."

Billy would gasp, take a deep breath and dive back in again whenever Bluey let him up for air.

The guys waiting must have been getting impatient for number four barged in.

"Fuck, Bluey, you gonna take all day. A man has needs, you know."

Bluey merely reached down and dragged Billy's legs up as a response. His ass was free and number four took full advantage of it as Bluey seem to be in no hurry to vacate the throne.

I lost count of the number of times the men used and abused Billy's holes, just as I lost count of how many times I blew a load against the wall. Billy was in a delirium of cock and come. His reliance on poppers became less and less until he was screaming for the men to come and take him, fill him full of spunk until it overflowed down his legs. They, of course, obliged his every command feeding his mouth with their hairy, funky holes or their hard, pointy cocks spewing their juice into his slutty stomach. But mainly stretching his gaping butthole, pounding their pricks and their fingers inside him.

When I looked at my watch three hours had passed. Some of the men had left already the rest were clearing up to go. Soon, only Howard and Buckling remained. Howard turned out the overhead lights before removing the mugs to the kitchen to wash up and clear away the debris from the evening. Buckling went to check on Billy. As he gazed down on the figure asleep on the divan, he said quietly, "You're going to make me a lot of money. Best slut we've ever had."

He shook Billy awake. "Time to go home."

Billy sat up. Although he was still sleepy he asked eagerly, "You think that first time was successful? Will I need many more meetings?"

"It's a long, tough process Billy. You think you'll be able to stay the course?"

"Will it be like tonight?"

"Even tougher."

"Then I'll have no trouble staying the course."

"Good. We'll see you next Friday. Let yourself out."

As Billy dressed, Buckling went to help Howard in the kitchen and I sneaked out in the darkness. I made one detour before I reached the top of the stairs. I had no need of the security code as I let myself out into the street. That would be Howard's responsibility. As I quietly closed the front door I heard loud curses from upstairs. "One of the fucking bastards has taken the money." Followed by Billy's, "What money?"

Back at our apartment, just shy of a couple of thousand dollars wealthier, enough to cover the mortgage for a month or two, I'd been in bed about ten minutes when Billy came home. He peeked in the door to see if he'd woken me.

"Hello, love," I said, feigning sleep. "How was it?"

"I learned a lot tonight. You got time to listen?"

"Of course."

I sat up, turning on the night light beside the bed. Billy stripped off his clothes and I could see the light reflected in the snail trails of dried spunk across his torso and his face.

"You going to have a shower first, love?" I asked.

"Not tonight," he said, sliding between the sheets.

He smelled of stale spunk and poppers as I kissed him, tasting the remnants of the men who'd fucked him that night. I pushed my fingers gently into his gaping ass as he opened his legs to welcome me, his sticky chest against mine.

"You like me like this." It was a statement of fact, not a question.

"Sometimes you go overboard," I said.

My cock was hard. I held him down on the bed as I entered him roughly. He pushed to meet me, grinning as I began to thrust.

"What did you learn tonight, baby?"

"That I don't need the groups. I'm not a sex addict." He was matter-of-fact about his discovery. "I may be a bit of a slut. I may be perverse."

"I wouldn't have you any other way. A bit of perversity adds spice to a relationship."

"Yeah, it does," he agreed.

I fucked him for a good twenty minutes before I dumped a load to mix with all the others already fermenting in his asshole.

We spooned that night and I awoke every few hours to bugger him again. He would be very sore in the morning but he didn't care. Nor did I. I didn't begrudge other men their moment of pleasure at Billy's butt. They might have boasting rights to it for a few minutes or even a few hours.

I had it for a lifetime

ABOUT THE AUTHOR

Barry Lowe writes about love and sex so he won't forget how to do it. When he's not scribbling his adventures for the Sydney gay weekly SX, or out doing field research, he's writing about love's wonderful variations for a series of smut eBooks, novels and anthologies for Lydian Press.

He lives in Sydney with his partner, Wally.

Check out his website at www.barrylowe.info

ANTHOLOGIES By Barry Lowe

ROMANCING THE BONE - eBook and Print

Carbon Dating
Let the Games Begin
Taking the Bait
Party Whip
Team Player
Davy Jones' Locker
Here's to You, Mr Robinson
Gay Dungeon for the Straight Boy
OMG! Santa's Got a Six-Pack
Vlad the Impaler
Meta-Analysis of the Effects of Love on Tofu

YOUR BOYFRIEND IS HOT - eBook and Print

From Here to Fraternity
Stripping His Assets
Indecent Exposure
Middle Man for Madame Blavatsky
A Cook's Tour
Topping the Pizza Delivery Boy

LIKE FATHER LIKE SON - eBook and Print

Man of the Hour
Like Father Like Son
Sonny & Shared
Sonny Side Up
Eclipse Of The Son
Son & Games
Where The Sun Don't Shine
The Sun Shines Out Of His Ass
Have Son Will Travel

BEAR SKIN - eBook & Print

> Carbon Dating the Bear
> Bumming a Fag
> Four on the Bear Floor
> Beauty, Mate
> There's a Bear in There
> Busting a Gut
> Steam Punk
> Piss Elegant
> The Bear's Guide to Depilatory Wax

ROUGH & READY - eBook and Print

> Stocks & Shared
> Scarface
> Ceps: Mad about Muscle
> The Plumbers' Mate*
> Climbing Up the Wall
> Little Red Rides da Hood
> The Dex Factor
> Jailhouse Cock
> The Skinhead Upstairs

THE MORE THE MERRIER - eBook and Print

> Marine Biology
> Flesh for Fantasy
> Buck's Night
> Four On The Floor
> Sluts & Satyrs
> Framing the Picture of Dorian Gray
> Fuck Buddy
> Seven Card Studs
> Dude, Where's The Bar?
> New Year's Steve

BABY, I'M NOT A MONSTER - eBook and Print

The Vampire's Guide to Dental Hygiene
Stupid Cupid
Gadigal
Pride & Joy
Seeing Things
My Dad's a Vampire
Guys & Trolls

THE MAJOR AND THE MINERS - eBook & Print

A Serpent in Paradise
Desperate Remedies
Joshua's Story
Emerald City
Danny's Revenge
Future Tense

THE GRAVY TRAIN - eBook & Print

In the Soup
Salad Days
Whores d'Oeuvres
Beefed Up and Porked
Torte A Lesson
Café or Lay

OMG! NOT ANOTHER GAY EROTICA ANTHOLOGY?

OMG! My Dad's a Stripper!
OMG! The College Jock's a Nudist!
OMG! Put Some Clothes On!
OMG! My Uncle's a Fairy!
OMG! Satan Wants a Blow Job!
OMG! My Dad's Got Tits!
OMG! Santa's Got a Six-pack!

THE BOY IS A BOTTOM - eBook and Print

Marine Biology
Marine Animals
Attack of the Ass Bandits
The Arab Downstairs
Clockwork Derriere
Creaming the Party Dip
Top of the World
Route 666: Signal Driver
The Butler Did Him
Fifty Shades of Fey
Spinning the Bottom

COCK-EYED OPTIMISTS - eBook & Print

A Red Rose Before Crying
Too Frocked to Care
The Three Spooges
Love and the Odor of Red Leatherette
It's All Greek to Me
Hard On His Heels
Salted Mixed Sluts
The New Dad's Club

For all Barry's titles please visit his page at:
lydianpress.com

Lydian Press is dedicated to bringing you the finest GLBTQ erotic literature on the web.

Visit us on the web at:

http://lydianpress.com

www.ingramcontent.com/pod-product-compliance
Lightning Source LLC
Chambersburg PA
CBHW051541030726
47592CB00001B/82